THE PARADISE
GHETTO

THE PARADISE GHETTO

FERGUS O'CONNELL

Published by Accent Press Ltd 2016

Paperback ISBN: 9781786150431
Ebook ISBN: 9781786151438

For my beautiful daughter, Ferga, who's been blessed
with so many talents

Potemkin village: Any construction (literal or figurative) built solely to deceive others into thinking that a situation is better than it really is.

1

The Amsterdam attic apartment is freezing and since she is working today, Julia has had to strip and wash all over, so she is still cold from that. She wears her coat, scarf, and mittens and tries to warm herself with the coffee. She drinks it almost painfully hot while holding her hands tightly around the cup. It is real coffee, not adulterated in any way. She hasn't had any for a long time and doesn't know when she will have more. Bert gets it and he gave her some last time in part payment. Of course, she had to give her usual part payment too.

She hates Bert. But at least you know where you stand with him. He seems to be one of those rare people – at least she's found them to be rare – who are completely honest. Apparently he has a wife. What she must be like – given that Bert does what he does – Julia can only imagine.

She stands by the small double window of her attic apartment. She is looking at the cobwebs on the outside. The night's frost has encrusted them in white and she imagines them as miniature ropes in the impossibly complex rigging of some tiny ghostly sailing ship. She is captivated by them and it is only the sense that time is moving on and that she might be late that eventually snaps her out of her reverie.

There are cobwebs on the inside too – there is one which has collapsed and bellies like a hammock. Julia never removes them. She thinks of them as the work of her little family, so that she is not alone. She really feels that she has built a home here. The last time she felt she had anything like this was that Christmas when her father gave her an elaborate doll's house. She hopes that it is still safe and that one day she'll be able to retrieve it.

She's glad to have some work at last. It's always quiet over Christmas – she had expected that. Men want to be, or have to be, with their families – fucking hypocrites – but this year, Christmas seems to be running well into January. Maybe it's the icy weather. Or maybe the Germans aren't spending like they used to.

The best thing is that it's Friday. Even though there is little to distinguish one day from the next, Julia thinks of it as nearly the weekend. She will have money tonight. Food. Enough, for once. She is becoming dangerously bony. She thinks that Bert noticed it the last time. She needs to fatten up a little. If he stopped giving her work she'd be completely fucked.

She looks round her eyrie, as she thinks of it. It may be grotty but it's neat, as she likes it to be. Dishes from last night washed and put away, bed made, everything in its place.

She looks at the picture, thumb-tacked to the wall. It is part of her ritual when she is heading out to work. The painting is called *A Kiss*, by someone called Lawrence Alma-Tadema. Julia found it in a magazine. In it, a little fair-haired girl proffers her cheek and receives a kiss from a woman with red hair. The red-haired woman lifts the little girl's cheek slightly and holds her hand in the gentlest of grips. A second woman with black hair looks on at the scene. She has a strange expression on her face, like she's not happy with what she's seeing.

In Julia's mind, the black-haired woman is the little girl's mother while the woman doing the kissing is a favourite aunt or friend of the family. It's only possible to see the side of the aunt's face but she looks kind and beautiful. From the expression on the little girl's face, she loves her aunt. Julia imagines she is the only person in the world that the little girl can confide in. Julia imagines the kiss.

But now she must go to work.

She sighs a deep sigh and takes the last mouthful of coffee. Then she tips up the cup and lets the last drops fall onto her tongue. Coffee is such a beautiful thing. After the war she will drink as much of it as she likes – she will never not have some in her cupboard. She rinses the cup, upends it on the draining board and buttons her coat. She looks through the contents of her bag to make sure she has everything – mascara, eyeliner, red lipstick, powder, hairpins and brush, spare black stockings and lingerie, garter belt.

Hanging on the inside of the front door is the 1944 calendar that Bert gave her – so that she'd never miss a session. Not that she ever has. At the end of every day, she crosses that day off. Another day closer to when the Germans will be gone. She just needs to hold on. Last night she drew a big 'X' through January 13th.

Finally, she checks herself in the small mirror by the front door and goes out, locking the door of the dingy, tiny apartment behind her. Her old place was nicer but more expensive, more obvious. Here, she goes unnoticed. People keep to themselves.

It's like everybody has a secret.

Outside it is bitterly cold, with a bone-chilling wind

and a leaden sky that hints at snow. As she walks, she feels her blood starting to move; she warms up slightly. She hears a car behind her. That can only be Germans and, sure enough, a black Citroën appears in her peripheral vision. It slows slightly and the driver stares at her. It's like the car hesitates but then it picks up speed again. She shudders and pulls her collar more closely around her neck.

She thinks it's funny how, once a thought comes into your head, it can keep coming back under similar circumstances. That first day she saw Germans, the first day of this new rule, it occurred to her that regimes may come and go, but lots of things don't change at all. People still have to eat, sleep, go to work just as she is doing now, have sex – as she will shortly be doing.

As she rounds the corner, she sees a couple of German soldiers on the other side of the street. They are not armed and one is not wearing a greatcoat – just his uniform with several of the tunic buttons open. They look like they've been on a night out and are both the worse for wear, walking along unsteadily. One is trying to light a cigarette but the lighter keeps missing the tip. Eventually, irritated, he pulls the cigarette from his mouth and throws it away. She thinks to wait until they have passed and then go and retrieve the cigarette.

But then they notice her. One of them wolf-whistles and Julia looks away and down at her feet. She walks faster.

'Hey,' one of them shouts in bad French. 'Come and meet my friend, Dutch girl. He likes dark-haired women.'

She is past them now and mercifully, they don't come after her.

Fuck them. Fucking Nazis. Fucking men. Fuck all of them.

As she turns on to the street along the Vondelpark, she

sees a discarded pear with a bite out of it on the pavement. She begins to salivate. She remembers the taste of pears. But you could catch anything from that ... She kicks it away savagely.

The address Bert gave her is a stylish townhouse from the last century with a balcony, large windows and a richly ornamented façade. How does he find these places? Presumably their owners are still wealthy because they side with the Nazis. But how does Bert get their permission to let him use their houses? Do they know what he uses them for? Of course Bert must be in bed with the Nazis too. That's where most of his business comes from.

The concierge is an old lady, who smells like she hasn't washed in a few days. She directs Julia to the stairs.

'Second floor, door facing you. Bert is already up there,' the woman says. Julia shakes her head. That's another thing about Bert. He either knows everybody or, if he doesn't, he's about to. It only takes him a minute or two to make them feel like they've known him all their lives. Why do people take to guys like that? The thought makes her sour, resentful.

She knocks on the door and a sharp-faced girl with dyed blonde hair, still in her street clothes, answers it. Julia doesn't know her. She's not one of Bert's regulars. She must be new. She's older than Julia – by maybe ten years, Julia reckons. Probably in her early thirties. Strange. Generally the girls are much younger. Sometimes *much* younger.

'I'm Julia.'

'Chantal,' says the girl, who is smoking.

She turns without another word and walks back down the hall, ass swaying, high heels clicking loudly on the parquet.

Bitch.

Julia has dark auburn hair. Bert likes to do this – blonde and black or blonde and brown. He's told Julia he thinks of it as one of his trademarks.

Fucking idiot. Bert thinks he's fucking Cecil B. DeMille. Pompous prick.

Now that she's here she just wants to be done with it. She imagines herself in a couple of hours, stepping out into the street, money in her pocket, ready to go and buy things. She puts down her bag on a chair and is taking off her coat when Chantal says aggressively, 'Are you Jewish?'

Julia is so surprised by both the question and the way it is asked that the first words that come into her head are, 'What if I am, you wizened old cunt?' She is about to say this but, mercifully on this occasion, her brain stays a fraction of a second ahead of her mouth.

'Of course not.'

But now Chantal is looking at her queerly.

'You are, aren't you?'

'Don't be fucking ridiculous,' says Julia.

A look of horror appears on Chantal's face. She turns and walks towards the other room.

'Bert!' she calls, going in and slamming the door behind her.

Julia finishes taking off her coat and goes to the door. Once again, her brain gets there before her. Rather than storming in as was her impulse, she stops and listens, ear against the door.

'I'm not working with that Jewish bitch,' Chantal says angrily.

'Listen to Betty Grable here,' Bert says.

'Fuck you. I'm not working with her.'

'She's not Jewish,' Bert says. 'And if you don't need the money, that's fine. Fuck off. I can have someone else here in an hour.'

6

'You should have told me,' says Chantal, but already the wind is going out of her argument.

'I told you she's not Jewish,' says Bert. 'And anyway, what difference would it make?

'It makes every difference,' says Chantal, but now she just sounds like a sulky teenager.

Julia breaks away from the door and moments later Chantal emerges. She flashes a look of absolute hatred at Julia.

'Come on then,' Bert calls from the other room. 'Time to go into wardrobe.'

Always with the Cecil B. DeMille. Dickhead.

'We need to know the script,' says Julia.

It's a dig at Bert. While it could be taken as just teasing, Julia doesn't intend it to be. He is as much a failed filmmaker as she is a failed actress. The thought makes a flame of anger flare inside her.

Bert emerges from the other room. He is a short dumpy man with a bald head, glasses and a light meter on a cord round his neck. Before the war he must have been very fat. Now, even though food is scarce, he has lost some weight but not that much. His shirt sticks out of the waistband of his trousers which are pressed down under his paunch. He is always sweating, especially when he is filming under lights. He is sweating now and carries a brown paper package tied with string.

'The story is in three acts,' he begins.

This just makes Julia angrier.

'In the first one, the postman delivers the package. Here, I've made up the package.'

He hands it to Chantal.

'You're going to be the postman, Chantal.'

'Why do I have to be the postman?'

'Just shut up and be the fucking postman,' Bert replies. He continues. 'The postman delivers the package. You take the package, Julia, and open it. It's a dress so you put it on. Then, the second act, Chantal – now no longer the postman but in character – comes along and finds you in the dress – the dress that she ordered. There's a bit of an argument. Third act. Well, you know, after that it's the usual. Clear?'

'Sure,' says Julia.

She suddenly feels weary even though the day is only beginning. Chantal, still being sulky, says nothing.

'So – wardrobe, ladies, please.'

Bert flashes them a smile without warmth – it's really pity. That or disgust.

In the bedroom where most of the filming is due to take place, Bert has set up a short rolling rail. There are only a few items of clothing on it, mostly underwear, hanging forlornly from hangers. Julia would much rather wear her own underwear – there's no telling where this stuff has been, who's been using it or what they've been doing in it. But she has found that often her lingerie gets damaged – pants get ripped, stockings get laddered – and she can't afford to keep replacing them. So reluctantly she will use some of the things on the rail.

Chantal undresses and puts on all black – bra, knickers, garter belt, stockings. She takes a pair of black boots with high heels from a suitcase full of shoes that Bert has brought. Julia glances across at her. She has a nice body that is not as bony as Julia's – Chantal is obviously getting food from some place – but her face isn't that pretty. It's kind of foxy.

Julia smiles as she is reminded of that last summer before the war, before she left home. They had gone on holiday, she and her parents, by the sea at Scheveningen. Julia met an English girl – Sheila. They became real friends. Julia told her about wanting to become an actress and Sheila said she must come to London to study. They would get a flat together. They had leant on the railing of the promenade, people-watching – mainly boys. Sheila, who was really quite beautiful, was also scathing about some of the girls they saw. It was cruel really, but Julia couldn't help but laugh when Sheila would call some girl 'a dog' or a 'bug-eyed Betty'. Chantal is a dog.

If Chantal is in black lingerie, then Julia goes in white. This is standard practice in Bert's films. She changes into a white bra, knickers and no stockings. She prefers not to think about the yellowish stains on the items she puts on. Over these, Julia adds a white blouse and a tight-fitting black skirt with a slit up the back. She picks a pair of black stilettos from the suitcase. The effect is demure – she looks like a perfectly flat-bellied secretary or office worker. Normally she and any other participants would have chatted while doing this – anything to make it bearable – but with Chantal there is an icy silence.

When all of this is complete they are ready to start. Chantal puts her coat back on over her underwear, wraps one side over the other, and pulls the belt tight. The three of them move out into the hall. Chantal brings the package, Bert carries the heavy movie camera on its wooden tripod, sweating and cursing its weight, and Julia brings the microphone on its stand. Bert switches on the light in the hall. It's not very bright and he looks at it with irritation. It's obvious that he's considering bringing the arc light from the bedroom. But he eventually decides he can't be bothered and that the hall light is sufficient. He checks the light meter just to be sure and confirms that it's acceptable. Bert is careful about attention to detail. Maybe, in another life, he might have been Cecil B. DeMille.

Now that they've started, Julia feels her anger slip away as the other, professional Julia, takes over. It may not be a very noble profession but it is the one she has.

The camera and mic are about four metres from the door. Bert looks through the viewfinder and adjusts a couple of things. Finally he is ready to start.

'All right, Chantal,' he says. 'Action!'

Chantal goes out the front door and closes it behind her. Julia stands to one side of Bert, out of shot.

'Rolling,' he calls loudly, so that Chantal can hear.

There is a knock on the door. Julia walks on in front of the camera, swinging her ass, and goes to the door. Just to irritate Chantal, she asks, 'Who is it?'

She can hear the annoyance in Chantal's voice as she calls back in a poor imitation of a male voice, 'Postman!' Julia opens the door slightly but not enough that the camera can see Chantal. Julia takes the package, thanks the 'postman' and closes the door again. Then she walks down the hall and past the camera. Bert yells 'Cut' and picks up the camera to take it back to the bedroom.

As he does so, he says to Julia, 'Let her back in.'

'Let the bitch stay out there,' says Julia, even though she goes to do as Bert asks.

The next set-up is in the bedroom.

As soon as Bert calls action, Julia walks in front of the camera carrying the package. The effect is that she has just entered the bedroom from some other part of the house. Chantal waits out of shot. She has taken her coat off and stands there in the underwear, stockings and boots. Beneath the arc light it is very hot.

While Bert might like to think of himself as DeMille, there is never a written script. As a result the girls have to make up most of the dialogue themselves. Julia doesn't mind this. She loves books and reading and making up the script is something that she is quite fond of. The dialogue comes easily to her – though it's hardly *Anna Karenina*.

She reads the address on the package.

'For Emily. Hmm – I wonder what this could be.

10

Maybe I'll just take a look.'

'Emily' is Chantal's name in the movie. Julia doesn't have a name. She unwraps the package and takes something out. She holds it up and lets it fall out. It is a red silk dress in a Chinese style.

'That is just – *gorgeous*,' Julia says. 'I'll bet it would look fabulous on me.'

She holds the dress to herself. 'I don't think she'll mind if I try it on and see. What's the harm?'

Julia puts the dress on the arm of a couch and begins to undress. She takes off her blouse. Then she turns her back to the camera, unzips her skirt, and pushes it down, wiggling her ass as she does so. She steps out of the skirt, picking it up and throwing it onto the couch with the blouse. The movement of the skirt has caused her knickers to slip down a fraction. She tucks her thumbs into the waistband and pulls them back up so that they cling to her, outlining the shape of her buttocks.

She holds the red dress to herself again, puts a dreamy look on her face and sighs. Again she turns her buttocks to the camera, then steps into the dress, wiggling her ass as she pulls it up. She reaches behind her for the zip and manages to get it about halfway up. But then there's a problem. She can't pull it the rest of the way. She struggles, tries by putting her hands over her shoulders instead of round by her shoulder blades but the effect is the same. Bert calls 'cut' in an exasperated voice.

He asks Chantal to do the zip but she refuses so Bert has to come out from behind the camera and do it himself. Bert is being smart – he'll give Chantal the odd little victory so that she'll stay in the game. He doesn't want her storming off when they're halfway through so that he'd have to re-shoot with a new actress. Julia saw this happen once and Bert's anger really was a Biblical epic.

Julia has never stormed off. She has never missed a

shoot, is always on time, and has always been able to do the things that Bert wanted. Even when she has felt terrible, she has done what needed to be done. But she has also set limits for herself. For example, she won't do more than one male/female scene in a week. Everything is too intense and usually with a much-larger-than-average man. Her body needs a few days to recover after that.

'Cow,' Bert mutters under his breath as he pulls up the zip. With that sorted out and the dress buttoned at the top, filming can resume. There is a cheval glass near the bed and Julia admires herself in it, turning this way and that. She pouts and smooths the silk down over her hips.

'Very nice,' she says. 'It fits me like a glove. I think I'll keep it.'

She holds up her hair.

'I think I should do something different with my hair – so it doesn't distract from this beautiful dress.'

Julia ties up her hair in a ponytail, looks in the mirror again and says, 'Perfect.'

'Where have you been?' Chantal snaps, walking on. 'I've been looking for you everywhere.' Then as she sees the dress, she says, 'Hey, isn't that the dress that I ordered from the catalogue?'

'It is,' says Julia, 'and doesn't it look fabulous on me?'

'Why are you wearing my dress? Opening my mail? I can't believe you're doing this.'

'Well, believe it. I'm sick of you flaunting everything you have. Constantly ordering gifts for yourself. You're very inconsiderate. You never buy me anything.'

'I don't like your attitude,' Chantal spits.

'I think at this stage in our relationship,' says Julia, 'I'm just going to reward myself.'

At this point she puts two fingers under Chantal's chin and tilts it up slightly. As she does, she says, 'For all the things I do for you.'

Chantal's eyes blaze and she is not acting.

Julia points a finger at her and adds, 'And you know what I mean.'

'I'll give you a little reward,' says Chantal. 'And you probably wanted me to do this.'

Julia had expected this build-up to take longer but it seems Chantal has jumped a page or two of the non-existent script. She grabs Julia's ponytail hard and says, 'Get down on your knees.'

The look in Chantal's eyes is vicious.

'Facing me,' Chantal commands.

It feels like Julia's hair is going to be torn out of her head.

With Julia kneeling, Chantal kneels opposite her. She takes a riding crop which Bert has placed conveniently on the couch and lifting up the hem of the red dress, she begins to spank Julia's buttocks.

Because of their relative positions, Chantal cannot swing the crop very much and the smacks do little more than sting. Julia can smell Chantal's perfume – it's something expensive – and the cigarette she smoked is still on her breath. Julia utters little whimpers every time the crop strikes.

'But I just love this dress,' Julia appeals.

Chantal continues to slap Julia with the crop.

'You're certainly in a bitchy mood today, mistress,' Julia says, trying to maintain the role that Bert had outlined to her when he booked her.

'I'm going to a party,' says Chantal. 'Without you, of course. And you're wearing my dress.'

Now Chantal moves on her knees behind Julia, hoists up the dress some more, pulls down Julia's knickers and begins to hit her hard with the crop. These strokes are really painful, strong enough that Julia is sure they're going to leave red marks. But she is reluctant to cry out.

For one thing, she wants this all to be over with as quickly as possible. She wants to get her money and get out of here. If she complains, Bert will have to call cut, there will probably be an argument, and will things be any better when filming starts again? And the other thing is that she is a professional. She is good at what she does. This is why Bert gives her so much work. And anyway, next time she will get Bert to make sure that she is the mistress and Chantal the servant. Or slave. Or whatever the fuck it is. That thought comforts her.

But it appears as if Bert has seen her predicament. He looks out from behind the camera and begins to make pouting expressions at Chantal. This means that he wants kissing. Chantal stops with the riding crop – but she doesn't seem to be finished yet.

'Do you know what bad girls get?' she says. 'They get spanked. You've been acting like a spoilt child so you need to be punished.'

She slaps Julia's buttocks with the palm of her hand. She reaches round to Julia's front, catches her groin between her fingers and the heel of her hand and squeezes hard. Then she slaps Julia a few times right in the groin. Each time she does so, Julia cries in pain or gasps. She's not acting now – the blows really hurt.

Bert is pouting manically, indicating, by stabbing his forefinger downwards, that he wants kissing right now. Still on her knees, Chantal goes round to Julia's front. She looks into Julia's eyes. Chantal's eyes are blue and alight with hatred.

'You know – you are going to have to work hard to earn my trust again. Give me a kiss and make it a good one.'

Chantal pulls Julia's head to her and Julia does indeed make it a good one. She slips in her tongue and groans with fake desire. It doesn't bother Julia for an instant that

Chantal is a woman – but it is a strange feeling indeed to be kissing someone as passionately as this when you loathe them and they you.

Chantal pulls away from the kiss and says, 'Now I'm going to give you a proper spanking.' She sits back on the couch.

'Over my knee,' she says. 'What are you waiting for?'

Julia stands up. With the waistband of her knickers just above her knees, it is difficult for her to walk. She lays herself across Chantal's knees. Chantal yanks on Julia's ponytail, jerking her head back, and spanks her hard. Julia makes the little whimpers and moans all the while. Chantal orders her to count the slaps and Julia does as she is told. Then Chantal tells her she must apologise and Julia does that too. Chantal makes her say 'I'm sorry' several times.

'I know you're enjoying this, aren't you?' says Chantal.

Julia says that she is.

'I don't think this is punishment enough for you,' says Chantal. 'And you know I can do what I want to you. So first of all – take the dress off, because it really doesn't suit you.'

Julia stands up and begins to take off the dress.

'Do a little strip show for me,' Chantal says.

Julia removes the dress while Chantal pushes Julia's knickers down to her ankles. Julia steps out of them and kicks them away. Now Julia is only wearing a bra. Chantal indicates that she should take that off too. When she does, Chantal kisses her breasts. Julia almost recoils when Chantal puts her mouth on her nipple and sure enough, Chantal nips her with her teeth. Julia makes a little yelp, repeated when Chantal does the same on the other side.

'Fucking bitch,' Julia hisses, soft enough so that

Chantal will hear but the mic won't pick it up.

Chantal grins at her. Julia has infused her moans and whimpers with weariness as though all of this punishment is wearing her out. She doesn't really have to act it.

'What am I going to do with you, you naughty girl?' asks Chantal rhetorically. As she says this she strokes Julia's breasts with the top of the riding crop. 'What do you think you can do to earn my trust again? Any ideas?'

Julia is not expected to reply to any of this so eventually Chantal says, 'Then it looks like I'll have to come up with something. Well that shouldn't be a problem.'

Chantal makes Julia kneel at the couch, with her elbows on its seat. Chantal disappears off camera and reappears a few moments later carrying a strap-on dildo. First she takes off her knickers and Julia is made to lick her. She tastes piss. Then Chantal puts the dildo on and begins to fuck Julia very hard, very painfully with it.

While this is going on Julia puts together her shopping list. She will have to go to three different shops – the grocer's, the baker's, and a third place to get wine. That's three queues. She could manage with just one but fresh bread and wine are her two big treats. The bread will probably be shit but at least it will be fresh out of an oven. And the wine – well, there's nothing but good to be said about that.

Chantal has been moaning while this was going on, but now her moans start to increase in volume. Her stroking in and out of Julia becomes deeper and more painful. Sometimes the people Julia works with get carried away, forgetting that they are meant to be acting. Julia can't see Chantal's face but it sounds very like that has happened to her now. Chantal announces that she is going to come and she commands Julia to come too. Julia fakes the orgasm. The movie ends with Julia still kneeling at the couch whimpering and Chantal trying on the dress. The last line is 'Hey, bitch, this dress fits me a lot better than it fits you.'

It has all taken little over an hour; the movie itself will run for about twenty minutes. Once Bert announces – as he likes to do – that it's a wrap, Chantal begins to change back into her street clothes while Bert packs up the equipment. Julia stays in her underwear, pulling her coat back on to keep warm. She takes one of Bert's cigarettes, lights it and goes into the living room. She is very sore.

Once Julia is out of the bedroom, Chantal slams the door, voices are raised and there is an argument. Chantal wants her money and there are going to be no extras today. It was bad enough that she had to fuck a Jew. After a few minutes, the door flies open and Chantal storms out, past Julia as though she doesn't exist and out the front door, slamming it so hard that the whole house shakes.

'Cunt,' says Julia.

Bert comes out of the bedroom. He is seething.

'No threesome then, Bert?' Julia says, delighted that this has probably ruined the rest of the morning for him.

'I'd drop the cow altogether except she does things that you aren't prepared to do.'

Julia remembers the first time she met Bert. He went through a whole list of things asking whether or not she would do them. Jesus – her innocence back then. Some of them she didn't even know what they meant.

'Did you tell her I was Jewish?' Julia demands.

'No, I didn't. It's just that, you know … in a certain kind of light … from a particular angle … your face…'

He leaves the sentence unfinished.

Always with the fucking Cecil B. DeMille.

There's one last thing to be done. Julia doesn't even ask. She just looks at him, waiting to be told. He has to be the most unattractive man in the world. Fat, sweaty face.

17

Grey and white stubble. Thin, greasy hair. Shirt hanging out of his trousers revealing a triangular patch of bulging, hairy belly. Smell of old sweat. A smile slowly breaks out on his face.

'No holes barred,' he says to himself, thoughtfully.

He thinks for a little while, obviously enjoying his moment of power. Eventually, he indicates with his forefinger that she should turn round. She does so, shrugging off the coat and then bending over.

When he is finished, he pays her.

'Don't spend it all at once,' he says. 'Though I may have something more for you before the end of the month. Depends on these Nazis. Some of them are starting to get a sense that they may not be around here for much longer. It's distracting them.'

Julia wouldn't have spent it all anyway. She'll put some away in case of emergency and spread the rest out equally over the seventeen remaining days of the month. She will treat herself today but do that by reducing the amount she can spend for the rest of the week. Ever since she left home and started supporting herself she has done this. She wonders if it's the Jew in her.

When Julia leaves the apartment, she finds it uncomfortable to walk but as the afternoon wears on, the discomfort eases.

With money in her purse, she spends the time until it gets dark queuing. As the long lines move slowly, she fantasizes about after the war. Then, she will try – again – to become an actress. A proper one. Maybe go to England and find Sheila – if she's still alive and hasn't been killed in the bombing. Or even America. Hollywood. Now that would be wonderful. It makes Julia angry to think of all the years of her life that she has wasted here.

Fucking war. Fucking Germans.

She manages to buy some bread, a little ham and

cheese, a couple of potatoes, two eggs for breakfast and a bottle of very cheap wine. She looks forward to the evening, a full belly for once and the pleasant numbness that the alcohol will bring.

She is exhausted by the time she gets home. It has been a long day – first at work and then all of the standing in line. She is cold. Being indoors seems to make little difference. She wonders if the temperature inside and outside are the same. And she is hungry, having eaten nothing since the two slices of sawdusty bread she had for breakfast with the coffee. Terrible bread that sucks all the moisture from your mouth. Slowly she climbs the stairs to the top floor, carrying the bag of food and wine. Before the war she would not have regarded it as heavy but now it seems like a dead weight and she has to stop halfway up and change it into her other hand. Her heart is beating fast and she is breathing heavily.

The food is delicious and everything she anticipated it would be. She finishes the wine so that she is slightly tipsy when she goes to bed and falls into an almost drugged sleep. But later that night, she catapults into waking, in a lather of sweat. Her heart is pounding, her face on fire, despite the frigid air of the apartment.

Chantal!

What if she goes to the authorities and says something? All it takes these days is a suspicion.

Julia checks her watch, the one her father gave her that last Christmas. She would throw it in a canal except she has come to depend on it. She feels that she has been asleep for hours but in fact, it is only just after midnight. She went to bed barely two hours ago.

She lies wide awake, staring at the ceiling. Or rather, where the ceiling is. She can't see it in the almost solid darkness caused by the blackout curtain. She tries to put the thoughts of Chantal out of her head. When that doesn't work, she tries not so much not to worry about it – going round in the same circles like a mule powering a grindstone – but to treat it as a problem to be solved.

What would she do if they came knocking on her door right now? She could climb out of the window and onto the roof but the tiles would be slippery with frost or ice. And it's a long way down. But if she was careful she could make it along to the next house, which is a direct copy of this one, and then break in the top floor window. She's already dressed – it's too cold to undress. If they came now, all she would need to do would be to put her shoes on. How long would that take? Should she try now and time it? But it is so cold beyond the bedcovers. Maybe in the morning, in daylight, she should check how doable it would be.

Julia ponders this and a dozen other details and scenarios until exhaustion eventually causes her to fall back asleep.

It is some time later when they kick in the door.

2

The first Julia knows of any of this is when the light
blazes on and a face appears, centimetres above hers. It is
the face of a big man, a bull face. His breath smells of
cigarettes and mints.

She begins to scream.

'No!'

She screams louder.

'Please!'

Until it is blood-curdling.

'Go away! Don't touch me!'

She sees surprise on the man's face but then he slaps
her hard across the cheek.

However, instead of making her go quiet, this only
causes her to get worse. She pulls the bedcovers over her
head. She tries to roll to the far side of the bed but strong
arms pinion her. She kicks, or at least tries to, but the
covers and the weight of the man, who has now spread
himself on top of her, mean she can't do much.

She struggles some more but she realises it's pointless.
His strength is way beyond anything she is capable of
fighting. Finally, she goes limp. He hesitates for a little
while and then pulls the covers off her face so that the
light and his bull face return. He is half on the bed,
pressing his hands onto her upper arms and with his thigh

and knee holding down her legs.

'We're not going to touch you,' he says quietly, almost tenderly, in Dutch. 'You just have to come with us. Understand?'

Her eyes slowly become used to the light and comprehension dawns. She returns.

'Understand?' he says again.

Eventually she nods.

'OK,' he says, climbing off the bed.

Slowly, she sits up. There are two of them – the one with the bull face who looks like a policeman out of uniform and one in a leather coat. He is short and thin and wears wire-rimmed glasses. Small and weaselly, he looks like a student.

A small man. Never good.

It occurs to her that it's lucky she's not naked, as she would have been had it been the summer. Tonight, this morning, whatever it is, she's fully dressed, having slept in her clothes.

'You have ten minutes to pack a case,' says the Dutchman, severely, this time.

She climbs slowly from bed, still somewhat stunned by what has just happened. She kneels down, groggily poking around under the bed for her suitcase. It is the same one she used when she left home three and a half years ago, just as the Germans were entering Amsterdam.

The Dutchman lights a cigarette, offering one to the other who declines with a curt 'Nein'.

So – the weasely one is a German.

While the Dutchman watches her, the German begins to search the place. He opens the wardrobe, his leather-gloved hand leafing through the few items of clothing that hang there. Then, he opens in turn the three drawers of the chest. The top one contains Julia's underwear and he seems to spend an inordinate amount of time with his hand in that. She can't be sure because he's got his back to her but she thinks he pockets something.

Now, at least, she is able to think a little more clearly. If she is packing it means they are not going to kill her. At least not yet. Not tonight. And it doesn't look like they're going to rape her. At least not here. Ever since she left home, Julia has kept a mental scale of the most frightening things she has done or that have happened to her. She decides that this would not be the top of her scale – maybe second. Up until tonight, second had been the first time she made a film. That's now slipped to third.

'You should bring food,' says the Dutchman. 'And a bowl and a spoon.'

Encouraged by his tone, Julia asks, trying to sound defiant but not really succeeding, 'Why are you arresting me? I haven't done anything.'

'Just pack, Jew,' the German says in a cold, toneless voice.

Chantal.

Julia packs any food she has into the suitcase and puts whatever warm clothes she has around that. She has a beautiful flowery summer dress. It's her favourite – the first thing she ever bought with money she had earned herself. No point in bringing that now.

On top of her chest of drawers are a dozen or so books that Julia either brought with her from home or that she has accumulated since then. She thinks of them as her 'library', a term that always causes her to smile inwardly. Now, she has to decide what she's going to do with them.

Julia loves books. With their ability to whisk her away to other places, to become part of amazing people's lives, books have been her solace ever since her mother first read to her and then taught her to read herself, so that Julia could get through grown-up books by the time she started school. She would love to bring them all but they will be too heavy. And picking just one of them, she thinks, is like being asked to choose between your children.

'*Schnell. Schnell*,' says the German. 'We haven't got all night.'

She wonders if she should take *Hollands Glorie* by Jan de Hartog but before she can decide, the Dutchman, who appears quite nervous despite his size, stubs his cigarette out on the floor and says, 'Come on, that's enough'. He shoves her aside and clicks her suitcase shut, before picking it up and thrusting it at her. Now that she's being taken, now that it's time to leave her little haven and she is fully awake, she's starting to feel very frightened. What is going to happen to her?

The Dutchman goes in front, the German behind. Julia has a sense that the whole building is wide awake and listening, but she doesn't see a soul as they descend the stairs. Outside in the icy night, a car waits for them, engine running. Its exhaust creates a small cloud of fog in the freezing air.

They drive her to a police station and she is reassured a little by this. She is taken down a corridor that is almost painfully bright – the lightbulbs protected by wire cages. Then she is pushed into a pitch dark cell.

The smell is the first thing that hits her. It is really bad – shit, piss, bad breath, the meaty smell of unwashed bodies. There is the sound of the heavy breathing of sleep. At first she can see nothing and stands by the door. But eventually her eyes adjust to the very faint light that comes in from a street lamp somewhere outside the thick, frosted glass window. She sees that the space is already crowded. There are at least eight other people there, as well as a pile of luggage in one of the corners near the door. There is a bed and there are people sitting on that, backs to the wall in various attitudes of sleep. There are more people on the floor, including some children. It reminds her of a photograph she once saw of a painting by Goya – something about a massacre. There is some space near the luggage so Julia steps across the prone bodies and inserts herself into it, back to the wall. She has just enough room to stretch out her legs. There is some coughing and snuffling. Somebody talks in their sleep. Someone else starts to snore. Despite all the bodies, the cell becomes very cold and Julia draws her coat around her and pulls the collar up. It doesn't make much difference.

The day, three and a half years ago, that Julia had resolved to leave home was in May. A Saturday. Shabbes. She feigned illness so that her parents would go to synagogue without her. The German invasion had started a few days previously and she had hesitated that Saturday morning after she heard the door close. Should she go ahead? She had a plan – she had had it for weeks. Everything was in place. She had found a place to live, she had a job. But now this – the Germans.

She didn't have much time to decide. Her parents would be back. She agonised. The minutes ticked by. Her suitcase sat on the bed, looking at her. Asking the question. 'Are we going? *I'm* ready.'

And finally she thought – if not now, when? If I am not for myself, who will be for me?

'Fuck it,' she said, and picked up the suitcase.

Julia wanted to be either a writer or an actress. Maybe both. Her job was at the Hollandsche Schouwburg theatre. It was menial – a dresser and general dogsbody. The pay was shit but just enough to cover the rent on a dump and cheap food. It was a start.

But things started to go wrong almost immediately. Her ration cards were sent to her home and she couldn't go back there. When she tried to re-register with her new address she was told that because she wasn't yet eighteen, she would have to get her parents' permission. That closed that door. Without ration cards, she couldn't get food. She eventually managed to get some cards on the black market – in the theatre somebody always knew somebody – and to get herself re-registered, but the cost was everything she earned. She needed money for the rent. That was when the idea came to her that she could use her looks and her body. That led her to the photographs. She only did them a few times to pay off the cost of the ration cards.

After that things were settled for a few months. She worked, she earned, she ate, she had a little money. But in October 1941, the Germans changed the name of the theatre to the Joodsche Schouwburg and decreed that only Jews could perform there. Julia had become friends with an old guy called Anton who had worked backstage there for ever.

'It's the beginning,' he said. 'You should get out of here while you can, kid. It's only going to get worse.'

She hadn't believed him until the following April when the order for the Star came.

'Get out,' Anton said again. 'Find some other way to make money. If you're really – and I mean *really* – stuck, call this guy.'

'This guy' had turned out to be Bert.

That first time, the first film, she had felt the same sense of dislocation she feels now. Obviously, her being here is only a temporary thing and they are going to take her somewhere else. She tries not to think about that. She tries to just be here now.

In the time since she left home, Julia has developed a skill that she calls 'moving her mind'. It was what she did during the films. She would be naked, legs open, and doing what she had to do, but her mind would be in a different place. It would be walking out the door after the shoot into the fresh air outside. Her body might be in front of the camera but she tried to make it that the rest of her was outside waiting for her. After the shooting, she and that other piece of herself would rendezvous. They would have money. They would go off and do things together.

Now it is like the opposite of that. Her mind wants to wander off, to try to anticipate what lies ahead, but Julia keeps bringing it back.

'Please stay with me,' she keeps saying to herself in her head. At some stage she must actually say it aloud because somebody shushes her and tells her to be quiet.

She dozes.

Some time later, while the night is still black outside, the cell door opens and a rectangle of light falls across the tangle of sleeping bodies. Julia's eyes snap open. Someone else is pushed into the cell and the door clangs shut again. A female silhouette in a coat stands there, unable to see after the brightness of the corridor outside.

'I can't see.'

'Over here,' says Julia. 'There's space.'

'But I can't see.'

The voice is young, fearful. Wet. She has been crying. Julia puts her hand up.

'Take my hand.'

Ice cold fingers find hers.

'Just be careful where you step.'

The girl steps over Julia's outstretched legs. Julia makes a space between herself and the piled-up suitcases. The girl puts her back against the wall and slides down, slotting into the space beside Julia. She can just make out a girl about her own age or maybe a bit younger. She is taller than Julia.

'Thank you,' the girl whispers.

Julia goes to take her hand away but the girl continues

to grip it tightly. Julia leaves it there. The girl is shaking. Julia just wants to go to sleep now. She is beyond exhausted. So much has happened it seems like months since she was filming with Bert – was it really only yesterday? But the girl has begun to cry and is soon sobbing.

This makes Julia angry. *She* wants to fucking cry. She wants somebody to hold her. To comfort her. Just once in her life to tell her it's all going to be all right. But this girl isn't going to do that.

The crying continues. It's really getting on Julia's nerves now. She sits there stonily until the girl goes silent. Eventually, Julia falls asleep. When she wakes, the girl's head is on Julia's shoulder and Julia's head rests against hers. The girl has drooled onto the sleeve of Julia's coat. When Julia lifts her head, the girl wakes. As soon as she becomes aware of her surroundings she starts to cry again.

Christ, Julia thinks, this one. She wants consoling. But nobody's consoling Julia. That's the way it's always been her whole fucking life – she's had to stand alone, with nobody to protect her. Julia ignores her, struggling with herself as her mind races off again, trying to anticipate what's coming.

The girl eventually stops, takes a handkerchief from her sleeve and wipes her nose. She is very skinny and wears a coat, beneath it a dark dress and black stockings. It's very hard to see what colour anything is in the weak light of the cell. The clothes look like they were expensive once but are now worn and shabby. The girl is maybe a year or two younger than Julia and unbelievably pale – more bone white than a corpse, with hollow dark circles around her eyes. Julia speculates that she might have worked in an expensive shop or maybe in De Bijenkorf, the department store – maybe the perfume department or expensive clothes or lingerie.

The girl returns the hankie to her sleeve and then takes a pair of glasses from the pocket of her cardigan. Putting them on, and with her blonde hair tied up, she suddenly doesn't look at all like a girl from De Bijenkorf. Rather, she reminds Julia of the girl who was top of the class in school. Julia can't even remember her name now – just that she hated her.

'I'm Suzanne,' the girl says.

She extends a hand. Reluctantly Julia takes it. The freezing fingers again.

'Julia,' she says shortly, not wanting to get involved.

'Pleased to meet you,' says Suzanne, with unexpected formality.

Julia says nothing. The rest of the occupants of the cell are waking up. People are having to go to the toilet. A coat is used as a screen. Somebody complains that the bucket is nearly full. The smell of shit and piss is suddenly much stronger. The children begin to moan and say that they're hungry.

'Are these some of your family?' asks Suzanne.

Julia shakes her head. *Don't talk.*

She does anyway.

'No, I'm by myself.'

'Me too.'

The implication seems to be that they should join forces in some way. Fuck that.

After a pause, Suzanne continues. 'I was in hiding. My parents found a place for me. But there was only room for me. I suppose my parents must be gone to the East now.'

Suzanne chokes back a sob. Julia remembers that that was why she hated that girl in school. Sara. That was her name. She hated her because she was so smart and seemed to have such a perfect life. It sounds like this one had had the same. *My parents found a place for me.*

'I hope they're still alive,' says Suzanne. 'I think

29

somebody betrayed me. What about you?'

'I just carried on. Didn't report. Didn't play their stupid fucking game.'

'You did? My God, that was so brave.'

Julia didn't think it was brave. Just smart. You can be smart in school and still be pretty stupid. Julia wonders where Sara is now. In hiding? Yes, her parents would probably have tried to find a hiding place for their darling daughter too.

Suzanne's face is not so much pretty as intriguing. She has high cheekbones and kind eyes. It's a face that invites questions. Curiosity. Julia both wants to ask but doesn't at the same time.

Suzanne says, 'You don't seem afraid.'

'I'm very afraid. But so far, it's not the worst thing that's ever happened to me.'

Julia knows she's bragging.

'No?'

'No.'

'Do you mind me asking –'

'Maybe some other time.'

An awkward silence follows. Suzanne asks the question that has been tormenting Julia.

'What do you think is going to happen to us?'

How the fuck should I know blazes in Julia's head but she manages to say, 'Ship us off to some place. A camp or something. If they were going to kill us they'd have already done it.'

The words come out without thinking. Julia doesn't know where they came from. Are they a wish or what she actually thinks? She finds though that, either way, they make her feel a bit braver. Despite herself, she says to Suzanne, 'It's better to be afraid. Makes you sharper.'

'You think so?'

Julia doesn't but she says that she does. Why is she

trying to make this girl she doesn't like feel better?

'I'm sorry I was so upset earlier on,' says Suzanne. 'I was in shock. I had been in hiding for two years. I thought I was going to get through. That I'd made it.'

'I can see how you would,' says Julia noncommittally.

'I'm better now,' says Suzanne. 'It won't happen again.'

This is too much for Julia. She cracks.

'How can you say that? How can you say such a stupid thing?'

'What's stupid?'

'"It won't happen again." What do you mean? You won't cry again? You won't be afraid again?'

'I might cry,' says Suzanne. 'And I'll certainly be afraid. But I'll try to control it. I'll try to control my fear.'

Julia's heard it all at this stage. 'And how the fuck are you going to do that?' she asks.

She's enjoying swearing in front of Suzanne who's clearly taken aback by it. Little daddy's girl never heard bad words.

'You know the weather?' says Suzanne. Her voice is even. Calm. Rational.

'Of course I know the weather,' says Julia.

'Our emotions are like the weather. They change from day to day, from hour to hour. Sometimes from minute to minute. Right?'

'Yeah'

'I try to make my own weather. Bring my own weather with me.'

'How do you do that?'

'It was something I realised while I was in hiding – that it's weakness to let your thoughts control your actions. You can let your actions control your thoughts. Then you'll be strong.'

'Like how?'

'Well, for example, I had these long days with almost nothing to do. So I made up these movies in my head. I would film a bit every day and assemble the movie in my head and then play it.' Suzanne has been speaking quietly but now is becoming more animated. 'Happy movies. Sad movies. Whatever mood I wanted to create I just played that movie.'

'Fucking weird,' says Julia.

But now the conversation stops because suddenly there is the sound of several sets of footsteps in the corridor. The cell goes silent. Everybody listens and stares at the door. The footsteps stop. There is a jangle of keys and then the metallic clatter of a key being put in the lock and turned. The cell door squeals open.

'Jesus, these Jews stink,' a voice says in Dutch.

3

They are taken, carrying their luggage, out into the rear yard of the police station where a truck waits, its engine running. It is still dark though the shell of night has cracked and the first traces of colour have appeared in a part of the sky.

Julia remembers the two eggs she bought; she had planned to fry them.

The cobblestones are slick with frost and the truck's exhaust smoke is grey in the bitterly cold air. Julia is shivering and she doesn't know whether it's from the cold or from fear. Suzanne is beside her, shaking too.

So much for bringing your weather with you.

Julia wishes Suzanne would go and cling on to somebody else; Julia needs to be alone. To think. To try and get to grips with all of this. To find a way out. There has to be a way. Last night, she was too tired and shocked to think but now her mind is racing again. She just needs to be by herself.

They are made to climb up into the back of the truck, the canvas cover is pulled down, tied and then the truck lurches off. A few rips in the canvas let a little light in. Julia and Suzanne sit beside each other in the semi-darkness. Nobody speaks.

They are not in the truck for long. When it stops again

and they emerge, they are at Muiderpoort station. The station is almost deserted at this time of the morning. They are taken inside and put on a regular passenger train in a compartment with other Jews. The doors are locked from the outside and the train pulls out.

Everyone is silent at first – even the children, who all sit by the windows. But once they have been going for a while, people begin to bring out some food. It's just as Julia has always said – people have to eat; life has to go on. Julia has the bread and ham from yesterday. She takes it out of her case and isn't in the least surprised to find that Suzanne has nothing. She apologises for this, explaining how it was the people hiding her who used to bring her food.

'What happened to them?' Julia asks.

Why do I keep doing this – entering into these conversations that I don't want?

Suzanne shakes her head, a forlorn expression on her face.

'I don't know. Nothing good, that's for sure.'

Julia feels she has no choice but to share her food. The result is that her portion hardly takes the edge off her hunger. Suzanne thanks her profusely but after that, she is silent as she gazes out the window as though entranced.

It is a blue and white winter's day lit by a bright, low sun. It's a day for skating or a long walk in the woods followed by a big dinner in front of a roaring fire, plenty of wine and then collapsing into a deep warm bed. Meadows and bare fields fly by, dusted with frost like icing sugar. There are the black limbs of bare trees, villages, people going about their business, three women in scarves chatting while they wait at a level crossing, two men meeting and shaking hands. The telephone wires along the track swoop up and down like swallows. The pale, wintry sun chases along beside them.

During the whole journey, Suzanne speaks only once. This is when she turns to Julia and with a radiant smile on her face, says, 'It's like freedom.'

'What direction are we going in?' asks Julia.

Julia isn't surprised that Suzanne knows. There are people who know which way north is and those who don't. Somehow, she knew Suzanne would be one of those who did.

'East. Towards Germany.'

This answer makes Julia even more afraid. For some reason, she thinks about her parents. She wonders if they are still alive.

The train stops numerous times and it is just after noon when they arrive at their destination. There was nothing to say they had crossed into Germany so Julia hopes that maybe they are still in the Netherlands.

The train has entered some kind of camp. The doors are unlocked and they disembark. There is a distant high barbed wire fence, watchtowers and a lot of long, low wooden huts that look like sheds with a few windows. There are no German soldiers to be seen – only members of the Dutch constabulary, the Marechaussee who guard the new arrivals.

'What do you think they're going to do to us, Julia?' Suzanne asks, inevitably, as she – equally inevitably – stands next to Julia.

'How the fuck would I know?'

Suzanne just stares at her. *Go on, the tears again.*

They find out soon enough. The constables herd them to a hut where they queue up and are registered. The people doing the registering are not Germans or constables but camp inmates. They sit at tables with typewriters. As she queues, Julia overhears the questions being asked – name, date of birth, occupation. Julia isn't quite sure what to say to that last question but something tells her that, in a place like this, 'actress' wouldn't really be a good answer. 'Cook,' she announces when her turn comes. The middle-aged man in the threadbare coat doing the registering looks up when she says this. He eyes her up and down, appears to consider it for a few moments and then writes it down as though it doesn't matter anyway. She is told she will be in hut sixty-five.

After registration, males and females are separated and Julia and Suzanne go, with other women and children, to another part of the camp where they find hut sixty-five. Inside are rows and rows of three-tier metal bunks and hundreds of people. The place smells of stale vegetables, bodies and dirty toilets. The huts have walls of thin wooden planks so that inside is as cold as outside. Clothes lines are strung between the bunks and there is washing everywhere. The women seem to all be washing clothes; children run about. One lot is playing a game of hide and seek. They stand in a circle, hands over their eyes, counting. As they reach a hundred, they scatter in different directions.

Julia and Suzanne manage to find a pair of bunks that are unoccupied. Suzanne takes the middle one, Julia the top – it feels less suffocating. Julia resigns herself to the fact that it looks like, for now, Suzanne is going to be her shadow. Julia tries to feel indifferent about it, consoling herself with the thought that if Suzanne finds somebody more like herself she'll be off. In the meantime, Julia will try to be as unpleasant as possible.

The end of each bunk consists of a series of steel bars and so she is able to climb up without standing on anyone else's bed. She puts her case on the bed and then clambers up onto the mattress, kneeling on it.

It is filled with straw, some of which escapes through rips in the seam. It is so thin that she can feel the slats of the bed underneath. There is also one weary blanket which was once yellow but is now brown and stained. While Julia's own apartment had been pretty run-down, the one thing about it was that it had had a really deep, comfortable mattress. And she had managed to accumulate a number of blankets so that it had been the one place where she was guaranteed to be warm. It is going to be cold here but she has brought a blanket of her own and remakes the bed with her blanket inside and the yellow-brown one on top. It's all about order. Julia likes order.

There is no place to put anything – no cupboards – so everything is either in her suitcase, on the bed or underneath the covers. She wonders how safe her things are going to be. She knows that it's not something she can really worry about or guard against. She resolves that if anybody steals any of her belongings, she will steal other people's. With that comforting decision made and as she is climbing down, there is a flurry of activity by the door of the hut. Apparently it's lunchtime.

Some inmates have pulled a cart into the room in which is set a big steel vat. Julia has a vision of battleships from the last war – great, grey steel. The occupants of the hut form a line carrying spoons and bowls. Julia returns to get hers and Suzanne says, 'Maybe they will give me one.'

They join the line and Julia engineers it that Suzanne is in front of her.

'I have no bowl,' she says when she reaches the head of the line.

'Just take your bread then,' says the woman who is ladling out the soup. 'And make it last. There'll be no more for three days.'

'But what about the soup?' asks Suzanne.

'No bowl, no soup,' says the woman. She has grey, stringy hair and an ashen face. 'Next.'

'Hey, that's not fair,' Julia says without thinking, stepping forward from behind Suzanne.

'Fair?' says the woman with an unpleasant smile. 'When was the last time you saw fair?'

Fucking bitch.

'There must be spare bowls,' Julia says. 'People who have left or –'

'Died?'

There is a man with the soup bitch – a big man. It looks like he must be there to guard the food. But he doesn't look like a guard or a bouncer – there is something refined, educated about him. Julia looks at him and flashes her warmest, most winning smile. It isn't sexy, exactly – she feels that would be wrong for this situation – but she reckons it is guaranteed to please.

'That woman who went during the night,' he says.

'It'll cost you,' says the woman. 'What do you have? Got any cigarettes?'

'I don't smoke –' Suzanne begins to say.

'I've got cigarettes,' says Julia.

The price is set at ten cigarettes, which enables Julia to hold on to the remaining three. She curses herself. She needs to cut Suzanne loose – the girl is way too much of a liability.

Suzanne is given a bowl and spoon. The two girls receive their so-called 'potato soup' and bread. They find a place to sit, against the wall of the hut.

'Thank you so much, Julia. I think you just saved my life.'

'Don't be stupid,' snaps Julia. 'You'd have figured it out. You'd have stolen somebody else's. Or something.'

Suzanne says nothing, the implication being that she wouldn't have done that at all. *Daddy's little angel.*

The soup looks like dishwater and smells awful so that Julia finds it difficult to pass it under her nose. There appears to be no nutrition to speak of in it. After it, she doesn't feel full or satisfied, just bloated. The pair go outside in the air. Julia wonders how she can get rid of Suzanne.

'What do you suppose happens here?' Suzanne asks, as they walk in the open space between the huts.

'How should I know? I suppose we'll have to do some kind of work. When they asked your profession, what did you say?'

'I told them I was a nurse.'

'A nurse. And are you?'

Suzanne smiles.

'I was studying English literature at university.'

Julia is both unsurprised and resentful. 'So what will you do if they ask you to do nursing?'

'I'll worry about that when it happens. My parents were both archaeologists at the university. They used to spend their summers on digs – once in England but mainly in Pompeii in Italy. I would go with them. I became the resident nurse on the site – if people cut themselves or got stung or bitten or something like that. That's about as much as I can do.'

'You've been to Pompeii?' asks Julia, annoyed because she is unable to say it without sounding awestruck. This girl has had it all – happy family, world travel...

'You've heard of it?' asks Suzanne.

'Of course I've heard of it,' Julia snaps. 'I may not have been to university but I'm not stupid. I've read about it.'

Julia's hoping Suzanne will get angry or walk away or just pick up that she's not wanted. But instead Suzanne says, 'You like to read,' and then, after a pause, 'I'm glad.'

They are silent for a while. Suzanne appears to be deep

in thought. Then she says, 'What about you?'

'What about me what?'

'Your profession.'

'I'm … an actress.'

'Really?' asks Suzanne. 'What kind of actress? Theatre? Movie?'

'Movie.'

'Would I have seen any of the movies you were in?'

Julia can't help smiling.

'I doubt it. I was just starting off my career. I only got small parts.'

Sometimes they were very big parts.

And now, weirdly, Julia feels unsettled. She thinks that she wouldn't ever want Suzanne to know what she did. After another long silence, Suzanne says, 'I wasn't very good at bringing my own weather with me during the night. I'm sorry for being so teary. You were so strong. I thought you were amazing. All along.'

'I was feeling the same as you,' says Julia. 'I just didn't want to show it. Didn't want to give the fuckers the satisfaction.'

She is annoyed to find that her swearing doesn't seem to shock Suzanne like it did at first.

They spend the rest of the day either trying to keep warm or aimlessly exploring their surroundings. They have to go to the toilet a lot because of the soup. There is a latrine building that consists of a long plank attached to the walls, above an evil-smelling ditch. The plank has a series of regular holes in it. You climb onto the plank, being careful not to slip into the ditch, and then sit on a hole. There is no privacy and no toilet paper.

Once it gets too cold to stay outside, they go back to the barracks. There is more potato soup for dinner. Julia reluctantly drinks it, knowing that she will be up and down to the toilet all night. They eat more of their bread ration. It is shitty bread. Julia would happily eat it all and she knows she still wouldn't be anywhere near full. With great difficulty she resists.

There is nothing much to do and anyway it is so cold. The girls decide to go to bed which is what most other people seem to be doing. As well as the latrine hut, there is a washroom at the end of this hut. It contains one long sink with taps spaced a metre or so apart and one toilet. They go to the toilet for what Julia hopes will be the last time until morning, wash in cold water and climb up onto their beds.

Suzanne says, 'Goodnight, Julia.'

The homely wish takes Julia by surprise. It's so long since anybody wished her goodnight or that there was anybody with her when she went to sleep.

'G'night,' she says, unable to bring herself to use Suzanne's name.

The soup goes through Julia rapidly so that she has to go to the washroom several times during the night. People complain whenever she climbs down as the rickety bunk shakes. There is often a queue in the darkness for the single toilet.

Sometime during the night, she thinks she can hear Suzanne crying.

There also turn out to be fleas in the bed. Julia starts to itch. She sleeps fitfully and when she wakes in the morning she has bite marks all over her body.

4

In the queue for breakfast – the inevitable potato soup – Julia and Suzanne get talking to the woman in front of them. She has a pale, gaunt face and wears an ancient overcoat with a scarf tied under her chin. There is a child with her, aged maybe three or four.

'Haven't seen you here before.'

'We came yesterday,' says Julia.

'What work are you doing?'

'They haven't given us any work yet.'

The woman's eyes widen. There is fear in them.

'What's wrong?' Julia asks, amazed by the woman's reaction.

'You must get some work,' she says. 'If not they will put you on the transport.'

'The transport?'

'Every Tuesday – they fill a train and send it to the East. They say it is to a work camp but…'

'But what?'

'They are Germans. Who can believe what they say? They are capable of anything.'

'What do you think?' Suzanne asks Julia, outside after breakfast, walking the perimeter of the camp to keep warm. 'Could it be worse than this?'

Why is it always thrown back on me? Why am I always the one?

There are a couple of things that Julia has always lived by. She thinks of them vaguely as 'principles'. They are things she has learned as she has grown up – especially in the last few years. One is that she is capable of dealing with anything. The second is that tomorrow is going to be a better day than today. It is this that guides her now.

'I don't see how,' Julia says. 'Anyway, how do we get work? Who do we go to? And you couldn't do any kind of hard work on this shit food they're giving us. I think we should just wait and see what happens. Conserve our energy. Save our strength.'

'I think you're right,' says Suzanne.

Of course you do. Anything rather than think for yourself.

Then Julia says, 'Was that you crying during the night?'

'I'm sorry,' says Suzanne. 'Did I wake you?'

'No.'

Suzanne says, 'I was just going through a "why me?" moment. Why was I born a Jew? In this time? In this place? You know how it can be in those dark hours of the night. I'm over it now.'

'You've got the weather back with you again?'

The words were intended to be mocking but if Suzanne notices, she doesn't respond. Instead, with a smile, she says, 'Exactly.'

Then she says, 'You said you like books. Reading.'

'I love books,' Julia says.

But it's not a conversation she wants to have with Suzanne. Julia regards books as part of her own intimate life.

'I love books too,' says Suzanne. 'I think I live my life by them. Sometimes I think they're my only real friends.'

After a silence, Suzanne says tentatively, 'I was

44

wondering … what would you think … if we wrote a book?'

'What – here in the camp?'

'That's right. Here in the camp.'

'You mean about the camp?'

'No, not about the camp. Not about the camp at all. It would be about anything but the camp. Something out in the world. It would be a way of escaping the camp.'

During the night, Julia has concluded that she can't get out of this camp. There is clearly no kind of escape. Between the Nazis and the collaborating Dutch they have set up what is obviously a watertight system. She knows enough about how life works – if you can't escape the system you have to work it. During the night, that's what she decided to do.

Though it is such a dismal system. The food, the camp. A book would be a way of leaving it behind.

But Julia could never write a book. She has always thought she would like to, has often scribbled random thoughts in a diary, stupid and bad little poems, or descriptions of beautiful things she saw – but the notion that she might write a book? It's absurd. Outrageous.

If this is what she is thinking, what she says is, 'We'd need a lot of paper. And pencils or pens. Where would we get all that?'

'When I went into hiding I took some notebooks with me. They were really just about the only thing I took.'

Again Julia's mouth goes first, opening up a conversation she doesn't at all want.

'How long were you in hiding for?'

'More than two years.'

'My God. In what kind of place?'

'A corner of an attic. The people who hid me built a sort of tiny room there. On one side of it – where the roof was highest – you could stand up.'

'And you stayed in that place for over two years?'

Suzanne nods.

Julia is appalled. 'Did you come out at all?'

'At first no. The people hiding me – they were an old couple – were too afraid that somebody might see me. But it became impossible. I can endure a lot…'

There is something about these words that resonates with Julia. Suzanne continues.

'But I was becoming weak, my muscles were wasting away from so little exercise. So I persuaded them to let me come out. At night. Just for a little while.'

Julia can see from Suzanne's face that she is becoming shaky at the memory.

'Eventually, every night, I would come out for a little while, go down into the house. I would just walk around – from one room to the next – endlessly. That nearly made us all crazy. Can you imagine it, just walking round a house from one room to another? Over and over again. Hundreds of times.'

Julia tries to imagine it. It occurs to her that there are many different ways that life can be unspeakable.

Suzanne has told Julia she is twenty. Julia looks at her now and all Julia can see – with the glasses and the pale face – is a fragile little girl who needs to be held. She is just a child, regardless of her university education. She has seen so little of the world despite all her travels.

'Sometimes, when they thought their neighbours were away, I was allowed out into their garden. Only at night of course. I can still remember how it felt to be out in the air. Breathing was like drinking wine, the air felt like silk on my skin. But in the end, I think that's what gave me away. There was a boy about my age next door. He heard me and started to call over the wall, asking who was there. I froze.'

It is as though Suzanne is reliving what happened.

'I crept back inside as quietly as I could. But the next day he called round and asked to see me. The old couple swore blind that there was nobody else in the house but he insisted he had heard somebody. Soon after that they came for me.

'In some ways it was a relief. The worst part was that I wasn't doing anything – I wasn't running away or fighting or anything. At least you did something. You lived every day. I was hardly living at all. I just waited. Like a cornered animal waiting for the hunter.'

Julia sees a small frightened rabbit cowering in a hedgerow.

'So anyway, I filled one notebook while I was there.'

'With a book?

'No, not a book. Short stories. My thoughts – a kind of diary. Things I would do after the war. Lists of the things I would eat. Places I would go. Anything really. Anyway, I left it behind, and hopefully I'll be able to pick it up when the war ends. I was ready to start a new one and managed to bring it with me. There are two hundred and forty pages in it. If we write small we could write a book.'

Suzanne looks into Julia's eyes. 'What do you think?'

'I've never written anything before,' says Julia and now, suddenly, she feels small and frightened.

'Nothing?'

'Well, you know, just childish things. Stupid things.'

'If you can read, you can write,' Suzanne announces, as thought that were the end of the matter.

Then she adds, 'Oh please, Julia, say that you will. I'm going to do it by myself anyway but it would be so much more fun to do it with somebody else. And anyway, can't you see – there's a reason why we've been thrown together.

There's no reason. It's just an accident. Chance.

'This is obviously the reason. What do you say?'

47

Julia is astonished at what Suzanne is proposing. The audacity of it. In this terrible place, in these circumstances, that she would even think up such an idea, much less voice it. And that she would ask Julia to be a part of it. In some ways that's the most extraordinary thing of all.

There seems no way out. And anyway, Julia is actually very taken with the idea, even though simultaneously, she is daunted – no, overwhelmed – no, terrified – at the prospect.

Suzanne looks at her. Suzanne has pushed her glasses up onto her head, so there are just her blue eyes framed in the blonde hair. She is smiling.

'But you know how to do it – you were learning it, in university. I know nothing about –'

'I've only ever written short stories before – or assignments for my professors. This would be the first time I'd tried to write a book. We'd both have to learn. We'd learn as we went along. We'd help each other. Come on, Julia.'

Julia feels tremendously inadequate at the thought of doing this with somebody who's been to university. But Suzanne's eyes are warm and her smile is inviting. And there is something else in her face – a frailness, even a vulnerability. Maybe Julia will be able to contribute something to this, instead of being just an incompetent passenger. After all, she has experience of the world.

'All right,' says Julia, 'I'll give it a try. But you have to swear that you'll tell me if what I'm writing is no good. I don't want to hold you back or ruin your book.'

'It's our book, Julia. And anyway, if you're a reader, you know good writing when you see it. You'll know if what you're doing isn't good enough. You won't need me to tell you. And you also have to tell me when mine's not up to scratch.'

The thought hadn't occurred to Julia.

'All right,' she says. 'I will.'

Suzanne extends her hand. Julia takes it and they shake.

'So when do we start?' asks Julia.

'We start right now,' says Suzanne.

'Oh,' Julia says, hesitantly. 'But how?'

'Well, we've got to have' – Suzanne counts the items off on her fingers – 'characters, action, setting, and atmosphere. How about we start with the setting?'

'All right,' says Julia and an idea immediately occurs to her. 'How about a big hotel. A luxury hotel. Since lots of people would be coming and going, we would have scope for lots of different characters.'

Suzanne considers this for a moment and then says, 'That's a really good idea.'

Julia is pleased – and not only that, but she was often in such hotels with her parents when she was younger. She'll have lots of information about them. Maybe there'll be stories and people she'll be able to remember if she thinks hard enough.

'And we'd be able to talk about food,' she adds. 'Beautiful food. Lots of it.'

'That'd be nice,' Suzanne says. 'So – a hotel. What century?'

'Just before the war?' Julia ventures. 'The thirties?'

'Makes sense,' says Suzanne. 'We both lived through that time so we wouldn't have to do much research. A hotel in Holland?'

'What if we just say somewhere in Western Europe?' suggests Julia. 'That should be all right, shouldn't it?'

Suzanne agrees.

'So that's the setting,' says Julia. She holds up four fingers, then lowers her little one. 'That leaves characters, action, atmosphere,' though she's not sure exactly what 'atmosphere' is. She asks Suzanne. That's another thing about Julia. She doesn't mind admitting that she doesn't know something. She tries to learn and learn quickly. Most other people seem to see not knowing things as a weakness but Julia sees it as a skill. The way she thinks about it is that it means she's expert in becoming expert. How stupid other people are not to see this.

'What kind of book we're going to write,' Suzanne explains, pushing a stray strand of her hair back behind her ear. 'You know. Whether it's a love story or a detective story. Serious or funny. Happy ending or sad. Those sorts of things.'

Julia likes the way Suzanne is explaining everything. She doesn't come across as some kind of know-it-all.

This one takes them quite a time to sort out. They do it by elimination. Finally, Suzanne says, 'What if we wrote a murder mystery? Set in the hotel.'

'That sounds really difficult,' says Julia. 'You know – we'd have to figure out all the twists and turns in the plot and keep the reader guessing.'

'But that would be part of the fun, wouldn't it?'

'Yes, I suppose it would be,' she says. Then she asks, 'And is it going to be a serious book or funny?'

'Well, murder's pretty serious,' says Suzanne.

'But that doesn't mean it all has to be serious.'

'That's true. But it's very hard to write stuff that's actually funny.'

'But that would be part of the fun, wouldn't it?' echoes Julia.

Suzanne looks into her eyes and laughs. 'We can but try. So – we have the setting and the atmosphere. Now we just need characters and action – the plot.'

'That's most of the story really. Isn't it?' says Julia.

'It is,' says Suzanne.

The two girls have been doing all of this while walking

around the open space between the huts. Dusk is coming on now and with it an intense, lung-searing cold.

'Maybe we should sleep on all that,' says Suzanne and that is what they decide to do.

The first Julia knows there is something very different about this day is when she gets up to go to the washroom sometime before dawn. The queue is far longer than usual, extending out the door, and there is the sound of somebody puking inside. By the time it's her turn, the bowl is overflowing and the floor is awash with urine and vomit.

After peeing, she goes back to bed and falls into a deep sleep. When she wakes, the sounds are very different from the ones she has become used to. There is a deathly silence about the place. The normal morning bustle is missing. People speak in whispers. Even the children aren't capering about as they normally do. And there is a smell that Julia knows very well. It is the smell of fear.

Today, they discover, is the day that the list of those to be transported is to be posted up. It usually happens in the evening.

'Pretty girls like you should be able to get off the list,' a woman tells them. 'The rate is one week's postponement. If I were you, college girl, I'd take off the glasses.'

'What did she mean?' Suzanne asks Julia as soon as they are alone. 'And how did she know – calling me "college girl", I mean?'

'Maybe you just look like a student with the glasses.'

'And what was the thing about the postponement?'

Julia tells her.

'My God, that's terrible,' Suzanne says.

If you only knew.

While they wait for the list, people don't know

whether they will be staying or going. Some try to go about their business as normal. Others gather their meagre belongings together on their beds, laying them out as though packing for a holiday. But nobody actually packs as that would be to invite calamity. Some people are unable to eat and give away their potato soup. Anxiously, Julia and Suzanne ask several people where the transports go but while nobody can tell them, they all reply with the same thing – that it's definitely nowhere good. And they tell blood-chilling stories of couples separated by the transports, children and parents torn apart, babies taken from their mothers, the separation of aging husbands and wives.

Julia and Suzanne had hoped to get on with their book today but the mood of raw terror that hangs over the camp takes hold of them too and means they are unable to focus on it. If people can be affected in this way, they reason, then whatever happens with these transports must be very, very bad. Julia finds she can hardly speak. Instead her thoughts go inwards. She is very frightened.

'Let's go out in the air,' says Suzanne.

Once outside they begin to walk – it is the only way to keep the cold at bay.

'Have you heard of Boudica?' asks Suzanne.

Julia feels like she is choking. She manages to say 'no'.

'One summer my parents took me to a dig – an archaeological dig – in England. They told me about Boudica.'

'What is it?' asks Julia.

'It's not a "what is it?" – it's a "who was she?",' replies Suzanne. 'In 60 AD the Romans had occupied Britain. They were just like the Germans – invading places, taking the land and all the wealth, enslaving people, torturing, killing. Boudica was the queen of one of the British tribes, the Iceni. She led a revolt against the Romans.'

'Good for her,' says Julia.

'She and her army attacked cities, burned them, killed many, many Romans and their collaborators.'

'And she freed the British?'

Suzanne shook her head. 'Sadly, she didn't. Eventually the Romans defeated her. Maybe she was killed in the last battle, maybe she killed herself afterwards. Nobody knows exactly what happened to her. But the reason I'm telling you this is that, when I first went into hiding, when I'd only been there a few days, I was in shock. I was thinking that I would never be able to survive this. I mean, I didn't even know how long it was going to go on for. Maybe I would grow old in that attic. If I hadn't been discovered, I'd still be there and who knows for how much longer.

'But then I remembered Boudica. The reason that she revolted was that Romans flogged her in public and raped her daughters.'

At this Julia shudders – actually, physically shudders. If Suzanne notices, she doesn't say anything. Instead she continues.

'I decided that she would be my heroine – that if I ever felt afraid or like giving up, I would remember Boudica. I started to talk to her. It became like she was there with me in the tiny attic. And I asked her to stay with me.'

Suzanne's face and eyes have become distant. She is back in the hiding hole in the attic. But suddenly she appears to return from wherever she was.

'This must sound very silly.'

'No, not at all,' says Julia, who is glad Suzanne is talking to her like this. She finds it's helping with her own fear.

'Is she with you now?' she asks.

'Yes, she's with me now. But you know, in some ways Julia – you remind me of Boudica.'

'Me?' says Julia in astonishment. 'How? Why?'

'Because you did something. You fought back. You were brave.'

Julia has never thought of it like this.

'I just carried on working,' she says. 'Trying to make enough to eat and pay the rent.'

But Suzanne ignores this. She says, 'You asked me if Boudica was here with me now. I think she is. I think you're Boudica.'

Julia laughs. The thought is too outrageous.

'You mean brought back to life or something?'

Suzanne shrugs. 'I don't know. Reincarnated –' Julia doesn't know what this means '– her soul, her spirit, something. I feel her very close to me now. Closer than ever before. And that is why there's no reason for us to be afraid. Imagine it. Feel it. You are Boudica and I am one of your army. Maybe one of your inner circle. Maybe your closest adviser. For now, the Germans have us in bondage.'

It's another word that resonates with Julia.

'But we will be free. We will defeat them. And most of all – we will have our revenge.'

While it all sounds a bit outlandish to Julia, she is startled to find that this talk of Boudica has helped. It has made her feel better, stronger, less fearful.

And Julia thinks how extraordinary this all is. A couple of days ago, she didn't even know of Suzanne's existence and she is very, very different from Julia. Suzanne is educated and dreamy and has travelled outside Holland. Julia could be wrong but she has a hunch that Suzanne has always lived with her parents – that she has led a pretty sheltered life. She's definitely a virgin. Julia doesn't know if Suzanne has brothers and sisters but she imagines that Suzanne's childhood was very happy, very protected.

But with all her university education and travel, Suzanne doesn't seem very smart about the world. Even if Julia's last few years had been relatively normal and she had worked in a shop or something like that, her knowledge of life would be so much more than Suzanne's.

Yet suddenly, bizarrely, Suzanne has – literally – become the dearest person in the world to Julia. Of course, this wouldn't be hard, Julia thinks bitterly. Who else is there? Suzanne is number one in a field of one. So now Julia asks the question that has leapt onto her back like a black, evil goblin.

'What if one of us is transported and the other isn't?' she asks.

They have been walking around to keep warm but now they stop and Suzanne turns to face Julia. Suzanne takes Julia's hands in her own.

'That's not going to happen,' she says, her eyes fixing Julia's and then Suzanne says it again with a terrible determination in her voice.

'That's not going to happen.'

The hours creep by with painful slowness. Darkness comes and there is still no sign of the list. By then they are back in the barracks and the smell of fear is acrid and overwhelming. The single toilet, which usually fills up some time during the night, is already overflowing and there is a constant queue for it.

Finally, the list is posted up. The occupants of the hut surge around it and the place descends into uproar. Those at the front who get to see the list first turn away, pushing their way back through the surging mass of people. Some are ashen-faced with relief. Some are hysterical and it's hard to tell whether from happiness or from terror. Some scream, some hold their heads in disbelief, women embrace one another, tears stream down the faces of those who are on the list. Some appear to be on the point of insanity and some seem to have tipped over into madness. There are wide eyes, people talking to themselves. There is urine on the floor and the sharp smell of faeces in the air. Mothers grip children until they cry out. Fathers look helpless, lost. A man in his thirties comforts a woman of the same age whose face is contorted with crying. 'I will come with you,' he says.

When the crowd thins and Julia and Suzanne get close enough to read, they find that they are both on the list.

5

A train is drawn up on the railway line that runs right through the centre of the camp. It is a regular passenger train of Pullman cars. The constabulary supervise the loading of the train while a few Germans stand in a group. Julia carries her suitcase while Suzanne has a cloth bag which she managed to pick up and which contains her bowl, spoon and the notebook. She has nothing else.

The two of them join the flow of people, all carrying luggage, that pass along the railway cars. The hysteria is pretty much over now. Everyone is muffled up as best they can against the cold – hats, scarves, coats. People wear what appear to be their best clothes but the shabbiness of these garments makes the whole scene appear a bit surreal. Julia sees a man and a woman shaking hands and she is reminded of the end of the summer holidays when she was a child – her parents saying goodbye to people they had met at the hotel.

Three Germans go by, an officer in the middle and two enlisted men. They wear heavy winter coats, caps and are all smoking. The officer is explaining something to the other two, accentuating his words with a chopping gesture of his gloved right hand that holds the cigarette.

An old woman is brought to one of the wagons on a wheelchair. Two men raise it and two other men gently lift her from the wheelchair into the interior of the car. A group of young women, looking like secretaries or shop assistants, crowd together in the doorway of one of the cars. There is much waving from people already on the train. Two middle-aged men shake hands and Julia has a sense of a friendship, forged in the camp, being sundered.

The loading is supervised by the constabulary. It is almost as if the Germans have nothing to do with it and are watching some local custom. Julia and Suzanne pass along the cars, looking into their interiors, trying to find one which isn't already too crowded. They choose one and climb aboard.

The car fills up quickly. A heavily pregnant woman comes into view. Julia watches from the window as a man helps her up the steps onto the train. Julia expects the man to join her but he doesn't – the pregnant woman appears to be quite alone. The woman enters the car and with a tortured look on her face and holding her belly, she eases herself down into a seat.

Outside, some constables can be seen approaching a knot of German officers. They hand over a sheaf of papers to one of the officers who leafs through the pages as though checking them. Having done this he gives them to the one who appears to be most senior. This man signs them before handing them back to the subordinate.

Meanwhile the doors of the cars are locked from the outside. Shortly afterwards, the locomotive whistle shrills and there is a hiss of steam. Couplings clank, the cars shudder and the train begins to move.

During all this time Julia and Suzanne have said very little. Julia feels that it has been like watching a movie. She knows this feeling too well. She experienced it the first time she did a film. She had thought it would be with one man, but it turned out to be with two. She realised afterwards that this was a thing Bert did. It was about showing who was in control. Julia nearly refused but the rent was due that day so she had no choice but to go through with it. When she made her painful way home afterwards she was in shock.

She is in shock now – in a train being carried away to an unknown destination. It is Suzanne who snaps out of it first. As the train begins to pick up speed and find its rhythm, she says, 'Now. Now we need to do the next piece of our book.'

Julia looks at her and at first she is astonished.

'Are you serious?' she asks.

But Suzanne is already rummaging in her cloth bag and produces the notebook along with a pencil that has been carefully sharpened with a knife.

The train is rocking along gently, rhythmically. For Julia, it is a rhythm familiar since childhood – it is the rhythm of going on family holidays. There is no conversation in the car. Most of the people seem locked inside their own thoughts. One or two people change places or help one another to get comfortable. An old man takes a blanket off his lap and drapes it over his wife's shoulders. She protests a little but he insists. The pregnant woman has a blanket over her lap and is staring off into space with a frightening intensity.

'You are serious, aren't you?' Julia says and she slowly breaks into a smile. It is the first time she has smiled today.

Suzanne smiles back.

'Of course – but let's have breakfast first. We can't work on an empty stomach.'

6

British newspaper report
October 1st 2015

Twenty-one transports went from Westerbork in 1944. Eight went to Bergen-Belsen. Eight went to Auschwitz. (The last of these – on September 3rd – was the one that took Anne Frank and her family.) The remaining five went not to a camp in the way we might normally imagine it – with watchtowers, barbed wire fences and gas chambers – but rather to a town in what is now the Czech Republic. These days it is called Terezin. In 1944 it was known by the Germans as Theresienstadt.

7

They eat some of the three days' bread ration they were given before boarding the train. Other people in the car are doing the same, carefully portioning out whatever food they have. There is a hum of conversation now. Julia thinks how strange it is that once there is food, everyone relaxes – a little.

She and Suzanne finish eating. Julia feels hungrier after the food than she did before but this is now becoming a familiar sensation to her. Just as Suzanne opens the notebook, a man with a grey beard across the aisle from them asks, 'What are you doing?'

'We're writing a book,' announces Suzanne cheerily.

'I don't know why you're starting something like that. You'll never get to finish it.'

At these words, Julia feels a churning in her stomach. It's as though a great dark cloud has gathered inside her head.

'Then we'll just have to write quickly, won't we?' Suzanne says jauntily.

'Fools,' he says, turning away.

Without missing a beat, Suzanne says, 'We're going to need a hero and a heroine. What if I come up with the heroine and you come up with the hero?'

Julia thinks about this for a moment.

'No, I don't think so,' she says.

'Why not?'

'If you have to think up a heroine, what will she be like?'

'Beautiful, smart, passionate –'

'There, you see, there's the problem. All women aren't beautiful and smart, you know. We want our heroine to be unusual, to stand out –'

'So, what, make her ugly with spots and hairy legs?'

'No, but she needs to stand out in other ways. Why don't I take care of the heroine and you do the hero?'

'Sure,' says Suzanne agreeably.

'And why don't we do this as well,' continues Julia. 'Why don't you make up your hero and I'll make up the heroine, but we won't tell each other what they're like. We'll just start the plot and we'll gradually find out what the hero and heroine are like – just the same way as the reader would find out. You know – as the plot gradually unfolds.'

Suzanne thinks about this and after what seems like a long time during which Julia wonders whether she had made a very stupid suggestion, Suzanne says, 'I think that's a brilliant idea.'

Julia spends most of the rest of the morning working out who her heroine is going to be. She decides to call her Fleur. Julia gives her long hair that is dark auburn – the same colour as Julia's. Fleur is tall, a bit taller than Julia – more Suzanne's height really – and she is given a fringe. Despite what Julia said to Suzanne, she makes Fleur pretty – very pretty, in fact. Fleur has long legs and breasts the size of big oranges. She is twenty, the same age as Julia, and she is also given the same birthday as Julia – December thirteenth, so she is a Sagittarius.

Now that Julia can picture her – and it doesn't take her that long to do all of that – she spends the rest of the time wondering why Fleur has come to the hotel. How can she afford it? If she is staying at the hotel she must be rich – or certainly well off. Is she alone? Is she married? Single? Even though she is young, does she have children? Is she a virgin? What part is she going to play in the murder mystery? Who is going to get murdered? And why?

There are so many questions to be answered that Julia reckons it will be impossible to answer them all before they start. Anyway, she decides that she is starting in the wrong place. Fleur must want something. That's why she's come to the hotel. And in their story, she will either have to get it and so, a happy ending, or not get it and thus, a sad ending.

And there has to be excitement. That in turn means that the stakes will have to be high. Fleur can't just want a couple of weeks of being pampered at a luxury hotel. What are the highest stakes of all? Well, they would have to be that Fleur's life was in danger. She has come to the hotel to get away from something. Somebody is pursuing her and wants to kill her. But why?

Maybe Julia doesn't need to figure that out now. Maybe she can get to that later. All she needs for now is that Fleur has a secret. There is something in her past that has made her flee wherever she was living and come here to the hotel.

And there's a related issue. Is she going to be fleeing for the rest of her life? Maybe. Julia could imagine an ending where Fleur gets safely away from the hotel but, whoever it is, is still pursuing her. That would leave the door open to a sequel. Or maybe even a series.

At this Julia has to laugh. It's a bitter laugh. As the man said, she'll be lucky to survive long enough to get one book written. Again the black cloud hovers in her brain but she dismisses it by throwing herself back into this other world that is starting to take shape in her head.

No, the ending – if it is to be a happy one, and right now that is what Julia would like – has to be final. Whoever was pursuing Fleur, whatever the secret was – all that has to be brought to a conclusion and resolved at the end of the book.

Julia ponders these and many other questions and later in the day, tells Suzanne that she has her heroine.

'And I've had some thoughts about the hero,' says Suzanne. 'I thought I would make him a –'

'No, don't tell me,' says Julia. 'Didn't we say we would find out as the story unfolded?'

'Oh yes, you're right,' says Suzanne. 'I'm dying to tell you about him. I think you'll really like him.'

'I'm sure I will – but I'll meet him soon, I'm sure.'

'So now,' Suzanne says, 'we have the characters. We have the setting and the atmosphere. Now we just need the plot.'

'Well, the start point is pretty simple,' Julia replies. 'The hero and heroine arrive at the hotel.'

'And the murder takes place,' says Suzanne.

'And then we take it from there,' says Julia. Then she asks, 'How are we going to write the book? You write a chapter and then I write a chapter? You write the hero parts and I write the heroine parts?'

'I don't really know. We only have two hundred and forty pages in the notebook. We need to make sure we don't waste any of them. How about we discuss what's going to happen next and then one of us goes away and writes it.'

'That sounds like the best idea,' agrees Julia. 'Let's try that and see how it goes. If it doesn't work we can always change it.'

Then Suzanne raises her index finger.

'We've forgotten one of the most important things,' she says.

'What's that?'

'A title. What are we going to call it? What title is really going to grab the attention of somebody looking at it in a bookshop?'

'A bookshop?'

Julia looks at Suzanne to see if she's kidding.

'Yes,' she says. 'A bookshop. If we're going to go to the trouble of writing this thing, we should be thinking of getting it published. After the war. After we get out of here – out of all of this.'

Julia suddenly feels like she is going to cry.

'Do you think we ever will?' she says.

'We have to believe it, Julia. You and I will leave here, alive and with the book. We'll go to America or some place. The book will be published. We'll make loads of money and live happily ever after.'

She pushes her glasses up her nose.

'That has to be the plan.'

Suzanne looks steadily into Julia's eyes. 'Agreed?' she asks, extending her hand.

Julia takes it. It is icy cold. 'Agreed. And the title?' she asks.

'*The Murder at the Grand Hotel*?' Suzanne ventures.

Julia frowns. 'Sounds like it's been done before.'

'Probably has,' Suzanne agrees. 'But it will do as a working title until we find something better.'

It's agreed.

'So the only remaining question now,' says Suzanne, 'is who goes first. Who arrives at the hotel first?'

'Ladies first?' Julia suggests.

'I don't see why not. And I guess we don't need to discuss this because you can decide the manner of your own arriving.'

'Sounds like a good title for a chapter – "The Manner of Her Arriving". Think we should have chapter titles?'

67

'Maybe' says Suzanne. 'Do whatever you think is best for the moment and we can decide that later. So – here, you take the book and the pencil. And remember to write small.'

Julia carefully opens the notebook. It has a black cover and marbling on the inside front and back covers. The marbling is beautiful in black and blue and white. She fans the pages and inhales the smell of new, unused paper.

Julia places the book on the table. Then, turning to the first blank, right hand page she writes at the top, 'The Murder at the Grand Hotel'. She does this in letters about a centimetre high. It is an extravagant use of paper but she hopes that Suzanne will understand. After all, it's the start of their novel.

After a moment's thought, underneath she adds in smaller writing, 'By Julia Snel & Suzanne…'

She pauses. 'What's your second name, Suzanne?'

Julia is aware that it is the first time she has used Suzanne's name.

'Helman.'

She adds the surname. Then she writes, 'Chapter One'.

Chapter One

The Manner of Her Arriving (Julia)

Well now it's done, thought Fleur as she came out of the police station, hailed a taxi and went to catch the train. She had relaxed somewhat during her interview but now her heart was pounding again. She had felt safe in the police station talking to the two officers. She had felt that at least while she was there, there was somebody to protect her, but now she was out in the world again she felt exposed, naked. She looked at her watch. Had she really been there for nearly four hours? She would be lucky to catch the last train to the Grand Hotel and there was no way she wanted to stay another night – so close to him.

Even though there was no rational reason for it, she kept looking over her shoulder. He was out for the night. Gone to a meeting from which he was scheduled to return late – so late that he wouldn't notice until the morning that she was gone. At least this was what she hoped. And by morning … hopefully the police would be there then.

So he couldn't possibly be here at the station. Unless his plans had changed. It had been known to happen. Or unless he had suspected something all along and the meeting was just a story to cover the fact that he was coming here to catch her. Even though she had confided in nobody, had written nothing in her diary, was it still possible that he knew what she was up to? That now he would appear smiling. Malevolent. Triumphant. It could happen here at the station, she thought as the taxi driver thanked her for her generous tip. The idea chilled her to the bone.

Once inside, she bought a ticket and retrieved her bag from the left luggage. A few days ago, she had managed to slip out of the house unseen and deposit it there. It was just a small, tired nondescript travelling case. She had other, newer, quite magnificent pieces of luggage but she had wanted everything to be as unremarkable as possible. The case contained a few of her favourite clothes, underwear and some toiletries.

The train sat hissing like some strange metal monster at the platform. Fleur could easily have afforded first class but once again she opted for something that would be less noticeable – a ticket in second class. Also he'd be less likely to look for her there. Him or the people he might send.

It wasn't 'might'. He *would* send them. There was no question of it.

The clothes she wore were drab. Those in her case were more suited to the Grand Hotel. There were only a few but they were beautiful – beautiful and the ones she liked most, the ones she thought she looked best in, the ones that she just couldn't bear to leave behind, the ones that were timeless. Between her dowdy clothes, her battered suitcase and sitting quietly in second class, looking like a mousy schoolteacher, she reckoned she had done everything she could do to make the manner of her going as unremarkable as possible.

He wasn't at the station. Nor did he board the train – at least, as far as she could see. As she settled into her seat and the gentle, rhythmic rocking of the train, she relaxed somewhat, undoing the buttons of her coat. It was mid-

September but it was not a cold evening and anyway, the train's heating was on and made for a warm, almost sleepy atmosphere. She loved September. She thought of the year as being like a deck of cards with four suits – spring, summer, autumn, winter. September was like a game where some of the days were played from summer and others were drawn from autumn.

She half-dozed, drifting into that strange place between sleeping and wakefulness that travelling often brings on.

The police had believed her. That was the important thing. At least she thought they had. There had been two of them – the young one at the desk and the second, much older one with a great moustache and kind eyes, that the young one had immediately called into the interview room. She had gone over her story once and then again and again. She had seen how they had done it. They asked her the same questions in different ways. After they had completed the first bout, Fleur had thought she would be free to go, but the older one had said, 'You know these are very serious accusations, miss. Your father is a very prominent figure in the city.'

'I realise that,' Fleur had said, 'but everything I'm telling you is true.'

'Let's go over it one more time, shall we?' the older one had said. But he had said it in a kindly way. He had the face and airs of a man who had seen it all – everything, no matter how bad – that mankind was capable of. If Fleur's story had surprised him, he gave no sign of it.

And so they did go over it one more time as the younger one scribbled furiously. After the third run through, during which they brought her tea, Fleur was almost in tears. She was weary from the talking, but really it was what she had to talk about.

'Don't you believe me?' she had asked in frustration,

71

at the end of that third run-through.

'It's not that we don't believe you, miss.' It was the older one again, the one that did most of the talking. 'Just that we have to be sure of the facts before we act on this.'

'And are you?' asked Fleur. 'Are you sure?'

'I think there's definitely something we have to investigate.'

'And so what are you going to do?'

'We'll pay your father a visit in the morning.'

It was just as she had hoped. She had deliberately gone in the evening so that they might leave any such visit until the morning. That gave her this evening and night to get away.

'When we do go round in the morning,' the older one said, and then Fleur saw that he really *was* kind, 'will you be there?'

Fleur shook her head. 'No, I didn't think that would be a good idea.'

'No, indeed it wouldn't. So you're going to stay with a friend?' he suggested.

'That's what I was thinking,' replied Fleur.

'Does your father know your friends?'

'Most of them.'

Then she thought again.

'Actually, all of them.'

'Then might I suggest that it might be good to go to some, er ... other ... different place. I assume you have some money, miss?'

Fleur did have money. She had been saving for this for nearly a year, steadily putting away the pocket money her father gave her. She had pretty much stopped buying anything except for essentials. Her father had even remarked on it, so that she had had to start spending a little again so that he wouldn't suspect anything.

She nodded.

'And it would be good if you could tell us where you're going to go – just so we can contact you, if we need to,' the older one said.

It had been the one moment when she had faltered. Now she really had to trust these two men – that they weren't, like most other people, in the pay of her father. She thought for a long time and then she answered, 'I am going to go and stay at the Grand Hotel.'

8

It takes Julia the rest of the day to write her chapter. If there are lights in the car they haven't been turned on, and so it is almost dark and she is having difficulty seeing when she writes that final sentence, 'I am going to go and stay at the Grand Hotel'.

She and Suzanne eat some more of their food. Suzanne says she's dying to read it and will do so as soon as it is light. Julia's eyes are tired but she is wide awake. She is exhilarated by what she has done and is wondering where it's going to go next. Part of her wishes there was enough light for her to read it again because she thinks it's really good and exciting. In fact, not just good – much better than she would have thought possible for a first effort. There is mystery in it and foreboding. There are hints of dark things and plenty of threads that can be picked up later in the story.

Now that she can't see the words, it's hard to stay in the story and she keeps coming back to reality. When she does she just feels terror. It wasn't so bad when they were setting out but now it is the feeling that each rhythmic clank of the wheels is bringing them closer to what? Something awful. She knows it. She feels it. She tries to keep her fear at bay. She tries to forget that she's in this car speeding to an unknown destination. But with that fear temporarily out of her mind, she finds that now, she has another fear as well. She is afraid that she will never get to finish this story that she has to tell, that she must tell.

And now she finds that the more she thinks about that opening chapter, turning the phrases over in her head, remembering how it flows from one piece to the next, picturing the characters – especially the policeman with the moustache and the kind eyes – the more she thinks it's really not that good at all. It's boring and pedestrian – little better than an essay she might have written in school years ago. And the characters are stock. Clichés.

What will Suzanne think when she reads it? Will she be gentle with her criticism? Tactful – trying to say it's shit without saying it's shit. Or will she just say it's shit? What is Suzanne like when she reads? Julia imagines that Suzanne loves literature so much that she wouldn't tolerate anything second-rate – and Julia's chapter must be fourth- or fifth-rate.

She sinks into an unbelievably deep sleep. Some time during the night, drifting near the surface of waking, she is dimly aware of the train stopping. She knows she should try to wake up fully but she is too tired – not just from the writing but from everything that has happened since Friday. Whatever the stop was for it doesn't last very long. The train resumes its journey, rattling relentlessly along, its sounds occasionally changing as it thunders through a station. In part it is the very familiarity of these sounds that makes all of this so frightening.

Falling asleep again, Julia dreams that she is on a train to the Grand Hotel. When she next wakes it is still night. She is momentarily devastated to find that she is on this train instead. She finds some comfort in thinking of Fleur – Julia and Fleur, their lives running in parallel on two sets of railway tracks.

9

When Julia next wakes it is fully morning. Her head is hanging forward and she has a stiff pain in her neck. The endless mechanical rhythm of the train continues. It is like they have always been on this train. She opens her eyes and rubs crusty sleep from them. There is bustle in the car as people eat and go to the toilet and begin another day. Suzanne, sitting opposite, smiles at her.

'You were out,' she says.

'This brain work is very tiring.'

They divide the bread they have in two and eat one half. While they are eating, Julia asks about Suzanne's hero.

'I was thinking of making him a conman,' says Suzanne. 'He comes to the hotel because that's what he does. He goes from one posh hotel to the next, tries to find some wealthy woman to link up with and gets as much as he can from her before moving on. That's as much as he has of a goal in life.'

Julia thinks that Suzanne really is making this up and that her hero is far removed from what Suzanne is like. Unlike her Fleur.

'What will happen is that when he meets your heroine –'

'Her name is Fleur,' says Julia.

'Fleur,' Suzanne continues. 'Fleur – flower. I like that. What will happen is that when he meets Fleur, her goal is going to – eventually – become his goal. So she'd better have something significant that she's chasing.'

'She does,' Julia says softly.

'And – obviously – they will fall in love.'

'So tell me more about him.'

'I'm going to call him Dirk. He has brown hair, green eyes, just under six foot, lean.'

Julia wonders if this was somebody Suzanne knew. A boyfriend, maybe? Did she ever have a boyfriend? Maybe Suzanne isn't a virgin. Somewhere, on one of those trips, while her parents were working, did she meet somebody? And did they…?

'He is charming, outgoing, extroverted, a ladies' man,' Suzanne continues. 'Has probably never read a book in his life. He's that boy in your class in school who always seemed to have a girlfriend and usually more than one. Why is he the way he is?'

When Suzanne asks this rhetorical question, Julia hopes that she won't ask her why Fleur is the way she is. As Suzanne talks, it is as though she is describing a real person.

'Maybe his family were very poor and he vowed that he would never be like that. He's European – in the sense that he's a citizen of the world and his nationality is of little importance. In fact it will never be made clear what his nationality is. Perhaps the most important thing is that he's not what he seems. So, does that give you a sense of him?'

'It does.'

'And now can I read what you've written?'

'I haven't had a chance to read back over it –'

'Never mind. I'm dying to read it.'

'I'm very nervous about showing it to you.'

'You shouldn't be. If you love books – and you do – then you know what's good.'

Julia hands over the book and Suzanne starts to read. Julia studies Suzanne's downturned face but can see nothing there. She looks around the car at the other people. She wonders what country the train is now in. She tries not to think about what their destination might be although at this stage, she would give anything just to get off this train. She fidgets. She keeps looking at Suzanne's face trying to gauge her reaction but Suzanne is deep in concentration.

Finally, she looks up. She is smiling. Julia has a momentary picture of a sunrise.

'It's good,' says Suzanne. 'It's really, really good.'

'Do you think so?'

'I do. There are people in my class in university who couldn't have written something this good.'

'You're not just saying it?'

'I'm not just saying it. You turn the key, you get the engine started.'

'What?'

'There's a point in every story where the story gets going – like starting the engine of a car. A lot of writers don't start the engine for ages – giving lots of background or setting or description. I think you start the engine in the first paragraph. By the end of it I'm hooked. Do you see?'

Suzanne hands the book back to Julia who reads the opening. Yes, she does see.

'Anything you didn't like?' asks Julia.

'Saying the train was like a "strange metal monster" – I thought that was a bit clichéd. You know – overused, ordinary. The kind of thing that a writer would say because it was the first thing that came into her head and she's too lazy or not good enough to think of anything better.'

Julia feels a bit stung by this, but then Suzanne adds, 'You're not that kind of writer. I can see already that you're not. You'll find something better than that. Believe me, Julia – if this is the way you write, then you have a talent. I just hope I can be as good.'

Julia surges with pride.

'What a good team we're going to be,' says Suzanne. 'But I have to tell you – I was thinking a lot during the night and maybe that's going to change what we're going to do.'

Julia is suddenly deflated again. Deflated and annoyed. Who does Suzanne think she is anyway, making all these decisions?

'I was thinking about the atmosphere – this plot is actually going to make for a very serious book. I don't see how we could add much humour, and it could be very dark. I don't know about you, Julia, but I've had enough of serious. There's been more than enough darkness in my life over the last few years. So I was thinking – what if we wrote a funny book? What would you think of that? That would be even harder to do than the one we were planning but if we managed to do it, it would be amazing.'

'But supposing the story is about something that isn't funny?' Julia asks. 'That couldn't be regarded as funny under any circumstances?'

'Heartbreak and humour,' says Suzanne. 'In some ways that's even more powerful. It could have an even bigger impact on the reader than just heartbreak on its own.'

Julia thinks about this. Could that first chapter be rewritten as the start of the kind of book Suzanne is describing? Yes, Julia thinks it probably could. Certainly the same beginning would pretty much work. She'd just have to add a couple of funny observations to it. And she thinks it would still be possible to tell the story she wants to tell. It actually might be good – humour and heartbreak, like Suzanne said – that's a good combination.

'It wouldn't have to start out hilariously funny from the beginning, would it?' Julia asks.

'No, I don't think so. We could build it as we go. And then bring out the darkness at the end. That would really hit the reader between the eyes.'

'All right then,' says Julia. 'We'll give it a try. I'll have to rewrite my first chapter a bit. And it means I'll have wasted some paper.'

'Don't worry about that. What's most important is that we get a good story. And the fact that we keep changing our mind –'

You keep changing your mind.

'– means we're on the right track. We're getting closer to what we're really meant to write.

'And let's not worry too much about the paper either. Maybe when we're about halfway through it we can see how we're doing in terms of the paper we've used. If it looks like we won't have enough, we'll see if we can get our hands on another notebook.'

Julia's irritation is brief, fading almost as quickly as it began. She's happy with the new direction. She starts to wonder about rewriting her chapter but she quickly finds herself stuck. She shakes her head.

'I need to know a bit more about what's going to happen,' she says. 'Even just the title. Is it still called *The Murder at the Grand Hotel*?'

'I was thinking about that,' said Suzanne. 'What about we do it as a farce? We don't just have one murder. We have lots of them. *The Murders at the Grand Hotel*. So something like this. Fleur arrives at the hotel. She is running away from something and somebody is pursuing her.'

Julia feels a funny sensation in her heart as Suzanne

says this. Suzanne continues, speaking quickly.

'Somebody gets murdered in the hotel. A young woman. But not Fleur. Maybe it's a case of mistaken identity. They call the police. On a train to the hotel, Dirk is in the same compartment as the detective who has been called to investigate the murder. The detective is a fat man with a soft spot for cream cakes. But he has eaten one cream cake too many.'

As Suzanne talks, Julia can see it all. It's starting to sound funny.

'The detective has a heart attack and dies. Dirk takes his papers – takes over his identity. Dirk has read Sherlock Holmes.'

Suzanne continues almost breathlessly.

'This is the manner of Dirk's arrival at the Grand Hotel. So his chapter – chapter two – will be entitled "Mr Dirk … er … er … Hoedemaker". Like the first chapter of *A Study in Scarlet*. It's called "Mr Sherlock Holmes".'

'Hoedemaker. The hat maker,' says Julia.

'I know,' says Suzanne. 'I wanted his name to be a bit silly. So the first murder is a mistake. It's a girl who looks like Fleur but isn't her. Then the people who are pursuing Fleur arrive. You'll have to work out why they're after her. Fleur goes to Dirk to look for protection and this is when their romance begins. Dirk begins his investigation though, in reality, he has no idea what he's doing.'

Suzanne is becoming really animated, so much so that several people in the carriage look around at her. She ignores them and carries on.

'However, Fleur's pursuers think that Dirk is getting close so they commit suicide. Or, no, they have an argument and one kills the other. Or there's an accident with a gun. I don't know. I'm not sure yet. But that makes it two unsolved deaths at the Grand Hotel.'

'All right,' says Julia. 'You start writing and I'll see if

82

I can figure out the things I have to figure out.'

This is how they spend the second day on the train. Julia finds it hard to work all this out in her head. Again and again she tries to work out the sequence of events but again and again, the pieces which she thought she had tied down, seem to float up and fly away from her like runaway balloons. Night comes on and she doesn't seem to have made much progress. Suzanne, who has been writing all day, has to stop as she can't see any more.

They eat silently in the semi-darkness. Suzanne looks exhausted. She pushes up her glasses onto her head and rubs her eyes. Julia is frustrated and anxious. What if they can't work out where to go next? She is loving this but hating it at the same time. She just wants to go to sleep and wake up with it all solved. As if echoing her thoughts, Suzanne says, 'It's really hard, isn't it?'

'It's really hard and it's brilliant at the same time.'

Suzanne nods wearily.

'That's what makes it so wonderful, I think.'

They fall asleep, Suzanne with her head thrown back, Julia with hers on the table. What wakes them is a sense that the train has begun to slow. Blearily, they open their eyes. There is darkness still outside. Yes, the train is *definitely* slowing. Julia looks across at Suzanne who has fear written all over her face. For some time the train travels at little more than walking speed and eventually squeals to a shuddering, shaking halt like a passionless orgasm.

And now Julia is very afraid

10

The doors are opened but the scene is not at all what Julia was expecting. Instead of a camp with huts and barbed wire and watchtowers, she is looking at the side of a building, a tall building with lots of windows. The building looks very run-down. Its walls were long ago painted yellow but now, chunks of plaster have fallen from the wall, exposing the red brickwork. Paint flakes off the window frames. Some of the panes of glass are broken and the holes are stuffed with paper or rags.

Julia and Suzanne get down from the train which has come to a steaming, hissing stop in the street of a town. The line of cars empties quickly. Most people alight unaided. Old people are passed down almost as if they were fragile pieces of pottery or glass.

The cobbles are broken in many places and there are large potholes filled with dirty water. There are tall buildings on either side, all looking very similar to one another, all painted the same ruined yellow colour and in the same state. There are Germans in helmets and heavy overcoats with dogs on leads and rifles on their shoulders. There are also men in other uniforms – they look like police – just like the Marechaussee in the Dutch camp. It is a foul day – dank, overcast, with air that feels like it's raining even though it isn't. Julia's hands are cold and an iciness seeps into her body, down her neck and into her spine. Her foot splashes into a chill puddle, wetting her shoe and her sock.

Julia and Suzanne look at each other in bewilderment. Inevitably Suzanne asks, 'What is this place? Where are we?'

Julia hardly notices the irritation this causes her. There is something very weird about this place.

The police organise the train's passengers into groups of four and then they are marched up some steps into the hall of a decrepit building. A queue forms. The place is dark due to both the leaden daylight outside and the lack of electric light inside. A single broken lightbulb hangs from a black wire that disappears into a hole in the plaster in the ceiling. Julia glances across at Suzanne, whose pale face is set rigid, her eyes unblinking. Becoming aware of Julia's gaze, Suzanne turns to look at her. Heroically, she manages a faint smile. Then she takes Julia's hand and squeezes it. Suzanne goes to let go but Julia holds on to the hand.

It is freezing cold. There is little difference between the temperature inside and outside. The queue shuffles forward slowly. There is a bad smell from the concentration of people. Julia knows that she smells awful. She hasn't been able to have a proper wash since Friday and now it's Thursday – she thinks. With unbelievable slowness, the queue wends its way into a room on one side of the hall. Here tables have been set up. It is the same registration process they went through in the last camp.

What is it with the Germans and their registration?

The process takes hours. The queue hardly moves at all. Some who go to sit down are made to stand up again – there is no sitting. Several people faint as the long morning moves into an even longer afternoon. Julia is hungry, incredibly thirsty and her back and legs ache from the standing.

Eventually their turn comes.

They approach a first table. An SS man sits at the table while a second one – an officer – stands beside it. Both wear heavy overcoats with the collars turned up and thick gloves. The standing SS man is tall with immaculately groomed hair and a handsome face. He speaks in German, telling them in a bored voice that they must hand over all valuables at this table. This includes money, whatever the currency, jewellery and watches. If they are in any doubt, they are to hand the item over and the SS man at the table will decide. Anybody caught trying to hide anything will be severely punished.

Reluctantly Julia gives up her watch. She hated it because it had come from her father but she loved the sense of order and control it gave her. Her wrist feels naked and her world feels that bit emptier without it. She also hands over the last of the money Bert gave her on Friday.

After the valuables, Julia's case is taken from her by one of the police. He places it on a table and rifles through it, removing the better items of clothing and underwear. She also has soap, sanitary towels and the remains of a roll of toilet paper. These are all taken. The case is then returned to her.

Now she is well and truly destitute.

Next a second man pats Julia down and discovers her last couple of cigarettes which he confiscates. He lets his hands linger on her breasts and then weighs them with his hands. Julia looks defiantly into the man's face as he does this but all she sees are dead eyes. He appears to be taking no pleasure from it. So why is he doing it? Because he can?

Julia is moved on to the next table as the man also

gropes Suzanne. Her processing is much quicker – she has nothing.

Finally comes the inevitable table and man with a list. Julia gives her personal information again. The man writes it down on an index card. She is given a number that the man calls a 'transport number'.

'This is your identification from now on,' he says.

He gives Julia a yellow star which he tells her she must sew on to the left-hand side of her coat and which must be visible at all times. She is also given a ration card for January – a small rectangle of cheap card with the days of the month on it. She has today off, she is told. Tomorrow she will be working in the old people's hospital. Finally he tells her that she will be housed in this building in the attic. He gives her a slip of paper and tells her to go right to the top of the building and hand it over to the person in charge.

With that, her processing is complete.

Julia waits for Suzanne who says that she is also going to be working in the old people's hospital. Then, together they climb the seemingly endless stairs with curved ceilings overhead. The girls' backs are bent – they are like old people. There are numerous people sitting on the stairs or lying on the landings. There is one old woman with wild hair who lies with her skirt and filthy knickers around her knees, exposing her hairy groin. She seems unaware of her surroundings and nobody pays her any attention.

On another landing a child that looks like it has only just learned to walk totters around. It is dressed in nothing but a fouled and reeking nappy. It is impossible to tell whether it is a boy or a girl. It has an unhealthy face and vacant eyes and seems to be quite alone.

They reach a landing and pause to catch their breath. As they do so a vile wave of shit smell comes down towards them. They look at each other. Julia is thinking that the place is a madhouse. Turning the corner and climbing the steps, they encounter a man squatting on the next landing taking a shit. Much as they try, it is impossible not to glance at him as they go past. He looks up and his eyes meet theirs. The man is crying and Julia thinks she has never seen such a mixture of humiliation, sadness and helplessness as she sees in that face. By now all Julia wants is to get warm, lie in a bed, sleep, forget about all this for a while.

They reach a door at the top of the building and enter. The room is crammed – people, bunks, washing – just like their last camp, but much more crowded. Inside the door is a rickety-looking wooden staircase that climbs higher. They are told to go right to the top so they take it, holding on to the rail. Julia feels weak from hunger. She is sweating. Overhead are huge rafters like the beams of a ship. Entering they find a room that is indeed the attic. It is small, with dirty whitewashed walls. Like everywhere else, it is crammed with three-tier bunks, people and washing. The people smells are quite overpowering.

They ask who is in charge and are directed to a man who is like a wraith, he is so thin.

'There are no bunks at the moment,' he says.

He points out a foul-looking mattress with a blanket on top lying in the aisle between two rows of bunks.

'Share that for tonight. It's never too long before bunks become available.'

'What is this place?' Julia asks. 'Where are we?'

'Where are you?'

A smile appears on the man's face, a smile that manages to be patronising or could be sly or even slightly insane, all at once.

'Why, pretty lady, you have come to the Paradise Ghetto.'

11

Some time after it grows dark. The attic begins to empty.

This has to be about food.

'Come on,' says Julia.

She and Suzanne grab their bowls and follow the flow of people downstairs. From what Julia has seen in the few hours she has been here, everybody seems to move in a sort of weary slow motion.

Except now.

Now everybody hurries as best they can.

Because lots of the people are old, Julia and Suzanne hurtle down the stairs, passing many of them. If Julia feels any tinge of guilt about this she pushes it to the back of her mind. They arrive out into the building's courtyard where stars glitter overhead, their brightness accentuated by the three storeys of the building. An arcade surrounds the courtyard on all sides and it is in this that they queue, Julia and Suzanne about midway along the line. People continue to arrive long after that. Julia pictures migrating birds gathering on telephone wires.

And there they wait.

And wait.

And wait.

Without her watch Julia has no way of knowing how long they are there. But by the time the line begins to move, she feels she has become a block of ice. Eventually they come to a window. In front of it, a woman takes Julia's ration card and tears off the coupon for today. Then she is given a brown liquid in her bowl and a third of a loaf of bread.

They are so hungry they eat the food there in the courtyard, even though the air is freezing and frost is starting to form on the cobbles and roofs. So do most of the other people. Eating seems to only take a couple of minutes. At least Julia now has something warm in her belly.

They drag themselves up the steps again, past occasional pools of piss or vomit, or scattered piles of turds. It is as though a dog has passed by – but they have seen no dogs. The attic is freezing. Their breath forms little clouds in the frosty air. Julia's fingers are like frozen sausages. They settle onto the mattress wearing all their clothes and their coats. Facing each other they pull Julia's blanket and the other threadbare one over themselves. It hardly makes any difference.

Julia doesn't know how she is going to get through all of this. She has only been here a few hours and already she feels like an old woman. She now knows that there is a very real possibility that she could die here – that the Germans have no particular interest in keeping the people in this camp, or town or whatever it is, alive.

'Are you warm?' asks Suzanne, interrupting her thoughts.

Julia is shivering.

'Are you fucking joking?'

'Maybe if we held each other? You know – the body heat.'

They try to do so face to face but it doesn't really help a lot – the great area of their backs remains chilled.

'What if we spooned?' Julia suggests.

'Spooned?' Suzanne asks, as Julia was almost certain she would.

'Like two spoons in a drawer. Your tummy to my back or the other way round. One of us can go first and then we swap.'

They do so, lying on their left sides, with Julia's front to Suzanne's back and Julia's right arm encircling Suzanne. Her hair tickles Julia's nose. Apart from when she was working, Julia hasn't been this close to another person since that boyfriend she'd had just after she left home. His name was Ad – short for Adriaan. It didn't last very long. Julia lost her virginity to him. He fucked her and then he fucked off.

Suzanne says that the new arrangement is really good and Julia finds that it helps a bit too. Her feet are still like blocks of ice though, the policeman having taken all her socks except the ones she was wearing.

'We'll do it every second night,' suggests Julia. 'Me on you and then you on me.'

'Or if we turn over during the night.'

'That's a better idea,' agrees Julia.

The two girls hold each other as other people also settle down in the attic. Eventually the single lightbulb goes out. In the darkness, Suzanne takes Julia's hand, which is closed in a fist, and holds it in hers, pressing it to her chest.

Suzanne has been almost completely silent since they arrived but now she says, 'You know that the book is the only way we'll survive this, don't you? We have to write the book.'

'Where are we going to get the energy for that? I feel half-dead already. If they're going to make us work…'

Julia leaves the sentence unfinished.

After a long silence, Suzanne says, 'We have to. I just know it. It's how we're going to get through this.'

Julia is angered by this but too tired to say anything more than, 'How do you know? How can you say something like that?'

'I just know, Julia,' Suzanne's voice comes back in the darkness.

And then she says, 'If we don't, we'll die. We'll die, for sure.'

Julia says nothing. There's no point in arguing. It's just going to make her weaker, weaker and pissed off with Suzanne whom she's now embracing like a lover – a strange, fragile thread running between them.

'But I don't think I can write the Grand Hotel book,' Suzanne says after a long silence. 'Not now. Not here. Not having seen this place.'

'What then?' asks Julia.

'A revenge book,' says Suzanne, and she says the word 'revenge' with a viciousness Julia would not have thought possible of her mild-mannered friend.

'A revenge book? How…?'

'I don't know exactly yet but it's going to be about someone who gets revenge on the people that have wronged her. Have you read *The Count of Monte Cristo*?

Julia has – an abridged version, when she was a kid. She knows the story.

'Like that.'

Suzanne is still holding Julia's hand. It is closed in a fist and becoming stiff. It is uncomfortable and Julia wants to flex it. She eases it open slightly and, as she does so, Suzanne leans back a fraction, opening a gap between her left breast and the mattress. It is like an invitation – or even if it isn't, almost without thinking, Julia takes it as such. She opens her hand and cups it around Suzanne's left breast. She can feel Suzanne's heart, beating sturdily. Julia has a picture of holding a little bird in the palm of her hand. It is like she is holding Suzanne's life. Suzanne settles back, closing her hand softly around Julia's hand once more.

And this is how they go to sleep.

12

During the night, Julia wakes with a full bladder. The fucking coffee – or whatever that brown piss was. She knows she won't make it until morning.

Since there is no bathroom in the attic, going to the toilet is going to be a huge undertaking. She disentangles herself from Suzanne, trying not to wake her and slips out from under the blankets. The icy cold makes Julia gasp. They're going to have to find more blankets – if they don't, they're will surely freeze to death. She puts her stockinged feet into her boots and begins the journey. In the pitch darkness she finds the doorway and then the staircase. Carefully she makes her way down, holding both rails. She is already shivering.

The toilet is at one end of the much larger room below. Julia gropes her way through the strata of sleeping figures and finds it. It has three cubicles and one of them is free. The stench from the other two is overpowering and Julia is aware of how bad she smells herself as she lowers her knickers and lifts up her skirt.

Having finished, she retraces her steps. When she arrives back at the mattress, she finds that Suzanne has turned onto her right side and is awake. Julia can see her eyes glinting in the faint light that comes through the single window. Suzanne holds up the blanket. Julia slips in underneath it.

'My God, you're so cold,' says Suzanne, enfolding her.

'Do you need to go?' asks Julia through chattering teeth.

'Not me. In the attic I developed a bladder of steel.'

It is still dark when the light goes on and there is the sound of much movement. Julia has slept the sleep of the dead. The effort to drag herself awake is monumental but she knows that if she doesn't get down to the courtyard now, she will miss whatever passes for breakfast. Suzanne is already sitting up rubbing her eyes. She looks confused, dazed – as though she's not quite sure where she is.

'Come on,' says Julia. 'We'll be late.'

Breakfast turns out to be nothing more than a bowl of the same brown 'coffee' they had the previous night.

'Isn't there any bread?' asks Julia at the window.

'You should have saved some of last night's, new girl. Next!'

Julia feels like throwing the coffee in the woman's face but thinks better of it.

Having drunk the coffee, the two girls ask the way to the old people's hospital. It is a short walk over icy cobbles through the gauzy, frost-laden air. They go down the street and round the corner – which brings them not to another building as they had expected but to the outer wall of the town.

This wall is not just a thin rampart sufficient for one or two men to stand on. Rather, it is wide enough to house large rooms embedded into it. They find themselves in front of a casemate with two barred windows and an entrance gate. They look at each other uncertainly and then enter what is for all the world a damp, dark, subterranean dungeon, feebly lit by naked electric bulbs. The place is unbelievably cold – colder, though Julia didn't think that was actually possible, than outside. There is a stone floor covered with filthy wood shavings and no beds – just mattresses with figures lying on them under single thin blankets. If this is a hospital, it is unlike any hospital that Julia has ever imagined.

She and Suzanne spend the rest of the day there. It turns out that this is the hospital for people who are dying – so there is no question of anybody getting better. Rather the job consists of trying to keep these emaciated figures on their mattresses as clean, as comfortable and as warm as possible while they see out their last days.

It is a quite impossible task.

There are no medicines to speak of, so anybody who is in pain just has to stay that way. And everybody is starving since these people get less food than anybody else. And people die of the cold. They just close their eyes and don't wake up again. The head nurse there is a short woman called Irena. She has thin blonde hair and what is still, despite her gauntness and a nose that looks like it was once broken, an extraordinarily beautiful face. She explains to them that here in the Paradise Ghetto, what food supplies are provided are rationed so that the people who do the heaviest work get the most. Children also get more 'since they are the one hope we have for the future'. She says these words looking in turn into Julia's face and then Suzanne's, as though trying to gauge their reaction.

Despite all these rules, Irena says, there is huge corruption in the way food is distributed. She says this placidly, almost matter-of-factly, with no sign of anger. The result however is that the people here are at the bottom of the list when it comes to food.

'There are people who feel they shouldn't be given any food at all – that it's only wasted if it ends up here,' says Irena.

With no nursing in the conventional sense, Julia and

Suzanne's job is straightforward. There is only cold water and with so many people so sick there is a never-ending round of trying to clean up people as they lie in their own waste. When she goes to one of the patients she has been allocated by Irena, Julia finds that the person is dead. Julia utters a gasp of surprise that brings Irena over. Realising what it is, Irena says emotionlessly, 'When somebody dies, this is what we have to do. First wrap them in their sheet if they have one or blanket if they don't. If there's a sheet that's good. It means we can keep the blanket for somebody else.

'Tie the ends. Then you need to carry the body down to the cellar. We use that as a morgue. You also need to tell me or the nurse on duty so that we can record their name and transport number for the central registry. They'll then give it to the Germans. They like everything to be precise, the Germans.'

Irena gives the two girls a break at lunchtime so that they can return to their barracks for lunch. By this time they have carried half a dozen bodies down to the cellar and Julia is weak and light-headed from the strenuous work. Something that she can only think of as a zig-zag electric snake runs across her eyes. She is sweating an icy cold sweat.

They emerge into a bitterly cold overcast day with small flurries of snow in the air. Their clothes smell of the dungeon. At the barracks, they queue as before. They are near the back of the line because they have arrived so late and it is a couple of hours before they are given their food. Since they are amongst the last, what 'soup' remains in the wooden barrel is merely lukewarm water. They are given a bowl of this and a boiled potato. The food doesn't even take the edge off their hunger.

They go back to the hospital after lunch and finally leave there in a cold darkness with no stars, linked to each other for warmth as they return to the barracks. The cobbles are icy underfoot so they proceed cautiously like two old women, holding on to each other.

As they turn the corner into the street where their barracks is – the street is known as Bahnhofstrasse – they see a figure coming towards them in the semi-darkness. It is a man, about twenty metres away. The confident crunch of boots, the faint glimmer of a belt buckle and a double row of buttons, the outline of a peaked cap and the skirt of a heavy overcoat tells Julia that he is SS.

As she recognises this, Suzanne hisses, 'Bow. We must bow.'

Suzanne is still linked to Julia and now she pulls her out of the way. Both girls stand and Julia feels Suzanne's hand pushing her head from behind. The result is that they bow at the waist as the SS man strides past, apparently oblivious to their presence. They continue their bow until they are certain he has turned the corner and is gone.

'Why did you do that?' asks Julia, angrily.

'They said we had to. You heard them. Severe punishment if we don't.'

'Fucking Germans,' says Julia. 'I'd rather die than ever do that again.'

'No, you wouldn't,' replies Suzanne.

Julia sulks while they queue for their bread and coffee. The line goes forward with dizzying slowness. It is an hour. Maybe two. Julia can no longer tell. Eventually, she snarls, 'Fucking penis.'

'What?' asks Suzanne, eyes wide in surprise.

'You heard me,' says Julia. 'That German. A fucking penis in a uniform.'

Suzanne starts to laugh.

'What's so funny?' asks Julia.

Suzanne is laughing really hard.

'What?'

Eventually, Suzanne manages to say, 'It's just such a funny picture.'

'What – a penis in a uniform?'

Suzanne nods – she's still laughing.

'And he did look like a penis,' she finally manages. 'That silly cap on top and then widening out with the skirts of his coat. All he needed was a melon in each coat pocket and it would have been perfect.'

Despite herself, Julia finds this picture very funny. But she's reluctant to let go of her anger.

'What would you know about it? I'll bet you've never seen one.'

'A melon?'

Julia nearly caves in at this but her anger keeps her going.

'A penis.'

'I've seen pictures of them.'

'Really? Where?'

'Pompeii. They're all over the place. And you – have you seen one? A real one, I mean.'

Julia is surprised at herself when she answers, 'No, I never have.'

Eventually they reach the window and are given their coffee and bread. They go indoors and find a spot on the crowded stairs to sit and eat. Julia breaks her bread in two, keeping half for the morning. The two girls eat in silence, as does everybody else around them. It's all gone in minutes.

Julia looks at Suzanne.

'I'm sorry,' says Julia. 'If you hadn't made us bow, who knows what might have happened?'

Suzanne acknowledges this with an upward nod. Julia continues to look into her eyes and then, after a long, long silence, Julia says, 'I want to write that revenge story too.'

13

'We'll talk about it in bed,' says Suzanne as they climb the stairs.

The two girls go to the toilet and despite the intense cold, wash themselves. Julia has always been fastidious anyway, especially after she began to make films, and she is pleased to see that Suzanne is too. They brush their teeth. Their toothpaste was taken on arrival so they have only water. Still, there is something comforting about these little rituals of civilisation. And anyway, Julia needs to get the smell of the dead hospital off her skin and out of her nostrils, though on this second she seems to fail because it lingers either there or in her memory.

In bed, facing each other and once they have stopped shivering and warmed up a little, Julia says, 'I nearly stole one of the dead people's blankets today.'

'We would have been a lot warmer,' says Suzanne.

'So you think I should have?'

'Of course not.'

'No. No, I didn't think you'd approve. It probably means we'll end up there, though.'

'We won't end up there,' says Suzanne.

It is another of these pronouncements that Suzanne is prone to making. Sometime Julia finds them irritating. Mostly she ignores them. Tonight, for some reason, she finds it strangely comforting.

'Last night I had a dream,' says Suzanne. 'I dreamt I was with my parents, in Italy. We went there before the war. They were working on a dig at Pompeii. When we were finished, we spent a week at Positano. By the sea. The dream was so real, I really thought we were back there. Then I woke up. I thought that us being at Pompeii and Positano was what was real and this ... this was just some horrible nightmare. Then I saw it was the other way round. I want to go back there when the war is over.'

'Pompeii – we could write a story about Pompeii,' suggests Julia. 'Two lovers who get caught in the volcano. I don't know anything about the history but you could provide all that, couldn't you?'

'I could. But where would the revenge come in?'

This causes them to go silent for a while. They pull the blanket more closely around their shoulders and move closer together. Suzanne smells of clothes that have been worn far too long but Julia knows that she does too. She thinks about the Count of Monte Cristo. He was betrayed and shipped from his home and his own country.

'What if,' says Julia, 'the hero or the heroine is betrayed and shipped to Pompeii from some other place? He gets caught in the volcano, but escapes and returns to get his revenge?'

'I like that,' says Suzanne. 'After the failure of Boudica's revolt, many of the Britons were taken as slaves to Rome. They could have ended up in Pompeii.'

'So that's what happens,' says Julia. 'They're taken to Rome, end up in Pompeii, escape during the eruption and return to Britain to take their revenge on the Romans, or maybe the people who betrayed them or whatever.'

'When you say "they",' asks Suzanne, 'you mean Fleur – except now in a Roman setting?'

'Yes, Fleur,' says Julia. 'I want it to be Fleur. And then

you can decide who the other person is going to be.'

'So it's a heroine, not a hero.'

'One of them is a heroine. The other can be a man or a woman. Whatever you want. It's your decision.'

'All right,' says Suzanne. 'Let me think some more about that. Maybe the conman again, but maybe not. Oh, Julia – I'm so glad that this is what we've decided to do. You know, all afternoon, I was thinking about this book of ours. I was thinking that I couldn't write the Grand Hotel one. Not here. Not in this place. The Grand Hotel is too far away from here. Maybe after the war, we'll go to America and become famous writers. Maybe when we're living in a Grand Hotel ourselves – like movie stars do – maybe then we can write it.'

Julia marvels at these fantasies that Suzanne weaves. She's a storyteller all right.

'You know, Julia – I think you're amazing. After all our various ideas and false starts, you're the one who got it. It's a revenge book. But it's also an allegory.'

Julia's not sure what an allegory is. 'Go on.'

'Boudica's revolt against the Romans – you see, the Romans, the Germans.' Suzanne is becoming really animated now and having difficulty keeping her voice down. This is different from the way she was with all the other ideas.

'Boudica's revolt happened in 60 AD. It failed and she died. So what happened after that? The Romans did just what the Germans do, attacking places, burning villages, killing and torturing people, taking people as slaves. So our heroine and this other person, whoever it turns out to be, will be two people of Boudica's tribe who are taken prisoner and sent to Pompeii as slaves.'

'To fight as gladiators?' asks Julia. 'Were there female gladiators?'

'Yes, there were. So maybe as gladiators. Or maybe

105

just as slaves. We can decide. Their master treats them very cruelly. But they help each other and support each other and gradually they fall in love. Vesuvius destroyed Pompeii in 79 AD, nineteen years after Boudica's revolt. We can't have them slaves for nineteen years. That'd be just too depressing. But in 62 AD, there was a big earthquake at Pompeii. It caused lots of damage. It was that that my parents were investigating when we were on the dig. During the earthquake, the pair kill their master and flee. They make their way back to Britain and live happily ever after.'

Julia likes it. She really does. 'It's good that you know all this,' she says. 'Otherwise we wouldn't be able to do it. We'd have to do all this research before we could figure out the plot.'

'That's the wonderful thing. The research *is* the plot.'

'The research is the plot,' Julia echoes and after a thoughtful pause, adds, 'Yes, I see it.'

She goes on, becoming excited now too. 'And how about we do it just like *The Count of Monte Cristo*? There are three people that they end up having to take revenge on. And they take it in different ways. Maybe somebody in their village in Britain betrays them to the Romans – just like what you think happened to you.'

'Brilliant,' replies Suzanne.

'So how do we start?' asks Julia.

'The news arrives at the village of the failure of Boudica's revolt. Now great fear. They are unprotected. Just like we were in Holland in 1940. The Romans are coming.

'Tomorrow – think it out while we're working in that awful place. I'll work out who the other character is going to be. Then, tomorrow night, we'll start writing. We should be able to do a couple of hours before the curfew at nine o'clock.'

'We certainly won't have to waste too much time eating,' says Julia. 'I need to know something about Britain in that time. What was it like? How did people live? What did they wear? Eat? What was the countryside like?'

'All right,' says Suzanne. 'It's my turn to spoon you so turn around and I'll start to tell you.'

Julia does as she is told, and Suzanne presses her chest, belly and thighs against her.

'What do you want to know first?' asks Suzanne. Her soft voice sounds comforting so close to Julia's ear.

'Describe the countryside, the landscape. Like in a movie. Start high up and then come down to earth.'

Julia recalls that what she just said was something she heard Bert say once. If she's correct today is Friday. Can it really only have been a week since she last saw him?

But now Suzanne has begun. 'A bird would see flat countryside, a bit like Holland,' she says, 'but heavily wooded.'

Some time after that Julia falls asleep so that next morning, she can't be sure whether the pictures in her head are what she heard or what she dreamt.

14

They spend the next day at the hospital – though Julia has started to call it 'the dungeon'. She has lots more questions for Suzanne. What kinds of names would they have had? What language did they speak? What food did they eat? Where did the last battle happen?

But by evening, after their meal, she is ready to write.

CHAPTER ONE

After the Battle (Julia)

It was that first column of black smoke rising slowly into the sky on the northwest horizon that told Birkita that something had gone terribly wrong. The smoke rose slantways, moved by the light summer breeze, before it began to diffuse.

Up until then, they had heard nothing of the great battle; the battle that was to be the last battle. They had burned the Romans' cities and now they would destroy its army. That would be the end of the Romans and Birkita's people could go back to the old ways. The land would be theirs again. They would be able to make weapons as they had before the Romans had prohibited it. There would be plenty of food, prosperity, no shortages or famine – just like it had been before the Romans came. The druids would walk amongst them once more.

The Romans had arrived the same year she had. 'The greatest blessing and the greatest curse a few weeks apart,' was what her mother always said. Now Birkita was seventeen and a warrior herself, left behind to guard the village along with her older brother Banning. He had pleaded to go and had railed at being told to mind the animals, the old people and the children. He argued with their father, saying how neighbouring villages had emptied completely as the entire population had gone to see the final destruction of the Romans and to loot their wealth.

'And while we're looting the Romans, who'll be looting us?' Caedmon, Birkita's father and headman of the village, had asked. Birkita wondered if she was the only one who had thought not about looting but what would happen if the Romans won the battle. Anyway, it had been settled. Birkita and Banning would stay.

And so this was why she was lying on her stomach in long grass, the summer sun on her back, watching a ladybird walk along a leaf. The ladybird was actually walking on the underside of the leaf. Birkita marvelled at this. Why didn't the tiny creature fall off? Was it because it was so tiny? Did it weigh nothing? Eventually it reached the edge of the leaf and like a fat woman scrambling over a wall, worked its way round to the upper side.

It was said that the Romans sometimes fought in formations that looked a bit like ladybirds. They would form an oblong with their rectangular shields over their heads and on all sides like a protective shell. Then they could attack the gate of a fortress or try to undermine a wall without being hurt. Nothing the defenders could do could touch them. Rocks and spears bounced off the shield roof, burning oil or pitch flowed harmlessly over the sides. Who had thought of this? Was it some Roman long ago, lying in a field and watching a ladybird just as she was now? Why did everything the Romans did have to end in destruction and killing and dying?

With Birkita were her dogs, Sun and Moon. Sun was two years old but still behaved like a puppy. He was small, short-haired and all black except for a grey moustache and beard around his muzzle. He lay on his side, his tail lazily swatting at flies. Moon was old, much older – furry, bone-creaky and in pain when winter came.

In summer Sun teased her mercilessly and forced her to play – which she did. It seemed to keep her young. But eventually she would lie exhausted and nothing Sun did could rouse her. She was like that now, deeply asleep, dog-dreaming in the summer heat.

Everybody said that after the victories at Camulodunum and Londinium and Verulamium and especially after the destruction of the Ninth Legion, that the Romans were beaten. The remainder were just a formality. Birkita prayed to all the gods that it was so even as she wondered why her heart felt heavy.

The ladybird disappeared amongst the innumerable stalks of grass. It must have appeared like a vast green world to a creature the size of a ladybird.

And that was when Birkita saw the first column of smoke.

Banning had seen it too and came running. They estimated it was somewhere between a day and two day's ride away. Banning said that he would take his horse and go northwest and try to find out what was happening.

'If it's coming our way, we must go to the Haven. I should be back before sunset.'

'Be careful,' she said, embracing him and kissing him on the cheek.

But he wasn't back before sunset. And before the sun had gone down, several more columns of smoke had risen into the sky so that the red and gold layers of cloud lit by the setting sun were as though dirt had been thrown on them. And the other thing was that the columns of smoke were coming closer.

With night, the pillars of smoke were replaced by sparkling clusters of yellow light low down on the ground. They looked as though stars had fallen to earth and begun to burn. Birkita stayed awake all night sitting in the ladybird grass along with her dogs, looking to the northwest. Back in the village, children and old people tried to catch what sleep they could. But very few slept. Maybe the smaller children. Everybody else was seized with an almost palpable feeling of dread.

'Where is Banning?' they asked.

The short summer night gave way to dawn. The unfolding light in the east was in stark contrast to the blackness that now smudged the north-western horizon. Birkita felt the hoof beats long before she heard anything. There was the faintest vibration transmitted through the iron-hard soil – hardly heavier than ladybird feet. She turned onto her stomach and hugged the earth. She could feel it now in her chest, like a second heartbeat.

Now she wasn't sure whether she was feeling the sound or hearing it, whether it was coming closer or becoming louder or both. She sat up. Sun was already up, sniffing the air. Moon rolled slowly from her side onto her stomach. Birkita gazed into the distant black that was slowly becoming grey. At first she could see nothing but then it was as though the horizon was bubbling or boiling. Something was moving. Coming closer. Becoming bigger. Moon hoisted herself up onto her feet and began to sniff the air. Sun's tail, which had been up and wagging furiously, stopped. Moon turned her head slowly, scenting an arc from west to north.

And then Birkita smelt it too, carried on whatever breeze there was. Through the sharp stench of burning came the acrid smell of sweating horses.

CHAPTER TWO

The Haven (Julia)

All during the night, while she had stayed awake and watched the distant fires twinkling, Birkita had endlessly gone over her three choices.

None of them was good.

She could stand and fight. But that would be pointless. She would be dead within minutes – not that she feared death – and then who would protect the village? Even if Banning got back and they fought together, they would be no match for a troop of Roman soldiers – which is what she assumed was coming now. She tried not to think about what this meant for their hopes and dreams of being free again – and for those from the village who had gone to fight the last great battle. What had happened to her parents?

The second possibility was to try and flee. But even if they left all the animals behind, with children and old people on foot, the Romans would be upon them before they knew it.

Finally, there was the Haven.

The Haven was an old underground tomb dating from the time of the ancestors. It was in thick woodland not far from the village. Some time in the past, long before anybody now living had been born, the interior of the tomb had been expanded – presumably to take further burials. But for whatever reason, there had been no more and now, with its remote location and tiny, hidden entrance it was a refuge, a place that could hold all the villagers, where they could hide and be safe.

It had never been used in living memory and Birkita had her doubts about it. If the Romans did find them there, they would be cornered like rats in a pit. Still – it wasn't like she had another choice.

With first light, she told the villagers they were going there.

'What about Banning?'

'Where is your brother?'

'What does he say?'

'Let us wait until Banning comes back.'

'There's no time for any of that,' said Birkita. 'Didn't you see the fires? Can't you smell the smoke? The Romans are coming. Who knows when they will be here?'

Reluctantly, the villagers began to move – old people, women with babies or very small children, pregnant women, children too young to go to war who had been left in the care of others while their parents went to fight.

Some began to round up their animals – chickens, goats, dogs, sheep, cattle, pigs.

'No,' insisted Birkita. 'There's no room for any of them.'

'The Romans will have them.'

'Would you rather they have your children?'

'Just the small ones then – the chickens and the dogs.'

'No. Chickens will squawk. Dogs will bark. We must be silent as ghosts. So you must kill your dogs – otherwise, they will follow you and betray us. And by all the gods, hurry. Please hurry.'

By mid-morning, all of the villagers were inside the tomb and only Birkita with Sun and Moon was still at the village. She released all of the animals from their paddocks. Ignoring their sudden freedom they just continued to graze placidly in their slightly newer surroundings. She took one last look around. It occurred to her that if the village was going to burn anyway, she should do it herself. If she did, the Romans might think that some of them had been there already and might bypass the place altogether. It was a slim chance but it was worth taking. Quickly, she took a torch from one of the huts, plunged it into a fire and then began to work her way around the twenty or so huts that made up the village. Soon the tinder-dry straw of the thatch was ablaze.

There was no wind so the black smoke swirled around her making her cough. Orange flames roared into the sky. Scattered around in front of the huts, the bodies of dead dogs lay on their sides. Their fur – white, black, brown – was speckled with red. With the smoke and fire and corpses, it was like the end of the world. Her two dogs were on either side of her. Sun sat staring at the flames with great interest, Moon looked up at her quizzically. The next thing she had to do broke her heart.

She drew her sword and with two quick movements, killed her dogs. Sun never knew what hit him. With Moon, Birkita knew that for however long she might live, she would never forget the look of sadness and confusion and fear as the sword came scything down.

Birkita was just backing out through the gate of the stockade that surrounded the village when she saw something white moving on the edge of her vision.

It was a dog.

Banning's dog, Bran – his favourite. Why hadn't Genovefa, her brother's wife, killed it?

'Bran,' she called gently. 'Here, Bran.'

The dog knew Birkita. If she was in her brother's house, Bran would lie at her feet and let himself be petted. Bran always came to her and would lie there for hours

116

provided she kept petting.

'Bran,' she called again, a little more loudly and insistently.

The dog looked at her.

He knew.

He gazed at her steadily for what seemed like ages and then turned away, disappearing between two flaming huts.

There was no more time to follow him. She had to get to the Haven herself. She began to run towards the woods.

The burial chamber was reached by a narrow passageway a couple of spear lengths long. The actual entrance to it lay hidden under the overhang of a huge boulder as big as a hut. If you didn't know it existed, it was impossible to see the entrance from outside. To get into the Haven someone had to crawl under the edge of the boulder. When their head and upper body were under the rock, and just when it seemed like they wouldn't be able to go any further, the entrance appeared. It was a masterful piece of concealment. Birkita crawled in now. Once inside, she was able to walk, crouching, along the passageway that sloped gently downwards to the room. Here, there was headroom and she was able to stand up fully.

There were about fifty people in the burial chamber itself. It was about half the population of the village. There was room for everyone to sit down but not much more than that. There were a couple of buckets in the corner for pissing and shitting. People had brought food and water to last maybe a couple of days. It should have been cool under the earth even in summer, but with the concentration of people it was already hot and starting to stink. There was a deathly silence as everybody strained to hear. The place was lit by a single torch so that the wavering shadows and pools of darkness and the pale faces of the people made it look like a vision of the underworld. The miasma of fear was almost palpable.

It wasn't long before they heard horse hooves – a lot of them. They approached quickly and soon Birkita could hear men's voices and horses snorting as they stopped. An order was given – it was in the Roman tongue so she didn't know what was said – but the men outside went silent. A horse whinnied and then the sound was cut off – Birkita could picture reins being pulled savagely.

A seemingly endless silence followed. Birkita could hear her own heart beating.

A child whimpered and was hushed by its mother.

Then came a soft rustling at the entrance. Birkita drew her sword and stepped forward. She braced herself, standing at this end of the passageway ready to meet the attacker. She steadied her shield.

Whatever comes.

A few moments later Bran came bounding happily into the chamber.

Birkita groaned.

Some of the children laughed and were cut short by their parents.

Now came another rustling, still soft but louder. Bigger. This was a man.

Birkita readied again. The passageway was only wide enough for a man and so the Romans would get no value from their numbers. In addition, they would have to crouch while Birkita could stand upright. This would be a succession of one-to-one fights. She would fight until they overcame her. Her eyes strained, peering along the dark entranceway, prepared for whatever might come out of the gloom. She would feint for the Roman's face and when his shield jerked upwards in a reflex, she would stab him in the belly. The first body would partly block the passage meaning that whoever came after him would have to clamber over him and this would make it easier for her to get the second one. And so on with the third and fourth.

That would be until they tried something different. The Romans always had something different. More awful. She tried not to think what that might be.

As all this was going through her head, a figure appeared and Birkita very nearly stabbed her brother.

Banning carried no weapons. His face was smeared with blood and he held up his left hand as though clenching his fist. A blood-soaked rag was wound around it and rivulets of blood ran down his arm and dripped onto the ground.

He was crying.

'Banning!'

'I thought I had outstripped them … but more of them surprised me at the village.'

He winced as a spasm of pain passed through him.

'They cut off my fingers, one by one … I was happy to die … I wasn't going to tell them anything … but then they saw Bran. "The dog," they said. "The dog will lead us to them." They said they would pour liquid fire in if you didn't come out. You must come out … otherwise you will all die.'

'We will die anyway.'

He shook his head.

'They said not.'

Birkita spat. 'You would take the word of a Roman?'

'You will all die for certain if you don't.'

Birkita wanted to hold her brother – just for a few moments. But he turned away, back the way he had come.

'Come,' he said, in a voice wet with tears.

With Banning leading and Birkita second, they emerged blinking into the sunlight that spilled into the clearing. Birds were singing. It took a few moments for Birkita's eyes to adjust to the dazzling light. As they did she saw that they were encircled by Romans on horseback with spears lowered, forming a hedge of steel. The Romans started to talk amongst themselves. They laughed as the villagers emerged one by one.

A heavily built Roman removed his helmet. He had a round head with a heavy, red face, reminding Birkita of a bull. He issued an order and three soldiers dismounted. One went to her, indicating that she should hand over her sword. She hesitated.

'You have to,' said Banning, standing beside her, his voice shot through with pain. 'If not, the killing will start.'

The bull Roman looked down at her. He had bushy eyebrows, probing eyes and a nose that made Birkita think of an axe. He said nothing but the question he was asking was eloquent. What are you going to do?

Birkita dropped the sword.

The bull Roman said something and his men laughed. He looked away from her as though discarding her. A soldier took her sword and shield and threw them between two horses out beyond the spear-hedge.

Then the three soldiers began to separate the old people from the rest, pushing them with the flats of their swords.

Banning spoke to the bull Roman.

'You said we would come to no harm.'

The bull Roman looked at another soldier who appeared to translate what Banning had said. The bull Roman smiled and said something. The translator too smiled.

To Banning he said, 'You will be walking far. My decurion says that the old people will not be able to walk.'

Just then, they heard the sound of more horses and wheels moving over the forest floor. An open-top wagon pulled by two horses emerged from the trees and stopped just beyond the circle of Roman horses.

'Also the children and babies. Give them to the old

people so that they can all be together.'

The remaining villagers hesitated. No one volunteered their offspring. The three soldiers began to take them. They were gentle at first but when some mothers resisted, the soldiers slapped their faces and tore the children from their arms. Women shouted, children screamed, babies began to cry. A pregnant woman was punched in the belly. She fell onto all fours gasping in pain. Another woman tried to help her to her feet.

When the children had all been placed with the old people, the bull Roman issued another order. A soldier drew a sheaf of short pieces of rope from his saddle bag and passed them down. The three soldiers began to bind the wrists of the remaining villagers. Birkita felt the hair on the back of her neck rising. She looked at Banning who seemed to be lost in a world of grief and pain. She held her hands out and the rope was tied savagely tightly around her wrists. The Roman who did it stank of sweat and horse and blood. He had bad teeth and his breath was vile. When he had finished he looked into her eyes and grinned at her. Soon everyone except the old people and children were tied.

The bull Roman spoke again.

'You,' the translator said to Banning, 'which ones are your family?'

'Don't tell him,' hissed Birkita. 'Don't tell him.'

But before Banning could do or say anything, Genovefa, his wife spoke.

'I am his wife,' she said almost haughtily. 'And these are my two children.'

The bull Roman seemed to think about this for a moment. Then, through the translator, he said, 'I said I would release you and your family and I will.'

15

It hasn't really gone like Julia or Suzanne thought it would. At different times they said that they would write on alternate days; that each would write their own character; that they would write every other chapter. They talked about how they would act out their characters' conversations and then one of them would write them down.

In the end it's almost as though the story itself decided.

Julia has been writing for a week. Each night, before going to sleep, she has asked Suzanne if she would like to see what she has written so that she can check if it's any good and whether she'd like to take over. Suzanne has always made the same answer: 'If it's flowing, keep going.' But after two full chapters, Julia can't wait any more. She needs somebody to read it. She needs to know. So on the last day of January, they sit on the edge of the mattress, knees up and blankets around them. Suzanne reads. Julia waits and watches her face nervously

Shortly after she turns the first page, Suzanne looks up and smiles.

'"Like a fat woman scrambling over a wall" – I love that.'

Eventually, she is finished.

'Well?' asks Julia.

'I like it. I want to know what happens next.'

Julia looks at her expectantly. She needs more and Suzanne seems subdued tonight.

'It's so authentic. There was no point in it where it jarred, where it didn't seem real and I was back there in Ancient Britain.'

'You gave me good information,' says Julia.

But she still needs to know about the writing. She looks expectantly at Suzanne who finally says, 'It's a book I'd buy and once I'd bought it, if I'd read this far I wouldn't stop until I'd finished.'

Julia is pleased. No, it's more than that. She's overwhelmed. Especially when Suzanne finishes by saying, 'I couldn't pay you any greater compliment, Julia.'

'So will you take over now?'

"I've been thinking about that,' says Suzanne. 'And no, I don't think so.'

'No?'

'No. I'll meet you in Pompeii.'

16

'So do you really not know who your character is going to be?' asks Julia.

It is later that night and the two girls lie in bed. Julia has managed to procure an extra blanket from the bed of somebody who died – she got there before anybody else did – and so they are warmer than they have ever been since coming here. They lie on their backs in the dark. It is after lights out.

'Not completely. But by the time you – Birkita – arrives in Pompeii and I meet you – her – I'll know.'

Julia has a sense that Suzanne doesn't really want to talk – that she is tired and wants to go to sleep. But Julia is excited about what she has written and is eager to talk about the story, to move it forward.

'Can't you even give me a hint?'

'Well, she's not British. I was going to make her from the same tribe as Birkita but then I thought it would be much more interesting if she came from another part of the world. That's what I haven't worked out yet.'

'And do you know what she's like?'

'Mostly. But you don't need to know that until you get to Pompeii and they meet.'

There is a finality about the way Suzanne says this which Julia accepts. The girls fall silent. Julia is exhausted but happy. She has found the writing to be immensely tiring – much more so than the physical work they do every day. But as each day went on she felt that what she was writing was good – maybe even very good, sometimes. And now Suzanne seems to agree. Julia can't wait to continue tomorrow.

She has fallen into something of a routine. Each night, before she goes to sleep, she tries to think through the next piece of the story. Usually she falls asleep before she has got very far. If she wakes in the middle of the night and has to go to the toilet, as she almost invariably does, she will return to bed and try to pick up the story where she left off. In the morning she can usually remember what passed through her head during the night. But more wonderfully, sometimes she wakes with a really clear picture of where the story must go next. Thoughts and whole sequences that never came into her head while she was awake have now suddenly appeared. It is almost like magic.

'I found out why this place is called the Paradise Ghetto,' Suzanne says.

Julia had thought her friend had fallen asleep. 'Why?'

'It was set up to house what the Germans called "privileged Jews".'

'Privileged?'

'Rich. Or famous. Or decorated in the last war. Apparently the place is full of famous musicians and artists and writers and scientists and doctors and university professors.'

'Who told you all this?'

'Irena. I realised,' Suzanne continues, 'that my parents were probably brought here. They were both university professors.'

Then she asks, 'What did your parents do?'

Julia feels a chill down her spine that has nothing to do

with the arctic conditions in the room.

'My father was a doctor.'

'An ordinary doctor?'

Anything but.

'A specialist. People came from all over Europe to see him.

'And your mother?'

'She was a housewife.'

'So that explains it,' says Suzanne. 'That's why you and I ended up here. Because of our parents. We're privileged Jews.'

'Some fucking privilege,' says Julia.

'Irena was saying that when people came here – especially Jews from Germany and Austria – they thought they were coming to a spa. That's why it's called the Paradise Ghetto. The Germans had painted a picture of nice apartments with views out over the lake. Some of the people were so shocked when they saw what the place was actually like that they died of it.'

'So our parents are here?' Julia asks with a growing sense of dread.

'No. That was what I thought – that I would get to see my parents. But then she said that thousands had been deported from here to the East. If my parents – or yours – came here in 1942 or 1943 – then there was a good chance they were no longer here. Irena was able to check for me. At the central registry.'

After a pause, Suzanne says in a voice that almost breaks, 'My parents came in 1943 and were deported later that year.'

'I need to check on mine,' says Julia urgently.

'I already did,' says Suzanne.

'And?'

'The same. They came and went last year.'

Julia emits a sigh of relief. Suzanne turns onto her

side – it is her turn to spoon Julia. Julia turns too and Suzanne's arm encircles her and settles on her breast in what has now become a familiar routine for both of them.

It is so cosy with the extra blanket.

'I'm so sorry,' says Suzanne, almost in a whisper.

'So am I,' says Julia. 'For you. It sounds like you and your parents were very happy.'

'We were. I'm sorry I had to be the one to tell you.'

'I'm glad I found out from you. Where do they go to in the East?'

'Don't know. Some kind of camp or something, I suppose. Maybe the same as this. Another camp for privileged Jews. It must be a terrible shock for you, Julia. I've had nearly a week to come to terms with it.'

'I'll get over it,' Julia says coldly.

Suzanne embraces her more closely, snuggling into her.

'You don't have to be strong all the time, Julia.'

'Yes, you do.'

CHAPTER THREE

To Pompeii (Julia)

Along with their hands being tied, the survivors of the village were now also chained. Each of them had an iron ring around their neck and a chain ran from this to the ring of the person in front and behind them. They trudged along a road that led south. The Romans rode in front and behind and one patrolled lazily up and down the line. He carried a whip and periodically lashed somebody at random with it.

There was no escape – other than the escape of death. Attack the whip-wielding Roman, drag him from his horse and hope that somebody would stab her with a sword or a lance. For several days, this was what Birkita had tried to find an opportunity to do. But she had never been able to get close enough to him. Still, she had focused on this – his position along the line of prisoners, his approach, whether she had the strength to drag the people in front and behind her when she moved and all the other minute factors that she allowed to crowd into her head so that she didn't have to think about other things.

More groups of prisoners had joined them, again in long chained lines and it was the third or fourth day when she acknowledged that she would never get close enough to the whip Roman to attack him. He was obviously experienced in this work and knew about such moves.

When she had finally given up on that – that was when she could no longer keep the images at bay.

First had come the old people. She could still see the bull Roman's upward nod of his head that indicated that the killing should begin. People suddenly collapsing. The screams of the mothers. The shrieks of the children. A baby crying before the sound was cut off. Blood. Blood everywhere. Spurting. Splashing. Pink clouds of it suddenly appearing in the air like the puff of a dandelion head. The smell. The smell of when an animal was butchered. The smile on the face of one of the Romans who was doing the killing.

It seemed to take only moments for the group of children and old people to become a bloody, tangled mound of bodies. There were still groans and wailing so now the three soldiers moved around the mound, plunging their swords savagely into the topmost bodies, the blades biting noisily into flesh and crunching through bone, until finally, there were no more sounds or movement.

There had been a break in the killing after that.

The survivors had waited in the hot day while crosses were assembled. The soldiers had brought timber with them on the wagon. But they seemed in no hurry. Skins of wine appeared. Birkita had an unbelievably clear picture of a soldier, head back, wine skin to his mouth while the red liquid dribbled down his chin. The sun was high by then, shining down into the clearing, baking them. The Romans had a couple of barrels of water on the wagon and they took ladlefuls of this from time to time. The prisoners were given nothing.

And all the while Banning looked across at her, his eyes pleading with her to do something.

And so she did.

When a Roman came to apply the neck chain, she head-butted him. There was a crunching of bone and blood erupted from his nose. She had intended to try to catch the handle of his sword and pull it from his sheath as he fell but just then she felt a crashing pain on the back of her head and the world went black.

When she same to, she was lying on the ground shackled hand and foot. After that all she could do was watch.

The Romans went about the assembly of the four crosses with the easy confidence of good tradesmen. Meanwhile, some of the Britons were made to dig holes. The sounds in the clearing were of birds singing, shovels biting into earth, hammers upon wood, a Roman whistling while he worked and Banning and Genovefa trying to comfort their two daughters. They were six and eight and knew what was coming.

Birkita closed her eyes and held them tightly shut.

But she couldn't block out the sound.

Eventually, there came a change. The hammering and shovelling ceased. Orders were shouted.

And suddenly there was the sound of a scuffle. Shouts. Running feet.

Birkita opened her eyes.

A couple of spear lengths away from her, Banning and Genovefa were each trying to strangle one of their children.

But it was no good. The Romans were upon them, beating them away.

After this both girls became hysterical as they were dragged screaming to the crosses.

Mercifully, Birkita couldn't fully remember everything which happened after that. The memories came in jagged fragments. All four bodies stripped naked. Those two frail children's bodies that she had known since they were born. The hammering. The animal shrieks of pain. The hollow thunk of the crosses being dropped into the holes and then the earth being shovelled in. The screaming that agonisingly slowly wound itself down to sobbing, gasping, moaning, laboured breathing.

Of course, she had tried most of the time not to look. But there were times when she had forced herself to.

To remember this.

The soldiers drank more and played dice. A decision appeared to be made that they would camp for the night. Fires were lit, food was prepared, guards posted. The crosses had been raised soon after the sun reached its highest point in the sky but as the late summer night fell, Birkita could see that her brother, sister-in-law and two nieces were still alive.

The terrible sounds continued intermittently during the night.

As dawn came, Birkita saw that Banning and Genovefa had died. But the girls were still breathing. Of course Birkita had known that would happen. The heavier bodies of the adults would have pulled them down and hastened death. The two children were as though drugged, lost in a world of pain.

With the sun, the Romans began to pack up. Soon everything was stowed on the wagon and horses were saddled. The bull Roman gave an order and a soldier took an iron bar from the wagon. With two easy swings he broke the legs of the two children, triggering new screams from them. Death would come more quickly now.

After that the convoy left the clearing.

Birkita took one more backward glance at the crosses silhouetted against the trees.

She would remember.

And somehow – she didn't know how yet, couldn't see a way forward right now – but somehow she would have her revenge.

She didn't remember much about the next few days.

They were a succession of baking heat and glaring light on the long white road that ribboned out ahead of them. She closed her eyes a lot. When she opened them, all she would see were chains. The neck ring of the man in front of her and the chain that connected her to him. And the crosses. Always the crosses.

Eventually they reached the great river where the Romans handed them over to a band of slavers. These put a heavy iron anklet on each of them and they were led up a gangplank on to a ship. Birkita had never seen a ship of such size before. Steps led down into a foetid hold smelling of shit and piss and vomit. Each anklet had a ring on it and now they were made to sit while a chain was passed through each ring. Then the rings around their necks were removed.

Throughout the afternoon and evening the hold continued to be loaded, filling up so that each person had room to lie down but nothing else. When it seemed like they couldn't possibly fit in any more and the smell had already become overpowering, the hatch was slid across slicing away the small square of blue sky. Shortly afterwards, the ship raised anchor and began to move.

For the first few days, they were kept below decks. They had to go to the toilet where they lay. Many were seasick so that a layer of human waste quickly built up on the wooden planking beneath them. They were given food once a day – sailors in boots stepped among them, giving each of them a bowl of some sort of porridge and a ladleful of water.

As the voyage went on, the hold became hotter. When it became so hot that some of the occupants started to die, the hatch was slid back again to reveal a glaring blue sky with a tracing of feathery white clouds high up.

There were women from the village chained on either side of Birkita. Both had lost children in the massacre.

One of them, Amena, sat or lay silently, endlessly staring at either the side of the ship or the underside of the deck. One day when the bowls of food were being passed along, Birkita nudged Amena and found that she was cold and stiff.

The woman on the other side of Birkita was called Kyna. She was petite, almost frail-looking, with thin arms and legs. The Romans had killed twins belonging to her. In the village, Kyna had always been viewed as mild-mannered, even timid. She seemed no different now as she sat, lay, ate and said little or nothing to Birkita or anybody else.

Even with the hatch pulled back, it continued to get hotter. During the middle part of the day, the sun would shine directly down into the hold, baking the people unfortunate enough to be caught in its beam. When more occupants of the hold had died, the slavers decided they needed to do something else. One morning as the sun began its ascent into the sky and was beginning to edge into the hold, Birkita heard the sound of the leg chain being pulled through the anklet rings. The slavers ordered them up on deck. Shakily, since they had hardly moved since the voyage started, they climbed the wooden steps out into the blinding light.

The first sensation Birkita felt was the warm breeze on her skin. It was like milk. As she became able to open her eyes, she saw that they were on a blue sea with an equally blue sky overhead. Sunlight glinted off the water sending up shards of light. There was a strong smell of salt and rope and grease. The ship whispered gently as it moved through the water. Ropes creaked and the sail made occasional swishing sounds. The air tasted like nectar as she took in great gulps of it.

A number of the slavers had lined the rails on each side of the deck. They were armed with swords, whips, cudgels. The slaves were made to shuffle round the deck for several laps and then they were returned to the hold.

This became part of the new routine. Each day the slaves were brought up in batches and spent some time on the deck in the air. The slavers prodded or whipped or hit them occasionally, but the slaves seemed happy just to be out of the hold and the routine soon became reasonably relaxed. It occurred to Birkita that in these circumstances it would be easy to escape – except where to? She knew how to swim but there was no land to be seen. She could drown herself but no, she would not do that. Not as long as the bull Roman lived.

One morning she and Kyna happened to be out on deck when a voice called down from the lookout's position high up on the mainmast. His extended hand was pointing off to the right of the bow of the ship. All eyes turned to look where he was indicating. There, on the horizon, faint but definite, was a thin purple stripe.

Land.

'They are nearly home,' said Kyna.

Startled, Birkita who was standing beside her, almost jumped.

'What?' she asked in surprise.

'They are almost home,' repeated Kyna. 'To their families and their children. And with plenty of gold in their pockets. It will be a joyous homecoming for them.'

Birkita looked at Kyna with one eyebrow raised. She had been looking ahead as she spoke but now she turned to Birkita and smiled, a gentle, almost shy smile.

'I suppose so –' Birkita began but then Kyna moved swiftly out of the shuffling line of slaves.

The nearest slaver to them was a tall, barrel-chested man with thighs like tree stumps. Kyna's move took him by surprise and he was slow to respond. His sword was in his sheath and his hand went for the handle. He gripped it and Birkita saw the sword sliding out slowly. But then Kyna – little, frail Kyna – had caught him around the waist and with a terrible roar lifted him off the deck, landing his lower back onto the rail with a loud thud. She paused for an instant. The slaver hung over the side, his head out over the water. The other slavers were moving now, barging through the slaves, knocking them aside so as to go to their comrade's assistance.

The barrel-chested slaver tried to recover. He groped to find the rail and grip it so that he could pull himself back in. But now Kyna moved her arms down and locked them around his thighs. With another shout – this time it seemed, of triumph – she upended him over the side. As she did so, a slaver reached her and drove his sword into the soft part of her back just above the waist.

The man in the water screamed. Even though she didn't know his language, Birkita understood what he was saying. It was well known that many sailors couldn't swim. If they went over the side, better to die straight away than linger.

And so it was. Before anyone could throw a rope to him, he was gone, dragged down and lost in the wash of the ship.

17

'Surely you must be ready to start now?' Julia says.

'Not quite yet,' Suzanne replies. 'You've nearly reached Pompeii. I'm in Pompeii waiting for you. Or at least my character is. You keep writing.'

'But how will your character and mine meet? How will I know where to find you?'

'You'll know,' says Suzanne. 'Now spoon me, please. I'm freezing.'

Julia does as she is told and they press together.

The first days of February. As cold as ever. Days of fog, of frost, of snow, of rain. Sometimes all four in the one day. Their work is hard and Julia is losing weight. Her clothes are loose upon her. But incredibly – miraculously even – she spends most of her time in the warm, sunny Mediterranean. There may not be much food there either, but at least she isn't cold.

She wonders briefly whether Suzanne has given up on the book and is just stringing her along. But she knows that actually, it doesn't matter. Julia would continue this on her own now. In some weird way, she is as happy – maybe happier, even – than she has ever been in her life.

CHAPTER FOUR

Arrival (Julia)

Kyna was still alive when they threw her over the side. The rest of the slaves were herded below decks again and kept there until the ship docked. As a punishment they were given no food or water. Several more died as a result. It was evening when the ship tied up. They were kept on board overnight.

In the morning a new slaver they hadn't seen before came down the stairs into the hold. He was accompanied by two of the crew and carried some kind of wooden tablet and a writing instrument. The leg chains were pulled through and the man stepped amongst the slaves, looking carefully at each one. Some he asked to stand and the crew members pulled them roughly to their feet. They were in no mood for gentleness after what had happened to their comrade. When the slaver asked Birkita to get up and the two men pulled her up, he said something in a tone that clearly sounded like a reprimand. Birkita was ordered to stay standing. Finally, she and about twenty other slaves were chained together and led up the stairs and out of the hold.

When her eyes adjusted to the dazzling light, she saw that they had arrived at some city. Sunlight danced on blue water. The port was crowded with ships and the quayside throbbed with activity. There were men, some women, animals, carts. Boxes, bales, amphorae were being loaded and unloaded. The land sloped gently upwards away from the harbour and was carpeted with buildings, all topped with red tiled roofs.

They were herded across the gangplank, along a stone pier that ran out from the shore and into a shed. Here, there was a large barrel of water, the height of a man's waist. Beside it were two men, one with a brush on a long handle and the other with a sponge. One by one the slaves were stripped of their stinking rags. A bucket of water was thrown over them and first, the man with the brush, then the other with the sponge, cleaned them down.

When she was being sponged, the man kneaded her breasts and pushed his fingers between her legs, probing. Birkita was only dimly aware of any of this – a state she had been in ever since what had happened in the forest clearing.

When the man with the sponge had finished she was handed on to another man who led her – completely naked – through a doorway into another part of the shed. Here there was some kind of stage or platform and beyond it a large crowd of people had gathered. Birkita's leg iron was taken off and then she was put in a line with some of the other recently arrived slaves. She tried to cover herself as best she could with her hands.

Eventually she was pushed up some steps onto the platform. There were two Romans on the platform. One was prosperous-looking in a short-sleeved white tunic that came down to his calves. The other was naked from the waist up with a hairy, bronzed chest and looked like a wrestler. He took Birkita by the upper arm and pushed her out to the front of the platform. He displayed her to the crowd. Then he forced her to turn round and showed her back. She was made to bend over. Then, facing the crowd again, the wrestler held her while the other Roman opened her mouth and pulled her lips back to show her teeth.

The Romans in the crowd began to call out words. Some raised their hands. One or two signalled with their eyes. One, who looked like a merchant, made the slightest of nods. Birkita saw that she was being traded. Sold. It went on like this for some time, with the merchant repeatedly nodding. Eventually, it all came to an end and Birkita saw that she had been sold to him. She was led down the stairs, a rough cloak was put around her shoulders and she was given a pair of sandals. Then she was led out of the shed and into the city.

The merchant walked in front of Birkita and another man walked behind. She guessed he must be some kind of bodyguard. He was built like a keg and carried a club as well as a vicious-looking knife in his belt. From time to time, he prodded her forward.

They walked along the side of the street on a raised stone walkway. The street itself was covered with brown mud mixed with the lighter colour of shit and pools of yellow water. Animals thronged the streets – heavily laden donkeys, carthorses, dogs, horses with riders. Carts trundled past, along with the occasional chariot. From time to time there were places where square blocks of stone had been set in the road like stepping-stones. They meant that vehicles could drive through but people could also cross without getting their feet dirty. Somewhere deep in the recesses of Birkita's mind, it occurred to her that it was a clever idea, but the thought was so far away, it might have been that she was thinking someone else's thoughts.

On either side of the street were houses and shops. They sold vegetables, nuts, fruit, chickens, bread. Many were cooking food and Birkita salivated as the smells were wafted on the air. She couldn't remember when she'd last eaten proper food. The place was noisy beyond

140

belief with the sound of animals and men.

Eventually, they came to a two-storey building on a V where a pair of streets came together. A few paces down one of the streets was a doorway. Birkita was led inside.

She found herself in a hallway with a series of two or three drawn curtains on either side. The place smelt faintly of a toilet. From either side came sounds which Birkita quickly identified as those of people having sex. A man grunting, a woman moaning and managing to sound bored at the same time, a second woman repeating the same word over and over again in an increasingly excited state.

A woman appeared from behind a curtain at the end of the hallway. She was tall and blonde with a hard face. Despite this, she smiled kindly at Birkita.

'I am Flavia,' she said.

18

'Flavia. It's a nice name.'

'Maybe she's a nice person,' says Suzanne.

'You understand the kind of place they're in?' says Julia, a little hesitantly.

'Of course I do. I'm not completely innocent.'

'It's just that – from everything you've told me about Ancient Rome – it seemed like the most likely thing that would happen to Birkita, if she was pretty.'

'And is she?'

'She is,' says Julia.

'All right. So now I think it's high time I started.'

'Yeah – give my hand a rest. I could do with it.'

Chapter Five

Flavia (Suzanne)

Flavia took Birkita upstairs into a room where there was a metal bath. She filled it with several jugs of steaming hot water that she brought from another part of the house.

'I must make you ready,' said Flavia. 'I will make you clean and beautiful. Though I can see you are already quite beautiful.'

Birkita's hands held the cloak shut but now Flavia gently prized her fingers open and slid the cloak off her shoulders. It whispered its way to the floor.

'Now, in you go.'

Birkita did as she was told. The water was very hot and she submerged herself into it. The cuts and bruises and whip-stripes on her body burned and stung but the feeling was not unpleasant. It was as though a layer was being peeled away.

'What is your name?' asked Flavia as she began to sponge Birkita's back.

'Birkita.'

'It's a nice name but when the men come, you must ask them what they want to call you.'

Birkita suddenly realised that she understood most of what Flavia was saying and the shock jolted her.

'You don't speak the Roman tongue.'

'I speak that too,' said Flavia.

'But you're speaking ... I understand...'

'I don't speak your tongue but one close to it. I am from Gaul. We are neighbours. Or we were once.'

Birkita looked properly at Flavia for the first time. She was older than Birkita – by about ten summers, Birkita reckoned. Flavia had obviously been beautiful once and still retained some of that, but she was past her peak. There were wrinkles around her mouth and eyes. Her teeth were yellowed and her skin was not as soft as Birkita's. And her eyes – there was something in them – a hardness, maybe, like she had seen too many things, not all of which were good. Birkita wondered if she had the same look in her own eyes.

'Where am I?' Birkita asked.

'You are in a city called Pompeii – in the same land as Rome.'

'And what will happen to me?'

'Happen? Why, nothing will happen to you. You are here to pleasure men. That's what you will do.'

'For the rest of my life?'

Flavia smiled.

'For the rest of your life? Who can say such a thing? For now. Who knows how things can change – what surprises the gods have in store for us?'

She moved round to Birkita's front, sponging her breasts, her belly and then between her legs.

'Here you must keep clean,' she said.

Flavia poured something cold from a small bottle onto Birkita's head. Then she massaged it into a soapy foam and washed her hair, combing it out afterwards and removing all the tangles. Birkita tried not to think about anything else and just focussed on the sensations in her body. The hot water had relaxed all her muscles. Flavia had put some sort of scent in the water and Birkita inhaled it. It was beautiful and reminded her of flowers in summer meadows. It was the scent of her life of long ago, lost now for ever. She wanted to cry but the tears wouldn't come. She closed her eyes and just allowed the water to take her.

'You have never been with a man before?'

'No.'

'Your master will be pleased.'

'I will kill him before I let him touch me.'

The words were out of Birkita's mouth before she knew she had said them aloud. She opened her eyes. It was as though she had suddenly returned from a far distant place.

'We all felt like that when we came here. All the girls.' Flavia shook her head. 'There's no point in thinking like that. Better to be alive. Life is sweet. Even this life.'

'I will kill him,' repeated Birkita.

Flavia spoke as though she hadn't heard.

'The first time will be the worst. It gets easier after that. After a while you'll hardly notice. The important thing will be not to have a child and I will tell you how to do that. Here you'll live well – enough food, wine, sleep – sleep mostly during the day. It's almost like not being a slave at all. Now, out you come. I'll dry you off and then there are clean clothes and food waiting for you. And after that a soft, warm bed. You will rest after your journey.'

146

19

British newspaper report
October 1st 2015

An extremely rich cultural life developed in Theresienstadt. There were lectures, recitals, poetry readings, concerts, and so on. At least four concert orchestras were organized, as well as chamber groups and jazz ensembles. Several stage performances were produced and attended by camp inmates. Many prominent artists from Czechoslovakia, Austria, and Germany were imprisoned at Theresienstadt, along with writers, scientists, jurists, diplomats, musicians, and scholars, and many of these contributed to the camp's cultural life.

Chapter Six

The Games (Suzanne)

Birkita's bed was indeed soft and warm and she slept the sleep of the dead. It was morning when Flavia woke her with a breakfast of freshly baked bread with honey, some fruit and a little wine.

'What time is it?'

'About noon. You were tired.'

Birkita was puzzled. There was something not right.

'I am a slave,' she said, 'but you are treating me like a mistress of the house.'

'This is the way Master Antonius likes it done,' said Flavia as she walked out.

Left alone, Birkita ate and drank. She had vague memories of the night she had slept through. Sounds from downstairs or out on the street – shouting, a woman laughing, a lot of groaning and whimpering and frantic, unintelligible sounds, something breaking – pottery perhaps.

She tried not to think about everything that had happened. She thought very briefly about escaping – there appeared to be no one at her door. But escape to where? She didn't even know where in the world she was. She couldn't speak their tongue. And anyway – return to what? Everything she had known and loved had been destroyed.

Some time later Flavia returned. She wore a floor-length sleeveless dress the same colour as autumn grass, trimmed with gold, and carried a second dress – a white one – over her arm.

'Come,' she said, 'it is time to get ready.'

Birkita didn't question her. She just did as she was told, putting on the dress, wrapping a gold coloured belt around her waist and stepping into gold sandals. Then Flavia applied something to Birkita's eyes and to her cheeks.

'You look beautiful,' said Flavia.

'Is all this for the men?' asked Birkita, dully.

Flavia laughed.

'No, of course not. We wouldn't go to that much trouble for those. No. This is for something else. You will see. Come.'

Flavia led Birkita down the stairway into the street. Here they waited on the walkway. People hurried past. Carts laden with goods trundled along. A chariot came by followed by a mule with two barrels strapped, one either side, on its back. The smell was overpowering – a combination of people and animals and food cooking and horse shit and toilets. Birkita tried to remember the smell of lying in a meadow amongst the fragrant grasses and wild flowers but found that she couldn't.

After a while they were joined by the merchant, Antonius and two men – the bodyguard and a second more compact man with curly hair who seemed to be one too. Birkita had not seen Antonius close up before or if she had, she had been in too much shock to notice much about him. Now she saw that he was short – not even as tall as her – and he reminded her of one of the Roman tax collectors that used to come to the village from time to time. He ignored the two women and set off towards the end of the street.

'Come on,' said Flavia, falling in behind him.

The two bodyguards brought up the rear.

At the corner they turned right and after two streets, turned left again. They were heading east. Over on their left, beyond the city a great mountain rose into the sky. Birkita had never seen anything like it. She tried to remember the way – she would need it when she came to escape – but she soon became totally confused. The streets all looked the same. They teemed with people, carts, chariots, animals. There was no grass or flowers – just stone everywhere, the buildings, the streets. And so many animals and people. And the noise – the shouts, the clamour. It was deafening. The only thing that seemed in any way familiar was the vivid blue sky like a ribbon overhead.

As they went further along, the flow of people increased. They all seemed to be moving in the same direction. The effect was like a river. Soon Birkita saw where they were going – a high, circular wall that extended off to either side and was inset with tall arches. There were stone stairs that led up onto the top of the wall and people were streaming towards the steps and going up them.

One of the bodyguards led the way and Birkita lifted the hem of her dress to climb the steps. The dress felt very strange on her. At home in summer she had worn a tunic that hung loosely on her and came down to her knees. Here, this dress seemed to have been fitted around her, moulded to her body. When they reached the top of the steps, she found that she was looking down into a huge elliptical depression in the ground. The bottom of the depression was covered in sand and a low wall encircled it. Tiers of seats mounted upwards from the wall. Overhead a great canopy shaded most of the seats from the sun. Birkita looked in a mixture of wonderment and confusion at Flavia. But Flavia said nothing – she just smiled.

They descended to seats about halfway down the stone stairs. Birkita sat on the cool stone with the original bodyguard on one side and Flavia on the other. Then she waited silently, wondering what was to happen next.

She had heard before that the Romans had places like this but she had never really been able to picture them. The scale of this was so far beyond anything she could have imagined. She knew too that it was a place where men fought each other. And so it turned out to be. When all the seats were filled, a trumpet blared, then a grey-haired Roman in a long red tunic made a speech. He signalled with his hand and things got under way.

Men in helmets and armour emerged from a tunnel and after saluting, began to fight each other. Birkita assumed that they were slaves or captives. She wondered for a moment whether, if she had been a man, she would have ended up down there rather than up here.

The crowds roared their approval. Soon men were dying. Birkita had seen fights to the death before, but to entertain a crowd? This was no way to die. What was it with the Romans and killing? What pleasure did they get from it? She watched the scene in front of her dully, trying to keep other thoughts and images at bay.

Finally, one warrior was left standing. He saluted and left the arena while men – Birkita assumed they were slaves – came in to remove the bodies. Using a large hammer and a knife, they finished off any that were still alive. Then they scattered fresh sand onto the bloodstains.

Once this was done, the same slaves carried in sections of timber which they quickly assembled into a low wooden platform. A man and a woman emerged from the tunnel and walked into the arena to the cheers of the crowd. Unlike the fighters who had looked around at the

151

crowd grimly, these two smiled and waved to the audience who whistled and cheered and waved back.

The man and the woman stepped onto the platform where a rug had been laid. Each briskly stripped the other naked, kissing one another as they did so. The man was black, muscular and well-built with a huge penis that was now erect. The woman was white with black hair, columnar thighs and large breasts. Now she lay back on the rug and parted her legs as the man lay on top of her and entered her. He began to pump her and the crowd cheered. After a few minutes, the couple changed position. The woman knelt down while the man entered her from behind, like a dog. The crowds applauded them. After a few minutes, they changed to another position, head to toe and toe to head and used their mouths. Then they changed again. Each time the crowd roared their delight, egging them on. And between each change of position, they waved to the crowd and bowed.

But then suddenly there was an unexpected hush. The couple ignored it and continued their latest coupling. This involved the man standing and holding the woman upside down, her thighs on his shoulders, his penis in her mouth. Suddenly the crowd began to roar with laughter. At this the man looked up and as he did so, a look of horror came over his face and he dropped the woman as his erection faded. She fell with a loud thud and a scream of pain onto the platform.

A huge brown beast with a great shaggy mane and a long tail had come down the tunnel and emerged from its semi-darkness into the sunlight of the arena. It padded along slowly, uneasily, looking around and sniffing the air, unsure. But then it noticed the man and the woman who were now standing on the platform in horror, staring at the beast. The crowd hushed as it waited to see what would happen next. The great beast stared at the couple.

They looked around frantically searching for some place where they could find safety. But there was nothing. They were alone in the arena with just the low platform. Then the great beast slowly broke into a loping run, moving incredibly quickly for such a large animal. The couple began to run away and the crowd roared with laughter. Most of the spectators were on their feet now, cheering and whistling and straining to see and make sure they missed nothing.

The man was much faster than the woman so that the beast caught her first, leaping onto her back. She uttered a wild, terrible shriek as she was brought down. The animal settled on top of her as she continued to scream. The man stopped, turned around, hesitated for a moment and then ran back. The beast already had the woman's shoulder in its mouth and was tearing at it. A spray of bright blood erupted splashing the beast, the sand and the woman's white skin with scarlet. The man tried to push the beast off but then the animal turned on him. He screamed, falling onto his back as the animal moved to lie on top of him and take his arm in its mouth. There was a loud crunching sound. Birkita looked to either side of her. On one side, Flavia stared down into the arena, her face impassive, unreadable. On the other, the bodyguard was laughing. After a few moments he seemed to become aware that he was being watched and he turned to Birkita. He looked at her with interest as though seeing her for the first time. Then he mimed a kiss at her before returning his gaze to the arena. Birkita kept her eyes averted until the screaming stopped.

The afternoon continued with more fights amongst men and between men and animals. The compact bodyguard bought snacks and wine from a seller and Birkita was given some of this. Towards evening, two saddled horses were led into the arena. At this the crowd fell silent. Moments later, a woman with wild blonde hair was led in by two soldiers, one holding each of her arms. The woman was bare-breasted and wore only a loincloth. Her wrists were chained together. She screamed and struggled like a madwoman but the soldiers grip was like iron. When they reached the centre of the arena where the horses were waiting, the woman suddenly went quiet. Her strength seemed to fail her and her legs folded beneath her.

Sitting in the sand, the two horses were backed up, one on either side of her. Then Birkita understood what was going to happen. She looked at Flavia who was staring intently down at the scene. The woman's chains were taken off but now her left wrist and ankle were tied by two ropes to the saddle of one horse. Then her other wrist and ankle were tied to the second one. Flavia became aware that Birkita was watching her because she suddenly turned.

'An escaped slave,' Flavia said by way of explanation before turning back. And now Birkita understood why she had been brought here. She kept looking away as she heard the horses urged forward, and then the screaming began.

20

'Did the Romans really do things like that?' asks Julia.
She is in some shock at what Suzanne has written.

'Apparently so,' says Suzanne. 'I'll keep going – OK?'

'Sure.'

Julia is glad to be out of it for a while.

CHAPTER SEVEN

Antonius (Suzanne)

They left shortly after the woman was torn apart by the horses, walking back to the building that Flavia told Julia was called the lupanar. She was in something of a daze. Upstairs, a boy brought her food from a nearby cookshop. Then Flavia came and took Birkita's dress from her. She gave her instead a long length of red cloth which she said was called a toga. It was made of much plainer, coarser material. Flavia showed Birkita how to tie it by wrapping it around herself and then over one shoulder.

While she was doing this, Flavia talked.

'Tonight you sleep here but from tomorrow, you will be downstairs. You will have your own cubicle. You can sleep late because we don't start until the middle of the afternoon. But then we are open until dawn.

'When the men come in, you will be standing in the corridor between the cubicles – you and anyone else who is not taken at the time. Smile at the man but don't say anything. The man chooses who he wants. If he wants you, you take him to your cubicle. You tell him your name. Sometimes they use your name but sometimes they want to call you the name of some other girl – a girlfriend or their wife or a woman they're in love with but they'll never be able to have.

'Next you undress him. If you see any cuts or sores of any kind on his thing, you can tell him you'll only give

156

him fellatus. With your mouth. You understand?'

Birkita understood.

'But please, be clear – you can only do that so often. If Antonius feels he is losing customers…'

She left the rest of the sentence unsaid.

'Then you find out what they want and how much they're going to spend.'

'I ask them how much they'd like to spend?'

'Not "like". Not "like" to spend. They don't *like* to spend anything. You say, "How much are you going to spend?" I will teach it to you in the Roman tongue – and also how to count. Numbers, so that you know the money and you won't get cheated. At first you may not be very good at all this. Most people say that you should hide your inexperience, but the thing is, you don't want to get complaints. If Antonius gets complaints…

'So – and this is what I did when I started – I think it's good to say that you're new. Then they'll be more tolerant of mistakes, they won't think you're cold, they'll be a bit more sympathetic. Most men aren't bastards – just the occasional one, and then our boys take care of them.'

Birkita assumed these were the two bodyguards.

'So give them what they paid for and then out as quickly as possible. If they give you any extra, you give me half – is that understood?'

Birkita nodded.

'But please listen to me.'

Flavia looked Birkita in the eye.

'Make sure that the customers are happy. Oh, there'll always be the ones who moan and want their money back. But try to make sure you send them away with a smile on their face. Master Antonius has paid a lot of money for you and he likes things to run smoothly. If they don't…'

It was the third time she had done this and this time, Birkita reacted.

'If they don't what?' she said, almost angrily.

'Understand, Birkita, you are now his property. That's all – property, the same as his dog or his shoe or a chair or this building. He can do what he likes with you. All he has to do is say that you tried to escape…'

'And what?'

'And you will end up in the arena.' Flavia quickly changed the subject. 'Now, you look beautiful. Tomorrow I will help you with your hair and your face. I will be there between customers in case anything needs looking after.'

'Flavia?'

'Yes?'

'You've done … what I will be doing tomorrow?'

'Of course. When I first came here.'

'When was that?'

'Ten summers ago.'

It was a lifetime. Birkita was appalled.

'And now?'

'Now, not very often. Only if someone is looking for an older woman. Which is not too often. Now I am called the ancilla ornatrice. This means I take care of everything.'

'Are you free?'

'No, I'm very expensive. More expensive than you.'

Birkita laughed. It was the first time she had laughed since that day in the forest.

'No, I mean are you a free woman?'

'I am a slave. As you are. As we both will be until we die. And now I must teach you some words.'

After Flavia left, Birkita lay down and closed her eyes. She tried to sleep, trying not to think about what had happened to her family, the events of this day and what was coming tomorrow.

Outside it grew dark. The earlier cooking smells had

faded away and now the street was becoming noisy again as people finished their evening meals and came out of their homes. Downstairs was open for business and Birkita could hear the sounds as the first men arrived. There was a greeting as though of old friends, a squeal of laughter, some heavy grunting as though of a pig, though she knew it was a man.

She lay on the bed, on her side, fully clothed. There was a stub of a candle on a little table beside the bed but she left it unlit. She kept her back to the door and she stared out the window. All she could see was the tiled roof of the building opposite but the window at least gave her the sense that there was a way out, a way back; that there was freedom somewhere. If she was a bird she could have just flown out the window and away. Back to ... where? Back to where?

She tried to sleep. She was bone weary but try as she might to block them, images of what she had seen kept coming, unbidden into her mind. She still found it hard to believe she had seen these things. But then everything was like a nightmare – everything since that day in the forest.

She wondered if the gods knew she was here in this place. Or were they still back in the fields and groves and rivers of home? Home. What did the word even mean now? How could she have any home when her parents, her brother, her village, everyone she knew, even her dogs, were gone?

A loud crash of something being broken came from downstairs. A male voice laughed loudly. But then a girl screamed and there was the sound of a scuffle. Birkita heard the sound of some punches and then a commotion out on the street. More laughter floated up on the warm air and in through the open window. When it had gone quiet again she heard footsteps on the stairs. Flavia.

The door of the room squealed open and Birkita knew

immediately, knew from the faint odour that whoever it was, it was not Flavia.

It was Antonius who approached her bed.

He uttered some words in his own tongue and shook her by the shoulder as if to wake her. She turned and looked up at him. He tugged at her clothes saying something else. She didn't understand the words but she knew what he meant.

Then he took her.

21

Julia reaches the end of the chapter and looks up. Suzanne is looking expectantly at her. Julia knows the feeling only too well – that terrible and exhilarating feeling of waiting to hear.

'I thought it was going fine until the end,' she says. 'This is a big thing for Birkita. What happens to her with Antonius and tomorrow when she starts work in the brothel. We need to describe it more fully. In more detail.'

'More graphic?'

'I suppose. Yes, I suppose … I suppose it is going to be more graphic.'

'You know, you're right. I think what I was thinking was that a publisher would never publish something that explicit.'

Suzanne with the publisher again. Julia can't help but smile.

'I think we'll worry about that when the time comes,' she says. 'Right now I think we just need to write the best book we can.'

'You're right. You're so right.'

Julia is very pleased. But it also occurs to her that Suzanne is extraordinarily open to criticism. It is a really attractive trait. Julia thinks Suzanne would have made a great teacher. Will make a great teacher.

'Actually you know what it is?' says Suzanne.

'What?'

'I funked it.'

'Funked what?'

'I thought it would be too hard to imagine what that would be like – you know, to be raped like that, so I … I funked it.'

'It's hard to imagine all right,' Julia says, almost in a whisper.

Then the words are out of her mouth before she has managed to think about them.

'I can try if you like,' she says.

Julia hopes Suzanne will say no. This is not a piece of the story that Julia wants to write.

'That would be great,' Suzanne says.

Julia groans inwardly. She takes the book and settles on the mattress, on her tummy resting on her elbows. She reads back.

"He uttered some words in his own tongue and shook her by the shoulder as if to wake her. She turned and looked up at him. He tugged at her clothes saying something else. She didn't understand the words but she knew what he meant."

She crosses out "Then he took her."

She takes a deep breath and continues.

CHAPTER EIGHT

Antonius – continued (Julia)

She sat up, climbed off the bed slowly and started to undress. Antonius was naked by the time she was and he was erect. He indicated that she should go down on all fours. Then kneeling behind her he entered her. She gasped as she felt the pain. Placing the palms of his hands on her hips he began to pump her. She panted as Flavia had told her to. The bed shook and made a rocking noise. Antonius began to ride her harder. She started to gasp just as Flavia had said. Antonius was thrusting in and out of her. More quickly. Breathing heavily. In the end, he climaxed, pressing himself hard against her and panting furiously.

Birkita moved gently back and forwards a few times. She sighed as though with blissful happiness. Both were nice final touches, Flavia had said. Antonius stayed inside her, kneeling, hands holding her until his breathing had subsided and returned to normal. Birkita could feel wetness on the inside of her thighs. She thought she smelt blood but she couldn't do anything about it. She just waited to see what Antonius wanted next or what he would do.

Sounds drifted up from the street. A man and a woman talking softly, sounding like lovers as they walked under the window. A dog barked somewhere, distantly.

Footsteps in a nearby street and the chink of metal – men marching. Normal sounds from the normal world.

She tried to think about something – anything – else. Something pleasant. But in all of the vast world that she had travelled, in all of the immense inside of her mind, she could find nothing.

Antonius had shrunk by then and eventually he slipped out of her. The bed creaked as he rose from it. Birkita stayed on all fours like some strange human beast of burden. She felt open, vulnerable, violated. Silently, Antonius dressed. Then, without so much as a word, he walked out.

22

The writing takes Julia less than an hour. When she is finished she passes the book to Suzanne who has been lying beside her on her back gazing up at the ceiling. It is something they have both come to do. While one of them is writing, the other is thinking about where the story might go next.

As Suzanne starts to read, Julia turns away onto her side. She finds that she is shaking and close to tears. She doesn't want Suzanne to see. A few minutes later lights out suddenly occurs and the room is plunged into darkness. Julia hears the book shut with a soft plop. They have made an incision in the side of the mattress and Suzanne stuffs the book into it. This is where they keep it hidden and where they hope it will be safe. Having done that, Suzanne turns onto her side too and spoons Julia.

'You're shaking,' Suzanne says softly.

Julia wants to cry. Her eyes have all watered up.

'It was … it was very difficult to write.'

It is all she can manage to say before the tears start flowing.

'Oh, my darling girl,' says Suzanne. 'Come here to me.'

Suzanne wraps herself around Julia, holding her breast in the palm of her hand. Julia feels Suzanne's lips on the back of her neck. Suzanne kisses her ever so softly, ever so tenderly and then gently caresses Julia's neck with her lips and cheek. It is the last sensation Julia feels before she falls asleep.

23

Usually Julia and Suzanne talk on their way to work. Ideas come to them during the night that they are anxious to share. They want to talk about the path the book is to take next. The following morning though, they are both strangely quiet.

It is a beautiful day. Though still very cold, it is nowhere near as cold as it was when they first arrived. The sky is cloudless and a perfect blue. There is a fresh fall of snow on the ground and on the ramparts. The sun has a little heat in it. There is a real sense of spring in the air. Rumours, or bonkes as they are called in the ghetto, abound. This morning's one over breakfast was that the Germans were suffering huge losses on a daily basis. Julia and Suzanne have managed to survive the winter. Spring is coming. Soon the summer will be here and then maybe the war will end.

Julia wonders what she would do then. What would happen to Suzanne? Would they just go their separate ways? Would they remain friends? Would they stay in touch? Would they finish the book? Or now that the real world would be calling them back, would they just forget this foolish project of theirs?

As soon as they arrive at the hospital, Irena asks if she can speak to them. They go to the corner where she has a table and chair – the place that she refers to jokingly as 'my office'. Julia and Suzanne laughed the first time she said it but it seems like it stopped being a joke a long time ago.

'I've been told I'm overstaffed,' says Irena.

Julia feels like the ground has given way under her. 'Deportation to the east.' What happened to her parents. And Suzanne's. From time to time the Germans decide that the Paradise Ghetto has become too overcrowded. Their solution is to deport people. Apparently the last deportations happened in December just gone.

'No – it's not what you're thinking, girls. Oh God, I'm sorry. I didn't mean to frighten you. One of you is just getting a transfer, that's all.'

'A transfer?'

'Yes. I've been told I'm overstaffed which, as you know, is just about the most ridiculous thing you've ever heard. But such is life – apparently I am. So I've been asked to provide one person for a new project the Council of Elders – in other words, the Germans – has decided to undertake. You were last in so I'm afraid it has to be one of you. That's the only fair way I can think of. I thought I'd let you decide.'

'Do you know what kind of work it is?' asks Suzanne.

'I don't. All I was told was that it was manual work. It would probably be more strenuous than what you do here but the rations would be better. You'd be out of doors, which sounds bad right now but spring is coming. Once the weather improves you'd be out in the air, which is healthier for you than being in this place. And when you're out and about there are more opportunities – to find food. To find ... well ... more opportunities.'

'I don't mind,' Suzanne says. Then she asks, 'Will we still be living together in the same barracks?'

'As far as I know.'

'I'll go,' says Julia.

To Suzanne, she says, 'I'm stronger than you and don't worry, I'll keep whatever extra food I get and share it with you.'

Julia's new job starts right away. She is assigned to a gang of male and female workers doing general labouring work around the ghetto. She spends the rest of the day painting some of the rooms of one of the barracks. One of her workmates tells her that there are going to be important visitors to the ghetto and it is being smartened up for that. There is indeed extra food which Julia pockets and brings home to Suzanne who argues with her.

'It's not fair,' she says. 'You're doing heavy work. You need to eat more.'

'We both need to survive,' says Julia. 'That's what matters.'

'Promise me you'll take more. If you just bring me one or two titbits now and again that would be wonderful.'

'We'll see,' says Julia.

What Suzanne is saying makes sense, but Julia feels responsible for her, feels – in a funny way – like the provider of the family. Their little family. The two of them.

CHAPTER NINE

Flavia Again (Suzanne)

Birkita lay on her mattress, the blanket pulled up around her shoulders, knees drawn up to her chest. She didn't know how much time had passed since Antonius had left her. She had crossed into a world of routine horror. What he had done to her had been the least of it.

Her life had become a journey along a narrow path through a dark forest of horrors. There had been the Games, the voyage here, that day in the forest which she still couldn't get herself to think about. And there would be tomorrow.

She thought of killing herself. Or of killing Antonius when he came again and then killing herself. What she knew for a certainty was that she would never die for the entertainment of other people. So if she killed him she would then have to take her own life. All she would need would be a knife. That couldn't be too hard to find. Maybe get one from one of her customers-to-be – charm him into giving it to her.

For a long time she imagined how blissful the sleep of death would be. She would cross over into the shadowlands and be with all of those people she had loved in life. They were waiting for her. She knew that. Maybe they were watching her now and wondering what kept her there, why she had not already come over.

She began to wonder this herself and slowly the answer came to her. Not until she had her revenge. Maybe on Antonius, but revenge for sure on the bull Roman who had tortured and killed her brother, his wife and their children. Little children. How could anybody do that?

No matter how impossible it seemed, no matter how far away her homeland was, she would somehow find a way back. At some point, she would turn around on this road of horrors. She would walk back the way she had come, retracing her steps through this evil forest. She would go back to the land where she had lived but which was now no longer her home, just a place of death. She would find the bull Roman and do to him what he had done to her kin.

Now, for the first time since she had been taken prisoner, she felt a glimmer of hope inside her. It felt like it was no more than a tiny lick of fire, a candle flame in a strong wind, but it was there. She felt it. And if it was there it could be fanned and if it was fanned it could grow. It would grow into a great blaze which would consume her enemies, the people she hated and who had wronged her so much.

Birkita became aware that it had gone quiet downstairs and out on the street. Beyond the window there was some light in the sky. A cock crowed somewhere, distantly. She began to cry. It was the first time she had cried since the Romans had enslaved her. And now that she had started she couldn't stop. The tears came in floods. So many tears. And she was sobbing so loudly that she didn't hear the footsteps on the stairs. It was only when the door creaked open that she knew someone had come into her room. Had Antonius come back? But then she recognised the perfume. It was Flavia.

She came to the bed and sat on the edge of it. Gently she wiped Birkita's wet hair off her cheek. She began to

stroke it and continued while Birkita cried herself out –
until there were no more tears.

When Birkita had finally gone silent, Flavia said, 'He
came to you.'

It was a statement. Birkita nodded.

'Come, you must wash him out of you,' said Flavia.

Flavia took her to the table by the wall where there
was a bowl, a jug of water and a sponge. Flavia showed
her what to do, how to squat down and wash herself out.
Birkita did as she was told like a woman in a dream.

'You must do this after every time,' Flavia said.

She led Birkita back to the bed and laid her down.
Birkita turned onto her side. Then she felt the bed shake
as Flavia climbed in beside her.

'Come to me, beautiful girl,' Flavia said.

She turned Birkita onto her back and then towards her,
enfolding her in her arms. In the dim light of pre-dawn
Birkita could see that Flavia's eyes were shining. Her lips
were moist.

Flavia kissed her.

Julia finishes reading and hands the book back to
Suzanne. They are in bed together – the eternal struggle to
keep warm. Spring may be hovering but will it ever
finally come?

Suzanne looks into Julia's eyes.

'So?' she says.

'So our lovers are going to be two women,' says Julia.

'So it would appear,' Suzanne replies.

'You know, when I met you I thought you were Little
Miss Innocent. The Bookish Virgin. But you're not like
that at all, are you?'

Suzanne smiles.

'I probably am. But when we were in Pompeii – my
parents and I – I had lots of time on my hands while they

172

were working. So I read – a lot. I was at that age. You know – I was curious. I wanted to know what the big mystery was all about.'

'The big mystery?'

'Sex. It was a big part of Ancient Rome.'

'But you never got to try it out for yourself?'

Not before I went into hiding. I hope I'll still get a chance to,' says Suzanne.

There is a tinge of sadness in her voice. This is the first time that Julia has heard Suzanne express any kind of doubt about the future. She touches her fingers against Suzanne's cheek.

'You will,' she says. 'I know you will.'

Julia wishes she believed it.

24

The painting gang of which Julia is a part is working its way down through a barracks. They started in the attic and have now moved on to the top floor proper. The foreman has explained the delicate balancing act he is trying to achieve. They will go as quickly as they can so as not to draw the wrath of the SS. But also, it is still winter outside and who knows what they will be sent to do once this job completes, so the longer they can make it last the better. They are indoors, it is relatively warm and their rations are merely poor – as opposed to completely inadequate.

Julia doesn't mind the work – it is better than being in that terrible hospital. She starts, gets into a rhythm and after that her mind is free to wander wherever it chooses. Most days she thinks about the book – though in Julia's mind it is 'The Book'. She imagines scenes, dialogue, surprises they might give the reader. But today she is thinking about something different. Today she is thinking about Suzanne and how you can be so wrong about somebody.

Julia really disliked her when she first met her. Suzanne had obviously had a pampered and happy childhood. She was a 'privileged Jew', to use that terrible ghetto phrase. She had travelled and seen all sorts of wonderful places.

Why couldn't Julia's childhood have been like that? Her father travelled a lot. Why could he not have taken Julia or her mother with him? While he was at all those conferences or whatever it was he used to do, she and her mother could have explored, seen things, gone shopping. Julia would never have gone with him by herself but she and her mother could certainly have gone. Apparently when her parents were first married, that was exactly what happened. But after Julia came along those days ended.

Suzanne hasn't at all turned out to be the spoilt daddy's girl Julia thought she was when she first met her. Julia sees that Suzanne is very grateful for all of the blessings that have been showered on her. She doesn't take them for granted. Julia likes that.

And Suzanne's parents may have loved their precious daughter so much that they did all they could to keep her safe – which was another thing that Julia resented. But Suzanne has suffered – every bit as much as Julia has. More in some ways.

She is amazing, Julia thinks. She endured two years in the attic without fresh air or sunlight. And she is so positive all the time, so convinced that they will get out of all this safely. And then it was Suzanne who thought up the idea of the book. Julia would be lost without that.

From all of the rumours, the bonkes, even if only a fraction of them are true it sounds like the Germans are losing the war and that it will end this year. With the spring coming, Julia is starting to feel a bit more confident now that they can hold out. What will happen when peace comes? Will they have finished the book by then? And if they haven't will they stay friends and finish it? Will they go back to Amsterdam? She imagines that that is probably what Suzanne will do – go back to Amsterdam to finish her university studies. Where will Julia go? Back to

Amsterdam to be near Suzanne or somewhere else? Where? England? America? Maybe they could get their book published in America. It would be made into a film with Julia starring in it. It would become her route to becoming a proper actress. Wouldn't that be something?

If all of this hadn't happened – the war, the Germans, their war on the Jews – then Julia would never have met Suzanne and there would be no book. It's something to think about. Julia feels so lucky that Suzanne has come into her life. How unbearable it would be without her and the book. That reminds her – they really must think up a title some time.

Julia's mind drifts off to other things. She remembers what Suzanne said last night about hoping she would get to have sex. She finds it hard to imagine a man that would be good enough for Suzanne.

Men.

They have really fucked up the world. From her father to stupid fucking Hitler – and every man in between. Bert, the fuckers that arrested her and every man she has encountered since then. That stupid prick that they had to get off the pavement for.

She tries to imagine the man that Suzanne would fall for. He would have to be someone pretty amazing, pretty special. Julia is not sure she could imagine such a man – what he would be like. And she finds herself feeling a tiny twinge of jealousy that any man would take Suzanne. Julia thinks that this word 'take' is a strange choice. What does she mean – 'take' Suzanne? From Julia? Or in the way Antonius 'took' Birkita?

Lunchtime comes and goes and the afternoon wears on. Julia's painting arm has become very tired and her stomach feels hollow. She hopes she won't get a headache as she often does when she is hungry. These last couple of hours are the hardest part of the day – it gets dark and still the work goes on. She hates this going to work and coming home from work in darkness. She looks forward to when there will be more light.

To take her mind off her discomfort, she tries to focus on the book. But she can't really concentrate on it because Julia finds that she misses Suzanne. When they were working together, they could chat, they ate their tiny lunch together, they talked about the book. Julia would ask research questions and Suzanne would answer. They could see each other. Julia remembers how occasionally they would happen to catch one another's eye across that dreadful hospital room and Suzanne's face would light up in a smile.

Then it suddenly comes back to Julia – how Suzanne held her the other night after she had finished the chapter about Birkita being raped. Julia had quite forgotten about it until now – how Suzanne kissed her on the neck.

And this leads her on to the character of Flavia.

With Birkita it's simple. Birkita is Julia, just transported back two thousand years. But Flavia – where did she come from? She doesn't appear to be just Suzanne in Roman times. Julia has a sense that she knows what the relationship between Flavia and Birkita is going to become.

She wonders. And she is still wondering when the foreman calls it a day and she can make her way back through the ankle-deep, dirty slush to the barracks.

'I missed you,' Julia tells Suzanne as they eat.

'I missed you,' replies Suzanne.

Apart from Julia's new job, their living conditions have also improved. This, of course, is by ghetto standards. They have been allocated a space on a bunk. As a result they have moved from the attic to the room underneath. Here they have taken possession of a middle bunk. Julia tries not to think about what it means – that somebody must have died for this to happen. The two of them have to share it but it's better than being in the freezing cold attic on a thin mattress on the icy, unyielding floor. The air feels slightly warmer down here. So they sit on their bunk now – Suzanne at one end, cross-legged with the notebook and pencil, and Julia at the other. With the bunk they have inherited another blanket, so each of them has one wrapped around their shoulders and the third one covers both their laps and legs.

Julia watches Suzanne who is deep in concentration. She has her glasses on her head and holds her face a bit closer than would be normal to the notebook as she scribbles away. She is short-sighted. 'At ten centimetres I have the eyes of an eagle,' she told Julia. 'It's after that it's a problem.'

A stray strand of blonde hair hangs down in front of Suzanne's face. She was thin when Julia first met her but she seems even frailer now. But she is so strong – inside. Julia always reckoned she was strong herself but Suzanne has a strength that seems to go beyond just being able to endure. Apart from that time that she first arrived in the prison cell, Julia has seen her radiate nothing but resolve and courage.

As though she became aware that Julia was watching her, Suzanne looks up. She smiles a tired smile.

'What?' she asks.

Suzanne's hair is thinning from the poor food. Julia knows that hers is too. Her friend's eyes are hollow, the effect even more stark because of the paleness of her skin. Julia imagines that whatever else about her, Suzanne must be aching to feel the sun again. Suzanne has perfect teeth even if they are dull from lack of toothpaste. She looks happy – but then she always does.

'What?' Suzanne asks again, her smile widening.

'My friend,' says Julia.

Suzanne reaches across and enfolds Julia's hand in hers. She squeezes it.

'My friend,' she says.

25

'So what's Birkita's plan?' asks Julia, the following evening as they sit on their bunk.

'Boudica's uprising was in either 60 or 61 AD. It's not known for sure. Let's assume it was 61 AD. Also, that it happened in the spring or summer because that was when people did their fighting in those days. Let's assume early summer when the British are defeated and late summer by the time Birkita has been shipped to Pompeii.

'She's going to learn as much as she can. She is going to learn Latin so she can get around. She is going to understand the geography of the world so she can figure out where she is and where she needs to get to. She's going to accumulate some money. Then, when she feels she has enough, she is going to run away, go down to the docks, find a ship that is going to Britain and pay the captain to take her home.'

'It's a pretty thin plan,' says Julia. 'I don't mean that as a criticism of you or us or our book – just that there's lots that could go wrong with it.'

'It's a thin plan all right,' agrees Suzanne. 'She doesn't have many options.'

'Which of us does?' says Julia.

The thought makes them go silent. At length, Julia asks, 'Do you think the war will end this year?'

'If even a fraction of the bonkes are true then it will.'

'Do you believe them?'

'I try not to think about it. Just get through every day. It's what I did in the attic.'

'Imagine when it does,' says Julia. 'What will you do then?'

Suzanne shakes her head. 'I don't know. Whenever I think of it, I try not to think of it.'

'But what if we think about it together?' asks Julia.

'OK.'

'So imagine – the war is ended, the Germans are defeated. We are free again.'

'And we're here in Theresienstadt?'

'I suppose so. Let's take it from here. Would you go back and finish your studies?'

'I don't think so. I can't imagine the thought of spending more years cooped up in some place – even if it was a library or a university. I think I'd travel. What about you?'

'I wouldn't go back to Amsterdam,' says Julia. 'That's for sure. There's nothing for me there.'

'Maybe not for me either … now.'

Suzanne is thinking about her parents. Julia has an image of her own mother and father. Where did they go? What happened to them? The image stays in her mind for a moment and then she banishes it.

'Would we finish the book?' she asks.

'Julia – of course we'd finish the book. And we'd find a publisher.'

'I was thinking,' says Julia. 'Wouldn't it be great if it got made into a movie?'

'And you played Birkita,' adds Suzanne.

'That would be unbelievable,' says Julia.

The girls go quiet again.

Then Suzanne asks, 'Why do you want to talk about

all this? Here? Now?'

'Because I don't want to lose you.'

The words are out before Julia has had time to think about them.

'I don't want you to go out of my life. I would want us still to be friends after this is all over. I really like you, Suzanne.'

'And I really like you,' Suzanne says, lifting the glasses off her nose, putting them on her head and looking at Julia in that blinky way she has when she's without them. Julia asked her once what it was like – to see the world in that way. 'Most of the time, it's a pain,' Suzanne told her. 'I'd love to have normal sight like most people. In my next life I'll be an eagle. But sometimes it's really beautiful – like a painting by Renoir or Monet.' Suzanne has asked if she knew any of their pictures. She doesn't. Suzanne said they will see them after the war.

'I'm glad,' Julia says.

Somebody announces that it will soon be lights out. The girls go to the bathroom, wash, brush their teeth. They climb back onto the bunk and settle in under their luxurious three blankets. They lie facing each other. It is what they normally do while they try to remember whose turn it is to spoon first.

'I think it's me on you,' says Julia.

Suzanne continues to gaze at her. The silence lengthens. Suzanne seems to be waiting for Julia to say or do something.

When Julia doesn't, Suzanne just turns over.

CHAPTER TEN

Birkita's Plan (Julia)

Birkita had counted four moons since she arrived in
Pompeii. Winter came. But it was not the kind of winter
she had known. There was no snow, no frozen rivers or
pools with thick layers of crunchy ice on top. No bitterly
cold, rainy days when all you wanted to do was huddle by
the fire and eat hot food and drink ale. Instead the weather
got colder but there were still sunshine and blue skies. It
was no different from summer really – except there wasn't
the great heat.

Everything here was wrong. Back in her old life her
day had been tied to the sun. She woke when the first hint
of daylight started to creep nervously into the hut. The
first thing she always did was to go outside and see the
sun. Make sure it was still there. What if a day happened
when it didn't rise? But it always did.

In winter – she could still picture this so clearly – the
grass and bushes and leaves would be white with frost, the
air thick and crackling with cold, the sky the faintest of
blues. The black figures of birds would flap across her eye
line and she would watch as the sun rose until it became a
blood-red disc in the sky.

Summer was so different. The ground would be warm
after the heat of the previous day and the only slightly
cooler night. There would be mist low in the hollows and

spread across the land like the breath of the gods. Birds would be twittering and singing madly – celebrating the warmth, the abundance of food, life itself. All the colours would be pale shades of their more vivid selves. And then would come the sun.

At first, light the colour of the centre of daisies in the east, as though a fire burned just below the horizon. Then a small orange bar colouring the edge of the world. It was the same vivid orange she had seen on butterfly wings. And finally, in all its glory the great glowing orb lifting itself up and pouring its blessings down on everybody.

How her body, her whole being ached for that time and place. And how she detested this one. Everything about it was so different from her old life. She no longer thought of 'home' now. She had no home. There was just her old life. Sometimes it seemed as though that time and all those people – her mother and father, her brother and sister-in-law, their children, even Moon and Sun – had all been just a dream, or a story told around the fire one night. She found too that their memory was becoming more and more faint. She could no longer remember their voices, picture their faces, recall the colour of their eyes.

It was late morning and she was still in bed in her cubicle. Her eyes were closed – trying to go back to sleep or feigning death – she wasn't quite sure which. She had been working until after dawn, had slept an exhausted sleep and been woken when the sounds out on the street became loud as lunchtime approached. She hated the way her days no longer followed the sun – in fact, the way they spat in its face. She slept when the sun woke; she was awake long after it had gone. She hated the people who had imposed this on her. She was revolted by what she was forced to do every day.

'In about an hour,' a voice said outside.

It was Cassius, the first of the two bodyguards.

Birkita's cubicle was one of the two beside the front door. Cassius was right outside talking to somebody on the street.

'Try to keep it in your pants until then,' Cassius said and the other man laughed.

The night after Antonius, Cassius had come to her. It had been her first full day in the lupanar. A slow day. Four, five, six men – she couldn't remember. After the first couple she was just in a daze. Eventually, Flavia had said that they were closing and Cassius had locked the door. Birkita's groin was in agony. Somebody had raked their nails down her back and only now was she feeling the pain. She lay on her bed in her cubicle, facing the wall. She tried to sleep, to forget.

But then the curtain rustled. She thought it was Flavia. But it was Cassius.

'Hello, new girl,' he said.

She rolled onto her back wondering what new horror this was. Cassius smiled.

'We have a tradition here in the lupanar,' he said. 'The master gets the first bite of the cherry. Then I get the second.

'You're too late,' said Birkita. 'There have been plenty of others today.'

He continued to smile.

'Not where I'm going there haven't.'

She looked at him uncomprehendingly.

'Face down,' he said.

Birkita tried to shake off the memory. It was time to get herself ready.

She got up and stretched. Overhead, through the small barred window that gave on to the street, smells wafted in – food being cooked; shit and piss, animal and human. The cubicle where Birkita lived and worked was slightly longer than she was tall. Along one wall was a stone bed

186

with a thin mattress upon it. After that it was less than two paces to the window. There was a table upon which lay a tiny hourglass, a simple oil lamp for after dark, a bowl, an empty water jug and a small wooden chest in which she kept the few possessions she had. She opened it now to take out the blanket she used for work and to fold away her sleeping blanket. She laid the blanket on top of the mattress.

She slipped her feet into her sandals and pushed past the curtain that screened the cubicle. Outside in the corridor, Cassius was at the door still chatting with somebody. He moved aside briefly so that Albinus the water boy could come in from outside. He carried a large earthenware amphora of water half as tall as himself and struggled under the weight. Birkita said hello to him – she never talked to Cassius if she could avoid it. Then she walked down the corridor to the toilet. Returning, she washed in the water that Albinus had brought in and changed into her other red toga. She would wash the first one later. Albinus looked in and handed her some food on a plate – some fruit, cheese, bread.

'Lunch, Birkita,' he said cheerily.

'Eat up,' called Cassius over his shoulder. 'Nobody likes a scrawny whore.'

He laughed, as did the man he was talking to.

She hated Cassius. During her first few days here she had eaten nothing. Looking back on it, she wasn't sure whether it was from revulsion at what she had to do or because she wanted to get her revenge by starving herself to death. Either way, after a couple of days, Cassius had noticed it and must have told Antonius. The result had been that Flavia had come to her and coaxed her into eating. Sly Cassius. Fawning Cassius. She would kill him if she ever got the chance.

More than anyone else, more than the men who came

to her, it was Cassius whom she hated. He tormented her constantly. 'Just one word from me,' he would say to her, 'just one word is all it needs and you'll find yourself doing what you do – but in the arena.'

He threatened that he would bring some of his friends and they would all enjoy her together. For a while, the terror of these threats kept her from sleeping. But after a while she saw that they were actually idle boasts. Cassius would have had to pay for this and he would never have paid for something which – on his own – he could get for free.

She sat on the edge of the bed while she ate. Apart from Flavia, Cassius, Crispus the other bodyguard and Albinus, the aquarius, there were five girls in the lupanar. There were two girls from Syria – twins. They occupied the two cubicles on the same side as Birkita. Sometimes customers asked for the two of them together. Opposite Birkita in the biggest cubicle was a girl called Claudia. She had been there the longest, Flavia told her. At one time, she had been the most popular girl there but she had become pregnant and had found out too late to have an abortion. When the child was born, just before Birkita arrived, it had been removed from her, taken somewhere and left to die. Flavia told Birkita that this was the Roman way. Ever since then Claudia had become more and more silent and withdrawn. She too had stopped eating and was becoming 'scrawny'. Birkita could see that Claudia was in serious danger of incurring Antonius' anger. Birkita had tried to talk to Claudia, to warn her but it was clear that Claudia was both completely aware of the risk she was running and, at the same time, quite indifferent to her fate.

'I've tried to tell her,' Flavia said, 'but she won't listen. Any more complaints and I won't be able to save her.'

The last girl was called Bakt and came from Egypt.

She had arrived just before Birkita. She had the most beautiful face that Birkita had ever seen – straight black hair, perfect creamy skin, beautiful lips, deep eyes. Of all of them she seemed the least bothered by what they had to do. She kept to herself and seemed to live a lot of her life inside her head. It was something Birkita wished she could do.

She dreaded the thought of what the day would hold. Things had been quiet this week but you never could tell. Some days, for no apparent reason, it could be unbelievably busy. Cassius would let in the first customers in the middle of the afternoon and from then on would come a succession of faceless men. Some talked, some didn't. Some were nervous, others were aggressive, hard. There were those that had washed and were scented and those who stank. Some looked as though they were disease-ridden. Almost all of them had bad teeth and vile breath that reeked. Birkita didn't know which disgusted her more – when they lay on top of her and put themselves into her or when she had to give them fellatus or when she had to submit to the other things they asked for.

Sometimes, a group of men came and asked to use the upstairs room and have several girls. Antonius wanted to hold more and more of those sessions, according to Flavia. He made a lot of money on them, overcharging for his cheap wine and for food brought in from down the street. Those sessions were generally the worst. The men became drunk and aggressive. Flavia told Birkita about a time the group of men had become so bad that they had done all sorts of damage to the upper room and Cassius had had to throw them out. A girl had nearly died and been good for nothing afterwards. Antonius had been furious about having to pay for the repairs.

'What happened to the girl?' asked Birkita.

Flavia looked at her, an expression of irritation on her face.

'She could hardly walk. Her face was a mess. You couldn't put her in front of clients. What do you suppose happened to her?'

Birkita had been involved in a number of these sessions. In some of them, several men would use one of the girls at the same time. All the girls would end up covered in bruises, with bite marks on their body and – usually – bleeding. There hadn't been one of these for nearly a month now but you never knew from day to day when Antonius might arrive and announce that such an event was to take place.

Normally, he wasn't around very much and Flavia pretty much ran the place. Apparently, he had several lupanars around the city but this was his biggest. Flavia told Birkita that Antonius had been some kind of moneyman in the army, responsible for paying the soldiers. He had left the army with a pile of money which he had invested in lupanars. While he was generally not there for most of the time it was open, he always arrived near the day's end to pick up the takings.

Birkita applied chalk powder to her face to whiten it. Then she dabbed some wine dregs onto her cheeks and rubbed them in to produce a pink effect. Finally she blackened around her eyes with soot as Flavia had taught her and touched some perfume made from rose petals to her neck, her throat, between her breasts, on her belly and the insides of her thighs. Just as she was finishing, Flavia clapped her hands and called the girls out into the corridor. A few moments later, Cassius let the first customer in.

He was little more than a youth – thin, spotty and nervous.

'Now sir, which of our beautiful girls would you like?'

190

Flavia began her patter. 'We have them from all corners of the world. Syria, Aegyptus, even as far away as Britannia. Take a look. What do you fancy, this fine day?'

Birkita smiled, as did the other girls. She pouted, pushed her breasts forward, and pulled up her toga to show her thigh. The spotty youth made a very short show of trying to choose, but in reality he chose the first girl he looked at. Birkita's heart sank – it was she. However, her smile widened as though she had just received a great surprise, she took his hand and led him into her cubicle.

'How much are you going to spend?' she asked, in the Roman tongue.

'How much is it?'

'Depends on what you want – fellatus, full sex, half and half.'

'What's half and half?'

'Some of each.'

'I'll have that.'

'That'll be twenty asses.'

The spotty youth looked shocked.

'That's a lot. It's more than I was –'

'You don't have it?'

If he didn't, Birkita's next question would be to ask how much he did have.

'No, I have it.'

'Would you like wine?'

'Is that extra?'

'Two asses.'

'All right.'

'Would you like to buy me one?'

The spotty youth gulped and nodded.

Birkita went to the curtain and called to Albinus to bring her two cups of the house's best wine. Returning with them, she asked, 'What would you like to call me?'

'Wha – what's your name?'

191

'That doesn't matter. While you're here I can be any woman you want me to be.'

'Really?'

'Really.'

'Aurelia,' he said.

Birkita often wondered about all these other women whose names were mentioned here and whom she briefly became. Who was Aurelia? Some wealthy woman whom the spotty youth admired from afar? Some girl his own age who lived in the house next door? The mother or older sister or aunt of one his friends?

She passed him the wine and then held out her empty hand for him to give her the money. The coins felt warm and damp, as though they had been clamped in his fist. She quickly checked that all the money was there and then, lifting the lid of the chest, dropped the coins into a bowl she kept inside. She upended the hourglass. By the time she turned back, the spotty youth had gulped down half the wine. She undressed while the spotty youth watched her with wide eyes.

'Do you like it?' she asked with a smile.

He drank down the rest of the wine and nodded. Birkita could almost have felt fond of him. He reminded her of her brother Banning when he was that age. She pushed the thought away.

When she was naked, she motioned to the spotty youth that he should sit on the bed. She knelt down, lifted the knee-length tunic he wore and went to work.

Birkita kept one eye on the hourglass. When the sands ran out, she stopped what she was doing, got up and climbed onto the bed. She lay on her back and indicated that he should take off his clothes. He undressed and got on top of her. He went to kiss her and she let him. Flavia said that men liked kissing and while not every lupanar allowed it, Antonius said his girls should do it. As the spotty youth entered her and began to pump her, Birkita closed her eyes.

'Aurelia,' he groaned. 'Oh, Aurelia!'

She moaned and whimpered and uttered compliments and encouragement as Flavia had taught her to do but her mind flew away.

It flew back to Britain and she imagined finding the bull Roman, taking him captive. She would bring him to exactly the same spot where he had killed her brother and his family. There, she would crucify him. She pictured his face as the nails were driven into his wrists. What he would look like as he hung from a cross looking down at her. She wondered how long it would take him to die. He was big and strong. He would take a long time. Much longer than the time it had taken Banning. More than a day, she thought. Maybe two. She hoped so. And she would stay there at the foot of the cross for all of it. She would revel in the bull Roman's suffering. She wondered if he would die bravely. She thought not. Like all bullies, he was a coward, she thought. He would grovel, weep, plead for mercy.

'I love you, Aurelia. I love you,' the spotty youth was saying as his tempo increased until finally he came to a shuddering halt.

In the end he had taken very little time. Birkita lay there for a minute or so until his breathing returned to normal and then she gently eased herself out from under him.

'Did you enjoy it?' she asked as she began to dress.

'It was amazing. What about you?'

'Unbelievable. You're an incredible lover. Aurelia is a very lucky woman.' They were the same phrases she always used.

The youth looked not just spent, but sad.

'Was it your first time?' she asked.

'First time with a –' He stopped.

'So you know that if you enjoyed it, it's lucky to give the girl something extra?'

The youth gave her an incredible five asses. It seemed to be the rest of the money he had.

'I hope you'll come again,' she said as he left.

She was pretty sure that he wouldn't – he had spent far more than he had intended. But at least he couldn't say he was unhappy.

And so the day wore on. It was a slow day. She had two other customers – a big man with a red angry face who hurt her, and one of the smelliest men she had ever had to endure. It grew dark. After the lamps were lit, Albinus brought her some hot food from the cookhouse down the street. As she sat on the edge of the bed and ate it, she thought through her plan again. There was so much that could go wrong.

She had waited four moons because she had needed to learn a little of the Roman tongue. She had that now. She had also learned something of the layout of Pompeii. Most importantly, from talking to customers, she knew where the harbour was. She had only been there that one time – the day she arrived – but she knew that once she escaped from here, if she went steadily downhill, she would come to where the ships were. Anyway, sometimes, depending on which way the wind was blowing, she could smell the salty, watery air and knew the direction in which to go.

She had earned some money. Her line about 'you know it's lucky to give the girl something extra?' hadn't always been successful. A lot of men were mean bastards but then there were some like the spotty youth who could be taken for a ride. Even with handing half the money over to Flavia, Birkita still had managed to put together a pile of coins. She kept them not in the wooden chest, but in a small hole she had managed to burrow out between the stone bed and the wall. She had no idea if it was enough to pay for a passage home. She would have to take a chance on that. Basically, she had decided that she would be prepared to fuck the entire crew if it was a case of getting away from here.

She had also needed time to study the routine in the lupanar. She had that now too. The event that signalled the end of the day was when Antonius showed up to collect the money. He would wait around for a while. As long as there was even the sniff of a customer who would pay, the lupanar would stay open. But eventually Antonius would collect the takings and go. According to Flavia he lived in another part of the city.

Once he was gone, Flavia sometimes left too – she lived in a room in a house up the street. With her gone, either Cassius or Crispus – only one of them was ever on duty – would close the front door and bar it from the inside. Two mattresses would be brought down from the room upstairs. Albinus slept on one which he placed in the central corridor near the toilet. Cassius or Crispus slept on the other and it was positioned right in front of the door, blocking it.

At first, Birkita had despaired when she had seen this arrangement. To get out, someone would have to either wake or kill the man sleeping in front of the door. But it didn't take long for Birkita to realise that while Crispus took his duties very seriously and performed them to the letter – he was terrified of Antonius – Cassius was a different proposition.

Cassius appeared to have three interests: chatting with his friends – he seemed to know everyone in Pompeii – drinking and women. His job at the lupanar enabled him to enjoy all three.

It turned out that if he got the chance, he would drink steadily through the day. It was in this that Birkita had seen the first dawning of an opportunity. Through Flavia, Antonius kept a strict watch on the consumption of the wine that was sold to the customers. This meant that there was no way that Cassius could have this without paying for it – which he couldn't afford. And he was too mean to pay for it in any of the local taverns. So Birkita had arranged from him to have a supply.

When she asked a customer whether they wanted wine, many said yes and in addition, they would often buy her one as well. She never drank any of it – she hated the Roman drink just as she hated everything Roman – and so she would save hers and after the customer had gone, give it to Cassius, if he was on duty. Otherwise, she gave it to Albinus or to one of the other girls. Cassius was a big man with a huge capacity, but if they were busy, she could give him enough that, by the end of the day, he was quite groggy.

This was where the sex came in. When Cassius was on duty, he rarely went to sleep on the mattress. As far as he was concerned, one of the perks of his job was that his working day always ended with sex. So he would go to one of the girls' cubicles – a different one every night – and have sex. After a noisy orgasm and with enough wine inside him, Cassius could be relied on to spend the next few hours out cold. Often he slept well into the morning, only being woken by Albinus just before he unbarred the door to Flavia's loud knock.

Here then, was the opportunity.

It would have to be a day when Birkita was very busy, when lots of customers asked for wine and bought her one and which she would then pass on to Cassius. After Antonius and Flavia had gone and Cassius had had his sex and was asleep, there was a period of time in which she might escape. All of that still left Albinus, but Birkita always tried to be nice to him and to treat him well.

Occasionally she bought him little treats from the cake shop down the street. The girls were allowed to go that far, provided Cassius or Crispus went with them. Birkita hoped that when the night came, Albinus would stay silent while she unbarred the door and stole out of the lupanar.

If he didn't, she had thought of that too.

There was a customer from whom she had bought a knife.

CHAPTER ELEVEN

Birkita's Plan Again (Suzanne)

There was one other complication.

Apart from a busy day resulting in enough wine to make Cassius drunk, Albinus keeping quiet or being killed, Birkita having enough time to get to the harbour, finding a ship that would take her to Britannia and having enough money to pay for her passage, there was one other thing that had to fall into place.

That first night that Flavia came to Birkita had not been the only one. Rather, it had turned out to be the first of many. As well as having to give sex to Cassius from time to time, Birkita also had to have sex with Flavia.

Flavia rarely had to take customers. In all the time she had been there, Birkita had only seen it happen twice. As a result, it seemed to Birkita that Flavia had a pretty easy life. When the end of the day came and Birkita was literally fucked to exhaustion, she then had to find the energy to be an enthusiastic lover to Flavia. Not that it happened every night. But two or three nights a week, Flavia ended up spending the night with Birkita in the bed in the upstairs room.

At first, she had shouldered this as just another burden. And as her plan began to form, she had added it to the list of conditions that would have to be met before she could escape. As well as all the other things, it would have to be a night when Flavia went home.

But after a while, a strange thing began to happen. Birkita found that she didn't mind when Flavia came to her. Apart from getting out of the cubicle which she hated and the more comfortable mattress upstairs, Birkita liked being in bed with Flavia. In comparison to any of the men, she was gentle and tender; she didn't just use Birkita as some kind of empty vessel to be filled up. After they had made love, Birkita would often fall asleep in Flavia's arms and Birkita found she slept deeply and had nice dreams, feeling safe in a way that she hadn't since she'd been made a slave.

She had a sense that Flavia cared about her. It was a feeling she had forgotten – that there had once been people in her life who loved her and who looked after her. It wasn't long before she found herself wondering throughout the day whether Flavia was going to come to her that night. Eventually, she looked forward to it and would be disappointed on the nights when it didn't happen.

So that as her plan began to take shape, she found herself picturing something else.

Birkita felt that she no longer had a home – a place to which she could return. Yes, she would escape – or die in the attempt. The gods could take her; she wasn't going to live the rest of her life here. Assuming she did get away she would go to the land of her birth and exact her revenge. But after that – what?

There was a good chance she would be a fugitive after killing the bull Roman and even if that wasn't the case, she felt there was no place for her in a land where there were Romans. But maybe she could find a place where the Romans hadn't come and spread their poison. And maybe … maybe … Flavia would come with her.

Birkita pictured them together living in a hut by a

stream in a forest. There was birdsong. The stream sparkled in the sunlight. They had a small garden where they grew vegetables and had some fruit trees. There were chickens and a pig and they kept bees for honey. Sometimes, they hunted for meat. They caught fish and baked bread. It was a vision which Birkita spent more and more time thinking about. As men sweated over her and pushed themselves into her, her mind would fly away to this faraway world which had now come to fill many of her waking hours.

But to make this dream come true, she would have to tell Flavia about it.

It was the night of the shortest day. Flavia had come to her and they had made love. It was afterwards and they were lying in bed naked. Birkita lay in the crook of Flavia's arm – something that Flavia said she liked – while she absent-mindedly stroked Birkita's breast and played with her nipple.

'What was it like – where you lived?' asked Birkita.

'It's so long ago now.'

'You don't remember?'

'Yes, I remember. The land was beautiful. There were forests and rivers and plenty of animals to hunt. We were free and had no shortage of food or drink – even in winter. The children were happy and played all the time. Men and women loved…'

Flavia's voice trailed off.

'Did you love?' asked Birkita.

After a silence Flavia said, 'There was a girl. We used to steal away to the woods. There we would lie amongst the flowers or in summer, in the water.'

'Was she very beautiful?'

'She was beautiful to me. We were going to run away and find a peaceful place to live. Then the Romans came.'

'What happened to her?'

'She became a slave – just like me. The last I saw of her was in a long column of us captives marching through a forest. She had golden hair so I could see her up ahead of me – a long way off. She was looking back trying to see me. Her face was bleeding where they had hit her. That was the last time I saw her face. I never saw her after that. I don't know what became of her. If she's alive or dead now, I don't know. But she's dead for me. I'll never find her again.'

'Were you warriors?' asked Birkita.

'We learned to use weapons and such but we had never used them in anger. There wasn't much fighting. It was a time of peace with most of the neighbouring tribes. If any trouble did break out – somebody stole cattle or something – the men took care of it.'

A thought suddenly occurred to Birkita.

'What's your real name? It's not Flavia.'

'No, it's not Flavia. My parents called me Sirona.'

'Sirona,' repeated Birkita, rolling it around on her tongue and tasting the word. 'I like it.'

'I liked it too,' said Flavia in a voice that sounded lost and distant.

She had stopped playing with Birkita's breast. Birkita put a hand across and stroked Flavia's belly down to where the hair began.

'That's nice,' said Flavia dreamily.

'Would you go back there?' Birkita asked.

'In a heartbeat. It would be changed I'm sure. It wouldn't be like it was. But to go back there ... why, it would be like being born again. To get out of this place. Not to die here.'

Birkita stopped stroking.

'I'm going to escape,' she said. 'Will you come with me?'

She had expected Flavia to be more shocked. Instead,

she almost sounded bored. And there was also a hint in her voice of the tone she used when she was instructing the girls to do something.

'It's not possible.'

'It is possible.'

'It's not. And even if it was, you would get caught and then … well, you know what would happen then.'

'If it was possible,' Birkita said, 'if it was – would you come with me?'

'To where?'

'Anywhere. Back to Gaul. Britannia. Any place but this shithole.'

Flavia went silent. Birkita knew that she might just have ruined whatever chance she had of escaping. Even if Flavia didn't tell Antonius, she would be on her guard now. If Birkita escaped, Flavia was bound to suffer in some way. She might even have ended up in the arena herself. It was too big a risk for her.

Birkita saw now the terrible mistake she had made. She was – or had been – a warrior. But Flavia wasn't. There had been some people like that in Birkita's village – one or two girls, one man. It was like they had been born gentle. The man would probably have become a druid. The women? Who knew? It mattered less with the women. She had assumed that Flavia would be prepared to take the risk. To Birkita it was just part of being a warrior. In fact, once she had decided to escape, it had been as though her power – which she had lost that day they had first put chains on her – had started to return. It had been like a drink, flowing back into her.

But it was a terrible risk she ran and while warriors took such risks all the time, not everyone was a warrior. Flavia clearly wasn't. Birkita had misjudged her completely and now her plan was stillborn. Dead before it began.

Flavia lay still, staring at the ceiling. Birkita wanted to say something but she didn't know what to say. What would undo the damage she had just done? Outside, the sky was showing the first hint of the day's colour. A cart was wheeled past on the street, the man pushing it whistling. A cock crowed. And a second time. And a third.

'Don't. Please don't try to escape,' Flavia said. 'It will only go wrong and you will die a terrible death.'

'Better death than this,' Birkita said without thinking.

Instantly she wished she hadn't.

'No,' said Flavia. 'No, you are wrong.'

With that, she rose from the bed and began to dress, her back turned to Birkita.

CHAPTER TWELVE

Flavia Changes Her Mind (Julia)

For the next few days Birkita lived in terror. If Flavia spoke to her at all it was only to issue instructions about work. Nor did Flavia come to her when the day was over. For more than a week, Flavia didn't invite her into the bed upstairs. It had never happened before.

The courage that Birkita had been painstakingly building up, spurred on by the vision of her idyllic life with Flavia, had evaporated. Now she found herself wondering when they would come for her. Whenever either Cassius or Crispus approached her, it was almost like her heart froze. When Antonius came into the lupanar her mind ran riot as she pictured herself being taken away and thrown into some awful dungeon. Then she would emerge, blinking in the sunlight, into the arena to die in a ghastly way for the entertainment of the crowd. The lupanar, with its horrible bed that was her home and workplace, its smell of candles and sweat and stale bodies and the toilet and semen, had suddenly become the dearest place in the world to her.

A few days into the month that the Romans called Januarius Birkita was lying awake in her cubicle. She was struggling to get some sleep, something that had pretty much eluded her since she had told Flavia of her plan. She changed position for the umpteenth time. Beyond the curtain, the lupanar was asleep. Albinus and Crispus were on their mattresses in the hallway, the latter snoring and making a sound like a cricket. The girls were silent in their cubicles except for Bakt, the Egyptian girl, who sounded like she was having a nightmare. Flavia had gone home. It was just after sunrise. Pompeii was hardly stirring with only the occasional sound floating in from the street. There were still hours before the lupanar would be open.

Next moment came a loud thumping of a fist on the front door.

'Open up! Open up!'

It was Antonius' voice.

Birkita's heart leapt with terror. She glanced up at the barred window. Crispus was right outside the curtain. There was no escape. In the hallway, Crispus groaned as he began to unbar the door. Birkita heard the hinges squeak as it was opened.

'Wake them!' Antonius said. 'Gather them all together. Now!'

Birkita had rarely heard Antonius speak and when she had, his voice had always been quiet, soft-spoken. Actually, she found he had a very boring voice. She had never heard him like this. As Birkita rose from the bed, she knew that there was only one option left for her. Quietly she lifted the lid of the chest, reached in and found the knife. Holding the handle in the palm of her hand, she laid the blade across her wrist and along her arm. He would not take her alive.

She pushed past the curtain.

Out in the hallway, the other girls were appearing. They were in various states of undress, hair tousled, yawning and wiping sleep from their eyes. Crispus and Albinus stood by the wall, almost at attention. Antonius, flanked by Flavia and another girl that Birkita had never

205

seen before, stood in front of the door which had been closed again. Cassius stood behind the three of them covering the door. The Syrian twins, Claudia, Bakt and Birkita stood close together, as though by doing so it would give them some protection. Antonius' face, which was normally very pale, was red. He looked at each of the girls in turn. Birkita was unable to hold his gaze. She looked down at her feet.

'Here in the lupanar,' Antonius began, 'do you think I treat you well? Cassius – what do you think?'

'Very well, master,' said Cassius.

Birkita glanced up. Cassius was clearly glad to be on Antonius' side of this exchange. Cassius looked at each of the girls, just as Antonius had done. Antonius continued.

'You have a place to live, good food, you get to sleep a lot of the day, you have clothes, there is wine. What do you think, Albinus? Are all these things true? '

'They're true, master,' said Albinus uncertainly, evidently unsure of where this was leading.

'But whether you are slaves or freemen, our world is a world where there must be give and take. Nothing is for free. And so in return for a place to live and the food and the sleeping and the clothes and the wine, I ask you to do some things for me. And so,' said Antonius, smiling very unpleasantly, 'we have a contract.'

'I have to say that I think your side of the contract is not all that difficult. I have to find the money to provide all these things for you and in return … well, some days you have little or nothing to do. You spend a lot of time on your back –'

At this Cassius snorted with laughter. Antonius turned and glared at him.

'In short, I think it is a fair contract. In fact, if anything, I think I have the harder side of the bargain. What would you say, Flavia? Is it a fair contract?'

'It's a fair contract,' said Flavia dully.

Birkita noticed Flavia for the first time. She looked very pale and clasped her hands together in front of her. And she had a black eye that Birkita only noticed now that Flavia had moved her head.

'It's more than fair, master,' chimed in Cassius, trying to make up for his snort of laughter earlier.

'More than fair. Do you hear that from one of your own? It's "more than fair", he says. Now of course, if somebody were to break that contract, that wouldn't be good, would it? Would it, Cassius?'

'No, master.'

'If I were to stop feeding you or throw you out on the street or take away your fine clothes, I would be breaking the contract. Isn't that true?'

It's not clear whether Antonius intends the question to be rhetorical but nobody replies anyway.

'But you could also break the contract,' he goes on.

Birkita glanced across at Bakt who was looking intensely bored as though all she wanted to do was to get this over with and go back to bed.

'How could somebody break the contract, Flavia?'

'If they tried to leave.'

Flavia said the words so softly that they were hardly audible. Birkita tightened her grip on the dagger. She would plunge it into her heart. She knew there would be terrible pain. But it would be over in a few heartbeats. And then there would be nothing.

'If they tried to leave,' Antonius repeated. 'If they tried to leave.'

He paused as though considering this.

'But somebody could stay here and still break the contract, couldn't they?'

The question wasn't directed at anybody. It was as though he were talking to himself, thinking out loud. The

207

effect was like an actor on a stage. In all the time she had been here, Birkita had never heard him say so much.

'If somebody didn't put their back into the work they had to do. If somebody didn't do an honest day's work, that would be breaking the contract too. Wouldn't it, Flavia?'

Birkita sensed a change in direction. Where was this leading? Had Flavia done something?

'They would,' said Flavia, becoming more and more mouse-like. Birkita had never seen her like this.

'Somebody here has broken the contract,' Antonius announced.

What had Flavia done?

'Somebody here is not putting their back into the work. And we have tried to fix this problem, haven't we, Flavia?'

'We have.'

Flavia's voice was little more than a croak.

'But I'm sorry to say it hasn't worked. So now we have to find new work for that person to do. Let me introduce you to Domitia.'

With a careless wave of his hand, Antonius indicated the new girl. She was tall and very thin. She had large breasts and long red hair that tumbled down to her waist. Her face was plain enough but Birkita could see how men would like the long body, the breasts, the red hair. Domitia stood, hands clasped looking down at the floor.

'Domitia wants to become part of our contract, don't you, Domitia?'

Domitia acted as though she hadn't heard. Birkita realised she couldn't speak the Roman tongue. Antonius glanced at her, irritated that she hadn't responded and that it had spoiled a piece of his performance. He continued.

'But as you know, we only have space for five here and so if Domitia is to come, somebody has to go.'

Suddenly there was an anguished cry. Birkita glanced across at Claudia. Her face, which had been dull and expressionless for as long as Birkita had known her, had suddenly come to life. It showed fear. It was as though she had just woken up or come out of a trance. She looked around like a cornered animal. But Cassius was already moving from his place near the door. Claudia tried to move away from him, to push her way through the other girls, but there was no space in the cramped hallway. Anyway, Cassius moved with surprising speed and had reached her and taken her upper arm in his hand the size of a ham.

'No,' Claudia said. 'No.'

Antonius smiled again, scanning their faces.

'Yes, I'm afraid Claudia is going to take up a new line of work. Something to which she might be more suited. Something that, whether she likes it or not, she'll be forced to put her back into.'

'No! Please, master! No!'

'Shut up, bitch!' said Cassius, turning to Claudia and slapping her hard across the face. The blow drew blood from her lip.

'Next week there will be a Games,' Antonius went on.

He was like an actor coming to the climax of his performance. 'My friend Sextus who organises the gladiatorial contests –'

'No, master – please!' Claudia interrupted again.

'Shut the fuck up,' Cassius said, slapping her twice, back and forth. Her nose started to bleed and she began to cry.

'My friend Sextus has decided it's time for something new. So he's putting together a team of women gladiators.'

Claudia's eyes widened in horror. All the other girls looked appalled.

'They're training even as we speak,' said Antonius. 'Claudia will be joining them. And Sextus has told me that he'll be making sure she puts her back into it.'

Antonius made an upward nod of his head and Cassius dragged Claudia towards the door. Her legs seemed to go from under her but it didn't make much difference to Cassius.

'Get the door, Crispus,' he said and then both men, with Claudia between them, disappeared out the door and into the street.

Antonius looked at them each again in turn. Then, without another word, he turned on his heel and went out.

Birkita and the other girls looked at Flavia. Nobody spoke. Birkita fingered the knife, praying that it wouldn't fall out of her hand. Relief flooded into her like sunlight suddenly appearing from behind a cloud. Whatever else had happened, Flavia hadn't told on her.

Then Flavia said, 'Birkita – you take the big room that Claudia used to have. Domitia will take yours.'

She clapped her hands.

'Come on now. Hurry. I want it all done before we open.'

Flavia took a step or two and Birkita noticed that she seemed to be limping and wincing when she moved.

The new cubicle was slightly bigger than Birkita's old one. She retrieved the money she had saved from its hiding place and put it in her chest. It would have to do for now until she had time to find or make a more secure place.

Flavia never came near her, instead spending most of the day with Domitia. The day turned out to be one of the busiest they had had and Birkita was exhausted when she finally, painfully was able to fall into bed. She immediately fell into a deep sleep. Some time later she became aware of a hand shaking her by the shoulder.

With some difficulty she rose from the depths where she had been sleeping.

'Shhh,' a voice said.

Birkita opened her eyes to yellow light.

It was Flavia, with a candle in one hand.

'Come,' she whispered. 'Upstairs.'

Groggily, Birkita pulled herself from the bed and followed Flavia.

She's moving like an old woman.

In the upstairs room, as Birkita closed the door behind her, Flavia set down the candleholder on the small table beside the bed. Then she turned to face Birkita and shrugged off the loose gown she was wearing. Birkita gasped.

In the soft candlelight, there were red stripes right across Flavia's breasts and belly and thighs. The weals looked like they had been done with a cane. Slowly she turned around to show the same on her back.

'Antonius,' she said, turning back again to look at Birkita.

'Why … What happened?'

'That's just the way he is. Oh, he's never been warm or friendly. But he is usually business-like. Sometimes even polite. But then out of nowhere – this.'

She spread her hands wide as if to display her body.

'Then he is like an animal. And I never know what I have done or not done. And I don't know from one moment to the next which Antonius I will be having to deal with.'

Flavia was almost in tears.

'At least this time he gave me a reason. He said he'd started to hear complaints from customers about Claudia and why hadn't I dealt with them.'

'And what did you say?'

'I didn't get a chance to say anything. He told me to

211

undress and … I suppose I'm lucky he didn't have me scourged. That would have been the end of me. And do you know what he did then?'

Birkita shook her head.

'He gave me some ointment – aloe to put on it. Said he didn't want any customers seeing me like that.'

'I'll put it on for you,' said Birkita.

'Birkita,' said Flavia. 'I've changed my mind. We have to escape. Otherwise we'll die here.'

She shook her head.

'Sooner or later. We'll die.'

26

The cold blue skies of February have given way to a March of grey days and low hanging clouds. Showers alternate with snow flurries. Julia is glad to be indoors. The crew of painters, of which she is part, has worked its way down to the ground floor but Julia's mind is not on painting or the Paradise Ghetto or the war or the book or anything else. She is thinking about Suzanne. Last night she wanted to kiss Suzanne – wanted Suzanne to kiss her. Why didn't she? Why didn't they?

Julia shakes her head. (She actually does shake her head.) She has kissed so many people – men and women – in the stuff she did for Bert. But now Julia is like a teenager with a crush. In fact, Julia had just such a crush in school – on a girl two classes ahead of her. Anika was her name. She was beautiful, great at sports, really smart in school. Julia feels just like that now – just as she did when she would see Anika across the playground or on the sports field.

Julia is sure that Anika is happily married by now – and she wasn't Jewish so she is probably safe in Amsterdam, or at least as safe as anyone can be. Maybe Anika even has a child. Or two. Julia imagines perfect, gorgeous little children. A boy and a girl. Or twins. When Julia thinks of the direction her life has taken in comparison, the things she has done, things she could never tell Suzanne … And yet now, Julia is just like the girl she was back in her second year in high school – melting at the sight of Anika.

Julia remembers how she used to try to catch sight of Anika by waiting until she went home from school. Julia used to spend hours awake at night trying to invent schemes so that she and Anika could become friends. Sure, she was two years older than Julia and had her own friends, but Julia was convinced that if only they could get to talk, Anika would see what a great person Julia was. How interesting. With such amusing things to say. And they would become best friends.

But then Julia would be overtaken by what she called the 'Anika feeling'. It was a feeling of being all weak and helpless. It was like she was Anika's little dog – with no mind of her own and anxious to please. She imagined that if she did ever get to talk to Anika that she would be like that – with nothing intelligent or witty to say – and Anika would just look at her pityingly and walk away.

In the end, of course, Julia never even got to speak to Anika. And it took another year before Julia's crush had faded away.

When Julia arrives back at the barracks from work, Suzanne is already there. She is beaming.

'I've got a surprise,' she says.

Julia is tired after her long day of physical work, hungry and frustrated.

'I've got a new job,' says Suzanne.

'Doing what?'

'They're going to be planting lots of flowers and plants for this big clean up that they're doing. I've been moved to the flower planting. I start tomorrow.'

Julia is pleased for Suzanne. She'll enjoy that more – and she'll get better rations.

'But that's not the best bit,' Suzanne continues, interrupting Julia's thoughts. 'I've already met the foreman. He's Austrian. He's really nice. He said he's looking for more people for his crew. He asked me if I knew anybody good and I told him about you. I gave him your name and he's going to arrange for you to be transferred too. Isn't it wonderful? We'll be working together again.'

It is wonderful and Julia is delighted. Hopefully, the spring will come in the next few days and then they will be outside and be together in the warmth and sunshine. She and Suzanne hug each other and go down to the courtyard to get their food. Meagre as it is, getting something into her belly restores Julia's humour. They go back to their bunk and discuss the next piece of the book. It's Suzanne's turn to write and they both agree that that's good. Flavia is her creation and Birkita's escape is now bound up with Flavia.

They spend some time talking about the whole revenge thing. *The Count of Monte Cristo* had three people on whom the hero sets out to exact revenge. So far they have only one – the bull Roman – or maybe two with Antonius. Suzanne says that they'll find somebody else along the way. She estimates they have written only somewhere between a quarter and a third of the book.

'There's still lots that can happen yet,' she says.

They wash and turn in. The lights are put out. Suzanne puts her glasses away carefully. They lie on their backs in the darkness.

'I'm glad we'll be working together again,' says Julia.

She suddenly feels the Anika feeling, wanting to say things – anything – that will make Suzanne find her interesting.

'Me too,' says Suzanne.

'Planting flowers will be nice.'

Julia has always been indifferent to flowers, plants or gardening of any kind. Her mother loved gardening. It was like she found refuge there. Refuge, or was it forgetting? Or pretending that the world was a flower garden.

'It will,' says Suzanne.

Julia can think of nothing more to say. She racks her brain but in all the vastness that she always imagines is there, she can find nothing. She is about to wish Suzanne good night when Suzanne rolls on to her side. She reaches across and gently turns Julia towards her. Their eyes have become accustomed to the dark so that Julia can see – faintly – Suzanne's face. It is quite beautiful, as though all the pain has been taken from it. Suzanne finds Julia's lips and kisses her. She slips her tongue into Julia's mouth. Suzanne closes her eyes.

For a moment Julia is so astonished that she doesn't know what to do. But then she returns the kiss, as passionately as Suzanne, and closes her eyes too. She opens them again only when Suzanne ceases to kiss her. Suzanne's lips are moist and slightly parted, her eyes bright. Her face wears a small, dreamy smile. Then she closes her eyes again so that she looks almost as though she were drugged. She puts her hand behind Julia's head and moves it forward kissing her again.

After the second kiss, Suzanne breathes, 'I love you.'

Julia moves closer – as close as she can – pressing herself against Suzanne's body. Her breasts against Suzanne's. Her groin pushed hard against Suzanne's. They are both wearing dresses and Julia feels Suzanne's hand through the material on her thigh. Then the hand has reached under the hem of Julia's dress and pushed it up. Suzanne's fingers feel gorgeous on Julia's skin. Suzanne continues to kiss her as her hand rises further until it has reached Julia's hip. Suzanne finds the waistband of Julia's knickers and pulls them down. Julia raises herself off the bed slightly so that Suzanne can get them down as far as she can as quickly as she can. There is an urgency in Suzanne's movements that Julia has never seen before. Suzanne has always seemed a bit dreamy. But not tonight. Not now.

Suzanne pushes the knickers until they are down below Julia knees. Julia can feel herself becoming wet. Suzanne's arm is at full stretch so now she shoves at the gusset of the knickers with her toes and they slide down around Julia's ankles. She thinks that one leg of them may have come off but she can't be sure. Julia parts her legs and a moment later Suzanne's fingers touch her there. Suzanne's index finger strokes along the line of her vulva.

And then Julia freezes. She clamps her legs together again, momentarily trapping Suzanne's hand. Suzanne pulls her hand away as though it had been burnt.

'What is it?' whispers Suzanne anxiously. 'What have I done?'

'I can't,' gasps Julia and she begins to sob. 'I can't.'

27

Julia wakes the next morning while it is still dark. The space beside her is empty and momentarily she panics. Where is Suzanne? But as Julia struggles to wake up, the bunk shakes as Suzanne returns and climbs back in. She turns away from Julia and pulls her knees up to her chest. Julia turns towards her. Suzanne's back is like a wall. Julia doesn't spoon her but just lies there. The gap between them is only a few centimetres but it might as well be the distance to the Moon.

Julia places a hand on Suzanne's arm but Suzanne pushes her off.

'Suzanne,' Julia whispers. 'Suzanne, please.'

'It's OK,' says Suzanne.

'No, it's not OK.'

'It is. Really.'

'Suzanne – please. Turn round. I can't talk to your back.'

After a long, long pause, Suzanne turns round. The pre-dawn light is very faint but she has clearly been crying.

'I want to explain.'

Suzanne shakes her head.

'No. There's no need. I ... I shouldn't –'

She stops. She is on the brink of tears.

'Please. Please can I explain?'

'Julia, I don't want you to. Can't you see? I just want to forget all about it. Forget it ever happened. Can't you do that for me? Please.'

'Yes,' says Julia slowly. 'I can do that.'

'That's all I ask.'

Suzanne turns away again. As she does she says, 'I'm just going to try to get some more sleep.'

Julia wants desperately to spoon Suzanne but she cannot, she dare not try to close the tiny gap that lies between them.

'Will ... will we still be friends?'

'Of course, we'll still be friends, Julia,' Suzanne's voice comes back.

It is the first time in the conversation that Suzanne has said her name and Julia takes some comfort from that.

'And the book?' she asks. 'Will we still write the book?'

Suzanne doesn't respond at once and in the silence Julia has a vision of herself on the scaffold with a noose around her neck and the executioner's fingers closing around the handle of the lever that will release the trapdoor. Everything happens in slow motion and she can see everything in extraordinary, almost supernatural, detail – the movements of the muscles in the executioner's hand, the tension in the lever and whatever mechanism it connects to, the grain of the wood in the planks of the floor.

Suzanne turns. She looks at Julia with eyes that are full of tears. Suzanne tries to speak, is unable to, gulps and then goes again.

'We'll finish the book, Julia,' says Suzanne. 'Don't you see? We have to. Until we do, the war won't end and we won't be able to leave this horrible place.'

CHAPTER THIRTEEN

The Escape (Suzanne)

For the next few nights, Birkita and Flavia lay in the upstairs room and talked through the plan. They tried to find flaws in it – something they'd forgotten or some eventuality they'd not anticipated or the kind of surprises that could occur. What if Cassius woke up? What if Antonius came back? It had never happened before but there was always a first time. Would Birkita really have the resolve to stab Albinus – innocent, cheery, hard-working Albinus? She prayed she wouldn't have to. Both Birkita and Flavia agreed that it was a thin plan. But equally, both agreed that there was no other way.

It would have to be a night when Cassius was on duty. It would have to be after a day that was busy enough and had generated wine enough to make him drunk. Albinus would either have to keep quiet or be killed. The thought that there would now be two of them – that Birkita wouldn't be by herself – buoyed up her courage. After leaving they would get to the harbour and find a ship. Flavia had pointed out that there would be no time to wait for a ship heading to a particular destination – Britannia, Gaul or anywhere else. Antonius might be on their heels. (The phrase had chilled Birkita.) They would just have to take the first ship that was leaving the harbour. After that, once they were away from Pompeii, in some other port, they could set their true course.

Birkita was terrified and excited.

Now, all they had to do was wait.

The days of Januarius passed slowly. Any night that Crispus was on duty was a night they knew they wouldn't be going anywhere. He dutifully lay on the mattress in front of the door blocking it with his body. Anyone trying to get out the door would have had to wake him – or kill him. Birkita didn't want to kill anybody.

On the days when Cassius was going to be on duty, Birkita started out wondering if tonight was going to be the night. But then the traffic through the lupanar turned out to be slow and during the early hours of the morning, it became clear to her and Flavia that nothing would happen.

Towards the end of Januarius came a Roman festival. The first day of it started out promising enough. The afternoon and early evening were busy so that by midnight, Birkita's body had already had more than enough. But the clients had been uniformly mean, buying little of Antonius' sour wine and even less of it for Birkita. And when somebody eventually did, there appeared to be something strange happening.

Birkita took the two cups from Albinus and placed them on the little wooden table by the bed. A tiny movement caught her eye. She looked down. The cup seemed to be shaking of its own accord and the red surface of the wine was vibrating in a series of tiny circles. She had never seen anything like it. After a little while the vibration stopped just as the customer said, 'Come on, bitch. I haven't got all night.'

On the second day though, everything seemed to change. The day was hectic – Birkita hardly got a break to eat – and many of the customers seemed to be already drunk before they started.

With drunken customers the amount of wine consumed went up – drunken customers meant generous ones. Birkita received a steady flow of cups of wine which she passed on to Cassius. Finally, several hours after midnight, the flow of men started to ease off. By then Birkita was in pain when she walked or even stood, but it was clear that this was going to be the night. Flavia confirmed it when she looked in while Birkita was between customers and mouthed, 'Tonight.'

The minutes passed agonisingly slowly as they waited for the last customer to leave and Antonius to arrive. Finally, he did. He talked with Flavia for a few minutes, as was his custom. Birkita pulled her curtain back a fraction and watched them as they stood in the yellow lamplight of the hallway. Everything seemed normal. Then, in the usual routine, Antonius took the bag of money which Flavia passed to him and emptied its contents into a leather satchel with a shoulder strap that he always carried. After that, he left.

Birkita waited in her cubicle. She heard Albinus struggling with the two mattresses. Cassius, who had been loud and obviously drunk earlier, had gone dead quiet when Antonius arrived. Birkita heard him walk along the hallway, stumble and curse. Then he belched loudly and sounded as though he'd bounced off one of the walls.

Birkita's curtain opened and Flavia came in. Her face was ghostly white. Birkita thought it was just the tension but then Flavia said, 'There's a problem.'

'What's wrong?'

'Antonius wants to come to me.'

'Come to you? But he's gone.'

'No, you don't understand. Sometimes he comes to me. In my house. Usually, it's after he's hurt me. He wants to make amends.'

'Amends?'

Birkita realised she was repeating everything that Flavia said.

'And he's coming tonight?' Birkita asked.

Flavia nodded.

'In a few minutes. He's just giving me some time to prepare.'

'Prepare?'

'Wash this place off me. Smell nice. Wear something pretty.'

Birkita's heart sank.

'So we can't do it?'

'No, we can,' whispered Flavia.

'How?'

'You know how he is. In and out. He won't be very long. Come in a little while. My house is five doors up on this side. I'll put a candle burning in the window while he's there. If you see no candle, you'll know that he's gone.'

Birkita smiled and nodded.

Flavia kissed her on the lips. A quick kiss. Urgent. She touched Birkita's cheek with her palm.

'See you in a while,' Flavia said.

She slipped out. Birkita checked the small bundle of things she was bringing. A cloak, her coins in a small bag made of sacking, the knife. She would wait six turns of the hourglass. That should give Antonius enough time. She had just set the first one when the curtain was pulled back. It was Cassius.

'British girl. How about a fuck to end the day?'

'Would you go ask somebody else? I'm tired – and anyway I gave you all that wine.'

Cassius stepped into the cubicle, lifted his hand and slapped her backhand across the face.

'You don't say no to me, British bitch.'

Wearily, Birkita went to the bed, lay back on it

and lifted her toga.

'That's more like it,' said Cassius.

He lifted up his tunic, climbed onto the bed and lay on top of her. Birkita closed her eyes. He reeked of wine, sweat and piss. A smell of shit wafted up past his back. She could feel that he had no erection. He lay on her for a while moving his groin up and down. He farted and sighed with satisfaction. But then his movement slowly came to a halt. Birkita opened her eyes.

He was asleep.

She waited a little while just to make absolutely sure. Then she rolled out from underneath him. He flopped against the wall like a sack of grain and began to snore loudly. Birkita was tempted to cut his throat but now she just wanted to be moving, to leave this place.

She put on her cloak and put the knife and bag of coins in a pocket on the inside. Then she slipped out past the curtain. The hallway was dark with no candles burning. She couldn't tell if Albinus was asleep or not. He seemed to be. He was turned on his side with his blanket pulled up over his shoulder. The rest of the place was in silence except for soft sleeping noises coming from one or two of the cubicles.

As silently as she could, Birkita lifted the heavy wooden beam that barred the door. It was much heavier than she had expected. She had grown soft in the time she had been here.

Please don't let me drop it.

She got it free of its iron mounts. It nearly fell from her hands but she was able to catch it on her knees, steady it and then, crouching down, she lowered it to the floor.

She straightened up. Her heart was racing and she was dripping in sweat. She looked around at where Albinus slept but there was no movement. The curtains on the cubicles were still. Cassius was snoring loudly.

Birkita lifted the latch and eased the heavy door back. Mercifully, the hinges didn't squeak – she had been regularly oiling them with lamp oil ever since she had decided to escape. She opened it just wide enough to slip through. Then she was out in the street, shutting it silently behind her.

She looked up and down. The street was deserted. It was the first time Birkita had been out here without somebody accompanying her. She was free.

She crossed to the other side of the street and staying in the shadows by the wall, moved silently, counting doorways. At the fifth one, there was no light in the window – it was a square of black.

She crossed back and tapped softly on the door with her knuckles. Flavia opened the door wide. Her face was still deathly pale.

'Are you ready?' hissed Birkita.

'Yes. Just come in a moment.'

Birkita did and Flavia closed the door. The room was in darkness.

Birkita was just about to whisper something when a figure stepped out of the shadows.

It was Antonius.

He carried a sword. Birkita noticed it was the short sword that the Roman army used.

She looked at Flavia in confusion.

'I'm sorry,' said Flavia.

CHAPTER FOURTEEN

You Betrayed Me (Julia)

'Take off that cloak and like down on the floor,' said Antonius. 'Face down.'

Birkita was reminded that Antonius had been a soldier. Maybe he hadn't been a fighting one but right now, she felt like it was a soldier facing her.

She hesitated, thinking about her knife.

She could try to get past the blade and cut his throat. Back, long ago, in another life, she had learned how to do that. But that had been a different time. She had had another body then. A warrior's body. Now she had a whore's body. And a weary, almost broken one at that.

She knew she wouldn't be able to reach him. Long before that, his sword would be slicing its way into her belly. She thought of the arena and what awaited her. Better to go now. Quick and clean. Here in the darkness. Fighting an enemy.

Fighting. That was the thing. Better to be fighting than just lying down like a lamb. A warrior again. If only for a brief instant. She would go to the gods as a warrior.

Antonius suddenly lifted the blade shoulder height.

Birkita's hand jabbed inside the cloak for the knife.

But then her head exploded and filled with light as he struck her hard with the flat of the blade across the side of her head. The last thing she heard was Antonius' voice saying, 'Go and get that drunken bastard, Cassius.'

When Birkita came to she was lying face down on the cold floor. Her cheek rested on the rough concrete. Opening her eyes she saw that a tiny amount of grey light had spilled into the room. Dawn was coming. She could see some small details. A pebble of concrete on the floor. The wooden leg of a bed. Some crumbs. A piece of lemon rind. She noticed that it was still bright yellow. It must have only fallen there recently.

Somebody had tied her arms behind her back. The cord was tight and bit into her wrists. Her legs had been spread-eagled so that she was completely open. Her head was pounding like a drum – on the side where Antonius had struck her, across her forehead, in her eyes. The room smelt bad. She knew Cassius must be there, behind her somewhere.

Next minute she felt what she knew to be the point of Antonius' sword poking softly between her legs.

'So – you're awake, British cunt,' said Cassius.

She felt the top of the blade, very sharp. She went to close her legs but Cassius stamped on her calf with his foot.

'Uh uh. Just stay as you are,' he said. 'I like it that way. It's my favourite view of you.'

He touched her vulva with the tip of the blade, stroking it.

'If you were mine,' he said, 'you know we'd be about to have some fun now.'

Gently, he inserted the tip of the blade into her, pushing it as far as he could without drawing blood or doing any damage.

'But sadly, you're not mine.'

He withdrew the point of the blade and began to stroke down the back of her thighs with the sword tip. It was gentle at first, almost tickling. But then he pressed the point into her more deeply so that it hurt.

'You got me into a lot of trouble,' said Cassius.

Suddenly, the floor beneath her began to vibrate. She could feel the vibrations in her chest and in all her limbs. Her first thought was that it was a chariot or a cart going past outside but she had heard nothing like that approach.

Cassius swore.

The floor was shaking now. It was as though waves were travelling through Birkita's body. It was like there was somebody upstairs – a huge, fat man walking across the wooden floor and causing the whole house to shake. A small statue fell onto the floor and shattered. Birkita felt some of the fragments spattering against her face and throat.

Then, as quickly as it had begun, the shaking stopped.

Cassius swore again. Then he resumed what he had been doing with the sword.

'Yes,' he said. 'You got me into a lot of trouble. But it's nothing like the trouble you're in.'

'Fuck you,' Birkita said.

She had wanted to say it ever since she got here.

'You want to?' asked Cassius. 'I don't think so. I think your fucking days are over. That is unless they find a horse for you to fuck. But if they do, that will be in the arena. I'd like to see that. Mmm, I'd really like to see that. I'll be going along, you know. I'll be there in the crowd next week to see your show.'

Birkita would have to kill herself. That was the only thing that remained now. She would have to find a way.

Cassius pressed the point of the sword hard into the back of her thigh so that it punctured the skin. Birkita gasped. Then she felt him score a line down her thigh just as far as the back of the knee. The movement was exquisitely light – but intended to open the flesh. She felt her skin puncture and warm blood trickle across her thigh and onto the floor.

Cassius did the same on the other leg.

'You have a nice ass, British bitch. I'll say that for you.' Birkita felt the point of the sword poke into one of her buttocks.

But just then the door opened.

A voice she didn't recognise in an accent that was unfamiliar said amiably, 'Don't worry about it, my friend. We are both businessmen. Night or day, whatever the hour, we must go where we can to make whatever small money we can.'

'What the fuck are you doing now, Cassius?'

It was Antonius.

'She tried to escape.'

'I'm sure she did,' said Antonius, wearily. 'Get her up.'

Cassius took Birkita by the arms and pulled her savagely to her feet. Then he stood behind her and just to one side. He was close enough that she could smell him and his breath when he exhaled.

The man with Antonius was about the same age as him but where Antonius was tall and lean, still having something of the soldier about him, this man was small and plump. He looked like he enjoyed his food and wine. He was deeply tanned with dark eyes. Birkita thought he had a look of the east about him. He wore good clothes. They looked expensive. If he had been woken unexpectedly, he didn't look it. Instead he had carefully prepared himself for the day. His black curly hair was brushed and oiled and he wore scent that filled the room.

'This is her, Sextus' said Antonius. 'Unlike the other one, this one's a warrior.'

'I see that,' said Sextus. 'She's been fighting already, eh?'

'It's a bit of a swelling and a black eye,' said Antonius carelessly. 'A few days and they'll be gone.'

'And of course the backs of her thighs. They'll need a bit of cleaning up.'

Antonius glared in Cassius' direction.

'She's well built, that's for sure,' said Sextus. 'I'm sure she's gone a bit soft in your establishment, lying on her back all the time, but that's nothing that a little training won't cure. Turn around,' he said to Birkita. His voice was gentle, almost kind. Birkita remembered the healer in the village a lifetime ago.

Before she could respond, Cassius seized her roughly by the shoulder and turned her back to the two men.

'And back again,' said Sextus.

He looked at Birkita appraisingly. Into her eyes. Then, as if for one last time, he sized her up from head to toe.

'I'll take her. And you'll give me a little discount for the face and the thighs.'

'Come up the street, we'll have a cup of wine and we can talk about that,' said Antonius.

'Excellent,' said Sextus. 'In fact,' he said, 'I'm thinking it must be nearly breakfast time.' He put his hand on his ample stomach. 'Throw in breakfast and you'll have yourself a deal.'

Antonius put his arm around Sextus' shoulder and ushered him out the door. Over his shoulder, Sextus said, 'Give her some water, for heaven's sake. And clean her up.'

After the door closed, Cassius called, 'Flavia?'

She stepped out of the shadows at the back of the small room in which she lived. She had been there all the time.

Flavia brought a bowl of water and a sponge and went down on her knees behind Birkita. She lifted her hem and began to wipe the back of one thigh gently. The wound stung. Birkita glanced down. The water in the bowl had turned red.

'The bleeding has stopped,' announced Flavia. 'That's good.'

She moved on to the other thigh.

'I'm just going to go outside and get some air,' said Cassius. 'There's only one way out, British bitch – and that's where I'll be.'

Cassius went out onto the street.

'See how the stink went with him,' said Flavia.

If it was intended as a joke, Birkita didn't laugh.

Instead, she looked around the room but Cassius was right – there was only the front door and a tiny window high up at the back. She would never have fitted through it.

Flavia finished the other thigh and got up off her knees. She went and changed the water, returned and started on Birkita's cheek and eye.

'When?' Birkita asked.

She tried to catch Flavia's eye but Flavia kept hers averted.

'When what?'

'When did you betray me?'

Flavia said nothing, dabbing away at the eye.

'When?' Birkita almost shouted.

'Just now … after he fucked me … he offered me my freedom.'

'And you believe him? You said it yourself – he's as changeable as the wind.'

'I have no reason to doubt him,' said Flavia, in a tone that sounded like she was trying to convince herself. 'On the first day of spring, the fifth day of Februarius, he will make me free. I must pay him, of course. But I have been saving the money. I told him what I have and he says it is enough. After that, I will be free. He says I can stay here and keep working in the lupanar or go, as I choose. If you had escaped that would have been the end of my freedom.'

'You don't care about anybody but yourself, do you?'

'I stopped caring for anybody else the day I came here,' said Flavia. 'I asked him to forgive you. I pleaded with him. But it was no good. He said if he did that, then it would only be a matter of time before one of the others tried it. He said he couldn't spend all his time watching you. That he had to make an example.'

Birkita said nothing, wincing as the sponge touched a cut near the corner of her eye.

'He was going to have you crucified. But I asked him to do with you what he'd done with Claudia. Send you to the arena.'

'It's the same thing,' said Birkita.

'No,' said Flavia and now she faced Birkita and looked into her eyes. 'It's not the same thing. Can't you see? This way you have a chance. You're a warrior. Claudia's not but you are. I knew it the first time I saw you. You have the body of a warrior. You can win. Win your freedom – just like me.'

'You betrayed me,' Birkita said again.

'What could I do?' Flavia appealed. 'What would you have done in my place?'

'We could both have been free,' said Birkita.

Flavia finished and dropped the sponge back in the pink water. It wasn't as bloody as the last time. As she stooped to pick up the bowl, Birkita said, 'Flavia, in my cloak is a dagger. Get it and please cut my throat.'

Flavia looked at her in horror.

'I can't do that,' she said.

'Please – you must.'

'I can't.'

'Flavia – they're going to put me in the arena.

You've seen what happens.'

'Birkita ... I can't. I ... I love you.'

It was the most outrageous thing Birkita had ever heard. She thought to spit in Flavia's face. Instead she said, 'If that's true ... If you have any feelings of love at all for me, you would do this. If you even cared for me the tiniest bit.'

'I can't.'

'Do you want me to die in the arena? For sport? Is that what you want?'

'I can't hurt you, Birkita.'

'And what do you think you've done already? What do you think they'll do to me in the arena?'

Before Flavia could answer, the door opened and Cassius came back in, the smell wafting in with him. He leant against the doorpost watching Birkita, leering at her. Flavia brought some water which Birkita drank greedily – she was unbelievably thirsty. Outside the sounds of the day waking started to drift in – traffic, people, animals. Birkita suddenly felt completely weary. She had had a long working day and no sleep. And then all this. She thought how delicious it would be to sleep and not wake up again.

Just then Antonius and Sextus returned. Sextus took her chin in his hand and moved her face up to the light.

'That looks better,' he said. 'Good. Time to go.'

'You go with him,' Antonius said to Cassius. 'I'll talk to you later.'

'Come then,' said Sextus cheerily. 'Time to show you your new home.'

28

Julia puts down the pencil. It's been one of the longer chapters and took her the best part of a week to write. She sits up in bed using her knees as a desk. Her writing hand is aching. She shakes it out.

It is nearly lights out. Julia looks down at Suzanne, but discovers that she is asleep, breathing deeply. She lies on her side, blanket pulled up around her shoulder. Both her hands lie on the pillow in front of her face, fingers interlaced. The effect is not so much like she is praying but rather that someone is holding her hand. Her hair is just starting to become tossed. People look so gentle and soft and vulnerable when they are asleep. Julia wonders if Nazis look like this when they are asleep. What does Hitler look like? Julia wonders when Suzanne fell asleep. She didn't say good night.

Birkita's words keep going around in Julia's head. *You betrayed me. You betrayed me.*

She had.

She has betrayed Suzanne.

Maybe not as bad as Flavia's but a betrayal just the same. She led Suzanne along and then walked away. As Julia was writing the bits about Cassius mistreating Birkita, she felt a certain grim satisfaction. Instead of Birkita, it was Julia being punished for her betrayal.

The lights go out and the place is plunged into darkness. Julia slides down into the bed wearily. The words keep buzzing around like angry bees in a disturbed hive.

You betrayed me. You betrayed me.

The next day Julia and Suzanne go their separate ways to their work. But when Julia arrives at hers, the painting foreman tells her that she has a new job. He tells her where to go and who to look for.

Her new boss, the Austrian that Suzanne told her about, is called Adolf.

'I share a name with our beloved Führer,' he says with a faint smile, as he shakes her hand and welcomes her.

Julia can't tell whether or not he is being sarcastic.

He has black hair and a long face with chiselled features – strong nose and chin, good cheekbones – that, if anything, have been even more accentuated by the poor food. He looks like he might have been some kind of athlete – he has that physical presence about him that sportsmen have. He is handsome in a craggy sort of way, reminding Julia of an eagle.

He seems an unlikely choice to be heading up the team that are planting flowers but he explains that it is more than that. They are one of a number of teams – he calls them 'kommandos' – who are turning 'desolate and decrepit areas of the ghetto into green and flowering spaces'.

'There will be a lot more nature in the ghetto,' he says.

Julia thinks that the whole ghetto is desolate and decrepit and should be blown up or bulldozed. She hopes that after the war it will be, though she knows this is a bit unlikely.

'Suzanne says you are a good worker,' says Adolf. 'You Dutch girls seem to be – that's if Suzanne is anything to go by. And not bad-looking either,' he adds, looking her in the eye and grinning.

In her old life Julia has heard this kind of shit a million times.

'What do you want me to do?' she asks as coldly as possible.

That night Julia tries to talk to Suzanne again.

'I didn't mean to hurt you,' Julia says while they are eating.

'I was upset at the time,' says Suzanne, 'but I'm OK now.'

'I don't know what it was,' says Julia.

Suzanne doesn't say anything to this but she looks into Julia's eyes. Suzanne's blue eyes are so striking.

'This place,' goes on Julia. 'The bad food. The war. We're so tired all the time.'

Suzanne's silence continues. This is not going at all the way Julia wanted it to go. She's on the point of starting to babble.

Suzanne says, 'It's OK. Really. Everyone does what they can.'

Julia feels a bit panicky.

'But … but what about after the war? When we get out of here?'

Suzanne shakes her head.

'You can't plan for everything, you know, Julia. You can't anticipate everything. Control everything. Sometimes you just have to wait and see what happens.'

'But I love you,' says Julia, unable to keep the desperation out of her voice.

'I love you, Julia, and I always will.'

Suzanne lowers her bowl and puts the spoon in it. 'Have you ever seen a full moon shining on the sea? It creates a silvery pathway on the water. It's like something has come down from some heavenly place and come among us. That was how I felt when I met you.'

At first Julia feels comforted by these words. It's more like the old, dreamy Suzanne with all her mystical talk. But then Julia realises that Suzanne said 'was' – 'that *was* how I felt when I met you.'

Before Julia can agonise any more about this, Suzanne says, 'So I'll always love you, Julia. No matter what happens.'

These last words chill Julia.

'But we have to stay together,' she says.

'That would be nice,' says Suzanne gently. 'I'd like that.'

'But if it's what we both want then we have to make sure it happens.'

'And we will,' says Suzanne.

She puts her hand on Julia's and holds it there for a few moments.

'We will.'

It is forgiveness.

Of sorts.

CHAPTER FIFTEEN

Gladiator School (Suzanne)

With Sextus leading and Cassius bringing up the rear, they made their way westwards across the city. Birkita's head pounded and her eye felt swollen. She thought to make a run for it but her hands were still tied behind her back. It would be pointless. Cassius would only pull her back again. She would at least have to wait until she was untied.

Sextus seemed to know everybody. He waved or said 'ave' or stopped to shake hands and have a little talk.

As they were walking down the street, Birkita noticed lots of frogs hopping around on the stones. Sextus noticed it too.

'There's a strange thing now,' he said to nobody in particular. 'Never seen that before.'

The low building into which she was led had a rectangular inner courtyard covered in sand. It was surrounded on all sides by a shaded colonnade. The sun was high enough now that it bathed the courtyard in warm lemon light.

At one end of the courtyard, men were fighting with swords, shields, nets and three-pronged forks. At the other, there was a group of about twenty girls and women. Their hair was tied up, they wore shabby, short tunics and they were fighting in pairs with wooden swords and shields.

Two men walked amongst the women, pushing them, shouting orders, urging them on. Occasionally they would take somebody's hand in theirs and show them how to hold the weapon. Sextus called one of the men over.

'Here's your latest recruit, Severus. She's from Britannia.'

The man called Severus was built like a barrel with short squat legs, powerful, muscular arms and a huge chest. He was naked to the waist and his chest and arms were covered in bushy black hair. He wore brown leather armbands on his wrists.

'I hope she can fight,' he said in a voice that was deep and seemed to resonate in the keg of his chest. 'Because precious few of these ones can.'

'Don't worry about it,' said Sextus, sounding like a man who never worried about anything. 'We're new to this. Nobody's seen women fight here in Pompeii before. It will be a novelty. They'll love it because it'll be something new. No matter how bad the fighting is.'

'We'll see,' said Severus, sounding unconvinced.

'And I've had another idea. I've been racking my brains trying to work out the best way to present this. If the fighting is not going to be up to scratch, then there has to be some other angle. So what I thought was – Amazons.'

'Amazons?'

'Yes – Amazons – Greek female warriors. With this one' – he indicated Birkita – 'that makes twenty. So we'll have two armies – Romans and Amazons. Of course the Romans will have to win, so you need them to be your best fighters. Oh – and one other thing. The Amazons used to wear tunics where one of their breasts was exposed.'

Severus grinned and shook his head.

'Boss, boss, boss. Always with the sex.'

Sextus smiled an almost boyish smile.

'Whenever I can. We provide entertainment, Severus. That's what we do. That's our job. And what better entertainment than sex? So what I was going to say was – make sure that the Amazons have the ones with the biggest breasts.'

'And the Romans have the best fighters?' asked Severus.

'Yes.'

'And suppose the best fighters have the biggest breasts?'

Sextus slapped Severus on the upper arm.

'I'm sure you'll work it out.'

'All right, British girl,' Severus said to Birkita. 'Let's see what you're made of. We'll get rid of this for starters.'

Severus pulled a knife from his belt and cut Birkita's bonds. One of her wrists was cut from the twine and the other had several deep red scores around it. She rubbed her wrists as Severus took her by the arm and led her towards the other women.

'Take a break,' he shouted to them. 'Get some water.'

The women did as they were told, carrying their weapons to where a barrel of water sat in the shade.

As Birkita approached, she saw a familiar face break out into an expression of complete happiness.

It was Claudia.

'Birkita!' she said, running towards her.

'You've come to save me,' Claudia said as she hugged Birkita.

Not to save you. I've come to kill you.

CHAPTER SIXTEEN

I'll Try to Protect You (Julia)

It wasn't so much training, as a rehearsal for a performance. Birkita had done weapons training. This wasn't it.

Most of the women were totally unsuited to what they were being asked to do. There were young girls – teenagers – who alternated between trying to master the weapons and breaking out into tears at the prospect of what lay in store for them. The rest were Birkita's age or a bit older. Some carried wounds – a limp, a livid scar across the face, a couple of broken noses, scars of a flogging, a forearm that had broken and not knit properly. One's face had some kind of pox on it – angry, red, weeping sores.

That first day Birkita was astonished at how poor her performance was. It had been so long since she had held a weapon. Almost every opponent she took on beat her. By the end of the day she was bruised and spent. Every bone and muscle in her body ached.

They were given a thick soup and bread for supper. The soup even had some meat in it. They ate in a room that smelt of sweat, moon blood, the toilet and fear. Afterwards, Birkita lay on the hard cot in the small cell that she shared with Claudia. She understood that what had happened today had been a blessing. The others would underestimate her – and that was always a good thing.

If she could get her strength and stamina back in time, she reckoned she had the beating of most of the women there. Most of them were slaves, not warriors. It would have taken several moons to transform them – and apparently, there weren't going to be several moons.

There were two women though, that Birkita was much less certain about. She called them the Cow and the Warrior. The Cow was a short, squat woman with one of the ugliest faces Birkita had ever seen. She was built like a small mountain – short thighs like tree trunks, gobbets of wobbly fat on her upper arms, bad teeth, breasts that spread all over her chest and belly.

At first Birkita had thought the Cow would be a pushover. But she moved extraordinarily fast and had fierce strength. She had broken numerous wooden swords – usually across her opponents' head or body – and a kick to another opponent when she was down had broken several of the young girl's ribs. Severus had just strapped up the ribs and the girl was made to carry on. Birkita reckoned she was as good as dead.

The Warrior was tall and lean. It was clear she *had* been a warrior. She handled her weapons with an easy familiarity. If Birkita came up against either one of these, she wasn't at all sure that she could win.

And then there was Claudia.

In the lupanar Claudia had been like a shadow. She rarely talked and really, Birkita had been surprised that she had lasted as long as she had. For customers, fucking her must have been like fucking a ghost.

But here, she seemed to have come back to life. Birkita didn't know if this had just happened since her arrival but whatever the reason, Claudia was like a real person again.

And it was as though Birkita was noticing her for the first time.

She was a few years older than Birkita. She was slim and in the lupanar had eaten so little that she had seemed like a dry stick that might snap at any moment. How she had managed with men on top of her, Birkita could only imagine. Claudia was graceful with fine legs and moved like a dancer. Had she had the proper training, starting in her childhood, she might well have become a very formidable warrior – strong and lithe.

And Birkita could see how Claudia had been the most in-demand girl in the lupanar. With her pert bottom, beautiful breasts and straight black hair that framed her face, she was very attractive indeed – or at least, had been one time. She had a long neck, oval face, a perfect nose and a determined chin. Her fingers were long and – Birkita thought – beautiful, unlike her own which were a warrior's. Up until recently Claudia's fingers had never held a weapon.

That night, Birkita explained to Claudia about the Amazons and Romans. Based on what she had heard it was clear that half of them would die. The thing was to not end up in the Amazons.

'You'll protect me, Birkita, won't you?'

'I'll do what I can, Claudia. But you have to try to learn how to fight.'

Over the next few days Birkita set out to teach Claudia and to remember herself. Birkita didn't know how much time she had. If what Cassius had said was true, it wasn't very much – only a few days.

So as much as she was allowed to, she trained with Claudia, showing her the basics of sword fighting – stance, position of the arms, stabbing, lunging, parrying. Claudia was a willing pupil, took it all in and came on rapidly. She was still too gentle but Birkita spent a whole day trying to make her more aggressive.

'Pretend I'm Cassius,' she would say. 'Or Antonius. Now – attack me!'

When Birkita had to fight against anyone else, she tried to be as bad as the worst of them. The Cow struck her numerous ferocious blows for her trouble – one that nearly knocked her out. The Warrior sensed what Birkita was doing and did the same thing herself. The result was a fight – if you could call it that – where they just circled each other endlessly and made half-hearted feints at each other. When Severus saw what they were doing he roared abuse at them and it was only when he threatened to put them in with the male gladiators for the night that they made any kind of an effort. In the end, they did enough to make him stop. When they were finished, and Severus had stopped swearing at them, the Warrior smiled a knowing smile at Birkita and walked away.

On the fourth day, they stopped using wooden weapons and moved on to real ones. Several of the women including Claudia sustained nasty cuts but Severus and his assistant stayed close trying to ensure that nobody was too badly hurt – or killed, which would have angered Sextus. Despite this, the Cow slashed another woman's arm so badly that it needed to be stitched. Severus' assistant did that while the woman screamed in agony.

Every evening after they had eaten their food, they were given some time to relax. On the third evening they were lying about and talking quietly. The Cow appeared to be asleep and the Warrior was sharpening a sword. Then – unusually – Severus came in.

'All right, ladies,' he said, briskly, 'line up and get your tits out.'

The women looked at each other. Nobody moved.

Sextus clapped his hands.

'Come on, come on,' he said. 'We don't have all night.'

Silently, hesitantly they got to their feet and started to do as they were told. One or two were still reluctant holding the fabric of their tunics against their chests.

'This is not the place for modesty, ladies,' said Severus, and with that, he ripped a couple of tunics down to the waist.

'Hands by your sides,' he ordered.

Then he walked down the line, with his hands behind his back, looking at each of their chests in turn.

'You'll be going into the arena in two days' time,' he announced.

An anguished groan went up.

'That's the bad news,' he said. 'The good news is that some of you will be coming out again. We will be dividing you into two "armies" – the Romans and the Amazons. You'll fight each other. The victorious army will be the one that inflicts the most casualties.'

He looked along the line, meeting each pair of eyes.

'You understand what this means, I hope. The losing side will be the one that has no soldiers standing.'

Birkita looked at Claudia who was beside her. Claudia's face was white and her eyes were wide and staring at some horror that Birkita could only imagine.

'So this evening I'm picking the armies.'

Starting at one end, Severus walked down the line again. To each woman he said either 'Amazon – over there' or 'Roman – here'.

When he was finished, Birkita stood in the same group as the Cow and the Warrior. They were the Amazons. Claudia was with the Romans. Her frantic eyes sought Birkita's who had to look away.

But there were eleven Romans and nine Amazons. Severus quickly sorted that problem out, taking what he judged to be the largest remaining pair of breasts from the Romans. But Severus still didn't seem happy. He stood in front of another Amazon, staring at her chest. Then he looked at Claudia's. He went back to the first girl and cradled one of her breasts in his hand as though weighing it. Then he did the same to Claudia. She stared straight ahead, unblinking.

Severus thought for a moment.

Then he exchanged Claudia for the other girl.

That night, as Claudia and Birkita lay on their bunk together, Claudia said, 'Have you noticed?'

'Noticed what?'

'The rats.'

'What about them?'

'There aren't any. All the other nights you could hear them rustling in the straw but listen – tonight there's nothing. They're gone.'

29

Julia and Suzanne are weeding. A patch of ground has been dug and now they must take out all the weeds before it is raked over and grass seed is planted. It is backbreaking work, the standing and bending over. Several times Julia feels dizzy and as if she is going to faint. They try kneeling down in the dirt and that helps a bit but the earth is cold and wet and they can only do that for so long before they have to stand again.

Suzanne points out that it is March 21st, the equinox. 'The days will be getting warmer now,' she says.

Julia notices the birds for the first time. Have they been there all along? Or were they hibernating for the winter? Julia is a city girl and knows little or nothing about these things. But today, the birds are singing their hearts out – twittering, whistling, cooing. She tries to think of other words. She has been doing this a lot lately – she'll think of a word and then try to find other words that mean the same thing. It's since she's become a writer – a notion that always makes her smile.

She comes up with other words – chirping, peeping, tweeting. Yes, the birds are doing all those things today.

'Why do birds sing?' she asks Suzanne.

'They're talking?' Suzanne suggests. 'They're marking their territory? They're happy?'

Julia likes this last explanation best. It strikes her how the birds here in the ghetto are unaware that they are in the ghetto. They're just doing what they've always done. Why can't people be that smart?

It is almost exactly two months that they have been here and Julia has lost so much weight in that time. Her clothes hang on her like a scarecrow's. She sees the same when she looks at Suzanne – she is skinny with a small waist and big eyes. Julia hopes that the weight loss will level off now that their bodies have adjusted to their new diet. It is something she tries not to think about too much.

She changes the subject to their book.

'I never saw that coming,' she says. 'In the book.'

'Saw what?'

'Claudia. I suppose when I dreamed up Birkita's character all I did was to try to imagine what I would like to have been like if I had lived in that time. I thought you'd do the same. But you did something much cleverer.'

'What did I do?'

'I thought you would be Flavia. You know – you, Flavia. But that's not what you did at all. You're going to be Claudia, aren't you?'

'I don't know really,' says Suzanne. 'When I started thinking about characters, I think betrayal was very much on my mind.'

Julia winces inwardly. A knife slices through her gut.

'The guy who betrayed me,' Suzanne continues. 'I wondered why he did that. Was it just a casual thing? Did he do it just because it was the law? Did he never think about the consequences – that there would be people who would be affected by what he did? Or did he hate Jews? And if he did, where did that hatred come from? Or was he – though I think this is a bit unlikely – placed in some kind of dilemma like Flavia, where she has a choice

250

between two options – a risky one that would help other people or a selfish one?'

'Or maybe he knew you were a girl,' says Julia. 'And he felt you had rejected him by not responding to him.'

'I guess that's possible too,' she says. 'I hadn't thought of that. So anyway, that's where Flavia came from. And then I guess, I'm in mourning for my parents. Even though I'm not really. Or rather I haven't started. That just seemed too much, along with everything else we had to cope with. So I thought I had just put them away in a place inside my head and then I would take them out when this was all over. Then I could grieve for them properly. But I guess the mind has its own paths. Even though I had locked them away, they came out in Claudia grieving for her child. So I think that's what happened.'

Julia is enjoying this. It is just like things are back to the way they were. But then, Julia's mouth runs ahead of her brain.

'So will they become lovers?' she asks. 'Birkita and Claudia?'

'I don't think so,' says Suzanne and that is the end of the conversation.

During the afternoon, Adolf appears. He calls Julia over and says he wants to explain to her the plans for this grassy area. He talks of important visitors and children playing on the grass and how long it will take to grow and how luxuriant it has to be. The conversation – well actually, Suzanne would call it a monologue – strikes Julia as a pretty stupid and pointless one. All he is really saying is that they need to get the grass planted in time which everybody knows anyway – and they have plenty of time.

Once during their discussion, as he is talking about what a great team they all are, he puts his arm around her shoulder. Three times – Julia counts them – Adolf points at something or other and each time he does, he contrives to touch Julia's breasts with his hand. Eventually he tells her she can go back to her work.

'What did he want?' asks Suzanne.

'He wants a good kick in the balls is what he wants,' says Julia.

Chapter Seventeen

Romans and Amazons (Suzanne)

On the morning of the day they were to fight, the women were led from their cells into the courtyard. Here two wagons had been drawn up, each of which carried a large iron cage. They were herded into the cages – one for the Romans and one for the Amazons – and then the wagons headed out of the school and into the city. Severus sat up front with one of the drivers while Severus' assistant rode on the other wagon.

People stared at them as they passed. The sight of wagonloads of gladiators heading for the arena was not uncommon, but wagonloads of women were something else. People stared. Insults were shouted. Children ran after the wagons and threw stones or rotten vegetables or balls of mud or shit. The Cow and some of the other women gave the finger and shouted insults back. The Warrior sat on the floor of the wagon quietly. Occasionally she looked at Birkita and whenever she did she smiled.

Claudia, who sat beside Birkita, was shaking.

Neither of them had got any sleep during the night just passed. For most of it, Birkita just held Claudia and tried alternately to sooth her and to convince her that she could survive. It was not something Birkita believed.

The wagons reached the amphitheatre and entered

through double doors into the interior, under the seats. Here the women climbed down and were taken through a succession of iron gates until they reached a torch-lit room. The place smelled of smoke and blood and excreta and fear. Two heavy wooden tables had been set up. On one lay Roman helmets, red tunics, swords and shields. The other had flimsy white tunics – more like short dresses really – and again, swords and shields.

Severus ordered them to take just swords and follow him out into the arena. They went through some more gates and along a torch-lit tunnel. They then passed under a low arch of brick and out from the darkness into the sunlight. At first it was so bright that Birkita was blinded. She shielded her eyes and was gradually able to open them.

From down here the place looked vast – much bigger than when she had sat on the stone benches. The tiers of white seats seemed to rise up endlessly towards a cloudless blue sky. High up, men were deploying the awnings that would shade the audience. They were like ships' sails supported on huge rectangular wooden beams. Other figures moved amongst the seats – they appeared to be sweeping or picking things up. Down in the arena two men were shovelling sand from the back of a cart drawn by a patient donkey. Other men used long-handled rakes to spread the sand and even it out.

Severus got the women to limber up and do some mild play fighting.

'I don't want anybody getting hurt,' he said.

It was as though the Cow hadn't heard him. She knocked one opponent out – she was resuscitated with a bucket of cold water – and a second, she struck her upper arm so hard that the woman was hardly able to lift it afterwards. Given that it was her sword arm it was another death sentence. Severus cursed the Cow.

Around midday when the sun was at its height, he called a halt and ordered them back into the room with the weapons and costumes. On their way in they met the male gladiators coming out. As they passed one another in the corridor, the men tried to grope them and shouted how they would fuck them in the arena or when the Games were over. The women shouted abuse back.

After that it was a just a question of waiting. Soon they started to hear the arena filling up outside. At first there were just the sounds of a few people but slowly this swelled into a buzz and then a roar like waves on the sea. The Warrior sharpened her sword endlessly. The Cow sat in what passed for cross-legged fashion for her and appeared to sleep. Claudia sat deathly pale and quiet. Birkita looked slowly around the room, going from person to person, trying to remember their strengths, their weaknesses, their habits when they were fighting. One of the things she didn't want to do was underestimate anybody. A small wound caused by a poor fighter could mean her death at the hands of someone like the Cow. And the Warrior was an unknown quantity. The hours dragged by mercilessly, Birkita simultaneously wishing they were over and not wanting them to end.

When the noise from the spectators outside and overhead had become constant, Severus reappeared and ordered them into their costumes. Birkita's Amazon costume was so flimsy she felt as though she was naked. With her right breast exposed she thought she might as well have been. Shortly afterwards the Games began. The crowd went quiet and somebody made a speech, though they couldn't hear what was said. When it concluded there was loud cheering. Then the first event – whatever it was – happened to roars of excitement, groans of disappointment, gasps of disbelief. Eventually it appeared to come to an end to tumultuous cheering and stamping of feet that echoed through the brickwork overhead.

A few moments later Severus ordered them to their feet. He formed them into pairs with the Romans in front. Then they went back out and down the tunnel which ended at double heavy wooden gates that opened out onto the arena. Someone behind Birkita was crying. Claudia, who stood beside Birkita, stared straight ahead, a sort of shivering tremor running through her body.

At a signal from Severus, two men opened the gates.

'Romans only,' he said and the first ten women made their way out into the arena. There were cheers and then gasps of surprise as the crowd saw that these were not men. Then came cheering and wolf whistles and a wave of stamping of feet so powerful it felt as though the archway overhead would collapse.

Severus organised the ten Amazons into three ranks with the Cow, the Warrior and Birkita in front. She could see the sense of it. If some of the weaker ones had been in front they might have had very little chance of getting out of the tunnel at all. Birkita glanced behind her. Claudia was in the second row. Now Birkita suddenly felt afraid too. She had only ever fought in practice – never fought to the death, never had people trying to kill her.

Out in the arena, the Romans disappeared out of sight. A few moments later, the women in the tunnel heard the words 'We, who are about to die, salute you' being recited. Somebody behind Birkita whimpered and whoever was crying continued to sob.

The Romans reappeared and gathered in a semicircle about ten paces back from the mouth of the tunnel. Birkita could see what they were doing – try to catch the Amazons when they would be temporarily blinded by the sun and with only three women in the front line.

The cheering in the arena sank to an expectant hush. The hush became a silence, a great stillness in which

256

coughs and the occasional shout or burst of laughter could be heard clearly. Birkita felt the balance of her shield one more time and gripped the hilt of her sword. She heard what sounded like the soft sound of pissing and then she smelt the smell. Behind her, looking down, she saw that a little pool had formed on the sand. When Severus judged that the silence had gone on long enough, he said, 'All right, out you go.'

The Cow shouted something unintelligible and plunged out into the arena like a sprinter. The Warrior and Birkita moved almost as quickly. As they did so all of the Romans charged forward. Everyone was shouting, screaming – urgent, animal cries.

Two women appeared in front of Birkita, hazy outlines in the sunlight. She feinted at the one on the right's head. The woman raised her shield in a reflex and Birkita whipped her sword down towards the woman's belly. The woman tried to bring the shield back down but it was too late. There was a soft sensation of resistance as the point of the blade pressed against the skin. Then the bitterly sharp steel punctured and sliced inwards easily. Blood sprayed out. Birkita's vision was suddenly clear and sharp. The woman dropped both arms. Her legs folded. She settled for a moment on her knees looking up at Birkita with sadness on her face. Then she fell face down on the ground.

It had seemed to happen so slowly yet it must have all been very quick because the second woman was still there with her sword arm coming down at Birkita. Had it hit, the blow would have cleaved her from her shoulder, but Birkita got her shield there just in time. The sword bit into the edge of the shield, sending splinters of wood flying in the sunlight.

Birkita charged her. The move took the woman by surprise. She tried to run backwards but stumbled. Terror flashed onto her face as she realised what was about to happen. Desperately she tried to hold her shield up but Birkita kicked it out of the way. Then she plunged her sword into the woman's heart.

Sweat ran down Birkita's face and forehead and stung her eyes. She was already panting and felt as though her heart would burst.

She looked around. There were two other Romans lying on the ground. One was still and the other was on her side trying to drag herself away from the fighting. Her belly and thighs were soaked in blood and more poured onto the yellow sand as she moved. There were three Amazons down – one was clearly dead, one had taken a terrible cut across the face and appeared to have been blinded, the third was shaking in what looked like death throes. Where was Claudia?

Everything was moving so quickly. The air was full of dust and the smell of animals being butchered. On the edge of her vision a Roman took a blow to the head that shattered her helmet and poleaxed her in a spray of vivid red blood. Another Amazon fell to her knees and a Roman almost decapitated her with a blow. The crowd cheered every time a good blow landed or somebody was hit.

Birkita thought she saw Claudia being pressed backwards by a Roman. There was the small frame and the black hair tied up with a thin strip of green cloth. The Roman was left-handed. Birkita had told Claudia what to do if she found herself facing a left-hander but all that appeared to be forgotten now. As Birkita watched, Claudia either dropped her sword or it slipped from her hand. She uttered an animal-like cry of despair. The Roman grinned and it was as though her whole body suddenly glowed with confidence. She rained blow after blow on Claudia's shield as Claudia stumbled backwards. Birkita ran to her, came at the Roman on her sword side and pushed the sword easily through her ribs.

And suddenly it was all over. There were no more Romans to fight. Six Amazons remained standing – the Cow, the Warrior, Claudia, Birkita and two others. All of them were panting. They stood, spattered with blood and some had cut wounds though none looked very severe. Glancing down, Birkita suddenly noticed that she had a deep gash across the front of her thigh and a sheet of blood had trickled down onto her knee. She had no idea when that had occurred. The crowd was on its feet and the cheering was deafening.

The Cow was walking purposefully from one fallen Roman to the next. Any she found alive she stabbed.

CHAPTER EIGHTEEN

The Earthquake (Julia)

With swords and shields raised in triumph, and to the roars of the crowd, the six women made their way back into the tunnel.

'I'm still alive,' Claudia gasped in disbelief.

'You did well,' said Birkita. 'Really well.'

When they returned to their room, they were surprised to find Sextus there. They were even more surprised at the state he was in. Any time Birkita had seen him, he had seemed imperturbable. Now he was like a different person. Face red, toga awry he held his face centimetres from Severus' and screamed at him. In the light of the torches they could see his spittle flying through the air.

'What the fuck just happened out there?' he asked.

Severus went to say something but Sextus just kept going.

'I'll tell you what happened. The Roman Army – the Imperial legions – were defeated by a crowd of women. That's what happened.'

Severus went to speak again but once more to no avail.

'What did I tell you about who was to win? By the gods, why should I even have had to tell you? It would have been obvious to a blind, deaf and dumb man.'

'You said you wanted sex. You wanted the Amazons to have big breasts. That's what I did.'

Severus' standing up for himself only seemed to make Sextus more angry, if that was possible.

'But not at the expense of a fucking Roman victory,' he shrieked.

'You should have been clearer. The best fighters had the biggest tits.'

'Oh, is that so? "The best fighters have the biggest tits."'

Sextus mimicked Severus' voice.

'"The best fighters have the biggest tits,"' he said again. 'Well thank you for explaining that to me. Now we have the secret. I'll be sure to tell all my friends. I'll shout it from the rooftops. "The best fighters have the biggest tits." I'd wondered what it was about my wife all these years. Now, at last, thanks to you, I've found out.'

Sextus paused to draw breath. Spittle dribbled from his lips. His eyes were flaring.

'Right, here's what we're going to do. Send them back out there.'

He indicated the bloodied group of Birkita, Claudia, the Cow, the Warrior and two others in their torn tunics.

'Six go out, one comes back.'

Severus seemed to have run out of things to try to say. A silence developed with Sextus' face still centimetres from his. It was as though everybody had become momentarily frozen.

Then a voice said, 'And what do we get if we're the one to come back?'

It was the Warrior.

It was the first time Birkita had heard her speak. She had a strong, deep voice and she stood confidently, almost haughtily.

Slowly, Sextus turned his head and looked at her in disbelief.

He seemed unable to speak. The Warrior just

261

gazed calmly at him.

Finally, Sextus raised his arm and pointed a finger at her as though it were a spear.

'You get to live,' he said, his voice suddenly going quiet. 'That's what you get to fucking do. You get to live. Now fuck off out there and give those people their money's worth.'

Somebody – it might have been Claudia – wailed in anguish.

They returned back down the way they had come, stopping by the wooden gates again while an announcement was made outside. Birkita glanced at Claudia who stood beside her. Claudia looked at her but it was like she didn't recognise Birkita or even see her. Claudia's face seemed to have altered – it suddenly appeared both familiar and unfamiliar. She was no longer crying or shivering. In some ways it looked as though her spirit had already left her body – that she was already dead.

The announcement ended, the gates were opened, the women ran out, the crowd roared its approval. The women fanned out.

'Stay near me,' Birkita shouted to Claudia above the noise of the crowd.

She positioned herself on Birkita's right.

In what seemed like moments, the Cow and the Warrior had dispatched the two other women. One moment they were six women standing, the next, two were lying on the ground, bloodied and unmoving.

Now the Cow and the Warrior turned towards Birkita and Claudia. The Cow immediately lunged at Claudia who stumbled backwards to get out of the way. She almost did. But then the crowd cheered, Claudia groaned and Birkita knew she had been stabbed. While the Cow was still at full stretch Birkita lunged at her but the Cow was too quick and pulled herself back out of sword range. Birkita glanced round at Claudia, expecting to see her fallen but she was still on her feet.

'I'm all right,' she said.

'Get behind me,' Birkita shouted, though she knew it was a pointless thing to do. She would be lucky to defeat one of these two; there was no way she could hope to win against both of them. They appeared to be working as a team now and suddenly it was clear to Birkita what was going to happen. They would kill Birkita. Then they would easily dispatch Claudia. After that they would fight it out between each other.

The Warrior closed in on Birkita on her left, the Cow on her right. Birkita fended the Warrior's blows with her shield. She parried the Cow's thrusts with her sword. All the while she backed away from them.

It went on like this with the spectators cheering every time Birkita managed to fend off another attack. But her arms were becoming heavy. They were dropping. She couldn't keep this up for much longer.

She hoisted up the heavy shield again but the Warrior continued to strike blow after blow against it. All the while the Cow lunged at her from the right. Birkita kept on trying to watch both adversaries at once, shielding herself from the Warrior's blows and deflecting cuts from the Cow's sword. It was becoming impossible. It must be only seconds before she would make a mistake, mis-time a move and then it would be all over.

She continued to retreat with Claudia – she assumed – behind her somewhere. The crowd began to boo. The spectators were becoming impatient. Birkita summoned up whatever strength she had left and tried to go on the offensive. She lunged at the Cow, but the blow was easily parried, the Cow batting it off almost negligently.

But the move seemed to aggravate the Cow.

'Come on,' she said to the Warrior. 'Let's get these bitches.'

The Warrior drove forward, leading with her leg and striking several huge downward blows against Birkita's shield, one after the other. Chunks of wood flew from the shield and Birkita thought it might have been cloven in two. The blows vibrated up her arm and through her whole body.

Then the Cow stabbed at her and caught her on her thigh where she was already cut. But this second cut was much deeper. Birkita gasped at the pain and felt her whole leg suddenly become weak as though the strength had been sucked out of it. On the downward periphery of her vision she saw bright red blood sprout from the wound.

Both the Warrior and the Cow were smiling now.

'You know where I'm going to cut you next?' said the Cow.

The fat woman lunged at Birkita's groin with a vicious downward stroke. She tried desperately to move out of the way but her leg failed to respond when she instructed it to move. She stumbled backwards narrowly avoiding the sword cut as it whistled down her belly but as she did so, another crashing blow came down on her shield and finally destroyed it. Chunks of wood tumbled onto the sand leaving a small piece of timber strapped to Birkita's arm. She just about managed to keep her feet but she knew it was the end.

But then there was a loud crack as though something huge – the amphitheatre itself – had broken. The ground began to shake. It was like what she had experienced in the last couple of days but much, much more severe. The loud crack became a steady rumbling that ran in chorus with the shaking. Screams came from the benches. Spectators rose from their seats and started to flee towards the exits. The awnings shading the crowd began to billow like ships' sails and clouds of dust fell from them.

The Warrior and the Cow stopped and looked up and around at the tiers of spectators. Birkita could have maybe taken one of them then but she suddenly felt immensely weary. The thundering and shaking subsided but the rumbling seemed to be still echoing a long way off. A sort of calm returned to the crowds on the benches. They could be seen turning back towards the arena. Some sat down again. The Warrior and the Cow both looked into Birkita's face and hoisted up their weapons for one last push.

But then the ground shook again. The shaking was so violent this time that it caused the Cow to fall onto her back, a sight that would almost have been funny. Her tunic flowered up, revealing flabby thighs and a vast black bush. The Warrior rocked and spread her feet to steady herself like somebody trying to balance on a small raft in a raging river. Somehow Birkita managed to stay standing.

The crowds screamed and began to flee again and this time it looked like everybody on the benches was moving. Large chunks of stonework seemed to rise up and then snap as though they were little more than chips of plaster. Then there was a deafening crack and it was like somebody had drawn a line through the tiers from the ground to the very top. The crack became a roar as a whole section of the amphitheatre, taking spectators with it, came tumbling down in a huge cloud of dust.

Out in the arena, the Cow had struggled to her feet but Birkita and the Warrior had stopped fighting and were staring in astonishment at what was happening.

Then there was another even louder crack and it was as though a long, wide trench, much deeper than a man, had suddenly appeared in the floor of the arena. Before their very eyes the trench lengthened and widened and great chunks of earth and sand and rocks tumbled into it.

The trench had opened up right behind the Cow and now she looked round in alarm. As she did so, the earth disappeared beneath her feet. She hung there for a moment as though suspended in air. Her face was a mixture of surprise and fear. Then she disappeared down into the bowels of earth as though she had been swallowed.

The great beams supporting the awnings began to sway wildly. Then, one by one in succession, the beams snapped as though they were twigs and came tumbling down onto the spectators who had not yet managed to get out of their seats. Crushing people as they went, the huge beams bounced down and eventually came to rest in the arena in a huge cloud of dust.

The Warrior flung down her weapons.

'Let's get out of here,' she said.

CHAPTER NINETEEN

Claudia (Suzanne)

It was an easy enough thing to do. With the Warrior leading the way, they ran round the great trench in the floor of the arena and over to the wall that encircled it. The wall was only the height of a man. With her powerful arms, the Warrior pulled herself up and over it. Then, standing on top, she reached down. She towered over them with her muscular arms and columnar thighs. Birkita knew then she would never have beaten her.

'You go next,' said Birkita to Claudia.

Claudia hesitated and seemed to stumble. Birkita suddenly noticed that Claudia was deathly pale and she was clutching her right side where the Cow had stabbed her.

'Your friend is bleeding,' said the Warrior.

'It must … It must have been deeper than I thought,' said Claudia in a voice thick with pain.

Birkita took Claudia around the waist and lifted her up. The Warrior did the rest, pulling Claudia up by her left arm. She gasped. Birkita followed.

Now it was simply a case of following the crowds who were fleeing towards the exits. The rumbling and shaking had subsided but huge clouds of dust filled the air where the sections of the amphitheatre had been wrecked. Birkita took Claudia's hand as, in front, the Warrior tried to push her way through the panic-stricken people.

Pulled along by the crowd, they flowed out through an exit and reached the top of one of the flights of steps that led down to ground level. Here there was a horrendous crush. People screamed. A man yelled for help as he was pressed against the stone balustrade of the stairway. He tried to extricate himself by pulling himself up on the shoulders of the people around him. But just as he pulled himself free and was half standing half sitting on the balustrade the crowd swayed and he fell off it, dropping to the ground with a scream. Birkita felt something soft underfoot which she knew must be a body but she was pressed in on all sides and could do nothing but stand on it. She squeezed Claudia's hand to make sure she was still there and felt a faint squeeze back. The crowd had carried the Warrior a couple of paces ahead but Birkita could still see her since she was taller than many of the other people. But now the surging crowd lifted Birkita off her feet and she was carried down the steps. Her hand still held Claudia's. Birkita squeezed it tight and prayed that she could hold on.

As they reached the bottom of the steps and people began to fan out over open ground, the crush suddenly eased. The spectators raced away from the amphitheatre as fast as they could. The Warrior was among them – Birkita saw her briefly before she disappeared into the crowd. But now as they tumbled out of the crush, Claudia stumbled and fell, dragging Birkita down with her.

Claudia had fallen on her back. She held both her hands against the side where she had been stabbed. Her once-white tunic was soaked in blood from her chest all the way down to its hem. Blood was bubbling through her fingers. Her eyes were closed.

Birkita found that she was still holding her sword. She dropped it in the dust and knelt by Claudia's head.

'Claudia! Claudia! Wake up!' Birkita said urgently.

Claudia's eyes opened slowly, almost dreamily.

She smiled a weary smile.

'It … It was too much –'

She winced as a spasm of pain passed through her. People continued to pour past them. Birkita didn't know what to do. Cry out for help? Carry Claudia to a physician?

'Too much to think…'

'Don't talk. Just rest. We'll get help for you.'

As she said the words she suddenly knew what to do. Flavia.

'I will take you to Flavia. She will know. She will find a physician.'

Claudia tried to shake her head.

'…that I would have gone into the arena…'

She winced again. Birkita placed her hands in under Claudia's back and knees and braced herself ready to lift her.

'…and survived,' Claudia said.

Then the smile froze on her face and her eyes looked vacantly at the heavens.

Julia gasps involuntarily.

She looks across at Suzanne who is eating, chewing her food slowly in that way that she does, savouring every mouthful.

'Claudia's dead,' she says.

Suzanne nods an almost imperceptible nod. It is more a movement of her eyes than her head.

'I thought they were going to become lovers,' blurts out Julia.

'So did I,' says Suzanne.

CHAPTER TWENTY

The Count of Monte Cristo (Julia)

Eyes blind with tears, Birkita walked away from where Claudia's body lay just outside the amphitheatre. As she looked back one last time, she saw that other people were starting to carry bodies out from the arena and lay them beside Claudia. *At least now you won't be alone.* Claudia had been alone for as long as Birkita had known her – wandering, lost in the darkness of grief. Now at least she would have company as she took the journey into the afterlife. But she had come to love Claudia – frail, gentle Claudia who had belonged no more in a whorehouse than in the arena.

Birkita had torn a strip from her tunic and tied it around the wound on the front of her thigh. It quickly became blood-soaked but no more blood seeped out underneath the rough bandage so she assumed the bleeding had stopped. Her tunic had been fashioned such that it ran across one shoulder leaving her right breast bare. She tore the fabric from her shoulder, ripped it down the centre and then tied it behind her neck, thereby managing to cover both her breasts. Satisfied that she looked just like someone who had been caught up in the collapse at the amphitheatre, she entered the maze of streets.

She wiped the tears from her eyes. She knew where

she needed to go – and she had taken up her sword again, holding it as unobtrusively as possible against her leg as she walked.

The narrow streets were heaving with people. There was a flow, of which Birkita was part, which was coming away from the direction of the amphitheatre. There was now an opposite flow of people who appeared to be struggling to get to it. A squad of soldiers came up the street at the trot, barging people out of the way with their shields.

The shaking had caused great damage in the city too. Statues had fallen, doorways had collapsed, roof tiles lay on the cobblestones and she saw a couple of buildings where the roofs had caved in entirely. Paving stones had been pushed up and stood at crazy angles. Walls had crumbled and in several places water was bubbling up through the cobblestones. One eating-house she passed was on fire inside as was a stable where men were frantically trying to get the wide-eyed, terror-stricken horses out of it.

The cramped streets all looked the same and she had no sense of direction but she asked people and eventually she found herself standing at the V in the road where the lupanar stood.

It appeared not to have suffered too badly. Some roof tiles had fallen off and lay shattered in the street. A huge crack ran up through the plaster on one of the walls. But the building was still standing. The front door was open but there was nobody visible, nobody standing where Cassius or Crispus should have been. Taking a firm grip on her sword, Birkita stepped into the cool shadow of the hallway.

It took her eyes a few moments to adjust. The hallway was deserted and there was no sound coming from any of the cubicles. But then a figure emerged from where the toilet was at the far end.

It was Cassius.

'We're closed,' he said, 'unless you're looking for a job. Then, you talk to me.'

He obviously hadn't recognised her.

But then suddenly, he did.

'British bitch! Wha –'

They were the last three words he uttered in this life.

Birkita charged him, sword arm extended. He put up his hands in a futile attempt to stop it but the sword went right through the palm of one of his hands and buried itself in his heart. He was dead before he hit the floor.

Behind her, the curtains on one of the cubicles rustled and Birkita spun round. It was Bakt, the Egyptian girl. She looked at Birkita, looked at the dead body on the floor and her hands went up to her mouth, so that the scream she might have intended came out as a gasp.

'Birkita!'

Behind Bakt, in the cubicle, the rest of the girls were huddled together, as though they had been trying to seek some kind of protection from the earth-shaking.

'You should escape,' said Birkita. 'You will never have a better chance than now.'

The girls looked at her in stunned silence.

'Escape,' she said again, as though they hadn't understood the first time. 'Go!'

Again nobody moved.

'Where is Flavia?' asked Birkita.

Several pairs of eyes looked upwards.

'Upstairs,' Bakt managed to say.

'Go,' Birkita said one more time before she left them and pounded up the stairs and into the upstairs room.

Where the tiles had fallen off, the roof was open to the sky. Flavia was inspecting the damage. When she saw Birkita she looked like she had seen a ghost. But she recovered almost instantaneously, while her eyes took in Birkita's bloodstained dress and the sword in her hand.

'Birkita – you survived!'

'I need clothes,' said Birkita.

'I can get you clothes,' Flavia said. 'There's probably nothing that would be right here – you know the only kind of clothes we have –'

Flavia laughed a thin, nervous laugh.

'But come up to my place and I will find something for you.'

They went downstairs, out and up the street, pausing only for Birkita to retrieve her money from its hiding place. Flavia talked non-stop about the earth-shaking.

'We thought the whole place would fall down. We thought we were all going to die. They say people have died,' she babbled on.

'Claudia died,' said Birkita.

'I'm sorry to hear that,' said Flavia, 'but it was her own fault. I warned her often enough.'

At Flavia's place, she lifted the lid on a wooden chest and took out several items of clothing. Birkita took a dark green tunic and belt and changed into them while Flavia watched uncertainly.

'Let me clean the wound on your leg,' she offered.

'It's fine,' said Birkita. 'But give me some water.'

Flavia did as she was told.

Birkita drank some of the water and splashed the rest in her face. Then she took up her sword again and moved to the door. Relief flooded Flavia's face like a sunrise.

She thinks this is finished.

'Now,' Birkita said, her body blocking the door. 'Give me the money.'

'What money?' Flavia said in alarm.

'The money you told me about. The money you were going to use to buy your freedom.'

'I've already given it to Antonius.'

'Liar.'

'It's the truth.'

'I've already killed people today,' said Birkita. 'And they were people I had no quarrel with. It wouldn't cost me a thought to kill you.'

'I swear. I gave it to him.'

Birkita stepped forward.

'I'm going to start cutting,' she said. 'I'll start with your hair. Then your face. Then one of your breasts. Then –'

'I'll give you the money,' said Flavia shrilly. 'All right, I'll give it to you.'

Flavia knelt down, rummaged in the bottom of the chest where the clothes were and withdrew a small leather bag of money. She handed it to Birkita who weighed it in her hand.

'There's more,' said Birkita.

'No, that's all of it.'

'You won't look nice with no hair. And when I cut your face, what will Antonius say then? You'll never work again. At least not in this business. Maybe as a beggar.'

Birkita raised the sword.

'All right, I'll give you the rest of it. Only – promise me. You have to take me with you.'

'The money?' said Birkita coldly.

Flavia went to the back of the room, knelt down and using the tips of her fingers, lifted up a flagstone. She lifted something out and handed it to Birkita who stood over her. It was a second leather purse, much heavier than the first one. Tears ran down Flavia's upturned face.

'Now, I will die here,' she said. 'Have pity on me, Birkita. Take me with you – please. Remember what we had.'

Birkita put the purses into the pocket of her tunic. She pointed the sword at Flavia.

'If you know what's good for you, you won't send anybody after me.'

Flavia began to sob. She put her hands together as though in prayer.

'Please, Birkita, please.'

Birkita turned and walked out the door.

She followed the smell of the sea, went downhill, had to ask a couple of people and made it to the port. Along the way she wondered what to do about the sword. She had money, she looked respectable – it would only be drawing unwelcome attention to herself, especially as there appeared to be a lot more soldiers on the street. After a moment's hesitation, she dumped it in a water trough.

At the port, a long breakwater with a tower at its end ran out into the sun-sparkled water. The harbour was crowded with ships moored along the quayside and at anchor further out in the bay. Smaller craft and rowing boats plied their way across the water, intent on their business. Seagulls screamed and laughed overhead.

Birkita hurried along the breakwater, trying to see which ship might be getting ready to sail. From time to time she looked back over her shoulder.

Halfway along she found a small ship where the sailors were in the process of setting the main sail. A short stocky man stood on the raised deck at the rear calmly giving orders. He had thick grey hair, a grey beard and a tunic of uncertain colour. His skin appeared grey. In fact, the overall effect was almost as though he were from the netherworld and didn't belong in this brightly coloured, sunlit scene.

'Hey, captain,' Birkita called. 'Are you sailing soon?'

The man looked at her.

'What's it to you?' he asked, though the words were spoken in a friendly enough way.

'Where are you going to?'

'All the questions. Yes, we're leaving now. And even though it's none of your business, we're going to Baeterrae.'

'Where's that?'

'Gaul.'

'Close to Britannia?'

The man shrugged. 'Closer than here.'

The man shouted an order at a sailor who grabbed a rope and began to pull it.

'Take me with you?' said Birkita.

The man raised a grey eyebrow. 'Don't be ridiculous. Woman on a ship. That's only going to be trouble.'

'Pull in the gangplank,' he shouted and two men came to the side of the ship and began to lift the wooden gangway that connected the ship to the quay.

'I can pay,' said Birkita, going to stand where the end of the gangplank had rested.

'How much?' said the captain.

'As much as you want.'

He named a figure.

'Agreed,' she said.

'Are you serious?' he asked.

'Let me on board and I'll show you how serious I am.'

She held up the purses.

The captain shouted to the two sailors to put back the gangplank. With his head he indicated that Birkita should come aboard. The sailors replaced the gangway and, lifting up the hem of her tunic, Birkita crossed it. As she did so, she heard shouting at the start of the breakwater where it met the land. A claw of fear seized her heart. Trying not to think what it might mean, she hurried across the deck and up the steps to the captain where she counted out the money. She emptied the larger purse and took a little from the other.

'Cast off,' the captain shouted.

Two sailors who were onshore lifted loops of thick rope from great wooden blocks and threw them onto the ship. Then they casually jumped the gap from the quayside to the ship as it began to open up.

The shouting became louder and there was a commotion on the breakwater. Then Birkita saw Antonius and two soldiers break from the crowd. One of his arms was raised and he was shouting.

'Friend of yours?' asked the captain, almost uninterestedly.

'Not a friend,' said Birkita.

She could think of nothing else to say. Was it all going to end here now? After everything she'd been through. She glanced at the rail of the ship. She would drown herself rather than be taken alive.

'Put back in!' one of the soldiers shouted. 'Return to port!'

He appeared to be some kind of officer, judging by the amount of red on his uniform.

'They're telling us to put back in,' a man behind Birkita called.

He was the steersman, manoeuvring a large oar at the rear of the ship. The gap between the ship and the quayside widened. It was already too far for anyone to jump. Birkita looked at the captain. He could put back in now – he had her money. However, he stood impassively, taking in the progress of his ship and the hullabaloo on the quay.

Antonius and the two soldiers had stopped now. They stood on the edge of the breakwater, in the gap where the ship had been, with the officer shouting, 'Return to port immediately! Return to port!'

'I'm sorry, sir,' the captain shouted back. 'After all that shaking I'm afraid it'll do damage to my ship. If that happens, the owner will have my hide.'

The gap between ship and quay continued to widen. The officer looked at Antonius and said something. Antonius' lips moved as he snapped something in reply. His face was red and contorted with anger

'Then drop anchor where you are. We'll send a boat out to you,' the officer shouted.

The captain moved to the edge of the deck and placed both his hands on the gunwale. He leant forward as though trying to hear even though the words being shouted were crystal clear.

'What was that?' he called.

'Change course, captain?' asked the steersman.

'Don't be ridiculous,' muttered the captain.

'I'm ordering you to drop anchor where you are. We're sending a boat out to you.'

The captain raised his hands to his ears and cupped them as though trying to hear better. The ship was far enough off now that the voices were starting to become indistinct. The sail bellied as a breeze filled it.

'What?' the captain shouted again.

The officer's lips moved. He gesticulated with a downward stabbing motion of his hand. The captain shrugged an enormous theatrical shrug and walked back to his spot on the raised deck.

'Fucking Romans,' he muttered to no one in particular.

'It'll probably mean trouble when we come back, captain,' said the steersman.

'It'll mean trouble if they send a ship after us,' said the captain.

'Do you think they will?' asked Birkita.

'Who can tell? They're Romans. They like everybody to do as they're told. Pisses them off when you don't.'

He looked at Birkita and his face broke into a smile.

'Looks like you must have pissed them off royally.'

By now, the figures on the quayside had become much smaller and silent. Birkita watched them until they became indistinct.

'Now, let's see just how much you upset them. If they send a ship after us, we'll know it was on a grand scale. And if they don't … well, it sounds like you might have a good story to tell.'

In the end, no ship came. Evening came on in glorious shades of purple and scarlet and orange and yellow as the sun gradually settled onto the western horizon. The air in Birkita's lungs was cool and fresh. It tasted better than anything she had ever drunk. There was no sign of another ship – they were alone on the ocean. It felt as though they could have been alone in the whole world.

She leant on the gunwale looking out at the setting sun. Only a tiny yellow slice of it remained and soon it too would be gone. She had escaped. And she had had her revenge. Or at least some of it. On Cassius and on Flavia.

How good it was to be free.

But even though the air and the ocean felt clean and unspoiled, her heart didn't feel that way. Claudia had died and Birkita felt a dark shadow upon her at the thought of what she had done to Flavia.

Yes, Flavia had betrayed her. And yes, she could have died in the arena because of Flavia. Why then did she not feel right about what she had done?

She sighed. It was done now and could not be undone; she must live with the consequences.

And just as she told herself not to think about the past, she tried not to think about the future. She was going back to Britain. But what would she find there? All she knew for now was what she would not find there.

30

There is a small wooden shed where Adolf keeps his work gang's tools. It is padlocked and Adolf holds the key. He also uses the place as a sort of office. Each morning when they arrive for work, the first thing he does is to unlock the shed. Then, if the weather is fine and increasingly now, as mid-April approaches, it is, the kommando will stand around in a rough semicircle while Adolf briefs them about what has to be done, allocates work and hands out tools. With the Germans' obsession for order and counting and recording everything, when each tool is handed out, Adolf records the allocation in a book. Each worker is then accountable for their tool and must return it when the day's work is done.

What Adolf does all day isn't a hundred per cent clear to Julia. He seems to go from one place where members of his kommando are working to the next. He will check on progress, muck in for a short while, helping them or – more often – showing them how to do something 'properly'. But then, he'll push off and they may not see him again for several hours. Julia reckons he spends most of his time doing damn all and smoking – he seems to be able to get more cigarettes than most.

Julia and Suzanne are weeding once again, this time on a new patch of dug-over soil. As usual, they alternate between bending down and kneeling in the dirt. A hoe would make all the difference and even though all the hoes were handed out this morning, Julia suggests that maybe one has been finished with and handed back to Adolf. She says she's going to go and see if she can get her hands on one.

The door of the shed is swung back and held in place with a red brick. She finds Adolf inside, sitting at the small table he uses as a desk and smoking. The book where he records everything is open on the table in front of him. As she enters, he becomes busy, picking up a pencil and appearing to study the book attentively.

It turns out there are no hoes available and Julia is about to return to work when Adolf says, 'Would you like a cigarette?' He reaches into a cardboard box, takes one out and hands it to her. Julia's always been able to take or leave cigarettes – and she definitely doesn't want to share one with Adolf.

'I don't smoke,' she says.

'You're a very beautiful girl,' says Adolf.

'Thank you,' Julia says as icily as possible. 'I'd better get back to work.'

'Don't be in such a hurry.'

He gets up and puts the cigarette down in an ashtray. He comes round the table.

'Even if you don't want to smoke, take a break. You won't find too many bosses who say that, now will you?'

Adolf stands a couple of steps away from her.

'I've been thinking about you a lot, Julia,' he says.

Julia says nothing, wondering what the best thing to do is.

'I've been wondering … wondering if you'd be interested in becoming my girlfriend?'

'I don't think so,' says Julia.

'There would be a lot of advantages. I could get you

282

extra food. You've seen – I have cigarettes. Even if you don't smoke you could trade them for something else.'

The prospect is attractive but that's about the only thing about the whole proposal that is. Julia dislikes Adolf and while this by itself wouldn't necessarily be a problem – she's fucked lots of people she didn't like, both men and women – she has another reason. Julia has slowly been coming to the conclusion that she never wants to have sex with a man again. Actually, if she thinks about it and judging by what happened with Suzanne, it seems like she never wants to have sex with anybody ever again – man or woman. Since she's been in the ghetto she hasn't had her period. She wonders if all that part of her body has shut down.

'Are you sure you don't want to think about it?' asks Adolf.

'I'm sure,' says Julia. 'I'm very flattered but I think not.'

'As you wish,' says Adolf.

'Will there be anything else?' she asks.

Adolf doesn't say anything but he lunges towards her and grabs her, putting his arms around her. She resists, she struggles but he is very strong. He tries to kiss her, but she turns her head away. She feels one of his hands make its way crablike from her ass down the front of her thigh and then, hoisting up her skirt, he puts his hand in between her legs. She wriggles and tries to escape but her arms are pinioned by her side.

'Just one kiss,' says Adolf, as he tries to get his hand inside her underwear.

'Let go of me, you fucker,' says Julia.

'Just one kiss,' Adolf repeats.

Julia tries to kick him in the balls but he holds her too tight and she can't lift her leg to get any kind of momentum. She can feel his fingertips trying to probe inside her. He is still trying to kiss her but so far all he has managed to do is to wet her face with saliva.

Julia suddenly relaxes and turns her lips to his.

'That's more like it,' he says and goes to kiss her.

He has eased his grip on her a bit. It is enough for her to raise her leg and stamp her heel down hard onto the top of his foot.

He shouts in pain and breaks away.

'Fucking bitch,' he says.

'Fuck you.'

Julia pushes her skirt back down and walks out of the shed.

This is going to be trouble.

CHAPTER TWENTY-ONE

The Voyage (Suzanne)

On the voyage Birkita learned a little more about the captain.

Contrary to appearances he was less than ten summers older than her – she had thought he was at least double that. His wife had died in childbirth taking the child – a little girl – with her.

'He left on a voyage with a beautiful wife and about to have a family,' the first mate, who was also the steersman, explained to Birkita. 'He came home to "dust", is the word he uses – everything gone.' After that he either sold or just walked away from his house – the first mate wasn't sure which. Now he lived on the ship which was called *Seva* after his wife.

If he had a name, Birkita never found out what it was and nobody on the crew seemed to know. He was simply 'Captain'. Birkita came to learn that the crew adored him – would go anywhere with him, do anything for him, risk anything if he asked them to. Of course the crew were well rewarded for their trouble. 'He shares the profits. There aren't too many captains do that.'

'Does he long for death?' Birkita asked the first mate, wondering if this meant the captain was rash and took wild risks.

'No. But he finds no pleasure in life.'

It might have been a description of her.

Birkita wondered if all of this explained why the captain seemed to have taken her under his wing. Was she the daughter he never had? When Birkita had first hailed him from the quayside, she had already decided that, in addition to paying him money, she would gladly have opened her legs for him. She was way past the point where that would have meant anything to her. But he had looked for nothing like that.

She ate her meals with him and the first mate and she occasionally managed to make the captain laugh. He seemed to like that, though his laughter was as though it came from another time and not something he did any more.

The days passed – an endless procession of blue skies and knife-sharp shards of sun on water. Occasionally they saw the sails of other ships but mostly they were alone upon the sea.

Birkita's skin started to brown under the sun – she had been so pale, had spent so much time indoors. Her body healed. In the lupanar she had felt as though she was little more than a vessel into which men pumped their poison. She had been beaten, bruised, bitten, punched and slapped. At times it had felt as though her insides were being destroyed. Here, on the ocean, with the warm breeze on her skin, the sun on her back, clean air in her nostrils, she felt her strength returning, her body becoming whole again.

She asked the captain about how they knew where they were and how they didn't get lost. He explained about navigating with the sun by day and the stars by night. He seemed to get great pleasure from showing these things to her. It was as though he had always intended to do them with his own daughter.

She asked if she could help and she was given menial chores to do – preparing vegetables, cleaning. She cooked a meal and the result was so successful that she was made the cook. Several of the crew looked at her in that way that she knew so well but under the captain's protection, there was never a problem. It was as though she was the captain's daughter with all the respect that that implied.

Being out there on the vast ocean, Birkita wondered if the gods really cared about her or anybody. She thought of the people who had come before her – not just the people that the bull Roman had killed but all of her ancestors way back to the first people. Why had they come into the world? What had their suffering been for? Did the gods really watch everything that went on? Did they care? Were there any gods? And if there were, what had she and her family and her village and her whole people done to deserve the punishment that had been visited on them? Soon she would die and it would be like she had never existed. There was nobody alive now who would even remember her.

But strangely enough, in this there was a certain comfort. She found she was able to stop thinking about the past – at least for long periods of time. And the future? That too she could forget about – at least for now. She found herself wishing that the voyage would never end. As she lay in bed, rocked by the gentle motion of the sea, she thought about asking the captain if she could join the crew but she laughed at the thought. It was a ridiculous idea. Anyway – there was something she had to do. Until that was done, there could be nothing else.

She had been surprised at how little the death of Cassius had satisfied her and as for Flavia, she still felt the guilt of that. They had been so close, so intimate. What would happen to Flavia now? If she was lucky, she would end her days in the lupanar.

And if she wasn't?

Birkita preferred not to think about that.

31

Next morning it looks as though Adolf has started to get his own back on Julia. Rather than letting her and Suzanne work together he sends them off in two different gangs. It is like this for the next few days. Julia consoles herself with the fact that once all this beautification of the ghetto is finished, she'll hopefully get moved into some other type of work and away from Adolf. Or the war might end. In the meantime, there is the book.

Though they didn't intend it this way – they hadn't really thought about it all – the book seems to be about to divide naturally into two parts. Part One is Birkita's outward journey from Britannia, Part Two is going to be her return and her search for revenge on the bull Roman.

Looking at them now, Julia thinks that there has been an inevitability to all of the chapters in Part One. Each one has flowed pretty inescapably from the one that came before it. Right now, Part Two is a blank canvas. Other than the business of Birkita getting her revenge, they have little else. It would have been nice to have been working side by side with Suzanne so that they could have started to talk about all of this but Adolf has put paid to that.

Birkita is going to land in Baeterrae which, as Suzanne has explained, is on the south coast of France – Gaul. Birkita then has to make her way to Britannia. Julia thinks there is no point in covering any of that in the story. The reader wants to know about Birkita's revenge. A journey through all of France, whatever adventures might occur along the way, is just going to bore people. They need to get Birkita to Britannia as quickly as possible. Of course, that's the great thing about writing a novel. They can get her there in just one line: 'As soon as the ship tied up in Londinium, Birkita walked down the gangplank and set off on the road that led north-east.'

So Julia starts to ponder what might happen next? What form will Birkita's revenge take? Will she really crucify the bull Roman or will it be something else? Does the bull Roman have a family? Children? That's another thing that Julia loves about writing – the possibilities.

That evening when they have handed in their tools and are heading wearily back to their barracks, Julia notices there is something different about Suzanne. Her usual dreaminess seems to have been replaced by something else. Is she smiling more than usual? She's always very optimistic and positive but there's something more this time. There is a sense about her of a secret she will never tell.

Before she has gone to sleep, Julia has worked out what it is. Suzanne has fallen in love.

Julia's theory is confirmed almost immediately. Suzanne is suddenly less interested in the book. When Julia starts to ask her about Birkita's revenge, Suzanne says she'll have to think about it, adding that it's good that Birkita is on the ship – while she is making the sea voyage, Suzanne and Julia can take their time thinking about what is to come next.

This is completely out of character for Suzanne. Up until now, it is she who has spoken of the urgency to get the book written – how the war won't end until it's done. And of course, there has always been – unspoken but constantly in the back of their minds – the worry that they might be separated or deported from the ghetto. After all, there was a deportation of nearly a thousand people as recently as February.

When Julia realises that this is indeed what has happened, the shock is really more than she can bear. And the Pandora's box that this has opened begins not with Suzanne but with Julia herself.

She has come to hate men. She has seen what they have done to the world. They are all about anger and aggression and violence. Even their bodies show it – the erect penis like a sword, wanting to hurt, to damage, to penetrate, to pierce. How different from the self-contained beauty of the female form. So Julia had come to the conclusion that she wants nothing further to do with men. If there is to be anyone in her life in the future, it will be a woman.

And she had thought that that woman would be Suzanne. Despite what happened the night of the betrayal (as Julia thinks of it), she had still hoped that she and Suzanne could build a future together; that after the war was over they would stay together. It is this prospect, as much as the book that has kept Julia going. Indeed, if it had been somebody other than Suzanne who had proposed the book, Julia sees now that she is not sure if she would have had much interest in it.

A future without Suzanne is the bleakest future Julia can imagine. In fact, it is not a future at all; not a future she would want.

Suzanne seems oblivious to all this and Julia is too distraught to speak to her about it.

Julia is even more distraught when she finds out that the man Suzanne has fallen for – for it is a man – is Adolf.

32

'I don't believe you,' Suzanne says angrily.

It's at this point Julia knows she should have stuck to her earlier instinct and not spoken about this to Suzanne. It's too late now, of course.

'Why would I lie? What reason would I have?' Julia asks.

'What reason? You're jealous. That's what reason. You wanted me and when I offered myself to you, you rejected me. And now you don't want anyone else to have me. Or maybe now you know what you've lost and you want it back. Well, it's too late, Julia. You had your chance.'

'Look, please – I'm telling you the truth. I know what happened between us can't be undone but not Adolf. Anyone but him.'

'He's a good man, Julia – and he can get extra food. I don't know about you but I can't take much more of this. We're dying on our feet. This can save us. And don't worry, I'll share the food with you, if that's what you're wondering about.'

'That's not fair, Suzanne. You know it's not the food.'

'He's a good man, Julia.'

'He's not a good man.'

'Oh, and you'd know, would you?'

'Yes, I would know.'

'Really. And how is that?'

Julia and Suzanne have been sitting against a wall out in the courtyard. It is April and the heat of the day hasn't quite evaporated yet. Now Suzanne gets up and stands opposite Julia, hands on her hips.

Julia had never intended that it would come to this – but now it seems like there's no going back. It is her last card.

'Sit down,' she says quietly.

'I'd prefer to stand,' says Suzanne, though her voice becomes a bit calmer.

'Remember I told you I was an actress,' Julia begins.

Suzanne nods.

'And you asked if you'd ever seen any of the films I was in.' Julia laughs a brittle laugh.

'I very much doubt if you would have. You see, they were … well, adult films.'

'Adult films?' asks Suzanne, uncomprehending.

She really is so innocent in so many ways.

'Dirty films! Sex films. I would have sex with men in them.'

The light has come on.

'And women,' Julia adds.

'What's that got to do with any of this?' asks Suzanne.

She tries to continue her angry tone but she is clearly taken aback.

'Because I've a lot more experience of men than you have. I've met his type a thousand times before. He's bad news. He'll break your heart … Or worse.'

'Well, it's my heart,' says Suzanne, and with that she storms off.

Suzanne doesn't come back that night. Julia assumes she is with Adolf. In the morning at the hut, waiting for their work assignments, Suzanne looks radiant despite her bony face, big eyes and shrunken frame. They stand at opposite ends of the semicircle of people and Suzanne looks defiantly at Julia. Mercifully, they are put in separate gangs and don't see each other for the rest of the day. Nor does Suzanne come back for food or bed that night.

Julia thinks she now knows what Birkita must feel like having lost everything. She finds herself thinking more and more about the girl on the ship in their story. Julia wonders if Birkita could have been an ancestor of hers, many, many generations back. She finds herself spending long hours thinking about this as she works silently, oblivious to her workmates around her. Could it have happened that an ancestor of hers had a life that mirrored Julia's?

And as Julia becomes more and more the girl on the ship, the girl who has suffered so much, Julia finds herself asking what Birkita would have done? What would she have done if she were here now instead of Julia?

The answer comes to her easily.

Birkita would have carried on.

CHAPTER TWENTY-TWO

Britannia (Julia)

As soon as the ship tied up in Londinium, Birkita walked down the gangplank and set off on the road that led north-east. It had been early spring when she had left Pompeii. It was the beginning of summer now.

The captain of the *Seva* had brought her to Baeterrae just as he had promised. She had been cheerless when the voyage ended. She would have happily stayed on the ocean for months – indeed for the rest of her life.

The captain embraced her before she left, holding her and whispering in her ear that she should be careful. He gave her food and some money – quite a lot of money – essentially what she had paid him in the first place. She had the feeling that there were lots of other things he wanted to say. She sensed that, had she asked him to let her become part of the crew, he would have agreed. Indeed, she felt that if she had asked him to adopt her, he would have said yes to that too.

She had had a lot of time to think on the voyage. Elbows on the wooden rail, looking out over the achingly beautiful blue of the Mediterranean, she had come to understand that everybody made the journey alone. Yes, maybe at times in our lives, we were thrown together with other people – our families through birth, friends and acquaintances that we met along the way – but ultimately we were alone. The gods just told this to some people more forcibly than others. In this she and the captain had a lot in common. Maybe – in this – they had everything in common.

In Baeterrae, Birkita had used some of the money to buy a horse, a saddle, clothes, shoes, a sword and a dagger. Thus equipped she'd set off for the north, arriving after a moon's travelling at a port called Caletum. Here she sold the horse and saddle and caught another ship to take her to Britannia. She had looked forward to another voyage but this one was very different. The sky was constantly overcast with low, grey pillows of cloud. There was a lot of rain. The iron-coloured sea was lashed by a vicious wind which drove waves over the sides of the ship. The captain said it was too dangerous for passengers to be above decks and so she stayed in a cabin with the other travellers. Like them, she spent most of the journey vomiting. When the sea eventually calmed, and she came out on deck, the sky had cleared to a washed-out blue and the ship was sailing sedately up a wide river. It docked just after noon.

The Romans were rebuilding Londinium. Last year – could it really have been such a short a time ago? – it had been sacked and razed to the ground by Boudica. Much of it looked like a drawing in charcoal. There were charred timbers, roofless shells of houses, piles of rubble, lone walls, fire-ravaged, blackened patches of ground overlaid with green weeds and bushes, boarded-up buildings. And then, almost as if by a miracle, a lone house or the odd tree that had escaped damage. There were also signs of rebuilding. Scaffolding around houses, masons or plasterers or carpenters whistling cheerily or calling to one another. No wonder they were happy – there would be work here for the rest of their lives.

Birkita had decided she would walk the rest of the

way. A horse would only draw attention to her. Anyway, the four days or so that it would take would give her time to think – because there was much to think about.

She had thought that being back in Britannia would fill her full of a vengeful energy. She had hoped that this would be the case. But instead, as she headed out into the countryside, she found she felt as desolate as the destroyed city she had just left behind. She would find the bull Roman and kill him or she would confirm that he was already dead. It was possible that he was no longer here – that he had been sent back to Rome or to some other part of their empire. If that was the case, he was probably lost to her – though she could have made it her life's quest to find him, to hunt him down wherever he was.

The thing though, was that it didn't seem to matter to her. She imagined herself actually finding him and killing him. The thought didn't give her a great deal of satisfaction. And even if all that happened what would she do then? Where would she go?

She tried not to dwell on this. When her mind pulled her into the swamp of these thoughts, she tried to haul herself back out again. She tried to focus on the sights and sounds around her. It had been around this time last year when she had travelled this road in the opposite direction. She had been in shock then and hardly remembered the days passing or the countryside she'd journeyed through.

Today, mercifully that was different. In at least one way it was good to be back in the land of her birth. She had forgotten how beautiful it was. The hypnotic effect of hour after hour walking on the grey stone of the Roman road freed her mind to travel wherever it would. She savoured the woods she passed through and the cool water of the rivers on her feet as she forded them. There was birdsong and bees and butterflies and the smells of the grasses and flowers and ferns. She saw hares and rabbits and foxes and badgers and deer. Once when she stopped for a break, to drink water and eat some bread and cheese, a ladybird landed on her knee and she remembered the ladybird she had watched all that time ago, before all this had happened. She felt her heart would break at the memory.

She shunned companionship. If she encountered people on the road, she quickly walked by them in silence. A few times she was harassed by men but a menacing look, some harsh words and showing them the handle of her sword peeping out of her pack was enough to keep them at bay.

At night, she didn't seek out an inn or any kind of resting place. Rather, she left the road and found a grassy place in a forest by a stream. There was no need for a fire – the summer nights were warm – and she was happy to eat bread, cold meat, cheese and fruit that she had bought along the way. She had also bought a skin of ale and it was good to drink that again after the Romans' wine-piss.

After that she would wrap herself in her cloak, use her pack as a pillow and gaze up at the stars – familiar from her childhood – until she fell asleep. In some ways, those few days brought her back to the sea voyage from Pompeii. Once again, it was like she was alone in the world with no past dragging at her and no future with which she would have to contend.

On the fifth day she found what remained of her village. It wasn't much. Where the houses had burned to the ground were scorched patches of earth. The stockade which had encircled the village was little more than a few sections of short blackened poles, no more than knee high, like rotten teeth. Nature had begun to reclaim the site. Weeds and grasses and some saplings were already starting to sprout across the patch of land. In another summer or two it would be like the place had never existed.

Birkita remembered how it had looked – people going about their business, carrying water, tending animals, cooking, talking, laughing. She pictured the animals that had been part of their lives – cattle, sheep, chickens. She thought of her two dogs and all the time they had spent together.

She thought about her parents. She had last seen them heading off to join Boudica's army. Her father – the headman of the village. A natural leader but never taking life too seriously. Funny, always laughing, cynical about anything that wasn't to do with what he called 'real life' – food, animals, crops, the seasons. She suspected he had known, at some level, that Boudica's rebellion was going to end in disaster but he had gone anyway. Really, he hadn't had any choice – there were times when things other than 'real life' took over – and what could you do then?

And then her mother. She adored her husband – her face seemed to light up every time she saw him or heard him speak. And yet she was so different from him. Serious a lot of the time – though maybe somebody had to be. Somebody had to suffer the pain to bring the children into the world and care for them and worry about them.

And what difference had any of her mother's fretting made in the end?

Birkita's mother had gone too, to be with her husband, to fight beside him as was the way. What had become of them? What had that last battle been like? How had they died? Had their deaths been clean or had they died slowly, agonizingly? Had they been together in each other's arms at the end? Or had the Romans taken them and tortured them? Birkita had once thought that they might have been made slaves just as she had been but something inside her told her that they were gone.

They were with the gods – all of them, all those she had known and loved. There were countless other people in the world, of course but these had been the ones she had loved and worked and played and laughed with. Now that she was here, she saw their smiling faces clearly, could picture them as they had been. All gone. They had created in this lovely land a place of tranquillity and beauty and it had all been destroyed. Why? What had anybody gained by that?

She remembered her dogs – Sun and Moon. Fleetingly, she wondered if what remained of their bodies was still around, but when she looked there was nothing. The bodies of all the dead dogs had been taken by other creatures. She hoped she would meet them too in the afterlife.

Birkita sat for a long time. The place still smelt faintly of fire and burning. She ran her fingertips through some new shoots of grass that had begun to emerge, moving them back and forth. She felt the sun on her back. Tears rolled down her cheeks until she wondered how there could be any tears left inside her.

She didn't have the courage to go to the Haven. Her stomach churned. She was too upset to eat anything. When it grew dark and it became time to sleep, she just lay down on the warm earth and prayed to the gods to give her strength for the next day.

CHAPTER TWENTY-THREE

Return to the Haven (Julia)

The crosses hadn't been touched.

The Romans would have left them there anyway and Birkita assumed that none of her own people had been left alive to return and take them down.

One cross had fallen down, one stood at a crazy angle and the other two – those of the two children – were still standing as upright as the day they had been put there. It was Banning's that had fallen. Birkita assumed it was his heavier weight that had brought the cross down in some winter storm. The wind that had felled him had come from the front, so that what remained of Banning's body lay face up.

Not that much remained of any of the bodies – just ghastly, grinning skulls and bones and some shreds of clothing. The birds and rats had done their work well and picked the bones clean.

Painstakingly, one by one, Birkita lowered the crosses, extracted the nails as gently as she could and freed the bodies. She laid them on the ground, beside one another. As she worked she prayed to the gods to take these four people that she had loved into their care. She felt a great weight on her, like the gods were pressing their feet on her back. At times she still found herself not believing that this had actually happened.

When the bodies were all down, Birkita used her sword to hack away the thorns and brambles and foliage that obscured the entrance to the Haven. Then using her cloak as a sort of litter, she dragged the skeletons one by one and carried them inside the Haven. They would be together in the next world.

She sealed up the entire entrance passageway with boulders and logs. The work took her two days. She stopped only to eat or drink or sleep. When the passageway was blocked she covered the entrance, pushing back everything she had cut down. She dug up saplings that the wind had sown and replanted them around the Haven. When she had finished her work, the place looked like nothing more than a great boulder resting on the ground in the middle of a forest. Very few people came here anyway and she assumed that any people that had known about its existence were dead now. In a few years the thorns and the trees would cover it and her brother and his wife and their two children could rest in peace, together, for ever.

When all of this was done, she made a fire from dead wood and burnt the four crosses, scattering the ashes once they had cooled. She slept one more night here lying face down on top of the boulder of the Haven, feeling her heart beat against the stone and remembering the people who lay beneath her.

Birdsong woke her the next morning. She had slept deeply. She rose, went to a pool she knew close by, stripped and washed her body all over. Then she ate some food, strapped on her weapons and went to seek her vengeance.

33

It has been five days since Julia and Suzanne argued; five nights that Julia has slept by herself. She assumes that Suzanne is safe – or rather, that she is with Adolf.

Julia has kept writing over these few days. Every day she has written at least two pages of tiny writing. This is about as much as she can manage given that she is writing by hand and also that there is a limited amount of time between when she gets back from work and has something to eat, and before lights out.

Adolf has taken to giving her harder work to do. If there is lifting of rocks or stones to be done, that is given to her. This means that she is even more bone-weary when she comes in from work. But despite this, no matter how physically tired she feels, she finds that her mind is fresh and ready to go. And she knows why.

The writing has saved her.

She can write from the heart about Birkita's desolation because that is exactly what Julia is feeling. The ghetto is hopelessly overcrowded yet Julia has never felt more alone. And she sees the writing as her only hope, the only light in her darkness.

She doesn't yet know how the book will end. She and Suzanne have never talked about this. Or rather, they have but it has always been to say, 'we'll see.' They want to see where the characters will take it. But by continuing to write, Julia is pushing Birkita's life forwards. Julia knows that Birkita will eventually get out of the terrible place she is in. She has to. If she didn't, if the book ended now, the reader would feel cheated. And it would be a drab ending. Actually, it would hardly be an ending at all – it would be like the book had been just abandoned, left there.

Julia thinks how wonderful it would be if her life moved forward as well. How great it would be for the war to end, the book to be finished, Suzanne to come back into her life and for them to do all the things they had talked about.

Of course, she has little confidence that this is what will happen. She hopes she will survive to the end of the war. No matter how desolate the future might be, she loves life. But after *that* – what she had with Suzanne, she feels is lost and can never return. Yet she does feel a faint glimmer of hope. She assumes that if she didn't she would be dead. Or at least have given up. She pictures this hope as a tiny, tiny candle flame burning, barely visible, glimpsed way off in the distance through the tall trees of a vast, dark forest – the way Birkita might have seen it.

Somehow, this hope is tied up with the book. Every day that Julia writes, every piece of the story that she adds, pushes Birkita forward, out of the darkness that she is in. And Julia hopes that just as Birkita is making slow but steady progress towards the light, then maybe Julia is too.

At least this is the thought that she comforts herself with as, writing finished for the day, mentally and physically exhausted, she closes her eyes and almost instantly falls asleep.

'Julia!'

Somebody shakes her. She moans, thrashes under the blanket as if that will push them away.

'Go away.'

'Julia! Wake up! Julia, I have to talk to you.'

Julia opens her eyes. Or maybe she doesn't.

But he is there. His face. The smell of him. The smell that she once loved because it comforted her. Protected her. Made her feel safe.

But now it's not like that.

How did he get here? She thought he was dead. But he's back. Here. In the Paradise Ghetto.

Was he here all along? Had he seen her? Was he watching her? Just waiting for the moment. Like he used to. When her mother was out. Is she here too? But that's no good because she will just do what she always did. Nothing. Even animals watch over their young.

'Julia!'

I can scream. I am in a room full of people. Surely one of them will come and save me.

'Go away! Please ... somebody save me!'

But of course she realises that nobody will come to her. People scream in their sleep all the time in the ghetto. Mostly, any screaming is just met with cries of 'Shut up!' and 'Go back to sleep!'

'Julia! Stop Julia! Stop. It's me – Suzanne.'

Julia opens her eyes. This time she is sure that she does. She screams again but then sees that Suzanne's face is above hers, looking down, her features just about visible in the faint light.

She has come back.

'Julia – it's me, Suzanne.'

'Suzanne – you've come back.'

Suzanne shakes her head. Or maybe she doesn't. Julia is still a bit groggy and can't be sure. She was sleeping so deeply. It was like death.

'I've brought you some food,' says Suzanne. 'Just like I said I would.'

'Thank you … that's … that's very good of you.'

'These last few days,' Suzanne says. 'I kept thinking about how we had left things. I said some horrible things. I just wanted to say I'm sorry. I want things to be good between us again.'

Julia is awake now. She lies on her back while Suzanne sits on the blanket.

'They are … it's all right,' Julia says. 'As you said, people do what they can … what are you doing here anyway?'

Adolf had to go to a meeting tonight. He won't be back until late. So I came here to see you.'

'After curfew?'

'He has friends. He was able to give me a pass in case anybody stopped me. Not that they did.'

'So everything's good with him?' asks Julia.

'I know what you think, Julia, but he's a good man. And now he's my man.'

Julia says nothing to this. Suzanne continues.

'After the war – when this is all over – we're going to get married.'

'That'll be nice,' Julia forces herself to say.

If Suzanne notices the grudging nature of the words, she doesn't remark on it. Instead she says, 'I'm in love, Julia. Be happy for me. Say that you are.'

'I am. I am happy for you.'

'I want you to be my bridesmaid,' says Suzanne. 'And then some day you'll find somebody and I'll be your bridesmaid. What do you think?'

'That'll be nice,' Julia says a second time.

Then she asks, 'What about the book?'

'You know – I'd forgotten all about it,' says Suzanne. 'Have you still been writing it?'

'I have.'

'So tell me everything that's been happening.'

Julia does so. Then she tells Suzanne that she has some questions about various 'research-type things'. Does Suzanne mind if she asks them before she goes? Suzanne says she doesn't, Julia asks and gets the answers she needs.

'Do you think you'll come back to it?' Julia asks.

'I don't know,' says Suzanne. 'I've got too much on my mind right now.'

34

It is while she is working the next day that Julia remembers her screaming of the previous night. Or more precisely she remembers those moments before it. Or were they hours?

And now she remembers.

She remembers it all. Everything.

It happened. There was a first time and then often after that, so that eventually, all the times ran into one.

Her mother was out. She can't remember how old she was. Nine? Ten? Somewhere around there.

The things he did. They did. There was something not right about them. There was a strange feeling.

She felt strange but he seemed strange too – like he was a different person.

He said nothing while it was happening. And she knew that if she told anybody they wouldn't believe it. For a long time she didn't believe it herself.

Where was her mother? How did she not know?

It hits Julia like an express train and an even more gaping abyss opens up.

She did know.

All the time she knew and she did nothing.

They might not have believed Julia but they would have believed her mother. Even an animal takes care of its young. The thought keeps going around in her head. A bitch. A she-fox – a vixen. A lioness. A swan. Julia has an image of a mother swan frantically trying to protect her eggs against men. Any of them – all of them – would have protected their young, would have given their lives to protect their young.

Her father had been a pillar of the community. At the synagogue. Not that that had saved her. Not that it had stopped him. She got some small satisfaction from the fact that, as soon as she left home, she had stopped going.

She assumed that when the Germans came for him, her father had been escorted away by police just as she had been. She smiles at that. But he should have been escorted away by police years earlier.

Now that this door has opened, the memories come tumbling in on her. What had been one incident starts to separate out into many different ones. Not just the times themselves but their whole lives together. Normal times – if, now, you could call anything in that house normal. Meals together – within hours of him having come to her. Holidays. Things they talked about and did while all the time this was going on.

No wonder she had been driven to get out. Julia thought back to that day when she had to decide – stay or go? She knows now she would have died had she stayed. Somehow some part of her – was it her body? – had known. Get out while there's still time. Before it kills you. Before he kills you.

No wonder she took so easily to the films. She had been doing that probably before any of the people she had worked with.

She remembers now how she used to wash, take baths. She never felt clean afterwards – no matter how hard she scrubbed herself or how fresh was the new underwear she put on.

And unlike Birkita, there is no revenge to be had here. Or is it that the Germans have already taken it for her? No – they have robbed her of the opportunity to see him stand in court and be accused and deny it.

But then nobody would have believed her. She's back to that. It would all have been for nothing. Even if it got that far it would have been her word against his. And her mother would have tried to stop her. And if, by some miracle, it had come to court, her mother would probably have spoken up for him. Spoken up for him. All she-animals protect their young. What had been wrong with her mother? What flaw was in her that stopped her from doing that? That allowed it all to happen?

All these questions and no answers. The perpetrators dead. Nobody even to talk to about this.

But would she? Even to Suzanne?

That's if Suzanne were here.

Maybe she would have. With the old Suzanne. But not now.

Julia's mind picks over these memories like the ghastly leftovers of some vast feast.

She thinks about the book and how Birkita is poised to get her revenge. But that is just in a book. Julia almost sneers at the thought. Real life is never like that.

CHAPTER TWENTY-FOUR

Birkita's Search (Julia)

Now that she was back in the place of her birth, Birkita began to talk to people, to understand what had gone on while she had been away. She learned that after the crushing of the rebellion, there was much killing and slave-taking. But with the onset of winter that had died down.

When spring had come, the Romans had begun to seize Iceni land and hand it out to their own people. When Birkita heard this, she was sure that it would only be a matter of time before the rich land that her village had farmed, would go that way. She was dismayed. Somewhere in the back of her mind, she had had the vague thought that when the bull Roman was dead, she would return to her village and start to rebuild it. If what she was hearing now was true, there would be no return and no rebuilt village. It was another door to the future closed. She tried not to dwell on it, to think about the job still to be done.

She had to assume that the Romans who had killed her family had come from some place close by. The nearest town was called Venta Icenorum by the Romans. That was where she would begin her search.

Venta Icenorum had started life as a Roman army camp. Birkita's father had recalled it being built. Since then, though the army was still quartered there, a civilian population had also grown up. Birkita had often been there to sell animals or crops and to buy supplies. She set off for there now. One of the people she had spoken to had told her that the Iceni were no longer allowed to carry weapons, other than a dagger for eating, so she hid her sword in some undergrowth near the village. She would return for it when the time came.

As she walked the road to Venta, Birkita's thoughts returned to the kind of vengeance she would exact. She had thought first to kill the bull Roman, to torture him to death by crucifixion, just as he had done to her loved ones. In reality though, there was no revenge that could fit the crime. The bull Roman had taken everything and everybody she loved – even down to her dogs. On the scales of justice, what could possibly balance that out? If he had a family she could kill all of them before she killed him. But these, if they existed, were innocent people. It wouldn't be right to kill them, no matter how much the sight of it might hurt him.

She began to understand that the best vengeance was the one she had taken on Flavia and that that was why it had troubled Birkita the most. Kill somebody and they were gone; their suffering was at an end. But the thing was to prolong that suffering – and not just for a few hours or days, by torturing them – but to condemn them to a lifetime's suffering. That was what the bull Roman had done to her. For as long as she lived she would endure the anguish that she woke to every day. Maybe it was possible that the years might lessen it a bit but it would always be there. That was what she needed to do to the bull Roman – to find a way to make him suffer for as long as he breathed.

But first she had to find him.

It was a market day and crowds of people with animals

315

and produce to sell were flocking to Venta. Birkita joined the throng queuing at the Eastern Gate. The town still showed its origins as a Roman camp. A deep ditch ran round the perimeter and inside that was a raised bank with a wooden palisade. A bridge of logs with beaten earth on top crossed the ditch to the gate. Inside the buildings were mostly single storey and of wood. Occasionally, there was one on two levels, built of stone with a tiled roof.

Birkita went to the market square. There she found an inn with tables outside. She ordered some ale, cheese and bread and settled down to wait.

The first day came and went. Lots of Roman soldiers passed through the square, sometimes in ones and twos wandering amongst the stalls looking to buy things, sometimes marching in squads – but none of them was the bull Roman. The innkeeper became irritated with her for holding on to a table all day so she inquired whether he rented any rooms. He did and she took one on the upper storey that overlooked the square. Here, she spent all of the second day gazing down on the activity below her but there was still no sign of her target.

On the third day, she thought she saw him – at the head of a squad of soldiers. The man had the same build and heavy features. But as she looked more closely, Birkita saw that the face under the helmet was very different – it was pale and with kinder, almost humorous, eyes.

As the fourth day dawned and Birkita took up her position at the upstairs window, it began to dawn on her just how stupid the quest she had set herself was. How was she going to find one Roman soldier in all of Britain? There must be thousands of them here. And this presumed that the bull Roman was still in Britain. He was a soldier – soldiers died, they got moved around. She wondered how many more days she should do this.

Then another idea came to her. She could go to the barracks and ask after him. That was it. She would pretend that she was pregnant and go to the gate and describe him to the guards. She could say that he had told her his name was ... Antonius. She could say that she wanted to speak to him.

But then what? Maybe the guards would just laugh at her and chase her away. And even if they didn't and they brought him to her, what would she say then? If it turned out to be him, she could always say that he wasn't the man. At least she would know then that he was there. It was a thin plan, but no thinner than what she was doing at the moment. She decided she would give it today and then see tonight whether this other idea was worth trying.

The sunlit square began to fill up. Farmers and stall holders set out their wares. People appeared in ones and twos and then gradually this became a steady flow as the morning progressed. It was nearly noon when Birkita saw a blocky man wearing a long brown tunic. The man's tunic was tied at the waist with a belt and his belly bulged over it pushing it downwards. His face was very florid.

She noticed him only because of who he was with – a tall, thin woman with jet black hair and a strikingly serene face. They seemed an odd combination – apart from anything else the woman was taller than the man. But what was most notable about the face was not so much its beauty – because Birkita thought it was beautiful – but rather that it carried a huge blue bruise around one eye and taking up most of one side of her face.

There were also two young girls – Birkita would have guessed their ages to be about six and eight – the same ages as Banning's daughters, her nieces. The two girls held one another's hands while the woman walked slightly ahead, looking at what was on offer, picking up items, sometimes smelling them or asking questions of the stall owners. She carried a basket and occasionally bought something and put it into it.

As Birkita watched them making their way through the crowded square, she found that she had jumped to her feet. She would hardly have noticed this pair at all had it not been for that huge bruise, so striking against the woman's pale face and red lips, framed in her straight black hair. She had only seen the man's face for an instant and now he had his back to her. But he was the right build. How could she have been so stupid? All along she had been looking only at soldiers but what if he had left the army but stayed here? That he was one of the people to whom the Romans were giving the stolen Iceni land?

She ran downstairs and out into the market square, threading her way through the crowd. She thought for an instant that she had lost them, but then she saw the top of the woman's head, her hair glossy in the sunlight. Birkita moved closer. Now she could see the man – but again it was his back, the thick neck with dark hairs on it, the powerful shoulders and muscular arms. Birkita squeezed her way between two stalls so that she was behind the stall holders. She worked her way along, moving in parallel with the man until she was slightly ahead of him.

From the side it could have been him. The build was right as was the ruddy face. One of the little girls must have said something because the man looked down. His lips moved as he replied. Then, as he was lifting his head back up, he seemed to sense that someone was looking at him. He looked directly at her and her eyes met his. They held for a few moments and then he looked away.

There was no doubt. It was the bull Roman.

CHAPTER TWENTY-FIVE

The Wheat Field (Julia)

It was early afternoon when the bull Roman, his woman and children finished whatever they had to do at the market. They stood in a little group while he appeared to issue the woman with orders. Then they split up. The woman and children went one way, disappearing off into the now-thinning crowds. Birkita followed the bull Roman. He made his way to the inn where she had been staying and, choosing a table in the shade, he ordered wine.

Birkita watched him from the corner of a building across the square. She was in absolutely no doubt. He had gone to seed a bit since leaving the army but it was the same man – the heavy build, florid complexion but most of all, it was the face that she remembered. The balding head, the thick eyebrows, the probing, ratty eyes, the nose like the prow of a ship, the thin mouth. He sat now looking like a labouring man at the end of a hard day's work enjoying a well-earned drink. Yet this was the same man who had casually given orders to crucify children.

During the rest of the afternoon, several of the man's friends came and joined him. They all had the look of ex-soldiers about them. They talked, laughed, made jokes, slapped or prodded one another playfully. The scene was redolent of sights Birkita had seen in her village before it had been destroyed.

Finally though, the bull Roman stood up, said farewell to his friends and began to make his way out of the square. Birkita followed him.

The town was emptying now. Stallholders were packing up what they hadn't sold and the last of those who didn't live in the town itself were heading out into the country and home.

The bull Roman took the West Gate. The road was busy enough that Birkita could follow him from about a hundred paces back and not be noticed.

Once beyond the gate, the road crossed a slow flowing river and then divided into two. The left hand road was the busier of the two but the bull Roman took the right hand road, as did a few others. Birkita allowed herself to fall further back but since the terrain was completely flat she was still able to keep him in view. They passed through land all of which had been cultivated. There were onions, cabbages, peas and golden fields of wheat. Dotted around were farmhouses – square or rectangular buildings with white walls and red tiled roofs. The Roman way of building was so different from the one she had known. Tracks led from this road to the various farmhouses and, as they went further out into the countryside, the number of people on the road reduced as, bit by bit, they took these tracks.

Finally, Birkita saw the bull Roman turn off to the left. She continued walking. The track the bull Roman had taken ran along the side of a wheat field. As Birkita got closer she saw that parallel to the track and to the left of it was a waist-deep drainage ditch. Then came the wheat field. The bottom of the ditch was dry now due to the summer weather. The bull Roman slid down into the ditch and then ran up the far side. Now he walked along the very edge of the field and ran the flat of his hand over the stalks of wheat. It was a tender action almost like a caress and she could almost feel the stalks tickling his palm. From time to time he would catch some heads of wheat, hold them for a moment and then let them slip through his fingers.

So. Our soldier is a farmer.

At the end of the track was a cluster of three buildings around a small yard. The largest was a square farmhouse with small windows high up in the white walls, the other two appeared to be barns or sheds of some kind. Looking back over her shoulder, she saw the bull Roman leave the field of wheat, re-cross the ditch and after a few paces, disappear into the house.

Birkita kept on walking for another ten minutes. Then she turned around and started back the way she had come. The summer sun hadn't quite set but it was low on the western horizon in a great bank of orange. A hawk hovered overhead floating on the warm air. There was no breeze and the golden field of wheat was quite still. Birkita smelt the air and looked to the south west. Clouds were gathering there. There were just a few and they were small and white and fluffy but they looked promising. And she had plenty of time.

She returned to the inn where she retrieved her dagger and a flint from her pack. Then she went downstairs and had some food and ale. When it began to grow dark, she put her cloak on and went outside and looked up. Just as she had suspected, the clear sky of earlier was gone. She could see no stars. Instead a blanket of cloud hung high overhead. And there was a slight breeze. She smiled.

She left Venta before the gates were closed for the night. Once clear of the town she found that the wind had come up and was now actually quite strong. It was from the south west and at her back as she walked, blowing her hair around her face. It would rain, of that she was certain, but not for a couple of hours.

The gods were with her.

The wheat field was an almost perfect rectangle. Its long side ran east-west parallel to the track that the bull Roman had taken and its short side lay along the road. The wind was blowing from the south west to the north east. The ceiling of cloud obscured the moon and the stars but Birkita had always had good eyesight, especially at night. She made her way along the field to the south west corner. Here she knelt down and using her cloak to provide shelter, she struck a spark on to a handful of dry grass. Her ear was almost to the ground as she blew on the spark gently and it became a tiny flicker of yellow flame consuming the grass.

She broke off a few stalks of wheat and twisting them together to make a torch, she lit one end of it. The flame ate up the dry stalks greedily. Now Birkita rose and with a whispered prayer to the gods, she set fire to the wheat. Quickly she moved along that side of the field touching her makeshift torch to the bone-dry stalks. Each time she did so the flames appeared to hesitate for a moment and then took off, scorching the stalks black and moving on to neighbouring ones. When her torch had finally burned down and she had to drop it, she looked back.

The fire had already eaten a good way into the field and it was moving at a frightening speed. By its light Birkita could see the golden swathe of wheat being turned to shrivelled black as though an invisible hand were sweeping across it. She made another torch and lit the rest of the southern side of the field. The wind took the flames and sent them tearing across the wheat towards the track and the farm buildings. Just as she finished lighting the last patch of wheat, she saw a light appear in one of the windows of the farmhouse. Moments later she heard shouting and saw silhouettes appear in the distance.

Her revenge had begun.

35

Julia is dreaming. In the dream she is a girl again – ten or eleven, around that age. She is at home but while it is definitely her parents' house, her parents are not her parents. They appear to be more like Suzanne's parents – or what she imagines Suzanne's parents to have been like. Julia's parents aren't actually in the dream but they are part of it – there in the background somewhere. Suzanne is also there – again, not in the dream but in the background. It feels as though Julia has a sister. Suzanne.

Nothing much happens in the dream. Julia is just around the house. In her room. Writing. Playing. Then she is out in the garden, lying on her tummy reading. The sun is shining and warm on her back. She is lost in the book. But soon, she knows, it will be teatime and her mum – Suzanne's mum – will call her in. There will be fresh bread and butter, ham and salad – luscious tomatoes that will explode in her mouth and creamy mayonnaise.

The dream is incredibly real so much so that Julia's mouth is watering at the thought of the food. When she wakes from it, she is desolate. She tries to call it back.

But of course, it is gone.

Julia thinks it's quite possible that she's going mad. First, there's the lack of food and the hard physical work.

Her body is weak and maybe that has started to weaken her brain too. It's coming loose. Unhinged.

She's starting to wonder which of any of this is real. The films, the war, coming here, this ghastly place, Suzanne, the book, the future that Suzanne used to constantly talk about until she went, Birkita and the things that happened to her. In Britannia. In Pompeii. Back in Britannia. Julia and the things that happened to her. Maybe none of it is real and she will wake and find herself living a normal life with a normal family and a normal job in an office or something.

Did those things really happen to her?

Did they?

Did they?

But yes, she can't deny her senses. At least she thinks she can't. She remembers the smell of him. She can still see – if she closes her eyes – the weird expression on his face when he was doing it. Familiar and yet, at the same time, unrecognisable. And there was the silence. Her father was normally a garrulous man. He loved to hear the sound of his own voice. He pontificated a lot. But – when he came to her – silence. Dead silence. Except for those first couple of times when he told her how good this would feel and that it would be their secret and how she must never tell. She could feel – could still feel – his whiskers on her skin. He shaved every day but he was still prickly. And the smell afterwards. After he had gone. The foxy, musky smell.

It really happened.

It did.

It did.

There was the time before it began. She had been a child. Happy. Innocent. Just she and her mother and father. The world had seemed perfect.

Or harmless.

And afterwards, she had come to understand that the world was nothing like that.

She remembered she had asked God to make it stop. She would kneel down every night by the side of her bed in her nightdress. Winter and summer. On the coldest night of the year, she would be on her knees. And this would be her only prayer. There had been a time when she had asked God to look after Mama and Papa and to watch over her while she slept and for other things that she wanted. But in the end there had just been that one prayer – that he would stop.

And when he didn't she knew that there was no God. Or if there was that he was too busy to listen to a little insect like her. Or if he was listening that he didn't care. And she knew then that there would be nobody she could rely on after this. She would have to take care of herself.

Yes – that had all been real. It had to have been. Because all of that had made her who she was now.

It is time to get up. Julia drags herself wearily from her bunk. She feels like she hasn't slept at all. During the day she tries to forget about how weak and hungry she is. She tries not to think about the future and when the war might end and whether her body still has the strength to make it that far. She has to force herself to think about the book. But that all seems so pointless now. And anyway she is stuck as to what Birkita might do next in terms of revenge. When work finishes, Julia just wants to get back to the barracks, eat whatever she can get to eat and go to sleep.

When she arrives back and goes to join the queue for food, Julia is astonished to find Suzanne there at the end of the line. She has been crying. Julia is at a loss for what to say – and anyway, she is too weary.

'I was waiting for you,' says Suzanne.

'How are you?' asks Julia automatically, not really

caring about the answer.

'Hungry,' says Suzanne.

'Me too,' says Julia. 'Always. I'm so fucking hungry.'

The words seem to take whatever remaining energy she had. They shuffle forward in silence. Julia wants to ask but she doesn't. She's just too tired. Too uncaring. When they have their food and are sitting on the stairs of the barracks eating, Suzanne asks, 'How is the book going?'

Julia feels angry at the presumption that she stayed at it while Suzanne was off doing whatever she was doing.

'It's stuck.'

'Maybe I could have a go at it again?'

Julia finally has had enough.

'So – you're back, are you?'

'Don't, Julia. Not now. Not this evening.'

Ordinarily Julia would have torn several strips off Suzanne at this point. She wants to. She really does. But she feels like somebody who is trying to lift something heavy over a wall and just can't get that last ounce of energy to lift it that last few centimetres.

'The book is in the mattress,' Julia says. 'Do whatever the fuck you like with it.'

Chapter Twenty-six

Meet the Family (Suzanne)

Birkita spent a night of broken sleep in some woods. The fire had been the easy bit. The next piece of her plan was where it could all go wrong.

In the morning, as soon as it got light and they opened the gates, she re-entered Venta, packed up her few possessions, paid the innkeeper and left the inn. Once again she took the West Gate and then the road out to the farm. It had rained during the night as she had predicted but the sky was clear now. Wet grass glistened in the sunlight and the clean air was just starting to warm up. Birds sang and twittered and called.

In the daylight, her handiwork was impressive. The field was a blackened, sodden mess. But the buildings had all survived, just as she had expected they would. The ditch around the field had stopped the fire from spreading. Indeed, her fire had been incredibly precise. There was the one large, black, incinerated patch and all around it green and gold crops flourished.

She turned off on the track that led up to the farm. As she approached the yard she saw the bull Roman and two other men, huddled together talking. Three to one. She hadn't anticipated that.

'How could it be a fucking accident?' the bull Roman said loudly, angrily. 'Some fucker did this and I'm going to find out who it was. When I do, they'll wish they'd never been born.'

Then he noticed Birkita.

'What the fuck do you want?' he said in the Roman tongue.

'Master,' she said. 'I'm looking for work.'

'Fuck off,' he replied. 'There's no work here.'

'I'm not looking for any money, master. If you give me a place to sleep and if I can eat the food that you eat, I will work hard for you.'

'That sounds like a good deal,' said one of the other men.

'She's strong,' said the other. 'Look at her.'

'And look at her tits,' said the first.

The remark made the bull Roman smile. Birkita pretended she hadn't understood.

'I could work in the fields,' she continued. 'I could look after your house. Cook your meals.'

'I have a wife that does that,' said the bull Roman.

'I can do whatever work you ask of me,' she said.

'You won't get a better offer than that,' said one of the men to the bull Roman, nudging him in the ribs.

'Can you plough?' the bull Roman asked.

'I can learn,' she said.

'What tribe are you?' he asked, stepping closer to her.

'I'm not any British tribe,' she said. 'I come from Gaul.'

The bull Roman looked into her eyes. This was the moment. Birkita returned his gaze, looking for any flash of recognition. As she did so she had a vision of the horror in the forest. Her dagger was in the pocket of her cloak. She could have taken him now. But maybe not. It was a long time since she had trained as a warrior. Maybe the three of them would have overpowered her before she got to him. And then it would have been over.

That look seemed to go on for ever. Finally, he said, 'All right. Today of all days, I could use help.'

He took her to the barn and showed her a corner where she could sleep.

'Leave your stuff there,' he said.

Then he took her to the door of the house.

'Wait here.'

He went inside and reappeared a few moments later with the woman with the black hair. The bruise on her face seemed even more livid close up and in the bright morning light. The two girls stood behind her, one on either side, looking up at Birkita.

'What's your name?' the bull Roman asked.

'Birkita.'

'She'll help you any way you want,' the bull Roman said to the woman. 'That's if she's not helping me. She'll sleep in the barn and you need to feed her.'

Then he said to Birkita, 'Come on and let's see what you're made of.'

CHAPTER TWENTY-SEVEN

The Farm – Settling In (Suzanne)

For that first day and the next one, nobody spoke to Birkita except for the bull Roman when he wanted to give her orders. Their initial job was to plough the burnt field and replant it. He ploughed, walking behind his one horse while she raked and took out clods of burnt, sodden wheat.

The bull Roman fumed the whole time they were working but his anger didn't seem directed at her. He cursed the gods but most of all he cursed the person who had burnt his field. He described the kind of retribution he would have when he caught them. With Birkita, however, he was just surly. He seemed happy enough with what she was doing and most of the time, just left her alone. Birkita was surprised to find herself enjoying the work. She lost herself in it and for hours at a time, was able to forget everything that had happened to her family and in the lupanar. It was almost like being back in the time before the rebellion.

Around noon, the woman appeared, bringing food and wine. She fed her husband first and then she brought what remained to Birkita.

'I brought you some food,' she said.

She smiled a small, sad smile and walked off. The food was plentiful and Birkita sat by herself on the edge of the field in the sunshine until the bull Roman shouted at her to get back to work.

She was glad that he stayed away from her. But he seemed so obsessed with the burning of his field and who might have done it, that there was nothing else he could think about. Birkita was happy to see the effect it had had on him. When he did happen to come near her for any reason, her skin crawled and it was everything she could do not to take her dagger and drive it through his heart. That time would come – but not yet.

They worked until the bull Roman decided it was time to stop. Then they returned to the yard, washed and Birkita was given a bowl of food and more wine. It was handed out to her from the door of the farmhouse as though she were a dog. But that suited her – anything rather than to have to sit with the bull Roman. She ate the food, sitting in the orange light of the westering sun, her back against the warm wall of the barn. After that she went into the barn and made her bed – spreading her cloak out on a pile of soft, fragrant straw.

As she settled down to sleep, Birkita heard noise coming from the farmhouse. The bull Roman was shouting. She heard furniture being scraped across a floor and then being overturned. There were screams – just the woman, no children. More shouting from the bull Roman – louder, even angrier. And more screams. But then suddenly the screaming stopped and there were just some muffled thuds.

Birkita slept badly that night. Despite being physically exhausted, she had nightmares. She was back in the forest. The bull Roman was there. The crucifixions were being carried out. She heard the metallic clanging of hammers on nails, the screams of the children, the routine conversation of the Romans as they went about their business. She remembered how one of them had whistled while he worked.

The following day, at noon, when the woman brought the food, Birkita asked for her name.

'Galena.'

It was a British name.

'You're not Roman?'

'No.'

'But you're married to a Roman.'

'We're not really married. He calls me his wife.'

The words were spoken wearily, the way someone might speak exhausted at the end of a long journey. She turned and trudged off.

The next morning, the bull Roman said he was going into Venta and would return that evening.

'No fucking slacking now just because I'm away. I want that field finished by the time I get home.'

Birkita made good progress and by noon, she could see that she would get the job done well before sunset. When Galena came with the food, Birkita asked, 'So how did you end up here?'

'My two girls. They're not his. Their father died in the great battle – the one that ended the rebellion. After that, the Romans were killing everybody. Killing and burning. Raping. We went into hiding, me and my girls. We hid in the forest and lived off whatever we could find there. So many times they nearly found us. But we were lucky.

'Except that we nearly starved to death over the winter. When the spring came I knew we couldn't go on. We came out. I did what you did. Came up here and asked for work. He said he didn't need any help – he needed a wife. And so he took me in. Me and my girls. We had food again. Even if I did have to share his bed. I … I only intended to do it for a while but now I can't leave. If I do he's said he'll kill me. Me and my girls.'

'He beats you,' said Birkita.

It was a statement.

'Only if I make him angry. He's been very angry since the field was burnt. And he wants a son. He wants me to give him one. Says girls are damn all use. He gets angry whenever he remembers I'm not carrying his child. But I'll never carry his child.'

Birkita remembered what they used to do in the lupanar to stop themselves from becoming pregnant.

'It means I'll be beaten for a long time yet.'

That night, Birkita tried to get clear in her own mind how she would exact her revenge. The burning of the field and coming to work here had just been spur of the moment things. She had hoped that after these two things, the path forward would become clear. But there had been no blinding flash of light. And if it had ever been her intention to murder his family, as he had done to hers, that was gone now. Galena and the girls were victims just as much as Birkita was.

She had decided she wouldn't kill him. Even crucifying him or torturing him to death would be too easy. She wanted him to live a long life of misery. She racked her brains to see if there was any way she could take his farm but that didn't seem like an option. She could destroy it. That might be worth considering at some point – burn the crops again but also burn the buildings. But before she could do that, Galena and her girls would have to be long gone. Then, with the farm gone, she needed to find a way to destroy him in some way – while still keeping him alive.

So the first thing was Galena and the girls.

36

Suzanne tries to make small talk with Julia on the way to work but she is having none of it. Adolf sends them off on separate work assignments. There is more silence when they return in the evening and eat. Afterwards Julia says she is going for a walk. When Suzanne asks if she can come, Julia says she'd rather go by herself.

She goes out to the ramparts and watches the swallows swooping. It is a sunny evening and spring feels like it has finally come out of hiding and won't be going back. Julia spends a long time sitting on the grass. She tries not to think of anything – is that actually possible? She tries just to become part of the scene – as though she were in a painting. Eventually she becomes aware that the people around her are starting to head back to their barracks. Soon it will be curfew. She gets up to go too.

When she returns, Suzanne is writing in the notebook. She looks up as Julia arrives at the bunk. Her eye sockets are big from hunger and red from crying.

'Can I tell you what happened?' she says.

Whatever anger was inside Julia is gone. It seems to have evaporated somewhere out there on the ramparts.

She nods.

'Want to come up here?'

Suzanne pats the mattress beside her.

Julia climbs up.

'I feel so stupid,' says Suzanne. 'All that talk of weddings and bridesmaids. It's just as you said. He just wants a girl. Any girl. And once he's had them, he's on to the next one.'

'He's a dickhead,' Julia says.

She puts an arm around her friend. 'Never mind. There are other things that are a lot more important.'

'I think part of me just wanted to find out what it was like.'

Suzanne looks into Julia's eyes. 'You know – before I died. I didn't want to have died and not experienced it.'

'You're not going to die,' says Julia. 'Not for many, many years.'

Suzanne smiles a small, sad smile. It's an unconvinced smile.

'And so?' asks Julia.

'And so?' echoes Suzanne.

'And so, what was it like?'

'What was it like? I'm wondering what all the fuss is about.'

After a long pause, she continues.

'You know … what you told me … about the films you were in. You weren't making that up, were you?'

'No,' Julia says softly. 'I wasn't making it up. It's true.'

She's not sure where this is leading.

'So you've done it a lot more than me. What's it been like for you?'

'Overrated,' says Julia.

She takes her arm off Suzanne's shoulder. She looks away.

'There's something else I need to tell you, Suzanne,' Julia says. 'I don't know where to start with this really but when I was young … my father –'

336

'I know that,' Suzanne blurts out.

'You know? How do you know?'

'Especially when you told me about the films. It was like everything – the way you are, what happened ... what happened between you and me ... it all made sense. Everything fell into place.'

'But –'

'When you met me, you thought I was an innocent in the world.'

Julia is so stunned she can only nod.

'I was a virgin, Julia. That didn't necessarily make me innocent. I had a lot of time while I was in that attic to think. To think about the world. To think about evil. I came to realise how blessed I was – that the childhood I had had was not the one that many people have. Once I unlocked that door into the world of evil, I saw it was a bottomless pit – that there was no end to the bad things that people could do. I'm sorry – I'm talking too much. You go on.'

'Before ... before it happened ... before the first time – I can remember so clearly, I was just a happy little kid. You know, you're born and of course you don't remember the first few years but then suddenly you're aware and you're in the world. And everything just is. Your parents, the house where you live, your room, the bed you sleep in. Everything. And meals appear and people give you presents and it's not so much that you take it for granted, although I suppose you do. It's that it just all seems to be right and it makes up the world. Your world. And every day you do things and there seem to be no restrictions or limits.

'When you go to school, the first restrictions happen. But even then – you've got all that time outside of school. And the holidays. So you put up with school – it's a bit of an inconvenience. But you still have all that time to live your life and be in the world that seems to be just there for your entertainment. Do you know what I'm talking about? Does this make sense?'

Suzanne nods, her eyes soft, the sides of her mouth turned up in the gentlest of smiles. 'That's just what it was like for me.'

'And so then, he did this to me. It doesn't matter how or when or how old I was. Just that I was a kid. And it changed everything. Everything.'

Suzanne takes the nearest one of Julia's hands in both of hers. Julia looks down at her other hand. It seems so alone. Just like her. Just like everything, all her life, she has been alone. She passes the other hand across and Suzanne takes that too, holding them both as though she were cupping a pair of birds.

'I had thought … I'm sure every kid thinks it – that I was beautiful. In fact, you don't really even think it. It's just another one of those things that you take for granted. It just is. Everyone else is and you are. Sure, people might call you names or do nasty things to you but their faces, their bodies – they're just part of all the wonderfulness of the world. But after that, after that first time, I knew I wasn't beautiful. If somebody could do that to me, then how could I be?'

Suzanne squeezes Julia's hands.

'And after that I was different from everybody else. I carried around this terrible secret. I used to imagine it like a black goblin on my back. Grinning. Laughing. And the worst part … you know what the worst part was?'

Suzanne's eyes ask the question. What? What was the worst part?

'The worst part was that I knew I was to blame.'

'No, Julia. No.'

Julia continues. She is starting to feel tears coming. She looks down at the dismal colour of the blanket they are sitting on. She takes her hands out of Suzanne's.

'I thought there was something about me…'

She bangs her hands on the mattress.

'Or something I had done…'

She bangs them again. With each piece of the sentence she bangs them.

'That had made him do this. I didn't know what it was. I couldn't even begin to work out what it was. Only that there was something … something…'

Julia looks up into Suzanne's face. Julia's eyes are full of tears so that Suzanne's face is not at all clear.

'I still don't know. I still don't know what that something was that made him do that to me.'

'Oh, Julia, come here to me, my sweet girl.'

Suzanne takes Julia in her arms and holds her as the tears finally start to flow freely. Suzanne rocks her gently and whispers to her. 'My sweet child. My dear, sweet child.'

Julia doesn't know how long they are like this. Eventually she eases herself away from Suzanne and wipes her eyes with her hands.

'You know none of this was your fault,' says Suzanne.

Julia nods a perfunctory nod. She's stopped crying now.

'So you can see – those films I made. They made complete sense. It was the only career for somebody like me. If it was all right for him to do it, it was all right for anybody and everybody to do it.'

Julia is finished. She has said everything she wanted to say. She feels like she has vomited. But it has been good vomiting. The vomiting after food poisoning. Something very bad inside her has come out.

For a long time neither of them says anything. But there is nothing awkward about the silence. Rather, Julia feels a great closeness to Suzanne. As if reading her thoughts, Suzanne says, 'I'm glad you told me.'

'I'm glad I told you too. It's been inside me for too long.'

Somebody shouts that lights out will be in fifteen minutes. Tonight, for some reason, the queue for the bathroom isn't so long. The two girls go to the toilet, wash, and brush their teeth. They return to their bunk and climb back up. Julia notices all these little activities as though they were happening for the first time. It is a strange feeling – as though she has never carried out these rituals a thousand times before.

They climb into bed. The weather is warm enough now that there is no longer any need for winter's spooning. They lie face to face. They are both smiling. A tiny smile of happiness on Suzanne's face. Julia feels her own to be weary. The lights go out. They move more closely together until they are embracing. They intertwine their legs.

And this is how they fall asleep.

37

Julia and Suzanne are stuck. They are stuck and they are arguing.

The story has ground to a halt. Suzanne explains that she thought she had done a really smart thing by having Birkita get into the bull Roman's family but now she doesn't see how it helped. Julia doesn't either. It's made the whole revenge thing much more complicated.

Julia has an even worse feeling. She thinks that they might have taken a wrong turning a long way back – maybe even as far back as the whole lupanar business and now they have ended up in a cul-de-sac. She fears they will have to redo months of work and throw away what could be a hundred pages or more. She knows she wouldn't have the strength for that. She's desperate to save what they have.

She says that it's all about what kind of ending they want – that that's where they should be starting from. Are they going for a happy ending? Suzanne says she doesn't know – it depends on what unfolds. Julia doesn't agree. They should fix the ending and then 'join up the dots'. And it should be a happy ending, Julia says. There's enough horror and grimness around them. As she says it, she wonders if 'grimness' is a word.

341

The characters mightn't allow that to happen, Suzanne says.

'Damn the characters,' replies Julia, 'They'll do what we tell them to do.'

'That's just the thing,' says Suzanne. 'They won't. Not now. Not now that we've come this far with them.'

And this remark stops Julia in her tracks. Suzanne's right – they won't. The characters are doing whatever they want now.

Julia tries another approach.

'So what do the characters want then?' she asks.

'Birkita wants revenge and to find some happiness. I think she also wants not to be alone any more – to find a new family in some way.'

'Maybe she needs to become pregnant then,' says Julia.

'Maybe,' says Suzanne.

It is the first sign of agreement they have had since they started this discussion.

'And Galena wants safety for herself and her girls,' Suzanne finishes.

'She could get that now,' says Julia. 'Birkita, Galena and the girls flee when the bull Roman is off drinking with his friends. Birkita burns the farm. Revenge, happiness, safety.'

'Or,' Julia continues. 'She cuts off the bull Roman's penis while he sleeps, then they flee.'

Suzanne starts to giggle at this.

'That'd be revenge all right,' she says.

'Well maybe not,' says Julia. 'But we could finish it now. We're very close.'

'We're not,' says Suzanne. 'We're not very close at all.'

'Why not?'

'We have to build up the tension to some incredible

climax.'

'We've already done that,' says Julia. 'Look at what Birkita's been through.'

'Yes, but that has to be nothing compared to what she has to go through next.'

'Are you serious?'

'I am. I am serious.'

Julia just wants to be done with the whole thing. To have it finished and then the war finished and just have a proper meal. One meal. Just one – with four courses – an appetizer, main course, dessert and cheese. And some wine. If she could just have that, she would die happy.

'It'll do,' she says. 'What we've done will do.'

The shocked look that appears on Suzanne's face is as though Julia has just slapped her. That expression turns to outrage.

'Don't ever … ever … say that again,' she says. 'Not about our book.'

They started this discussion as soon as they got up this morning. It continued over breakfast. They have been on their way to work for the last few minutes of it. Now they both go silent and stay like that for the rest of the way. Adolf gives them separate assignments and they don't see each other until evening when they are handing back their tools. It has been a warm day and Julia stinks of sweat and is weak from hunger. She salivates at the thought of food.

'Cut off his penis while he sleeps,' says Suzanne as they walk back to the barracks. 'I'd like to cut off Adolf's penis while he sleeps.'

Julia has just about enough energy to laugh.

'If you like I'll write the next chapter,' says Suzanne.

'That would be good,' says Julia. 'I don't think I have the strength for it right now.'

343

CHAPTER TWENTY-EIGHT

The Farm Again (Suzanne)

Birkita learned from Galena that the bull Roman's name was Lucius, but Birkita continued to think of him as the bull Roman. He had quite a large amount of land – all of it stolen from the Iceni – so there was plenty of work to be done. He was also a man who liked order. She had to admit that he cultivated the land well. His fields were neat, the rows of crops straight, his schedule for care and maintenance unbending. He also liked routine so that twice a week, without fail, he would go into Venta to drink with his friends. Galena said she dreaded those nights the most. Then, invariably, he would come home drunk and angry. She almost always got beatings on those nights.

One evening, after he had left, Galena came out of the farmhouse carrying grain for the chickens. Birkita had finished eating her food and sat against the wall of the barn, in the setting sun, her eyes closed. Colours swam before her eyes. A dark pink that boiled up to red. Then it changed into hundreds of tiny turquoise and dark green triangles. Wasn't the body an amazing thing? Especially the eyes. They did so much – not just seeing but they were part of a person's beauty. And they told you all kinds of things about the person themselves. When she heard Galena talking to the chickens, Birkita opened her eyes.

'You're alone for the evening,' called Birkita.

'For a few hours anyway,' Galena said wearily.

She upended the bowl to empty out the last of the chicken feed and then came over and sat down with a loud sigh, next to Birkita. She was surprised – Galena had never done this before. The bruise on her face had almost faded away but her lip was cut from a more recent beating.

Galena closed her eyes and looked up at the sun, bathing her face. Birkita studied her. She could almost see the tension draining out of Galena's face, so that it softened and became beautiful again, framed in the glossy black hair.

'He'll kill you if you stay with him,' said Birkita. 'You know that, don't you? Eventually.'

Without opening her eyes, Galena said, 'Yes, I know that.'

The unasked question hung in the air. It was a while before Galena answered it.

'But by then maybe my two girls will be able to fend for themselves.'

'What makes you think they'd be safe?' asked Birkita. 'The Romans kill children.'

Galena's eyes flipped open. She looked into Birkita's.

'That was during the rebellion. They wouldn't do it now. He wouldn't do it. Maybe he doesn't love them but he's kind to them. He often brings them back little presents from his nights in town.'

'And what about the presents he brings you? I hear him. I hear the two of you. What he's doing to you.'

'I told you – he gets angry that I'm not pregnant. I've been thinking lately that maybe I should let it happen. The only thing is ... if it turned out to be another girl ... he wouldn't be happy about that. But maybe for nine months it would mean that he wouldn't beat me. Not too much anyway.' Galena closes her eyes again and returns her face to the sun.

'You could escape,' said Birkita.

'How? Where to? Don't be silly. He'd find me and then he'd kill me for sure. For making a fool of him in front of his friends.'

'I could help you. We could go, the four of us. You, me, your girls.'

As she said this, Birkita wondered how much this was about her own vengeance and how much was about saving Galena.

'What … why would you do that?' Galena asked. 'Why would you want to help me? Why put yourself in danger like that?'

'I have my reasons,' said Birkita. 'I hate the Romans.'

'We all hate the Romans. But they're here to stay. We may as well get used to it.'

'We could go to a place where he would never find us.'

'Like where?'

'Gaul.'

Galena opens her eyes again. They are big and blue.

'Across the sea. Are you crazy?'

'I'm from there' – the lie was easy – 'It's not too different from here.'

'He'd come after us. He'd never stop until he found us. And then … his revenge would be terrible.'

Birkita had hoped she wouldn't have to say what she says next.

'We could kill him. I … I would kill him. Burn the farmhouse with him inside. Pretend it was an accident.'

'The Romans would never believe us. They'd say we did it. They'd crucify us – all of us. Even the girls.'

Birkita has a momentary, ghastly vision. She gives it one more try.

'Kill him, burn the farmhouse and flee all in the same night.'

'You're mad, Birkita. They'd come after us. We'd all die. Stop talking like this.'

Without another word, Galena gets up, picks up her bowl and walks away.

38

'You don't have to write this chapter, Julia,' Suzanne says. 'I can write it.'

'No. No. I want to … I have to.'

CHAPTER TWENTY-NINE

The Farm at Night (Julia)

The sound of the barn door squealing open woke Birkita. She heard soft footsteps. For a few moments she thought she was back in the lupanar and Antonius or Cassius had come into her cubicle. But then her senses cleared and she remembered where she was. It was very dark with just some small squares of starlight where the windows were. Her knife was under her pillow. She reached in, took it in her hand and turned onto her back. She held the knife under her blanket.

The bull Roman was standing over her. She could smell him. Sweat and stale wine and urine.

'You're awake,' he said.

His voice didn't sound in the least drunk and suddenly, Birkita was very afraid.

'What do you want?' she asked, trying to keep her voice calm.

'I just wanted to renew an old acquaintance,' he said.

'What old acquaintance?'

'Oh, come now. Don't play games with me. I knew that first time you came into the yard that I'd seen you before. It just took me a while to work it out. And then this evening, it came to me. A few of us were talking about the old times and then I remembered. I never forget a face. I always get them in the end. Yours just took me more time than most.

'That village … you had this sort of underground cave. The dog gave you away. You were the sister of the fellow we crucified. A real warrior. You, I mean – not your brother.'

'I don't know what you're talking about.'

'Don't you, indeed?' Well, it doesn't matter – because I just wanted to welcome you to the family. I think we're going to be very happy here, the five of us together.'

Birkita said nothing. She was aghast. Speechless. The bull Roman continued.

'Galena – well, her body isn't like it used to be. Childbirth takes its toll. But yours? You've not had children. And a pretty face, nice shape. I'd really like to see what's under your clothes.'

Birkita gripped the knife. When he came down on her she would kill him. There was nothing else for it now. Whatever plans she had, whatever about what might happen to Galena and girls – all of that was irrelevant now. Birkita would take her revenge on the bull Roman in the next few minutes and then she would be gone. Galena would have to decide then what she would do.

And Birkita understood now that it would be good. She would have done what she came to do. Then, somehow, she might finally be able to throw off the shackles of the past. Then it might be possible to get on with her life – to build some kind of new life – somewhere. Somehow.

'So here's how it will work,' the bull Roman continued. 'You let me fuck you whenever I want and, in return, Galena and her girls get to live. And you know how serious I am about this. You know I have no problem killing children. And you wouldn't want that on your conscience, now would you?

'So be a good girl now. Put the knife down and open your legs.'

351

Julia is crying as she finishes. She is sitting on the bed with Suzanne. Julia realises that Suzanne has been watching her all the time that she was writing this chapter. She has written quickly – she has filled almost two pages and it is still nowhere near lights out. Gently, Suzanne takes the notebook out of Julia's hands. She looks at her friend. Julia is slumped, feels defeated, beaten down.

'That was what he used to say. That's what he said that first time. "Be a good girl now." And then after that. Before he – "Be a good girl." Always "Be a good girl." And afterwards. "You're a good girl. You're a very good girl."'

Suzanne holds her, embraces her, stroking her hair. They stay like this until the lights are turned out.

39

Julia hums to herself while they wait in the queue for breakfast.

'You're very happy this morning,' says Suzanne.

'It's the first of May. Didn't you know?'

'I didn't,' says Suzanne in surprise. 'I hadn't realised that.'

Julia nods. 'Summer,' she says and indeed it is already warm in the courtyard of the barracks.

They are given their food and sit side by side on the cobbles, backs against a wall, to eat.

'I knew that it wasn't my fault,' says Julia. 'Last night … writing that chapter … I realised that it wasn't anything I did or didn't do. It was him.

'Whatever twisted thing was inside him – that's what caused it. It was him. All him. Completely him.'

Suzanne has turned her face to Julia and has stopped eating.

'Oh, I don't know why he came into my life. Why I got a father like that when most other people got normal fathers. I'll probably never know that. And I don't know what made him that way. And I don't know why I deserved that to happen to me. I know that sounds terribly self-pitying.'

Suzanne shakes her head. 'No,' she says softly.

'It doesn't at all.'

'But it wasn't my fault. That's what matters. It wasn't my fault. And you know what the really strange thing is?'

Suzanne's eyes ask the question. What?

'That if I hadn't come here … if I hadn't met you … if we hadn't started writing this damn book' – Julia smiles as she says this – 'and if this book hadn't gone the way it has gone – the plot and everything – if all of that hadn't happened, then I might never have found this out.'

She shakes her head slowly. 'Isn't that strange? Isn't that so strange?'

They have to go to work and it is evening before they get to talk again.

'The funny thing is that I don't feel any anger towards him now. And I don't know if that's because he's dead. And he can't have died a happy death. But he's gone now. Disappeared from the face of the earth. It's like he was never born. And yes, for a time in my life, he was with me. But now he's gone. Gone!'

CHAPTER THIRTY

The Farm – Family of Five (Suzanne)

After the first night with the bull Roman in the barn, Galena stopped speaking to Birkita and avoided her as much as she could. At lunchtime, Galena came with her girls to the field. Galena would go to the bull Roman and the girls would bring Birkita's food. Once or twice Galena did bring the food to Birkita – it looked to her as though the bull Roman had forced Galena to do it. But now there was no conversation. Instead, Galena handed over the food, eyes averted, and walked off. The first time it happened, Birkita was too surprised to say anything. After that, she just accepted it.

In the evenings Galena had always handed Birkita out her food – sometimes with a smile, sometimes with a wish that she enjoy it. Now it was one of the girls who gave Birkita her bowl – and the two children, who had just been starting to come out of their shyness with her, now avoided her as though she had the plague. Galena did her best not to be out in the yard when Birkita was around.

The bull Roman was happy. He whistled while he worked and his previous angry mood and peremptory tone in giving orders were gone. Sometimes, he would make remarks to Birkita about things he had done to her in the barn. He often slapped her buttocks or felt her breasts or grabbed her between her legs. Several times, he didn't

355

wait until nightfall and the barn but took her in the field amongst the crops which were now in the full leafiness of summer.

It was worse than the lupanar. It was worse than the arena. This was the worst of all.

Every day, Birkita resolved that she would kill the bull Roman but every day something stopped her. And she knew what that something was – it was a picture in her head of the clearing in the forest and the four crosses. Except this time, the figures on the crosses were Galena, her two daughters, and Birkita herself.

Birkita told herself that she didn't fear for her own life. But she wondered just how true that was. She had never feared death before the Romans came. Indeed she had thought that it would be her destiny to die in battle. She had never feared death in the arena. She had felt outrage, of course – outrage that she should die for somebody else's entertainment – but never fear. But the deaths she had imagined or faced had always been quick, clean ones. A cut from a sword or a spear and then she would find herself on the journey into the lands of the gods.

Crucifixion was something different. She had been there when her brother and sister-in-law and their girls had died. She had seen how long it took the adults to die. Maybe somewhere, deep inside her, the life that Birkita now led was better than what she might have to endure if she ended up on a cross.

Nearly a moon passed. The summer started to turn. It was harvest time and they were all in the fields – the bull Roman, Galena, the two girls and Birkita. The bull Roman gave orders, the girls chattered or teased each other or played while they worked, Birkita and Galena worked in a hard silence.

They had finished a field that was called the North Field. Evening had come and the barn was filled with so many sacks of grain and so many bales of straw that Birkita was hard put to find a spot in which to sleep. She didn't mind. It was warm enough that she could sleep out under the stars. The bull Roman had gone to Venta to celebrate. Birkita was washing herself in the horse trough in the yard when Galena came out the back door of the farmhouse and came towards her.

'Birkita – you are a warrior, aren't you?'

Birkita stood up, surprised, the water draining down her face onto her chest.

'I am. At least I was one time.'

'As was I,' said Galena. 'Before I became a mother first of all. And then a mouse.'

She said the last words bitterly. Birkita looked at her in puzzlement. 'A mouse?'

'Look at us,' said Galena. 'Look at me. This is no way to live. We're not slaves. We're not whores. We're warriors.'

Birkita wasn't sure what to say. She half-nodded in agreement.

'I just want you to promise me one thing,' Galena continued. 'If we are captured … each of us must kill one of the girls.'

Galena's eyes looked haunted.

'We will agree,' she said the words slowly, deliberately. 'You and I – which one we will kill. Then, if it happens … if we are not able to escape … if we are taken … you will kill your chosen one and I will kill the other. My beautiful girls are not going to be raped and tortured for the amusement of Romans.

'Promise me … Promise me that and we will come with you. We will escape.'

357

CHAPTER THIRTY-ONE

The Farm – Night (Julia)

They left under a clear sky full of stars and a waning crescent moon which gave them just enough light to see by. It was a beautiful, late-summer night – still warm after the heat of the day. They travelled light, bringing only food – bread, cheese, smoked meat – tied up in bundles in their cloaks. Because of its weight, they brought no water – they would find streams along the way. They took two short army swords belonging to the bull Roman and the money that he kept in a box under a flagstone. There was quite a bit since he had been paid for some of the crops he had just harvested and sold. Birkita reckoned it would be enough to pay for their passage to Gaul and perhaps see them through the first couple of months of winter – if they were frugal. Galena and Birkita hid the swords in the bundles that they carried slung over their shoulders – the British were forbidden to carry swords.

Birkita had spent whole nights before their departure agonizing over whether or not to burn the farm. She pictured the bull Roman, coming home drunk, wanting sex and finding all the buildings intact but everybody gone. How would he react? Birkita sensed that his military training would kick in, he would sober up instantly, realise what had happened and come after them. On a horse, the chances were that he would catch up with them quickly.

Burning the buildings would cause confusion. He would try to save what he could. Birkita would also let the animals loose by opening gates. Hopefully he would try to round those up and that would buy them more time.

Then there was the question of where they would go – what direction. A few nights before they left, when the bull Roman came to Birkita in the barn, she pretended to be crying. In truth it hadn't taken much pretending – though she hated for him to see her like this, even if she was faking it.

'What's wrong with you?' he demanded, angrily. 'You have food in your belly and a roof over your head. So you have to spread your legs once in a while.'

'I was thinking about my home,' Birkita sobbed. 'Where we lived. I miss it so much.'

That was it. That was all she said. Her idea was to try and plant in the bull Roman's mind the thought that she was homesick. Maybe – just maybe – he might assume that that's where she had headed. She knew it was a thin enough hope.

As soon as he had disappeared out of sight on the road to Venta, Birkita ran round and opened all the gates to release the animals. By the time she got back, freed chickens and geese flustered around the farmyard. Galena and the girls stood in the yard with their bundles. Galena may have been a warrior one time but she didn't look much like one now. Instead she and her girls looked like three lost souls waiting to be given orders.

'The girls know what we're doing?' Birkita asked.

'I told them.'

Birkita squatted down in front of the two girls. They were clearly terrified. She gave them a big smile.

'You know what,' she said, 'I'm always mixing you two up. I can never remember which of you is Kelyn and which of you is Sevi.'

'I'm Kelyn,' said the older of the two.

'And I'm Sevi.'

Birkita knew who they were only too well. Kelyn was the one that she was to kill if they were caught. In all likelihood, Birkita knew that, if that happened, she would probably have to try and kill both girls. She couldn't see Galena having the strength to do it. And then she would have to kill Galena. And then herself. She prayed it would not come to that.

'Good, I'll remember that now,' Birkita said. 'So your mother has told you what we're doing.'

They nodded, their small faces almost frozen with fear.

'You've got to be very brave now but your mother was once a great warrior and so was I. We'll take care of you. We're going to go on a long journey and find a beautiful, happy place to live. Would you like that?'

The two girls looked at her with big round eyes. They nodded again.

'And he's not coming?' said Kelyn.

'No, he's not coming. He's been cruel to your mum and hurt her very much. So now we're going to hurt him.'

'He's a mentula,' said Kelyn.

Birkita looked up at Galena. 'Mentula?'

The stress etched on Galena's face broke into a smile.

'Penis,' she said. 'Prick.'

Birkita laughed.

'He is. He's a big mentula. The biggest mentula of all.'

Galena set fire to the barn. Meanwhile Birkita carried a couple of bales of straw into the house and set them alight. The barn went up like a torch. The house took a little bit longer but soon it too was on fire, bright yellow and orange flames dancing, framed in the windows and doors. By then the barn was already whooshing like some kind of monstrous animal. They gathered up their bundles,

Birkita checked the stars just as the captain had shown her, and they turned south. Venta lay to the east and Birkita's old home east of that again. She prayed that when the bull Roman returned and set out to find them, as she knew he would, that was the way he would go.

Her plan was to go south west to Londinium and from there, take a ship to Gaul. Surely there, they would be beyond his reach. As for her revenge, she had taken his family and destroyed much of his property. She felt grimly satisfied. Maybe he would not suffer for the rest of his life as she would have liked, but there were a couple of year's grief and heartache in that for him. On the great scales of the gods, what she had done hardly registered against his acts – but it was something. And she could always come back again, she thought. Just as he was getting his farm back on its feet. Destroy it all again. That and whatever else he had in his life. That would be something. And then again and again – for as long as he lived. She could keep doing it every few years. She might end up driving him into madness. She smiled at the prospect. That would be revenge indeed.

They walked until a bar of light appeared on the eastern horizon. By then, the girls looked exhausted and footsore but if they were, they didn't complain. As the first colour started to return to the black and grey world through which they had been journeying, they took to the woods which bounded the road on either side. Here they found a small stream where they made camp. They lit no fire and ate their cold food. Enveloped in the warmth of summer, it was no hardship. Then they slept, with Galena and Birkita keeping watch alternately. The two girls slept the sleep of the dead. Birkita found it hard to sleep. She was not confident that Galena would be alert enough to danger – and Birkita also enjoyed imagining in detail the bull Roman's return from Venta.

She was not sure if he would have smelt the fire first or seen the column of black smoke against the night sky. He would eventually have seen the flames. Then would have come the realisation that they were coming from his own farm. She could picture him running as fast he could, his squat body on thick thighs. He couldn't run fast and looked foolish on those rare occasions when she had seen him do it.

She pictured him arriving into the farmyard. He would have known even before he got there. He would have known that this was no accident. And he would have known who was responsible. He might still have expected Galena and her girls to be there. Or he might have thought for a while that they had died in the farmhouse. But when the flames died away and the ashes cooled and he sifted through the ruins, he would have known then that they had gone too. His anger would have been a wonderful thing to behold.

They slept by day and travelled by night, meeting almost nobody – just the occasional drunk or tramp. As they walked through the darkness, Birkita strained all her senses in search of danger. She listened for the sound of hoof beats coming from behind but nothing like that came. She wondered if the bull Roman might have got ahead of them and be lying in wait somewhere. But night after night, there were just the sounds of owls and frogs and the occasional cracking of a twig as an animal moved in the undergrowth.

They reached Londinium on the eighth day, timing their arrival for just after sunrise. It had taken much longer than Birkita's original journey when she had landed in Britannia but the short summer nights had limited how much they could travel. Anyway, she wasn't sure the two girls could have done much more walking than they had done. As the four of them moved through the crowded streets of the city towards the port and as Galena and the girls gazed wide-eyed at the buildings and the people and the traffic, Birkita saw that a subtle change had come over her little band.

Both Kelyn and Sevi, while they were certainly in awe of their surroundings, didn't give off that air of frightened little rabbits that they had always exuded when they were at the farm. Their permanent nervousness had been replaced by curiosity, even excitement. Sevi even had a bit of a swagger about her as she walked.

And it was their mother who had undergone the biggest transformation. Galena was several years older than Birkita but she had always seemed younger, more like the bull Roman's cowed, frightened daughter rather than his woman. Now that was gone. Now Galena walked with a confident stride, her head up, her beauty – those vivid blue eyes and shiny black hair – striking once more. It was like her real self had been hidden before – as if behind a veil. Now it was on display. Birkita was starting to get a sense of the warrior Galena had once been – and might be again.

If the other three were confident that they had escaped, Birkita stayed watchful. She told Galena to do the same. Birkita wouldn't rest until they were on a ship and out of sight of Britannia.

In her imaginings, she had pictured herself going down to the port and finding the captain of the *Seva* there. Had that happened, the gods would truly have been smiling on her. But she wasn't surprised when he wasn't. The gods had been good to have got them this far.

Down at the river they found a captain who said he was sailing for a place called Gesoriacum in Gaul. Birkita remembered it from the time when she had pored over maps with the *Seva*'s captain. It was not too far away from Caletum, the port she had sailed from a few months ago. The captain, a short man with a pot belly, had an honest manner about him. His opening bid, when she asked him how much he would charge for passage for the four of them, wasn't outrageously high. In the end it was agreed that he would charge for the two girls as though they were one adult. The negotiation was good-humoured and the captain was happy with half the money now and half just before they disembarked. Birkita found out that he had children of his own and that reassured her a bit. He also seemed impressed with her apparent knowledge of ships and sailing. Her main concerns had been that he would have his crew throw them over the side once they were out at sea or try to take their money while they slept. For the first of these, she would just have to trust to her assessment of him. For the second she had her sword.

The vessel set sail late in the morning under a blue sky and with very little wind. Kelyn and Sevi were completely entranced, running from one side of the ship to the other as it pulled away from its moorings. As it sailed down the river, Birkita and Galena leant on the stern rail watching the land recede. Gulls screamed overhead, the sails flapped in what breeze there was, the wake of the ship paid out behind them.

For a long time they were silent. Then Birkita became aware that Galena was looking at her. Birkita turned her head. Galena's face had become a little tanned during their journey. Her eyes were bright.

'Thank you, Birkita,' she said. 'Thank you.'

40

It is just before the lunch break on May 11th when Julia hears the news. (She has started to track the days.) She has been clearing rocks and stones from a patch of earth so that it can be planted with grass when Erika, one of the women who works with her, comes over and says simply, 'There are to be more transports.'

By lunchtime it is clear that this is more than just a rumour. When Julia sits down to eat her meagre lunch, Suzanne has heard it too and what she has is more definite. Seventy-five hundred people are to be deported to the East. It is clear that it has to be true because of the logic and the detail of it. The ghetto is being beautified because some important people are coming to visit. But one of the things that can't be 'beautified' or hidden away or papered over is the fact that there are just too many people in this small town. So with the implacable logic that is so characteristic of them, the Germans are going to ship out seventy-five hundred people on three transports, thereby reducing the overcrowding.

Now the rumours take over, lift off and begin to fly. Some say that it is the old people who will be shipped out because they make the ghetto 'unsightly' and – terrible though they know this is – Julia and Suzanne take comfort from this. But others say that it is able-bodied workers who will go – because the destination is some labour camp in the East and old people would be of no value there – it's workers that are needed. People dare not ask themselves what this might mean for the old people – there are some things that it is best not to think about.

And for the first time, Julia and Suzanne hear the story of the children who came from Poland. It happened in the late summer of last year. One day, a train arrived in the ghetto and the wagons disgorged not adults but children, nothing but children, hundreds of them. They were emaciated and their clothes were little more than dirty rags. They looked like scarecrows and were covered in lice and sores. They held each other's hands. The older ones helped the younger ones, trying to comfort those that were crying. It was raining the day they arrived and the bedraggled column of children was accompanied by a squad of SS men.

These children were placed in a special camp outside the Theresienstadt fortress itself. They were kept away from everybody else. A team of doctors and nurses was recruited from those already in the ghetto and was placed in isolation with the children. Nobody – neither children nor the medical staff – was allowed to leave this camp.

The children were given excellent care, special food, new clothes. They didn't have to do any work. Slowly they began to recover from whatever terrible ordeals they had been through and appalling sights they had seen. They began to behave like normal kids again – playing, drawing pictures, making friends. But then one night, the children and all their caregivers disappeared – presumably put on a transport to the East.

So it is clear that whatever this phrase 'transport to the East' actually means, knowing the Germans, it is nothing good. The ghetto, which up until now is one of the most awful, meanest, most dismal places on the planet has now indeed become the Paradise Ghetto and people will do anything to stay here.

The ghetto is its own weird world with its own rules and so, while no one considers themselves a hundred per cent safe from transportation, some people almost certainly are. Children of mixed – that is, Jew and non-Jew – marriages; those who were awarded medals for outstanding bravery during World War One as well as their families; people who are classified as 'prominent'; the municipal orchestra, the community guards – a sort of Jewish police force with no power to speak of – and the fire department are also, more than likely, excluded.

Julia and Suzanne are swept up in the contagion of fear which takes over the ghetto. The transports are all that people can talk about. About their destination, Suzanne says bravely, 'It could hardly be worse than this', but it is obvious that even she doesn't believe these words. They are unable to write or even talk about the book. It still doesn't have a title – they have only ever referred to it as 'the book'. They are unable to sleep or think about anything but the transports.

Early on the morning of the 13th, the list for the first transport is posted and having fought their way through the milling crowd, Julia and Suzanne almost faint with relief to find that they are not on it.

However, the ghetto descends into turmoil.

People try to pull whatever strings they can to get themselves removed from the list. It appears that lots of children are going on the first transport. Inevitably this has resulted in situations where children are on the list but their parents are being left behind. Whether this has been by accident or by design is now of less concern to frantic mothers and fathers than that they try to get the situation remedied. They either want themselves added to the transport or their children removed. But the Germans have strict quotas – twenty-five hundred people per transport. Some parents find themselves in the bizarre position of trying to trade with other people to get *on* the transport. There are stories doing the rounds of parents not being able to arrange any of this and Julia can't even begin to imagine what the torment of those parents must be like.

In the barracks, people are packing and saying their goodbyes. There is much crying. While Julia and Suzanne have mostly kept to themselves, this doesn't mean that they haven't made friends. Now, many of these are scheduled to leave on the 15th. They say their goodbyes. People make arrangements to meet after the war. In Prague. In Amsterdam. In Vienna. Wherever they happen to be from. All these different nationalities. Some talk of emigrating to Eretz Israel when the war is finally over.

There are tears and hugs. People offer words of comfort. Julia and Suzanne offer them to the people they have known but the words sound empty to Julia's ears. Some people have made little gifts for those leaving – a drawing, a card – or they have given them a little bit of food – a slice of bread, a potato.

Finally, the lights are put out on the night of the 14th. With full suitcases and backpacks everywhere an uneasy quiet settles over the barracks. Julia can't imagine that anybody sleeps.

In the morning at first light she goes to the window and looks out. People are already moving down the street, hauling their suitcases and bags. Around each person's neck is a string attached to a card bearing their transport number. For those left behind in the barracks there is a sense of unbelievable relief. But it only seems to last for an instant because everybody knows that, even now, the list for the next transport is already being drawn up.

It appears later that day. Julia has a blinding stress headache by the time she and Suzanne repeat their fight through the crowd. Julia checks and checks again. She asks Suzanne just to be sure.

'We're not on it, are we?'

Although trying to retain an outward calm, Suzanne is as pale as a ghost and her face is almost rigid with fear.

'No, we're not,' Suzanne says.

The two girls embrace.

But of course, then the cycle starts again for the third transport, which is to leave on the 18th. Julia believes that their luck has to run out soon and her headache doesn't lift. Her old life in Amsterdam, the book, everything is forgotten now as Julia's life comes down to this transport. Where is it going? Will Suzanne be coming too or is it just Julia? What should she bring? Not that she has very much.

Suzanne makes one of those pronouncements that she is prone to making.

'We're not going to be on the third one,' she says.

This just causes Julia to fly into a rage.

'How the fuck can you say that?' she screams. 'You stupid fucking bitch and the stupid fucking things you say.'

But it turns out that Suzanne is right. There is no sign of either of their names on the third and final list. Julia can't pull herself away. She keeps checking until Suzanne says to her softly, 'We're not there, Julia. We're not.'

It is evening as they return to the barracks. There is a mournful calmness and sense of loneliness in the air. Julia has apologised to Suzanne who tells her she understands and that Julia has nothing to be sorry for. A lot of the time Julia finds Suzanne's equilibrium anything from irritating through obnoxious to unbearable but tonight it is so comforting.

The barrack they return to is a mess. There are discarded items of clothing, broken crockery and papers scattered about the floor. Books have been discarded as no longer being of any use. There are empty or broken washing lines. Suzanne picks up a photograph of a family – it looks like three generations, grandparents, parents and children.

Under one of the bunks, Julia finds a little book. About the size of her hand and bound in dark blue, it has 'AUTOGRAPHS' written in ornate gold letters on the front. She leafs through it. It looks like many of the friends of whoever owned this book have signed it. 'Best wishes,' it says over and over again. 'Best wishes for '42-'43.' 'Best of luck.' 'Yours ever.' 'Love and best wishes.' The last page reads, 'To sweet, dear and fair Claire' with an illegible flourish of a signature after it. Julia guesses it is male handwriting.

She closes the book. She isn't sure whether to take it or leave it there. She hesitates but finally she takes it and puts it in the pocket of her cardigan.

Later, as she falls into an utterly exhausted and dreamless sleep, her last conscious thought is of 'sweet, dear and fair Claire' and to wonder who she was.

41

The next morning Julia wakes to a world without transport lists. Already the people who survived the last few days are getting on with their lives. Much of the debris of yesterday evening that was scattered around the barrack floor has already disappeared. Even things that might have appeared broken and beyond any kind of use or recovery in the normal world, have gone. Such things can be made to serve some kind of purpose in the ghetto – its occupants are infinitely inventive. And there's something else – something that had never occurred to Julia before. There are lots of spare bunks.

It turns out there are ones right under and over the middle bunk that she and Suzanne have been sharing up until now. Julia takes possession of the lower one straight away. For the moment they have an entire three-bunk bed to themselves.

'Now we have my place and your place,' Julia says to Suzanne.

'That's a step in the right direction,' says Suzanne with her usual glass-half-full view of things which, at least on this occasion, Julia is happy to accept.

It turns out too that whoever doles out the rations hasn't yet got the amounts reduced proportionately and so for this breakfast, there is extra food. The quantity is almost enough to be satisfying but because her stomach has been used to so little, for a few hours at least, Julia has the illusion of being full.

The day is fine and she and Suzanne are put together in a gang with others cleaning a side street. This involves picking up all the garbage, then going back down the street, clearing any dirt or mud from between the cobbles, before finally mopping the street.

'Mopping the street – have you ever heard of anything so fucking stupid?' says Julia.

But the work is not too demanding, the warm sun is on their backs – at least for some of the day – and they are together. They talk about the plot and what is to happen next to Birkita. They talk too about the significance of the big clean-up.

Ever since it began at the start of the year, there were bonkes that the great beautification was for a visit to be made by the International Committee of the Red Cross. Now it appears that that is indeed what is going to happen. Nobody knows when it will be yet but the thought cheers Julia enormously. If somebody like the Red Cross is visiting here then maybe the war is indeed coming to an end. Maybe after this visit conditions will improve, there will be more food, and they can start thinking about when they will eventually leave here.

Julia is hesitant to talk about it. She doesn't want to jinx anything by building up hopes. But she and Suzanne work away contentedly and by the time they are finished and head back to the barracks – Julia refuses to call or think of it as 'home' – they think they have worked out where the book is going next.

Julia is going to spend her first night in her new bed. To mark this occasion, and even though there is only cold water, she strips completely and washes herself all over. She doesn't just feel she is washing away the dirt and sweat of the day. She has a real sense that she is erasing the horror of the last few days and the transport lists. Her skin feels tingly afterwards and she smells of soap as opposed to just smelling which is how she normally is.

Suzanne has had an all-over wash too and she is just sitting on her bunk, brushing out her hair when Julia returns. On an impulse, Julia asks, 'Want to sleep at my place tonight?'

Suzanne looks up and laughs.

'Your place,' she says. 'Yes. That'd be nice. Want me to bring anything? Wine? Some food? A house-warming present?'

'No, no,' says Julia, playing along. 'Just yourself.'

The girls settle in together on the lower bunk. For a while they just lie facing each other looking into each other's eyes. At length, Julia says, 'We made it. We're still here.'

'I think this means we're going to make it right to the –'

Julia puts a finger on Suzanne's lips. No pronouncements. No jinxing. Not tonight.

Suzanne's eyes are bright.

Julia leans forward and kisses Suzanne on the lips.

In the hours that follow, try as Julia does to imprint every moment, every feeling, every sensation, on her brain, to lose nothing, to forget nothing, to remember everything, it is just too much. The avalanche of bliss that descends upon her in the next few hours is such that she can only remember a handful of things – though more will return to her, often unexpectedly, in the weeks and months that are to follow. Sometimes they will be triggered by a word or a gesture of Suzanne's. Or an expression on her face or a note in her voice. Or a smell – maybe the most evocative of the senses. Or sometimes an urgent need not to forget. Or sometimes – it seems – by nothing at all. Vaguely too, on the edge of her consciousness, Julia becomes aware that other people in the barracks are doing what they are doing. It is survival. A celebration of life.

Julia remembers Suzanne showering – literally showering – kisses on her face. It is like it is raining kisses.

Later there is Suzanne with her face between Julia's thighs. She cannot see Suzanne's face – only the top of her head, her beautiful blonde hair. But Suzanne is using her tongue to bring Julia to the biggest, most long-lasting, most shuddering climax she has ever had. It is as though Julia has left her body and that everything – the ghetto, life in Amsterdam, her childhood, everything – are just small figures acting out dramas and glimpsed from a very long way off. Like through the wrong end of a telescope. After, Suzanne will say that she didn't really know what she was doing – just that she'd always wanted to do it to Julia.

And then there is Suzanne lying open to Julia and she is doing to Suzanne what Suzanne did to her. And Suzanne is soon whimpering and then panting and then squealing with squeals that could be pain except Julia knows they are not. And then one of Suzanne's hands grabs one of Julia's, fingers interlaced, and squeezes it with a strength that Julia would not have thought Suzanne possessed. And Suzanne is trying to push Julia off with her hands, with her knees, and Julia sticks to her like a limpet until Suzanne gasps, 'Stop, Julia. Stop. You're killing me.' And eventually Julia does stop and Suzanne moans softly as though she has just been badly hurt or even tortured.

Later they do the same thing to each other with their fingers. Maybe they sleep for a while during that night – Julia is not sure. In fact, there are times when Julia doesn't know if she is waking or sleeping or dreaming or died and gone to a heaven she doesn't believe in.

They breathe and whisper words of endearment to each other. 'My darling.' 'Love.' 'You beautiful girl.' Sometimes Julia doesn't know if she is the one saying the words or hearing them. They touch each other's faces, tracing features with fingertips – eyebrows, lips. They kiss fingertips. Eyes. They caress the curves of each other's bodies. They stroke each other's hair until their fingers become entangled in it. Julia is astonished at how Suzanne's face seems to change when she comes close to orgasm.

And in the morning when they wake, Suzanne says simply, 'I love you, Julia.'

42

'How do you know?' asks Julia.

'How do I know what?' replies Suzanne.

'You said this morning that you love me. How do you know?'

It is evening. Work is finished, they have eaten and are sitting on the grassy ramparts of Theresienstadt in the May warmth. The setting sun has turned Suzanne's skin a sort of golden-orange colour.

Julia has never felt so confident about her relationship with another person. She has no fears about it; no fears that Suzanne will go out of her life or do something to hurt her. She feels she can say anything to Suzanne and this is what she is doing now. She also sees that she wants Suzanne to talk about what has happened between them. She wants to hear it confirmed not out of any sense of unease but just for the sheer pleasure of hearing what it looks like from Suzanne's side.

'It's like I got a letter,' says Suzanne.

Julia raises an eyebrow.

'A letter?'

'You get a feeling and something tells you that it's right, that you can trust it. Remember I told you about the boy next door to where I was hiding, the fellow that I thought betrayed me? Well, when he was asking over the wall, who was there, I had a feeling, a really strong feeling, that nothing good would come of replying to him. It was like I got a letter, the feeling was so strong. And I see now I didn't get that feeling with Adolf.'

'No letter,' says Julia.

'Exactly. No letter.'

'And you got a letter with me?'

'I did,' says Suzanne.

She takes a deep breath.

'When I was in school, I fell in love with a girl in my class. For a brief time – maybe a week or two – it felt wonderful. But then I realised – I'm in love with a girl. I was terrified. What if people found out? And even if they didn't, what was wrong with me? There was nobody I could turn to. I tried praying but that did no good. It was like I was talking to the air – to nothing. And so I tried to be 'normal'. I started to walk home from school with a boy but he seemed so uninteresting and he soon lost interest in me. After that, whenever my father asked me whether there was anybody in school that I fancied, I would invent a boyfriend.

'So I poured myself into studying. I didn't have many friends and I kept to myself. I was afraid I would get too close to somebody and that my secret might get out. One summer there was a girl – in Pompeii, actually – on a dig. An Italian girl. She was so beautiful. But I said and did nothing, just longed to be with her all the time I was there and pined for her for years afterwards.

'That whole thing with Adolf. I think it was one last effort to be "normal". To want to be with boys, just like other girls. But now I know I'm not ... I'm not that way. And will never be. Couldn't be. You know, looking back on it, I think wanting to sleep with him was just to confirm that I wasn't interested and would never do that again. Have you never had a feeling like that, Julia? A certainty?'

After a long silence, Julia says, 'I know now that what happened with my father … I knew it wasn't right … that I should have gone to somebody. My mother. The Rabbi. The police. Somebody. Even if they all hadn't believed me, even if they had tried to lock me up in a madhouse, I should have shouted it from the rooftops. If I could put the clock back now, that is what I would do…'

Julia's voice drifts off.

'You were a child,' says Suzanne. 'How could you have known?'

'I got a letter – just like you say. But I tore it up. Or hid it in a drawer. It's taken all this time to come out.'

'But now it's out,' says Suzanne. 'And you'll never ignore a letter again.'

'No, I won't.'

That night Julia has a dream. When she wakes in the morning she only has fragments of it – a bicycle leaning against a wall by a back door painted red. A little plot of ground that has been dug over, raked and seeded with vegetables. The plot is criss-crossed with string upon which strips of newspaper or rag have been tied. The strips flap and keep the birds away from the seeds. As they are walking to work and as Julia tells Suzanne about these images, other details return to her so that she is able to reconstruct the dream in full.

'It is where we are going to live after the war,' says Julia. 'You and I. It is a little cottage in a little village or maybe a small town. It is maybe outside Amsterdam. Or it could be in Amsterdam. Or somewhere else altogether. One of those places that gets swallowed up by a city but never really loses its feeling of being a village. It has a small sunlit square where you can go and just sit for hours. Have coffee or a drink. It's one of those little places where everybody knows everybody else. Everyone smiles. Strangers say hello.

'So our cottage has a little garden where we're growing vegetables. Well – we've just started. And it has a red back door. And two bikes. And in my dream it wasn't the summer. It was cold and had started to rain so that the gardening had been called off. Actually, it was a slow Sunday afternoon where we have work the next day.'

'What kind of work?' asks Suzanne.

'Dunno. Writers? Aren't we going to be writers?'

'We are,' smiles Suzanne. 'Words have power. We need to keep saying it.'

'OK, so next day, we'll be working on our current novel. But today we've lit the fire and we're cooking. Or maybe baking. Stew or a cake or biscuits. The kitchen is full of the most wonderful smells.'

Suzanne pushes Julia playfully on the shoulder.

'Stop,' she says. 'You're driving me crazy.'

'It's going to happen,' says Julia. 'Just you wait and see. I know. That dream. I got a letter.'

43

'So they land in Gaul,' says Julia, 'and then what?'

She and Suzanne are working side by side, mopping their way down the street outside the Magdeburg barracks. It is completely pointless work. Despite the deportations, this small town normally home to around five thousand people is housing many times more than that. It seethes with people. Anything that is cleaned will be dirty again an hour later. So this will all have to be done again many, many times before the important visitors come. But Julia and Suzanne don't mind. They are together and they are talking about the book.

'They go inland. They find a place to live,' Suzanne says.

'What kind of a place?'

'By a stream or a river, so they can have water. I see an open, grassy area by the water's edge and then beyond that a forest.'

'Do they live by themselves?'

'I don't think so. I think they find a village and ask the headman if they can come to live there.'

'And he lets them?'

'He turns out to be a nice guy and he's been fighting the Romans all his life. Birkita explains what the Romans did to her family and that gets his sympathy. Then, she tells them about Galena and the farm and everything that happened. And then you can imagine the headman roaring with laughter when she tells them how they let out all the animals and burned the farm. So yes, I think he would let them stay. Women and children aren't any threat. And it's always good to have women. Life was precarious then. Battle, disease, illness. The more women, the more babies. The more babies, the more likely the tribe are to continue and have a future.'

It makes sense.

'So they should really just live happily ever after now,' says Julia.

'That'd be nice,' says Suzanne. 'For them.'

44

Suzanne begins the writing of chapter thirty-two. She has already mapped it out with Julia. This will cover the arrival in Gaul, finding the village and the headman telling them they can stay. It will describe how the village bands together to build a hut for the new arrivals. Then will come the onset of winter and how Birkita's little family is warm and snug and has enough food. The girls will pick up the Gaulish language very quickly and, in that way that children have, soon make friends.

At different times over the winter, young men in the village will approach Birkita and Galena but they make it clear that they are not interested. The headman will come to them and tell them that the men of the village are completely confused by these two women – something he finds hugely amusing. After a time, the approaches will stop.

The writing takes Julia and Suzanne into June and covers chapters thirty-two through to thirty-six. They alternate – when one feels they're getting a bit tired or their ideas are drying up, the other takes over. They are working together most days and they do their writing after dinner in the evenings.

The days get longer, the weather is good a lot of the time. They are still achingly hungry but their weight loss doesn't seem as dramatic now and Julia feels it may even have stopped. Whether it has or not, she has ceased to think about it much.

One evening, Julia writes the last few words of chapter thirty-three. Ever since they began writing, whenever they finished a chapter they always have a little celebration. It might only be a hug or to eat a piece of food that they had saved for the occasion. Then they always write the chapter heading of the next chapter. It is a reminder that they will have to do it all again tomorrow, that no matter how well they think they had done today or how far they have travelled, tomorrow – once again – the blank page will be waiting for them.

Julia is about to write the heading for chapter thirty-four when she does something else. Quickly she scribbles down, 'For me, the last few days have been like reading the first pages of a big fat novel that I've not read before, hearing the opening bars of a symphony that I've never heard, seeing the first moments of a long movie that I've not seen: There is so much to be discovered.'

Then she writes 'Chapter Thirty-four' and draws a line under it.

'May I see?' asks Suzanne.

Julia hands her the book and watches while Suzanne reads. Then she looks up and smiles.

'Me too,' she says.

Later that night, after they have made love and lie sweating in the warm June night, Julia bursts into tears. One of the things she loves about Suzanne is that, when it really, really matters, she always seems to know the right thing to do or say. Now Suzanne just holds Julia while she cries.

When she has finished, Julia says, 'Tell me about your childhood.'

'I was lucky,' begins Suzanne. 'My parents loved me. And they were well off. They had to work, of course, but they loved their work. To them it wasn't like work. We lived in a nice house. We always had plenty. In the summers we travelled. It was perfect. I was lucky,' she says again. 'Very lucky.'

After a long silence, Julia says, 'Every childhood should be like that.'

'They should.'

The next silence is so long that Julia thinks Suzanne may have fallen asleep. She lies in the crook of Suzanne's arm and looks up now to see. But Suzanne's eyes are open and bright.

"I don't mean to make light of all you've suffered,' says Suzanne, 'but it's made you who you are. You know that, don't you? You wouldn't be the Julia I love – in fact, we probably wouldn't even have met if it wasn't for your past and everything you've gone through.'

Julia knows it's true. Had she had the same kind of loving family as Suzanne, she would never have left home. That would probably have meant she would have been rounded up during the deportations of 1942 and 1943. Or else she would have gone into hiding like Suzanne. But yes, the chances they would have met would have been miniscule.

'I just wish I could leave it all behind me,' she says. 'All that … that stuff. Everything that happened. I feel … I don't know … cheated or something. No, it's more than that. It's like I was given something and then I lost it. And I keep looking for it even though I know … I know I can never find it again. If I could just stop this stupid fucking searching…'

Julia goes silent. Her head lies near Suzanne's breast and she can feel and hear her heart beating. It is rhythmic. Big. Solid. Almost permanent – like it might never stop.

'You'll find a way,' whispers Suzanne. 'I know you will. That's what you do.'

45

Disaster is looming. As Julia and Suzanne have been writing, they have been getting closer and closer to the end of the notebook. Each night, they count the remaining pages. There is now only a handful. No matter how small they make their writing, they know they're not going to have enough paper. They ask around on their barrack floor. Does anybody have a notebook they'd be prepared to give up? Or even sell – for food? When that fails they ask for paper – even loose sheets.

Suzanne says that Adolf would have paper and that she could go to him. She'd even be prepared to – but as she starts to say this, Julia silences her. They ask their workmates, some of whom are in other barracks but nobody has paper – or if they do, they're not prepared to part with it.

Then Julia has an idea. What about Irena at the hospital? Maybe she could spare some paper. They go there after work but there is no Irena. It turns out she was deported in the May deportations. Beautiful, gentle Irena, who was given an impossible job and managed it with unbelievable dignity. Julia shakes her head. Is there no end to it?

A new woman is in Irena's place – Eva. In her fifties, she has raven coloured hair without the slightest hint of

387

grey in it. The girls explain their plight. The expression on Eva's face changes from interest to intrigue until finally, she is smiling.

'I think I may have just the thing,' she says.

Eva uses the same desk and chair that Irena used to use. She reaches into one of the drawers and extracts – a notebook. It has a soft cardboard cover with pictures of fruit on it – peaches, cherries, apples, pears. Eva opens it. The first page has writing on it in blue fountain pen. Reading upside down, Julia can see that it is a diary. There are two blocks of writing each of which begins with a date. Eva turns the first few pages. There are more entries but then, after about the fifth or sixth page, they stop.

'May the fourteenth, 1943,' she says.

She looks up at them.

'He either died then or gave up writing or was deported.'

Eva tears out the pages with entries on them and hands over the notebook.

'Good luck,' she says. 'Oh, and here's something else that might be useful.'

She gives them two rubber bands.

'Keep your story all together.'

Outside the hospital, the girls are jubilant. The notebook is about half the thickness of the other one but it should be enough to finish the book. They know they're coming into the closing stages of it.

'We must celebrate,' says Suzanne.

'But maybe not tonight,' says Julia, thinking of Irena.

They do the next night. That is the way in the ghetto. Always life has to go on. People have to find a way. They keep some of their food from dinner and on the first page of the new notebook, Suzanne begins writing the menu for the celebratory dinner. 'Bean soup with noodles.' Julia takes the book from her and writes 'hearty' in front of 'bean soup'. Then she hands it back.

'Roast chicken with spring vegetables,' Suzanne continues, speaking as she writes.

'We have to say what the vegetables are,' says Julia.

'Carrots, peas, roast potatoes. Golden brown. Very crispy outside and soft and fluffy inside.

'Onions,' adds Julia. 'Lots of them. Fried.'

'Asparagus,' says Suzanne. 'The most perfect vegetable in the whole world.'

'Gravy.'

And for dessert a selection of cakes. They spend a long time discussing what kinds of cakes. Eventually, they are ready to start and they eat their food, mouthful by mouthful, imagining this feast.

'It's dining "as if"', says Suzanne. 'Welcome to the Restaurant As-If.'

46

Julia is angry. She's angry at her father, at her mother for not protecting her, at herself for not acting on her feelings and going to somebody – the Rabbi, her schoolteacher, the police, anybody who might have listened. She's angry that she can't rewind the clock and do any of that now. She's angry that her parents are dead and that she can't confront them.

She has an image in her head of this anger. It is of a barrel of gunpowder with a long fuse on it. The fuse has already been lit and it is burning, running across the ground. It runs across sand, through grass, across mud, along city streets, along by tram tracks, across bridges, up a garden path, through doorways, up stairs, across floors but no matter how much it burns, it never reaches the barrel of gunpowder. If it did, she has a feeling that that would be the end of her anger. And she wants to be done with this anger. But instead, the fuse just sputters along its way. One night she even dreams about the fuse.

'You know we'll have to go to Pompeii,' says Suzanne one evening towards the middle of June.

They have finished chapter thirty-five – they wrote the last paragraphs while sitting on the grass – and there is still some time before lights out. They are on the ramparts while swallows swoop overhead like tiny curved axe blades in the sky.

'I hadn't thought,' says Julia.

'Of course we will. You have to see it – especially the lupanar. I have to see it – my memory may not have been completely accurate. After all, it was seven years ago. And you have to get a sense of the place. We both do. Actually – what we have to do is take the book and read it there, at least the chapters that are set there. It'll be like opening the door to the past. Who knows – we might even have dreams or visions while we're there. Anyway, I think it will cause us to make changes – even if they're only small ones. But it will all heighten the authenticity. And what we certainly don't want is that somebody reads our book and we have got something wildly wrong and it bounces them out of our imaginary world. That'd be a disaster.'

'How far is it?' askes Julia.

'From here? I don't know. Maybe a couple of thousand kilometres.'

That night as she drifts between wakefulness and sleeping, Julia imagines going to Pompeii. She sees herself walking in the gate – which gate she'll ask Suzanne in the morning – but some gate. When she walks in that gate she'll know finally that she is free and her life can start again.

How will they get there? Train, she imagines. What does it cost? Will they have money? What's going to happen when they leave here? How will it happen? Will somebody free them? The Russians? The Americans? Or will the Germans just pack up and leave?

So now she goes over it again, trying to answer all these questions. They arrive by train in Pompeii. Or is it Naples? Ask Suzanne in the morning. They have money. Maybe they were given some by whoever freed them or maybe they got a job. Yes, that's better. They were freed by the Americans, she imagines. She'd prefer that. And she and Suzanne got jobs working for the Americans. Doing what, it doesn't matter. Waitress. Working in a kitchen. Or an office. The important thing is that they have money.

And if they are freed this year, then they can work all winter and have enough money to go to Pompeii in the spring. April, maybe.

And now a very strange thing happens.

Because Julia suddenly has a vision of the fuse again. And it has been set alight at Pompeii – an unseen person has touched a match to it. But the barrel of gunpowder is in Theresienstadt – here in the barracks, in fact. Right under her bed, actually. And now the fuse begins to burn.

Down from Pompeii to the railway station in Naples – along the narrow roads that run along the coast that Suzanne has described to her. With blue water twinkling silver in the distance and huge lemons growing on the trees.

And then running alongside the railway track where the train that will bring them to Pompeii will run. All that distance. The two thousand kilometres or whatever it is. She assumes they will have to change trains from time to time, that there isn't a direct route, but that's OK. Every time they get off the train to wait for the next one, the fuse burns along the blackened cinders in the railway bed. Julia sees it, bright yellow in the black.

And then they're back on next train and the fuse is running beside the rail. They can see it out the window. At least Julia can see it.

It's almost become like a happy little companion. When night falls, it is bright, a sort of bluish white sizzling along as Julia gazes at it through the big window while the train rackets along. It goes all up Italy. Across the Alps. Julia's knowledge of geography isn't very good but she knows that much. Along valleys, yellow on green, over passes, sizzling across snow, the blue flame vivid against the blinding white.

And then down again onto the plains. Is that Switzerland? Or Austria? Julia is not sure. But it doesn't matter anyway. Then the fuse turns north east crossing into Czechoslovakia. And then on up, burning across fields, over countryside, finding bridges to cross rivers, through villages and towns and cities.

Finally, the fuse burns right up to the gates of the base where the Americans are and where Julia and Suzanne are working. It passes under the barrier at the gate, unseen by the sentries, and crosses the parade ground. The tiny blazing light flies up some steps and in through a doorway. It burns across the floor of the hall where the Americans eat. It shoots under the swing door of the kitchen and Julia, standing at a sink washing dishes, hears it as it sizzles behind her. She glances over her shoulder and she just has time to see it disappear round the corner of a cooker. Then it is out under the wire fence that surrounds the base and it is heading for its final destination.

And now, at last, it comes through the gate at Theresienstadt – the same one through which their train came through all that time ago. The fuse wire has settled in the bottom of one of the tracks that runs up Bahnhofstrasse and so the flame burns brightly there. But then the wire takes a sudden ninety degree turn like a racing driver on a bend and climbs the steps of the very barracks in which Julia lies asleep.

She knows that the barrel of gunpowder is under her bed but she feels no fear. The fuse wire snakes up the stairs, climbing steps, turning corners. The black wire is consumed as the tiny, fizzing yellow flame hurtles upwards. It is going very fast now. Much faster than a fuse could in real life. It is as though it knows its journey is coming to an end. It's like a marathon runner who knows that the race is won and has begun to sprint the last two hundred metres.

The fuse rounds the door frame of the room in which Julia lies asleep. It whizzes across the floor and in under her bed. She still feels no fear. It is as though she is watching this from somewhere else. The flame rockets up the side of the barrel and onto the lid. There, there is a small hole into which the fuse wire disappears. The yellow-blue flame seems to hesitate for a second. It has stopped. It is still burning but it is not moving. The hole in the lid of the barrel waits like an open mouth but the flame refuses to go in.

And then, with a faint sputtering sound almost like a sigh of weariness, it goes out. There is a tiny puff of black smoke that quickly diffuses into the air leaving only the smell of burnt cord behind.

When Julia wakes in the morning, her anger is gone.

47

Adolf is handing out their work assignments for the day. It is the eve of the visit of the International Committee of the Red Cross.

Julia stands to one side of Suzanne and studies her face. Even though it has become painfully thin with her hollow cheeks and shadowed eyes, Suzanne's face is usually relaxed and – as Julia sees it – always ready to break into a smile. But the morning allocation of work, when she has to deal with Adolf, is the one exception. Here, Suzanne's face is immobile, unsmiling, as though it were carved out of rock.

This morning Adolf has allocated work to everybody except the two girls.

'It's your lucky day,' he says with a smile without warmth.

Julia feels Suzanne stiffen beside her.

'Take these and report to the Marktplatz,' says Adolf. 'Don't open them until you get there.'

He hands them each a brown paper parcel tied with string. Julia has a momentary flashback to Bert's film and Chantal being the postman. And of course, the first thing she does when she is out of sight of Adolf, is to open the parcel. It contains a dark blue skirt and a white blouse, so clean and possibly new that it seems to almost shimmer in the sunlight. The yellow star is bright on the left breast. Julia and Suzanne look at each other quizzically. They shrug and tie up the parcel again before heading for the Marktplatz.

A final frenzy of activity is going on. A man on a stepladder paints the top of a door frame. A signwriter puts the final touches to the last letter of a shop sign in gold. A sign reading ZUR BUCHEREI, 'To the library', is attached to a wall. There are shrubs and flowers and plants everywhere. The ghetto has been transformed. Now, in many ways, it *is* the Paradise Ghetto.

They pass a sign advertising an evening of lieder sung by Karel Berman with Rafael Schichter on the piano. There will be songs by Wolf, Beethoven, Haas and Dvorak. On their right, a street has been roped off. The walls of the buildings are pristine and the cobblestones there almost glow, they are so clean. There are signs everywhere: TO THE BANK. TO THE POST OFFICE. TO THE COFFEEHOUSE. TO THE BATHS.

They pass a building that was an old school and which had been used as a hospital. A few weeks ago, the patients were cleared out and the rooms were given a fresh coat of paint. School benches were installed and the place now has a sign above the entrance in gold letters that reads: SCHOOL FOR BOYS AND GIRLS. Pinned to the door is a piece of paper with the single word, VACATION, written on it.

Some of the barracks have been renovated apparently. One, that houses young girls, has been repainted, given brand new furniture – bunks, desks, tables, benches. Each girl, so the rumour goes, has her own locker, all different colours, decorated with pictures of animals. The lockers apparently have been filled with food. There is an art exhibition on the second floor of the Magdeburg Barracks with paintings of different aspects of Theresienstadt.

And it isn't just renovation that has gone on in the ghetto. There are whole new constructions. There is a newly built children's pavilion, all done in glass and wood. There's a nursery for the very smallest children and a playground with a merry-go-round, swings and monkey bars.

The girls reach the town's main square, Marktplatz. Now that the work is pretty much complete, the town's new appearance is quite unbelievable. The main square used to be surrounded by barbed wire, inside which was a huge circus tent. The tent housed over a thousand people who worked making boxes. Now, all of that is gone. In its place there is a vibrant green lawn interspersed with flower beds and snapdragons. Newly sanded paths intersect the lawns and these are lined with freshly painted benches, set on concrete supports. And there are not just one or two benches. Suzanne deliberately counts them. There are seventy three of them. Julia watches an old man in a threadbare overcoat and battered hat gingerly sit on one. It is as though he is afraid it will explode or collapse or fold shut and swallow him up. But it does none of these things and eventually his shoulders settle and he relaxes in the sunshine. The black coat and hat seem at odds with the white light of the morning and the soft pastel colours with which everything has been painted.

A rectangular bandstand has been erected in the centre of the square. Square pillars at each of the four corners support a roof with gaily painted sides. Two or three steps lead up to the bandstand and a group of musicians are just packing up their instruments as the girls arrive. It looks like the musicians have been rehearsing. Around the bandstand, a crowd of people that had been listening is gradually beginning to disperse.

There have always been so-called 'shops' in the ghetto. Items stolen from the people when they arrived –

in other words, almost anything of any possible value – would reappear in the shops a few days later. New arrivals often found themselves buying back their own possessions. It was a joke in the ghetto that you could go into a shop and find a shirt with your monogram already on it. Now, all the shops around Marktplatz have been given new signs: PERFUMERY, DRUGSTORE, GROCERY, SHOES, CLOTHING, LADIES' UNDERWEAR. Only the best goods are on show in window displays and with advertising boards that wouldn't have been out of place in a smart boutique in any capital city. The window of the grocery store contains things that some of the ghetto inmates – those that have managed to survive that long – haven't seen for years. There is fresh meat, freshly baked bread – white and dark – sausage, fruit, vegetables.

They see a group of young girls all holding brown paper parcels and Julia nudges Suzanne.

'There,' she says.

They join the rest of the girls. Nobody knows what is happening and an anxious feeling about the whole thing starts to build. But shortly afterwards two men arrive, each carrying an armful of garden rakes, which they deposit near the girls. Minutes later a third man appears. He explains what they have to do. Tomorrow, they must wear the new clothes and during the visit, they must 'happen' to cross the visitors' path, with the rakes over their shoulders, as if going to work. He also explains that they must be whistling or singing happily while doing this.

Julia and Suzanne look at each other. Suzanne's eyes are bright with laughter. Julia shakes her head in disbelief. But it is better than work. They spend the rest of the morning rehearsing this. They try it with both singing and whistling and in the end, the man decides that singing is better. After that, they are told to be back here at eight in the morning and are given the rest of the day off.

The girls wander out towards the ramparts, one of the few places in the ghetto where they can be in nature and find beauty. They find a path that, up until now, had been barricaded with barbed wire. Now, the wire is gone and the path is open. They look at one another, puzzled. They look around. But there are no guards, no Germans with rifles. Hesitantly they take a first few steps down the path, waiting to hear an angry shout. But no shout comes. With a little more confidence now, they proceed down the path. It leads into a meadow full of flowers in bloom.

The girls sit down in the meadow and talk. What does it all mean? Is the war almost over? Is this all just for the Red Cross visit? Is it to fool them? They ask the questions but they have no answers. Eventually, as dinner time approaches, they leave and return to their barracks.

The Red Cross visit itself takes place on June 23rd. Julia and Suzanne, dressed in their new clothes, are in the Marktplatz by eight along with all the other girls. They all look pretty in their white blouses and dark blue skirts but Julia thinks that the vomit-coloured yellow star on each of the blouses ruins the whole effect. The man who rehearsed them yesterday is already there. He seems very nervous. The girls are formed into pairs and marched off down a side street. Here they wait while the man stands at the top of the street, repeatedly looking at his watch and glancing out around the corner.

In the end it is nearly noon before anything happens. By then, the girls are weary from standing, but when one of them goes to sit down, the man barks at her to stay standing, that otherwise she would dirty her skirt. Eventually, a boy appears and says something to the man. He buttons up his jacket and straightens his hat – he is overdressed for what is turning out to be a warm day.

The girls are ordered to shoulder their rakes. They do so like a well-drilled squad of soldiers. The man continues to look around the corner. He appears to get some kind of signal because he tells the girls to start singing which they do. He's not happy so he tells them that they must do it louder. They do. He glances round the corner again, hesitates for a few seconds and then, judging the moment to be right, says – just as though he were an army drill sergeant – 'Quick ... march! And don't forget – plenty of smiling and laughing and joking.'

'What's the difference between a smart German and a unicorn?' hisses Suzanne, as they wait for the girls in front to move off.

'Dunno,' says Julia.

'No difference,' says Suzanne. 'They're both fictional creatures.'

Julia snorts with laughter.

The girls walk out of the side street. Over on the left are a cluster of men, some in German uniforms, some in their best ghetto clothes. They pause as the singing squad of girls walk across their path and into a neighbouring side street. Here, another man is waiting for them. He leads them to the end of the street where they turn left. He orders them to halt.

'Thank you, ladies,' he says and Julia is struck by the look of disgust and self-loathing on his face. 'Now we wait.'

They spend the rest of the day waiting here until a signal finally comes that the visit is over. By then it is dinner time and everybody is weak from hunger and thirst. The girls are given leave to disperse and go back to their rooms with the proviso that they must hand back the white blouses and blue skirts before the day is out.

Most people are confined to barracks for the duration of the visit and so see very little of what takes place. But for weeks afterwards gossip swirls about things people witnessed and it is possible to get a picture of what happened.

The visitors were taken along a carefully planned route, the streets that had been roped off being where they travelled. A number of men – ghetto residents – went ahead of the visitors. The job of these men was to signal to the appropriate groups of people when they should do what they were meant to do. Thus the visitors saw Julia and Suzanne's group walk past, laughing and singing, as they supposedly headed off to work in the fields. A soccer match was in progress and a goal just happened to be scored as the visitors paused for a few moments to watch the game.

In the bakery, bakers wore white gloves as they handled white bread. Elderly people sat around the bandstand and listened to a concert. Chess players sat at tables studiously pondering their next move.

At the children's pavilion, healthy-looking children played happily with dolls and teddy bears that they had been given only an hour before. They called to the camp commandant, Rahm, saying, 'When are you going to play with us again, Uncle Rahm?' to which the commandant replied, 'I'm sorry. Not now, children. Another time.' The children were being given slices of bread and butter just as the visitors arrived.

At the bank they met the 'manager' who smoked a cigar and offered them cigarettes. Parcels were being passed out at the post office. In the hospital, healthy people lay between clean white sheets – the sick had been moved somewhere else.

In the coffee house there were elegantly dressed women in silk stockings, stylish dresses, hats, scarves and handbags. Men in well-cut suits accompanied them as they sipped real coffee and ate cake.

'How could anyone with half a brain be fooled by that?' asks Julia as they sit exhausted in the warm courtyard eating their evening meal.

48

'I've got you a present,' says Suzanne.

'What is it?' asks Julia excitedly. She loves presents. She can't remember when last someone gave her one. It must have been the Christmas before she left home. Bert used to give her what he called 'presents' but they weren't really – she always had to give him something in return.

Suzanne hands Julia two small pieces of rectangular pink card with some printing and perforations on them. Julia looks up, puzzled.

'Tickets,' says Suzanne. 'For *Brundibár*.'

Brundibár is a children's opera written by a composer who is actually a ghetto inmate. Whenever it is performed – which is often – signs are posted up and, even though it is the ghetto, tickets are printed. The signs show a group of children peeping over a wooden fence. *Brundibár* is so popular that it is almost impossible to get tickets for it.

'How did you get these?' asks Julia, holding the two tickets in the upturned palm of her hand.

'Traded some food for them,' says Suzanne.

She is grinning from ear to ear.

'What food? Your food?'

'Yes, my food.'

Julia is at a loss. 'But why –?'

'It's our anniversary. We've been … well, you know – for six weeks.'

'But Suzanne … we … you … have so little food.'

'I love you, Julia. You know that. Come on. It's on tonight.'

Everyone in the ghetto knows the story of *Brundibár*. Two children, Aninka and Pepicek, want to buy milk for their sick mother – the doctor says she has to have milk. But the children have no money and they don't know how to get any. But then they have an idea. There's an organ grinder who plays tunes and people put money into his hat. So the children try that too – singing for money. However, the organ grinder is evil and he tries to drown out their voices. But then a miracle happens. With the help of a sparrow, a cat, and a dog, and the children of the town, Aninka and Pepicek sing louder than the evil organ grinder. In the end they are victorious.

Brundibár is held in the new cultural hall in the Sokol building on the outskirts of the ghetto. The cultural hall was specifically built as part of the Great Beautification. When Julia and Suzanne walk in, the hall is almost full. On this warm June night, the smell in the room is like something solid that hangs over the crowd – old clothes, unwashed or starved or diseased bodies. Still, everyone is talking excitedly while, up in front of the stage, the musicians are tuning their instruments. Julia and Suzanne take their seats. Then, the last few seats are filled, the hall slowly goes quiet, the lights go down and an expectant hush settles on the audience. The curtains open to reveal the set – the buildings of a town in the background and in front the wooden fence just as in the poster.

And so it begins. *Brundibár* is sung in Czech but even so, it's not too difficult to follow the action. It starts with the doctor coming to visit the children's mother. Then they go into town to buy the milk. The opera takes its title from the evil organ grinder whose name is Brundibár. There is a great cheer when he comes out on stage. This is because the boy who plays Brundibár – his name is Honza Treichlinger and he is only thirteen or fourteen – has become well known in the ghetto because of his role in the show.

And the cheer is because Brundibár – Honza – sports a great pasted-on black moustache which he wiggles from time to time, causing huge amusement in the audience. The villain has a black moustache. The symbolism is so obvious that people in the ghetto wonder how the Germans have not seen it and closed the show down ages ago. *Brundibár* was even performed for the Red Cross visitors. It's true what Suzanne said – a smart German is an imaginary creature.

Julia is entranced. It seems to her that this is what life should be all about. Creating beauty. Art. Those things that happened to her – at this moment they seem unimportant. This – in front of her – is what really matters. Those things that happened to her – it is like they are floating away from her, becoming smaller and smaller. She's not forgetting them; that's not what it is. Is she forgiving? She's not sure. She frowns at this – she actually frowns. If she's not forgiving, maybe she's just saying that what happened to her in the past isn't going to determine what happens from now on. This – the here and now – and art – these are the things that matter.

And Julia understands that what she and Suzanne have been doing with their book – this too is part of it. They too have been creating beauty. Making people feel and think so that they don't just eat and make love and fight and – here in the ghetto – try to survive.

Julia becomes aware that Suzanne is looking at her. Julia turns. Suzanne smiles at her in the semi darkness.

'Thank you,' Julia mouths.

Suzanne takes her hand and squeezes it.

Finally, the children get their milk and Brundibár is defeated. The final song is the 'Victory Song' that everybody joins in singing. By then Julia's eyes are smarting and as the song comes to an end, she is weeping.

She and Suzanne sit for a long time afterwards as the hall empties. Eventually Julia's tears stop. Suzanne stands and Julia looks up at her. Julia blows her nose and smiles wearily. Together they make their way out into the gathering twilight.

There is a half moon high up and just visible against the darkening blue of the sky. Suzanne stops to look at it.

'She's my favourite planet,' says Suzanne. 'I love the moon.'

And then Julia says the words she has never said to anybody in all of her twenty-one years.

'I love you, Suzanne.'

CHAPTER THIRTY-SEVEN

Kelyn (Suzanne)

Birkita lay in bed savouring a few more moments before it would be time to get up. Through the doorway of the hut, with its cover pulled back to try to keep the place a bit cooler, she could see the sky becoming brighter. Soon, the sun would pull itself over the horizon and then it would be time to move. She had slept so deeply it was almost as though she had been drugged. The others – Galena, Kelyn and Sevi – were still asleep.

It had been a beautiful summer – an endless procession of misty early mornings that gave way to scorching hot days with cloudless blue skies. Now, it was harvest time and the early spring rains followed by dry weather just when it was needed meant that the harvest was plentiful. For days, Birkita, Galena and the girls had been working in the fields bringing in the crops. The muscle pains that Birkita had felt – that they had all felt after the first few days of work – had now faded so that her body felt taut and hard and strong. She couldn't help comparing this harvest with the last one she had experienced a year earlier with the bull Roman. How things had changed in that time.

Now whole days went by when she didn't find herself thinking about her parents and her brother and his family. She found the memory of Pompeii was fading so that sometimes it seemed like all of that was something that had happened to someone else. Or it was like a story she had been told, with the captain and all the other people she had met, simply characters in it.

Most of all, Birkita felt she had a home again. This unusual, all-female household that she was part of – it really did feel like her family.

The sun slipped above the edge of the field across the river sending a shaft of red-orange light into Birkita's eyes. It was time to get up. She called the others and with a mixture of groans and heavy silences, they began to stir.

'Will you get some water, Kelyn?' asked Galena.

Kelyn let out a sound that was part moan, part complaint. Nevertheless she stood up, took the two buckets from their place by the door and went out. Birkita began to feed twigs onto the fire, blowing under it gently so that the grey embers gradually became scarlet and the fire came back to life. They had some fish, taken from the river yesterday. Galena took a knife and began to prepare it, cutting it expertly. It had turned out that Galena cooked beautiful food. 'It was one of the things the Roman liked,' she said. Birkita took satisfaction from the fact that this was yet another thing she had taken from him.

'What's taking Kelyn so long?' asked Galena as she finished the fish and began to break a loaf of bread into chunks.

'That girl – she gets distracted so easily. I ask her to do one thing and she ends up doing anything but.'

'Maybe she's talking to one of the boys,' said Birkita. 'She's very pretty. Haven't you noticed – several of them have their eye on her.'

'Sevi, go and see what's happened to your sister. And if she has stopped to talk to one of them, at least bring back the water.'

It was some time before Sevi returned. Birkita was in

the back of the hut with her back to the door, bent over and tidying away their blankets.

'She's not at the river,' said Sevi.

'That girl! Where's she gone now? Is she in one of the other houses?' asked Galena.

'No, I went round them all. Nobody's seen her.'

Birkita straightened up and turned round. It was like a sliver of ice had run through her veins and entered her heart.

'Come on,' she said.

In summer, the river was about two spear throws wide and maybe the depth of a small child. The far bank was high and steep but on this side, the slope was much gentler. The river flowed from left to right. At the village there was a brief patch of open ground – a grassy bank that eased its way down to the water's edge. Here, the villagers drew water and women washed clothes. But on either side of this open area, the bank was heavily overgrown with gorse and wind-sown saplings and thorn bushes. This had never been cleared and so the years of growth were high enough that a man sitting on a horse would have been invisible there. A narrow path wove its way through all of this along the riverbank.

It was clear that Kelyn had got as far as the river. Footsteps were clearly visible in the dew. But they only went one way. There was no return track. Birkita looked up and down the river. There was not a soul to be seen, neither animal nor human. There were no tracks along the river bank so Birkita could only assume that Kelyn had been in the river. Walking? Being carried? Taken? On a horse?

In the time they had been here, there had been no trouble with the surrounding tribes. As far as Birkita could judge, Guidgen, the headman, seemed to be sensible, practical and wise. In that respect, he reminded her a lot

411

of her father. However he had done it, he seemed to have established peace with all of their neighbours. Of course, it was always possible that that would come to an end. Birkita wondered if that was what was happening now. Had Kelyn been kidnapped and would whoever had taken her ransom her and was this to be the start of something? Birkita prayed that it was only that.

'Sevi, go back and round up as many people as you can,' said Galena. 'Tell them what's happened – that Kelyn is missing.'

Within minutes, Guidgen had arrived and taken command. He organised four search parties. Two went upriver, one on either bank, the other two in the opposite direction. Between them all, they would see anything that might be on either bank and also anything in the river. Birkita tried not to think about that. Galena was silent, doing whatever she was told to do, but fear was etched into her face.

When the sun was at its highest, the four parties met up again back at the village but there was no trace of Kelyn.

Now, Guidgen sent riders out to all of the neighbouring villages. If they were still friendly, his rationale went, it could only help and if, for some reason, they had gone to war, then that would become apparent pretty soon too.

The sun was low in the sky when the riders returned. All was peaceful. Nothing had changed. But nobody had seen Kelyn.

Birkita convinced a distraught Galena that she needed to have some food. They hadn't eaten since the previous evening. Then with something in their belly, they could carry on looking. The moon was close to full. It would give plenty of light and they could comb through the forest which is what Guidgen proposed to do next.

Birkita cooked the morning's fish and she, Galena and Sevi ate in silence. Galena didn't touch her food. The other two finished quickly and went out of the hut, heading down the gentle slope that led to the river.

But now there was a crowd of villagers down there, gathered in the blue moonlight. Clearly, they had found something. Galena began to run. Birkita and Sevi ran with her. As they got near the group of people it parted. Guidgen stood on the river bank, tall, well-built, like a bear with his back to them. Galena ran past him and stood on the edge of the bank. Birkita arrived a moment later.

Face down, arms and legs outstretched, a figure floated in the water. The blue dress was unmistakeable. It was Kelyn.

And then Birkita knew.

49

'I knew you were going to do that,' says Julia.

'We both knew,' says Suzanne.

'We could have ended it there,' Julia goes on. 'They could all have lived happily ever after.'

Julia's not complaining. She and Suzanne are just discussing the latest turn their book has taken and what has to happen next.

'But you know we would have been cheating,' says Suzanne. 'Cheating our reader.'

'I think some writers wouldn't have felt that,' says Julia. 'Bring the reader to the safe shore of a happy ending and drop them there.'

'But we're not some writers,' says Suzanne. 'There has to be a last trial that our character goes through. The hardest trial of all.'

'So now what? asks Julia.

'Now, Birkita has to hunt down the bull Roman. He's discovered they crossed to Gaul so he's come after them and found them. Now he's stalking them. He's killed one daughter. He'll kill again. His plan is to kill them all. They have to find him.'

Finding the bull Roman turns out to be nearly as difficult as it must have been for him to find Birkita, Galena and the girls. Julia starts on the chapter on the first day of July but runs into problems almost straight away. The story just becomes episodic. And then. And then. And then. When she shows it to Suzanne, Suzanne reads a couple of pages and looks up frowning.

'I know,' says Julia. 'What's gone wrong?'

Suzanne takes a turn but after the few days, the result is no better. They decide to take a break in the hope that that will make a difference. They take a week off, agreeing to restart on July 17th. They become irritable with one another. The war will end when their book ends – but at this rate, it looks like their book will never end.

Just as they are about to restart, a bonke goes round that a group of people who had been painting pictures of the ghetto have been arrested and sent, with their families, to the Little Fortress. The place called the Little Fortress is a part of the Theresienstadt complex but separate from the ghetto itself. The Gestapo uses it as a prison. Terrible rumours circulate about what is done to people who are taken there, Mention of the Little Fortress is probably the only thing more terrible in the ghetto than the phrase 'transport to the East'.

When Julia and Suzanne hear about the artists, they are truly terrified. They talk of burning their two notebooks. They consider it seriously. They are close to going off and trying to find a place to do exactly that. But in the end, between them, they manage to talk themselves out of it. They have put too much into their story. It would be criminal to destroy it.

However, for the rest of July and early August they do no writing. Instead they spend it trying to find a safe place to store their notebooks. They don't want to store them on the floor on which they sleep. If the books were found in a search, the Germans are quite likely to send all the occupants of the floor to the Little Fortress. In fact, Julia and Suzanne decide it would be best if they didn't store them in their barracks at all – or in any barracks, but rather in some kind of public place. Eventually, after much searching, they find a place. It is not ideal because it is in the washroom on their floor but it will have to do. And the notion that they would have destroyed the notebooks is too unbearable. And anyway, they have to finish the story so that the war will end.

Low down on the wall of the washroom there is a loose tile. When pulled away it reveals a hole in the wall about the size of a small fist. Putting a hand through the hole – and it took them some courage to do that until eventually Julia said 'Fuck it, I'll do it' – they find that the hole extends back quite a way. Julia can put her arm in up to her shoulder and still the hole doesn't come to an end. While Suzanne keeps watch early one morning, Julia widens the hold just enough to be able to push the notebooks through. The final thing they need is that they manage to get their hands on a piece of oil cloth and they use this to wrap the books to keep them dry. They stow them away and for several days, neither of them dares even talk about what lies hidden in the washroom.

In the middle of August, a new piece of excitement sweeps the ghetto. Apparently the Red Cross visit was a complete success. The visitors were completely taken in by everything they saw and heard. In a place where disbelief has become something of an everyday occurrence, the ghetto residents still find this jaw-droppingly incredible. Anyway, the Germans are so pleased that they have decided to make a movie about Theresienstadt. So another beautification takes place – everything is smartened up again so that a camera crew can film many of the things that the Red Cross visitors saw on the day. And of course, with typical German economy, the filmmakers themselves are ghetto residents with a couple of Germans in overall charge.

Julia and Suzanne have to do their laughing and singing with rakes on their shoulder act again. This time, the group have to go to Adolf to draw their rakes and costumes. Adolf makes them line up outside his shed and then, one by one, they come in. He hands each of them a brown paper package with the clothes and they take a rake from a pile of them leaning against the wall of the shed. He records all of this in his book. When it is Julia's turn, Adolf hands her the package and says, 'You can change here if you want.'

'No, that's all right, thank you,' Julia says as icily politely as she can.

'I could insist, you know.'

And that does it for Julia.

'Adolf,' she says, 'why don't you go fuck yourself.'

Julia had hoped for some kind of shocked reaction from Adolf but instead his smile just becomes unpleasant and he says, 'You know, Dutch girl, before too long don't be surprised if you're begging me to fuck *you*.'

Filming finishes in mid-September. By then, it is more than two months since they have worked on the book. Partly this is due to the block they were experiencing before they hid the notebooks. Neither of them wants to be the one to have to restart. Each is hoping that the other one will volunteer. But then there is also the fear of their being discovered. For as long as the filming has been going on, there has been more renovation, snap inspections and Germans popping up everywhere. It has just been too dangerous.

But with filming over, things settle back into some kind of normality. Each day, the girls discuss whether today will be the day when they pick up their story again. But each day, they take no action. The notebooks remain undiscovered and untouched.

Then, towards the end of September, matters are taken

out of their hands when it is announced that there are to be a new series of transports.

That evening they retrieve the notebooks.

'I'll restart, if you like,' sys Julia.

'Sure,' says Suzanne, 'but I want to write something first.'

When she's finished she hands it to Julia who reads.

The last piece of filming had hardly been completed when the Great Unbeautification – would you call it an 'Uglification'? – began.

Just as with Grigory Potemkin a hundred and sixty years earlier, dismantling the fake settlements he had built along the banks of the river Dnieper once the Empress Catherine II had passed, the Paradise Ghetto, the Theresienstadt that its occupants had spent six months building, was dismantled.

Claw hammers hooked the heads of nails and extracted them slowly like teeth, all the time trying to keep the nails straight so that they could be used again. (Nothing must be wasted in the ghetto.) Screwdrivers turned screws counter clockwise. Walls could hardly be unpainted but there was still plenty of time for overcrowding, diarrhoea and infestation to take its toll on the paintwork. And anyway – it was only the bits along the route of the tour and the filming that had been painted.

Bunks that had been moved out of barracks to relieve the overcrowding were put back. The third tier on the bunks, that had been removed temporarily, was replaced. The bandstand in the square was dismantled, carefully, of course, the timber being used for other, more pressing purposes – beds, partition walls, barracks.

The clean clothes that had been given to the inhabitants were taken back, fumigated (since Jews had been wearing them) and would eventually find their way –

one assumed – to bombed-out families in German cities.
The toys that the Jewish children had played with would
end up in the hands of orphaned German children. At
least the extra food that some of the inmates had been
given during the Red Cross tour and the filming couldn't
be taken back – though if that had been possible, then
surely the Germans would have done that too.

And continuing the theatrical theme that had
characterised the Paradise Ghetto, since there was no
further need for a set, there was no point in having actors
or a cast, so once the autumn came, the deportations
resumed.

Julia looks at Suzanne.

'It's wonderful,' says Julia. 'It's vivid and fierce and
angry – *so* angry. It seethes with anger –'

Suzanne acknowledges the compliment with her eyes.

'And if anyone finds it, we're dead,' says Julia.

'They won't find it,' pronounces Suzanne and Julia
finds herself believing completely that Suzanne is right.

'These things have to be recorded,' says Suzanne.
'And now – off you go. Your chapter.

CHAPTER THIRTY-EIGHT

A Trap (Julia)

Galena shook her head.

'I won't do it, Birkita. I can't. I can't ask her. Sevi's still in shock.'

'It's the only way,' said Birkita.

'How can you ask me to do this – after everything that's happened? After what I've lost?'

'It will work, I swear it will.'

'It was an accident, Birkita. An accident.'

'It wasn't an accident. You know it wasn't. He's found us. He's out there somewhere, watching us. You know him. He'll kill Sevi next. That's the way he works. He'll want you to suffer as much as possible. Then he'll kill you. Or maybe me. Maybe I'll be next – because he knows how much you mean to me.'

It was about the last appeal that Birkita could make.

Galena looked up. Her face was tear-streaked.

'And what if it goes wrong?'

'It won't go wrong. We'll have all the men of the village there. How can it go wrong?'

'All the men of the village? Are you mad? He may be a Roman but he's not an idiot.'

'Then just me. I'll go by myself. I'll either kill him or bring him back alive and you can kill him.'

'And what if Sevi is the one who gets killed?'

'She won't be. I swear it.'

Galena shook her head.

'How can you say that? How can you promise such a thing?'

'We can't live our whole lives in fear, Galena. We have to do something and rid ourselves of this threat for once and for all.'

Birkita could think of nothing more to say, no other argument. Galena's gaze became distant. Birkita couldn't tell whether she was considering all of this or whether the argument was over. The silence lengthened. Outside, a horse neighed. A dog barked. In the silence which followed, Birkita could hear birds singing. In the normal world.

She had lost. She could feel it. Now, she would just have to try to go and find the bull Roman herself. But she knew that wouldn't work. While she was hunting him he would find a way to kill Sevi. If he had abandoned his farm and come all this way, there was only one thing on his mind now – vengeance. And Birkita knew that feeling. She knew that only too well – with nothing to lose, how single-minded you could become.

Galena's focus returned to the here and now. She looked at Birkita.

'Please,' she said, 'please – don't be wrong about this.'

50

The transports that are to go are to consist of men only. According to Communications of the Jewish Self-Administration – in other words, the SS – these men will 'be employed in priority tasks outside Theresienstadt'. A first transport of men leaves at noon on September 28th.

Then a flyer is circulated saying that a limited number of family members can go with the men, if they like. On this basis, a large number of women volunteer for the next two transports that leave on September 29th and October 1st.

CHAPTER THIRTY-NINE

Sevi (Suzanne)

Birkita knelt in front of Sevi. The little girl's face looked resolute but Birkita could see it in her eyes – she was terrified. Galena looked on, stony-faced and saying nothing.

'You understand, don't you, Sevi? The Roman has come back. He tried to make Kelyn's death look like an accident but we know that it wasn't.'

'How do you know?' asked Sevi.

'This is what we think happened. She went to get water. He surprised her and captured her. Then he took her upstream somewhere and killed her. Then he let the body float back down the river. So now he thinks he has us really frightened. We don't know whether it was an accident or not. We think it might have been. We hope it might have been. But we're not sure. It's worked before so now he thinks it will work again.'

Sevi listened to all of this, her eyes becoming more and more frightened.

'You know you don't have to do this if you don't want,' said Birkita.

'It's dangerous, isn't it?' said Sevi.

'It's dangerous,' said Birkita, 'but I'll be there with you, watching over you. You'll be safe. I won't let anything happen to you.'

Sevi looked at her mother but Galena's face remained expressionless. Then Sevi looked back to Birkita. Her eyes held Birkita's. Eventually, Sevi said, 'What do you want me to do?'

'We're going to set a trap for him. You'll do exactly as Kelyn did. Go to get water. First thing in the morning. When he tries to take you, I'll be waiting for him. We'll capture him – you and I – and then your mother can kill him.'

'Can I help to kill him?' asked Sevi.

Birkita looked at Galena.

'Yes,' said Galena. 'You can help.'

The plan was simple. Since Kelyn's lifeless body had been floated downriver with the current, it was clear that the bull Roman was hiding upriver somewhere. Birkita assumed he had some kind of camp there. So he had come down from there to stalk the riverbank. Presumably he had hidden somewhere in the undergrowth off to the left of the open area, waiting for Kelyn or Sevi to appear. Then, when Kelyn had gone down there, he had surprised her. Maybe he had crept up on her and overpowered her. Perhaps he had stepped from the bushes and spoken to her. Her surprise might have given him just enough time to seize her.

Now, Sevi was going to act as the bait but Birkita would hide in the undergrowth on the downriver side. When the bull Roman appeared, as Birkita was convinced he would, she would confront him. Sevi would run back the short distance to the village and bring Guidgen and the men. Meanwhile, Birkita would take the bull Roman. If she failed, if he got the better of her, then by the time that had happened, the men would have arrived and he would either be killed or captured.

Birkita hoped she would live to see it.

That night, Birkita took enough food and water for

several days and found a place to hide in the dense undergrowth. It was an opening, almost like a spherical cave, underneath some high, thick gorse bushes, just off the riverbank path. She cut some branches with her sword and camouflaged her position further. From where she sat, she could observe the open grassy area that led to the river. The spot where Sevi would kneel to draw water was no more than ten paces away.

Sevi came for water just after sunrise. She was alone. Birkita crouched down ready to move. Sevi knelt down and slowly filled each bucket in turn. Having done so, she carried them back up to the house.

Soon after that, the village came to life and there were lots of comings and goings throughout the day. Birkita relaxed though she continued to observe everything. He wasn't going to strike while there were lots of people there. The day passed slowly. As it started to grow dark, the river bank became quiet again and finally, Sevi came down one more time alone. However, just as before, she drew her water and made her way back home.

It was in the morning they discovered that a different little girl was missing.

51

The small piece of flimsy yellowish paper that Suzanne holds by one corner is a deportation notice.

She hands it to Julia as though it were diseased. Julia reads. It says that Suzanne is to report for the transport designated Eo, leaving on October 6th. It takes Julia a minute to work it out. October 6th is Friday. Today is Tuesday.

'We have to finish the book,' says Suzanne, her face suddenly becoming bright. 'We're so close. We're nearly there. Come on. Let's think what happens next. What does Birkita do now?'

'Fuck Birkita,' says Julia. 'We have to get you off the transport.'

'You know that's not possible, Julia. We're not prominent or important or anything. We're just two insignificant Dutch girls. What matters now is the book. We get it finished, we hide it. Then we come back after the war and we find it. If we finish it, we'll survive. I know we will.'

'You finish it,' says Julia. 'There's something I need to do.'

Adolf is working at his ledger when he looks up and sees Julia. He doesn't seem surprised to see her. Julia wonders if he had something to do with Suzanne's ending

427

up on the transport list. He continues working for several minutes. Julia waits silently. Eventually he puts the pen down.

'What can I do for you, Dutch girl?'

'My friend has been put on the transport list for Friday. Can you get her taken off?'

Adolf sits back in his chair and steeples his fingers. He looks into Julia's eyes. A smile plays around lips. For a long time he is silent. Julia wants to pick him up and shake him. She actually wants to strangle him. Instead, she manages to stand patiently. She holds her hands behind her back and interlaces her fingers in case she does something she'll regret.

'It's possible I could help her,' he says eventually, speaking the words slowly, easing them out one at a time.

'How quickly can you do it?' blurts out Julia, despite herself. 'We don't have much time.'

'No, we don't, do we?' says Adolf.

After another long, trying to appear thoughtful, pause, he says, 'I could do it straight away.'

Julia is struck by the word 'could'.

She can't stop herself.

'And so will you?'

'Funny, isn't it, Dutch girl – how things turn out.'

Julia knows what's coming.

'Remember what I said the last time we spoke – how you'd end up begging me … And here we are now.'

'If that's what you want,' says Julia, 'if that's your price – then OK. But first you have to get her off the list.'

'You're hardly in a position to bargain,' says Adolf. 'So first – before anything else – I'll be needing a down payment.'

CHAPTER FORTY

Banished (Suzanne)

'They must leave,' somebody shouted.

'They're cursed and they've brought the curse with them,' another voice said.

'It's not them – it's the Romans,' said a third person.

Guidgen called for quiet. The meeting was taking place in the open area outside his house. All of the villagers were there.

'What says the woman whose daughter has been lost?'

The crowd went silent. All eyes turned on the short woman with a thin frame and blonde hair scraped back. Her eyes were swollen and her face was dirty with tears.

'Haven't we lost enough?' she asked, looking around at them all. Then she added, 'I don't care. Decide for yourselves.'

It was Galena who spoke next. The crowd went silent.

'You have been good friends to us. Even though we came from another place, you took us in. We fled from another land so that we could escape all of this. We are truly, truly sorry that it has followed us here and brought such tragedy upon you good people. We will leave here now … at once.'

It was Birkita who suggested they follow the path upriver. It would take them inland, she said. They would find a new place. Galena said she didn't care and Sevi just looked stunned. It was after noon when they left, marching until the sun had begun to settle and had dropped below the surrounding trees.

They found a grassy spot beside the river and lit a fire. They ate some food. Nobody spoke. Once it got dark, Galena and Birkita spread out their cloaks and the three of them lay down, side by side, with Sevi in the middle. The night was warm – there was no need for any covering. Birkita asked to borrow Sevi's cloak and placed it beside her. It concealed her sword. Then she settled down to wait, wide awake, eyes not quite closed.

He came, as she had known he would.

She heard no sound. For such a squat, heavy man he had moved incredibly silently. The first she became aware of him was when she saw his dark shape suddenly blot out a piece of the starlit sky. And then she smelt him – a mixture of sweat and horse.

He was strong and his plan seemed to have been to seize Sevi, who wasn't very heavy, and carry her off as he might have carried a sack of grain. He was bent over, legs parted for balance, hands reaching down when, in one smooth movement, Birkita reached under the cloak, pulled out the sword, lifted it and placed its point into his groin. She stopped just short of stabbing him.

'Leave her,' she said.

Birkita began to rise and was on one knee, in the act of standing, when she felt a terrible blow to the back of her head, a light seemed to flash for a moment and then there was darkness.

When she came to, the first thing she was aware of was grass – blades of it that seemed incredibly big. They were spattered with droplets of dew and the light sparkled through them with all the colours of the rainbow. A ladybird was walking up one of the stalks and passed through a droplet, destroying it. Birkita remembered a

430

faraway time and place, several lifetimes ago.

Her head throbbed, a savage pain at the base of her skull and another across her forehead. Her hands were tied behind her back and she was half on her side, half on her belly, face down in the hard ground. She rolled onto her side and lifted her head, trying to look around.

They were in a small clearing. In the background, everywhere she looked, were trees. This seemed to be deep forest. Galena and Sevi lay a few paces away, tied up the same way. Their backs were to her. Birkita was glad she couldn't see their faces.

Beyond them, the bull Roman and another man were working. Birkita could just see the top halves of their bodies above Galena's prone figure. They appeared to be digging. Birkita lifted her head and it was as though she had been hit again as her whole skull seemed to be one mass of pain. She had to ease her head back down until the wave of pain passed. Then she lifted it again, higher this time.

The bull Roman and the other man were digging all right. Each was digging a hole. Beside them, on the ground was a pile of heavy timber beams.

And Birkita knew what they were for.

52

The next day, Wednesday, October 4th, Suzanne gets notification that she has been taken off the list for the Friday transport.

Suzanne's face seems like it has been washed with relief.

'How did you do it?' she asks Julia.

'I just talked to some people,' says Julia quietly.

The ghetto is in uproar. Transport summonses are being issued day and night. It is said that the transport office is working round the clock and certainly lights are burning there twenty-four hours a day. People are packing, giving away their belongings, saying goodbye. There are huge crowds at all of the Jewish self-administration offices – anywhere people feel they might be able to get an exemption, on whatever pretext.

That day, Wednesday, there is a steady stream of people, in as much clothing as they can wear, carrying luggage and heading to the Hamburg Barracks from where they are processed onto the train that waits on Bahnhofstrasse.

While all of this is going on, Julia has to go to Adolf's quarters again that night and the following night, Thursday. It is almost like Suzanne doesn't notice, she is so intent on the book.

On Friday, Julia visits Adolf again for the last payment. When she returns, Suzanne is holding another deportation notice. This one is for the transport leaving on the coming Monday, the 9th.

'I just have the last chapter to do,' Suzanne says, wearily.

Equally wearily, Julia returns to Adolf's quarters. She is angry but now her anger feels crushed under something else. It is as though a great weight has settled on it, taking all the life out of it so that what remains behind is little more than a husk of anger. Julia has never felt like this before.

'You told me she would be exempt,' she says.

'I got her exempted from today's transport. There's no such thing as a permanent exemption.'

'So what can I do?' Julia asks.

'Haven't you wondered why you have haven't been getting these notices, Dutch girl?'

The thought had flickered from time to time on the edge of Julia's consciousness but now the realisation flares into life.

'Yes, that's right. I've been keeping you exempt.'

'So that you could fuck me?' blurts out Julia.

'Does it matter what the reason was?'

'Please, Adolf,' – Julia has deliberately never said his name before – 'can't you exempt her instead of me? Please?'

He shakes his head.

'It's too late for that.' His voice has suddenly become soft, quiet. 'You'll be lucky if I can manage to stop you from getting a summons.'

'I'll give you … I'll do … anything.'

'I'm sorry, Dutch girl,' he says in a desperate voice. 'It's out of my hands now.'

Then he reaches into his pocket and takes out a crumpled, flimsy yellow piece of paper.

'I got mine today.'

CHAPTER FORTY-ONE

The End (Suzanne)

The bull Roman and the other man lifted a cross and it thudded into its hole.

'Yes, that's deep enough,' said the bull Roman.

They lifted the cross out again and laid it on the ground.

Overhead, the open sky was blue and clear. The autumn air was warm and scented of woodland. Somewhere amongst the trees, birds were singing.

Sevi, still with her back to Birkita was crying and through the tears, made some incomprehensible sound that could have been her saying her mother's name.

The bull Roman turned towards the three figures on the ground.

'Now,' he said brightly. 'Who's first?'

And then, after a few moment's thought, 'You, I think.'

Sevi screamed as the two men came towards her. She called her mother's name over and over again. Galena began to scream too, a sound that quickly became an unearthly wailing, sobbing. It was like no sound Birkita had ever heard before.

The bull Roman picked Sevi up as though she were a doll and carried her to where the crosses were. Birkita strained, lifting her head to see what was happening. She tried to force her hands apart, to snap the rope that held them together but it was impossible – she already knew that.

The bull Roman took out a knife and cut the rope that bound Sevi's wrists. Then, with him taking one of her arms and his partner, the other, they pushed her down onto the cross. Sevi struggled and screamed and shrieked for her mother. Galena kept on calling Sevi's name over and over again.

The two men pinioned Sevi to the cross. The bull Roman placed his knee on her forearm and Birkita saw him reach for something. Then she saw a large iron nail in his left hand. He lowered it onto Sevi's wrist and raised his right arm. It held a square, heavy hammer.

But then he paused. He put the hammer down again, stood up and said to the other man, 'Hold her'.

The bull Roman walked over to where Birkita and Galena lay. 'We need a proper audience for this,' he said.

He straddled Galena and pulled her up into a sitting position, facing her towards where Sevi lay on the cross. He then came to Birkita to do the same. Just as he planted his feet either side of her, Birkita saw a tiny chance. She pivoted at her hips, brought her legs up and smashed her feet as hard as she could into the underside of the bull Roman's balls. He shouted in pain and stumbled. Clumsily, Birkita got to her feet. The bull Roman hadn't fallen but he was winded. She could see that as he turned to face her. He clutched his groin, his face was red, his eyes were watering, he groaned.

'Fucking bitch,' he said.

With a strength she didn't think she possessed, with a savagery born of all the humiliations and brutality that she and those she loved had endured at his hands, with a terrible scream, Birkita stepped forward and delivered a second kick to his groin. This one brought him down.

Even as it did, on her peripheral vision, Birkita saw the bull Roman's partner stand up. He drew a sword and ran towards her.

But then Galena stood up.

Intent on Birkita, it was like the partner didn't see Galena at all. As he went to run by her, she extended a foot and tripped him. He stumbled, looked like he might actually fall, tried to regain his balance. As he did so, Birkita ran at him from the side that didn't hold the sword. He looked up, surprised as she closed the gap in a few strides. Then she headbutted him savagely. The man dropped the sword, his hands going to his face.

'Sevi!' screamed Birkita. 'Get the hammer.'

By now the bull Roman was back on his feet. He was panting and his red face was crimson with pain and rage. Birkita lowered her head and charged him like a bull, screaming as she did so. The sound she made was a war cry, a sound she had forgotten, a cry she had learned long before any of this had happened. He fell backwards wrapping his hands around her so that she fell with him into the dust. He gripped her tightly as though they were lovers.

'I should have hung you on a cross that day too,' he grunted.

But now Birkita no longer felt entirely human. Like an animal she put her mouth on his cheek just under his eye. She found skin and sank her teeth into it until she tasted blood. The bull Roman bellowed and his grip slackened. Birkita headbutted him again and this time, heard his nose crack. His arms released her and she got shakily to her feet. Her heart was pounding. She was panting as though her lungs would burst. She looked over to where the bull Roman's partner was. What she saw astonished her.

The partner had picked up the sword again and had been coming for Galena. But Sevi had jumped on his back

438

and Birkita was just in time to see Sevi's hand bring the hammer down onto the partner's head. Once. Twice. Three times. Birkita heard his skull break. He collapsed and Birkita knew he was dead.

Sevi jumped down and grabbed the sword. She turned towards her mother. 'No,' Galena said. 'Birkita. Do Birkita's.'

Sevi did as she was told. She came to Birkita and sawed through the rope that bound her hands. Birkita felt the blade cut her skin somewhere but it didn't matter. Her hands were free. She grabbed the sword from Sevi.

The bull Roman was on his feet. His face was a mask of blood from the broken nose and the wound gouged in his cheek. He took a step towards her but stopped when he saw the sword. He hesitated. She saw fear in his eyes, something she had never seen before. Then he turned and began to run, his shaky stride becoming firmer after a couple of paces.

He would never have outrun her – even unwounded.

His heavy body and fat legs would not have taken him far. He was built for strength, not for speed. And now Birkita seemed to have the strength and speed of two people.

She allowed him to run ahead of her. His panting quickly became a series of frenzied gasps. He speeded up. She did too, staying about ten paces behind him. He was unable to maintain that pace and he slackened. She slowed too keeping the same distance. It was easy running.

'How does it feel, Roman?' she called. 'Knowing that you're going to die?'

He tried to speed up again but now, whatever rhythm he had had was starting to falter. Birkita maintained the gap between them.

'And you're hoping it'll be a fast death, aren't you? A quick thrust of the sword. Over in a heartbeat.'

439

His run had now just become a scurry, his breathing loud and fast and terror stricken.

'But that's not what I have in mind for you. Your last days on earth are going to be the longest ones of your life.'

The Roman stumbled and fell. Birkita stopped, waiting for him to rise again. He did and began to run, though now it was little more than slow jogging. He fell again and got up once more. He walked a few more steps, head bowed, his breathing sounding like crying. Finally, he fell again and this time he didn't get up. Instead he rolled onto his back and looked up at her. His face was a mask of terror.

Galena and Sevi caught up with Birkita and Sevi was sent to bring men from the village. While they waited for everyone to arrive, Galena tied up the bull Roman while Birkita held the sword to his throat. When he tried to push himself onto the sword she knocked him unconscious with several blows of the flat of the blade.

Not just the men but the whole village came.

The bull Roman's ankles were tied to a horse and he was dragged back to the clearing where the crosses were. By then he was whimpering and pleading for his life in the Roman tongue. Birkita was asked if she wanted to drive in the nails but she was happy to let one of the men do it. The Roman screamed and screamed and screamed until long after the cross had been hoisted.

Birkita was right. It took him the rest of that day, all of the next day and some of the one after to die. Sevi went back to the village with some of the women but Birkita and Galena stayed there. They made no effort to break his legs or do anything to speed him on his way.

When it was done, Galena said, 'So now what?'

'Now?' said Birkita. 'Now, we go home.'

53

Suzanne has been writing furiously but now suddenly, she stops, puts the pen down and looks at the page. Julia watches her. After a good fifteen or twenty seconds, Suzanne hands the notebook to Julia. With an upwards nod of her head, Suzanne says, 'Here – you write the last two words.'

They sit, side by side, on Julia's bunk. It is Saturday night. The train is on Monday.

Julia takes the book, looks at it and is mystified for a moment. Then she understands. Suzanne is offering the pencil to her. She takes it and writes, 'THE END' in capital letters. Then she draws a short line underneath it.

For a while neither of them speaks. Julia feels overwhelmed. Birkita's journey is over. The journey that began in that railway car as they left Westerbork is done.

'I can't believe it,' says Julia eventually.

'It always seems impossible until it's done,' says Suzanne.

'What are we going to call it?' asks Julia. 'We don't have a title.'

'You're right,' says Suzanne. 'We don't. We never have.'

'Pompeii?' suggests Julia.

'It'll do for now – until we find a better one. A working title. Anyway – that was kind of always the working title, wasn't it?'

Julia agrees. She takes out the first notebook, the one with the black cover, which was hidden under the blankets and hands it to Suzanne along with the pencil.

'You write it.'

Suzanne does so, writing on the marbling of the inside front cover, 'POMPEII'.

'Now what?' asks Julia, deliberately echoing Birkita's last words in the story.

'Now we have to hide it. Then, when this is all over, we'll come back for it.'

They put the two notebooks together and wrap them carefully in the oilcloth. Then they snap the rubber bands around the oilcloth to hold it in place. They take it to the washroom and hide it behind the tile. Because Suzanne is taller than Julia, she has a slightly longer arm. Lying on the filthy washroom floor, she pushes the package in as far as she can, until she is all the way up to her shoulder.

'I hope it will be safe,' says Julia.

'It will,' pronounces Suzanne.

Julia thinks that it will be as safe there as any place that either of them is likely to end up.

That night, lying in bed together, they both still can't believe that it's over.

'Do you think the war will end now?' whispers Julia.

'It has to. Very soon, I'd say. You saw those planes the other day.'

And indeed the whole ghetto has seen aircraft like tiny silver birds high up in the sky. It has happened on several days now.

The two girls hold each other. Suzanne initiates lovemaking and Julia is astonished that her lover can feel like doing it. But Julia has seen it before – how Suzanne

442

seems to be able to block out any thought of the future and just focus on now.

Since Julia cannot get Suzanne off the deportation list, she has decided to go with her. She tells Suzanne of her decision first thing on Sunday morning. Julia has also worked out how to do it.

Those being deported are always required to report to the Hamburg Barracks. Here is the so-called 'sluice' – the room through which people are processed onto the train. When people are being deported it is forbidden for their loved ones to accompany them to the sluice. It is also very dangerous – for the loved ones. There have been occasions when loved ones, who weren't on the deportation list, were shoved onto the train and the doors closed.

Julia plans to use this to get onto the train. So both she and Suzanne spend Sunday packing. The book is finished. They just managed to finish it in time. It is as Suzanne said when they lay in each other's arms the previous night after making love: 'The gods have been watching over us.'

And it seems like they have. Now, as they leave the ghetto, they will be together.

A desperate atmosphere hangs over the rest of their floor where other people too are packing. There is a silence the like of which Julia has never been conscious of before. There seem to be no words to describe it. In the time she has known Suzanne, Julia has become very conscious of words – just the right word. Maybe, icy or deathlike are the words here. But maybe there are actually no words. Occasionally the silence is broken by sobbing or wailing.

Suzanne keeps talking about after the war. They will come back, find the book and then get a publisher. It will sell millions and with the money, they'll buy the place

443

that was originally in Julia's dream and of which they've now created such a clear picture. There, they will write more books.

'I'd really like to write *The Murders at the Grand Hotel*,' says Suzanne.

They discuss whether they'll use their own names or pen names. Should they just pretend to be one author? Could they combine their names into one? Julia Snel and Suzanne Helman. They decide that Julius Snelman has a ring to it – in a ridiculous sort of way. In the end, they are laughing and people look strangely at them as though they've lost their minds.

On Monday, they get up early, wash and dress in their warmest clothes. They finish the last details of their packing including whatever food they've managed to hold on to. They step out into the street just as it is getting bright. They've decided there's no point in waiting around. Better to get there. Anyway, they might find a better spot in the freight car – against a wall.

Even though it is early, there is already a steady stream of stooped, shabby people, heading in the one direction. They join a long line of people and begin to move forward slowly. They put their cases on the ground and nudge them forwards with their feet.

At the entrance to the courtyard of the Hamburg Barracks, Suzanne shows her deportation notice to an SS man in a heavy coat with a rifle on his shoulder. He waves her past. Julia goes next. She has been rehearsing what she would say in her head. In her school German, she explains that she has just come to see her friend off. The SS man is probably no older than Julia. His face is pink from where he's shaved earlier.

'That's not allowed,' he says. 'Get out. Next.'

His tone isn't unkind – just bored. He probably says this a hundred times a day when there's a deportation.

444

'I want to go with her,' Julia blurts out.

Suzanne stands just on the far side of the SS man under the arch of the courtyard entrance. Her face is anxious.

Now, the SS man seems to come alive.

'You're better off here, pretty lady,' he says. 'Don't you see that?'

'But I want to –'

'Believe me,' he says.

Gently, he pushes her out of the line.

'Next,' he says, his tone as before.

Julia half shrugs and looks at Suzanne helplessly.

Suzanne calls, 'Look after yourself. And I'll see you when it's all over.'

Another SS man begins to push Suzanne into the courtyard.

'I love you,' Suzanne mouths.

And then she turns and is gone, her blonde hair swallowed up in moments in the brown and grey crowd of people.

54

Towards the end of October, Julia receives her deportation notice. On October 28th, she makes the journey to the Hamburg Barracks a second time. She is processed through the sluice and boards the train.

The cattle cars are filled and the doors slid shut. The locomotive whistle shrills and there is a hiss of steam. Couplings clank, the wagons shudder and the train begins to move. At first it is travelling at no more than walking pace. But then it picks up speed – somebody would have to run to stay with it now. And soon it is going too fast for anyone to keep up with it at all.

By then it has passed out of the Paradise Ghetto.

55

The Paradise Ghetto was a Potemkin village – a construction built solely to deceive others into thinking that some situation was better than it really was.

But what if our story too was a Potemkin village?

An eraser removes words and a hand brushes the specks of black residue away leaving only tiny indentations in the weave of the paper. A fountain pen draws a line through a phrase. A back button obliterates a sentence. Words are deleted, phrases peeled back, whole sentences are torn up like a partisan attack on a railway track. A ball of paper rolls like tumbleweed down the main street of an empty shtetl. Pages are lifted, like the paving slabs that were taken up in the square in Theresienstadt so that it could be seeded with grass, and these pages fly away in the wind, across the vast plain of Eastern Europe – devoid now of its Jews. Handfuls of pages flop wearily into the bin, leaning against its inside as though exhausted from everything that has happened or drunk, as the Nazi Einsatzgruppen executioners often were.

Because Julia could have slept through that night in January 1944 and woken on the Saturday morning. With the day would have come the realisation that maybe she

449

misjudged Chantal. Yes, the girl was a bigoted cunt but lots of people are like that. It's a long way from that to betraying somebody so that they will be killed. When it's not the dark waking hours of the night, when the sun is shining outside, it's easier to think like that.

With nothing for Julia to do and with the intense cold she would have stayed in bed, sleeping late. But eventually she would have had to go to the toilet. She would have jumped out to use the chamber pot and having done that, pulled the blackout curtain aside. Then swiftly back into bed to assess the twin rectangles of sky in the attic window.

It is a blue sky that Saturday – pure blue.

It is that blue which, along with the glancing light from a low winter sun and the heavy condensation on the inside of the windows that has turned to thin sheets of ice, dazzles her as though both panes of glass were encrusted with sapphires.

Eventually her curiosity about the day outside and what it holds draws her from bed. By then it is about noon.

Breakfast. And for once there is enough – bread, ham, cheese, the two eggs and some tea. In comparison to coffee, Julia doesn't really rate tea but that Saturday morning, it is hot and warming.

Unbeknown to her, Julia has less reason than most other Dutch Jews to worry about Chantal or anybody else betraying her to the Germans. This is because – amazingly – Julia has slipped between the cracks. With all their filing systems and lists and transport numbers and thoroughness, their liking of order and discipline and everything else, the Nazis still make occasional mistakes. After all, they are human – though some would definitely argue with that statement. Julia is one of those mistakes and for it – though she will never know this – she has to thank Karl Maurer.

It came about like this.

The Nazis have a card index of all the Jews in the Netherlands. The index shows Julia as still living with her parents. Julia's mother and father were deported to Theresienstadt in 1943. (From there, some time after that, they were deported again, this time to Auschwitz. Upon arrival, considered too old to work, not to mention physically and mentally destroyed after their short stay in Theresienstadt, they were gassed within an hour and their bodies burned.)

After a deportation from Westerbork takes place, there is a job to be done to update the card index to reflect the new situation. What is done is that the cards of the Jews who have been deported are removed from the main index and filed separately.

It is a Friday after the deportation of Julia's parents when a German soldier – a clerk, the aforementioned Karl Maurer – is carrying out this task. His system is simple. Using a ruler to underline each name on the deportation list, he then finds the corresponding card in the card index and removes it to a separate pile – the pile of dead Jews, as he thinks of it. It is dull work, even though he enjoys seeing the dead Jews pile grow like winnings in a card game.

This task is the last thing Maurer has to do this week. His boss, a tidy-minded bureaucrat, insists on the card index being updated the same week as the deportation. Normally, there wouldn't have been any problem doing this. Since only a little over three hundred Jews were deported and there are about fifty names per page on a deportation list, Maurer has about six pages to process. He had been intending to spend most of the day doing this at a leisurely pace with plenty of breaks for coffee and to chat with his colleagues. But that plan got ruined when his boss gave him another supposedly high-priority thing to do. The result is that Maurer started the deportation list late and is now under pressure.

Because there is another thing.

Karl Maurer has a seventy-two hour pass to Paris and his train leaves at seven this evening. It is just after six now and he is nearing the end of the list – he is into the S's. He can still make it to the station. He has to make it to the station. If he doesn't he will be forced to spend one of his three precious leave nights in Amsterdam rather than in the (blacked out) City of Light.

Maurer has never been to Paris before and has visions of spending a long weekend fucking some beautiful French girl – in fact, more than one. Three of them in a bed in a fine hotel with champagne and good food. He sees himself eating food off their bellies and their tits – strawberries from other places. He is hard now just thinking about it. Ordinarily, he would go to the bathroom to relieve his tension but he doesn't have time for that now – anyway, better to save that for Paris.

When his ruler reaches Julia's father, Maurer quickly finds the card for him and places it on the desk in front of him. The card lists his wife – Julia's mother – and Julia as being dependents. Maurer moves the ruler. As he expected, just below her husband on the transportation list is Julia's mother. He finds her card and removes it, tossing it onto the dead Jew pile.

Then a picture comes into Maurer's head. It is of himself and the two French girls. Naturally one is a blonde and the other a brunette – just like a dirty movie he saw recently. The three of them are naked on a huge bed. The blonde is on all fours. Maurer is on his back with his head between her legs looking up at her pussy. The other girl pours champagne into the crack of the blonde's ass and it flows from there down into his mouth.

He enjoys this picture for several minutes and then snaps out of it.

He refocuses on the index card for Julia's father. He recalls that he already found the card for the mother. Now he finds Julia's card and tosses it, along with the father's card onto the dead Jew pile. He moves the ruler down one, finds the next name and his short, pudgy fingers begin to flick through the card index. The S's. He is nearly there. It looks like he's going to make his train after all.

It is a mistake, of course. After his daydream, he should have moved the ruler down one on the transportation list expecting to find Julia's name. If she was there it would have been correct to place her on the dead Jew pile – but if she wasn't, her card should have stayed in the card index.

It is on this insignificant, almost atomic event that everything changes.

With the records showing that Julia has been deported from the Netherlands, there is no likelihood that the Germans will try to deport her again. Their faith in the accuracy of their card index is as strong as their faith in their Führer.

This means that the only way Julia can be caught is if somebody brings her to the authorities' attention. Chantal had been tempted to do this because she is convinced that Julia is a Jew and Chantal hates Jews. (Bert is right – in certain light, at certain angles with her dark hair and brown eyes, Julia does look Jewish.) But after Chantal leaves the shoot, she has other things on her mind.

A German who has seen her in a film has tracked her down through Bert. He wants to become a private client. (This is something that Julia has always refused to do. She sees having sex on film and getting paid for it as being quite different from prostitution. Also some of those things that men look for are pretty weird. And anyway, being that close to Germans, for they are the only people who have any money, is something too terrifying for her – a Jewess – to contemplate.)

So Chantal is off to meet this man, find out what he wants and put a price on it. Apparently, according to Bert, this German is very high-ranking so Chantal is thinking in terms of outrageously big numbers – 'telephone numbers' to use a term favoured by bankers. She is hoping that her film days are over, that the peanuts Bert pays her will be as nothing compared to what she could get from this. She is conscious – more so than Julia because Chantal is older – that she cannot stay at this for ever. Gravity will start to take its toll, her age will begin to tell against her. Chantal also wants to have a baby, though at the moment there is no man in her life to facilitate this. So for all these reasons, she is hoping that she will be able to get enough money from this, not just to survive but to save so that she can start to make her dream come true.

Thus, though Julia does not know it, she is pretty much as safe as any Dutch person can be in Nazi-occupied Amsterdam in January 1944.

She eats breakfast and goes out for a walk. She returns, cooks dinner – though without any wine this time and goes to bed early to keep warm and to read. She takes with her *Anna Karenina* which she loves and which she has just restarted for the umpteenth time.

Spring eventually comes and with it, warmer weather. Julia gets reasonably steady work from Bert which keeps her fed and a roof over her head. She never works with Chantal again so she never gets to have her revenge – at least not directly.

In June the Allied invasion takes place in France and the southern part of the Netherlands is liberated. But with the failure to capture the Rhine bridge at Arnhem it is to be nearly another year and the terrible Hunger Winter of 1944-45 before the Allies eventually liberate Amsterdam and the war ends.

Julia survives all this. Work from Bert dries up in the second half of 1944 and she is skin and bone by the time May 1945 comes and the Germans surrender. But at least she is alive. Thousands are not.

It is the day after the Liberation when Julia is walking down a street in Amsterdam that she encounters Chantal again.

Chantal did indeed make a lot of money from her German benefactor. He set her up in a nice little apartment – taken from Jews, of course – and she survived the winter quite happily. As it became clear that the Germans were going to lose the war, she contrived to get everything she could from her German – this by offering him ever more inventive delights. Simultaneously, she decided that as soon as the Allies came, she needed to find a British or Canadian or – best of all – an American officer who would bring her to America. There she could leave the past behind her.

Except that the past has a way of not wanting to be left behind. Like trying to get rid of an unwanted dog, you drive it out into a secluded country lane and open the car door. You use some treats and endearments to entice it out. It does – bounding out happily to find out what this new game is. You jump back in quickly and drive off, trying not to look in the mirror. But when you eventually do, as you inevitably will, you don't see a tiny, devastated face receding into the distance or a frantic and hopeless effort of short legs to catch up with you. Rather, sitting up in the back seat, face filling the mirror and eager to find out what we're doing next, is the self-same dog.

So with Chantal.

Unfortunately for her, her presence in the apartment

hadn't gone unnoticed. Nor could her relative affluence which contrasted so obviously with that of her neighbours. How could it have? At a time when people were starving to death, Chantal made little effort to hide her prosperity. (From a poor childhood, Chantal had money for the first time in her life – and lots of it. Which of us mightn't have done the same?)

The result is that what Julia sees are two men dragging an expensively dressed, nicely coiffeured woman from a doorway into the centre of the street. Julia recognises Chantal instantly. The dyed blonde hair is perfectly styled. How did the stupid bitch ever think that would go unnoticed?

There is a large crowd on the street and the men push Chantal through it. Julia hurries to the edge of the crowd and by standing on her tiptoes she can just about see what is happening.

Chantal is pushed down onto the cobbles and her dress is ripped off her shoulders, revealing her bra and slip. They are expensive – not the endlessly washed, weary garments that Julia wears. A woman stands over Chantal and grasps a fistful of her thick hair. Then the woman hacks it off with scissors. She takes a second clump and repeats the process, then a third and a fourth, working her way methodically across Chantal's head. The woman is not being gentle. At one stage Julia winces as the point of one of the arms of the scissors jabs into Chantal's skull. A rivulet of blood trickles down the side of her face. The woman nicks Chantal's ear and there is another flow of blood, this time more copious. Chantal cries. At one stage Chantal looks up at the crowd. It may have been intended as a gesture of defiance but all she manages to do is to look pitiful. Her eyes meet Julia's for an instant but there is no recognition.

When Chantal's head is no more than a field of bloody

stubble, a man with a paint pot and paintbrush carefully paints a black swastika on her forehead. By then another woman has already been brought into the centre of the crowd and Chantal is shoved aside. Kneeling on the cobbles, she gathers the remains of her dress around herself, covering her underwear as best she can. She stands up and due to the angle Chantal happens to be standing at, Julia notices the swelling in the other woman's belly.

Chantal is pregnant.

Julia is not sure what she feels about all of this. Certainly it's not the kind of revenge she would have wanted. Chantal hugs the torn fabric to her and pushes her way through the crowd. She is jostled. Several people spit at her. The last sight Julia has of her is of spit and tears beginning to dilute the blood on Chantal's face.

Julia notices another girl in the crowd. She is looking on just as Julia is. The girl is painfully thin, as are most other people, but what is striking about her is how pale she is. The combination of blonde hair and an unbelievably white face makes her look like a ghost. Or a corpse. She seems to be made of a different colour palate from the rest of the people in the crowd. It is as though they are in oils while she is drawn in pastels. Where they are red she is a faint, dusty pink; their strong blues contrast with hers, the faintest wash of dawn; their sturdy greens and browns and blacks all seem faded or seen through gauze on this girl. The girl wears glasses but Julia thinks she is pretty – or at least she would be if she looked less ghostly.

The girl is Suzanne, of course.

It is the only time that her and Julia's paths will cross. This is the first full day Suzanne has spent outside her attic in three and a half years. She has yet to get used to the light, the people, the smells, the noise. Her muscles are weak, almost withered. She has wandered around in something of a daze, touching the stone of buildings, the wood of canal locks, grass. She has not been out in daylight in three and a half years and her eyes squint against the brightness. She feels the warm May air and the sunshine. She marvels that she is alive and hasn't yet begun to think about her parents or the rest of her extended family. She looks on quizzically at the scene in front of her as though at a movie that she doesn't quite understand. Eventually she shakes her head to snap out of it and slips out of the press of people.

It is the first and only time Julia will ever see Suzanne.

Come the autumn Suzanne will resume her studies. In due course she will graduate, then study for a masters and finally get a doctorate. She will go on to teach English literature in a variety of European universities. She will spend some time in similar institutions in America. She will get married – to another academic – but it won't be a happy marriage and in time, they will divorce. Suzanne will have a child, a daughter, called Theresa – though she will be known as Tess, a small homage to Mr Hardy's heroine.

As for Julia, she will become a proper actress just as she had dreamed. She will move first to Paris, then to England and finally to New York where she will make a career – taking whatever work comes her way, voice work in radio advertisements, small, off-Broadway productions, bit-parts in movies, in time some television. Nothing major but it will be a living.

She will have numerous relationships – with the occasional man but mainly with women.

She will always find herself disappointed.

56

We forget that there was a time when nobody smiled in photographs. But that was in the early days of photography. By the time the thirties had come everybody smiled and laughed and looked happy just as they do today. Look at any of the pre-war pictures to be found in Holocaust museums – there's plenty of smiling and laughing and happiness.

Nobody smiles in the Theresienstadt propaganda film.

This is a film of the entire population of a town on Death Row.

Although as I write these words, I realise it's not strictly true.

The children smile.

The children smile and they laugh.

Especially when they are eating.

And it's good to be able to think that at least Julia and Suzanne aren't two of the lost, unsmiling faces looking out at us from that movie.

That would be almost like saving them.

Like bringing them back.

Imagine if that were possible – to bring back one, just one of the six million.

What about one of the children?

Just one.

So that they could live out their life and die a gentle death. It seems so little to ask and how wonderful a thing it would be.

But of course it's impossible.

And so it eases things for us a little to be able to think that at least Julia and Suzanne escaped all of that.

57

British newspaper report
November 28th 2015

They are two tattered notebooks that have lain undisturbed for over seventy years. One has a black cover, the other faded pictures of what were once brightly coloured images of fruit. The curling, yellowed pages, some spattered with brown spots of damp, tell a remarkable story.

The notebooks were found during some renovation work in the Czech town of Terezin. These days a small, picturesque town inside what was once a military installation, Terezin holds a dark secret.

During WWII it was a Nazi ghetto for Jews. Known as 'the model ghetto' or 'the paradise ghetto', thousands died there of starvation, disease and ill-treatment. Thousands more were shipped from there to Auschwitz to be murdered.

Despite the appalling conditions in Terezin, there was a vibrant cultural life. There were book clubs, discussion groups and theatrical and musical performances. Now a new element of that cultural life has been uncovered with the discovery of these notebooks.

Written in pencil, the notebooks contain a complete (and rather exciting) novel set during Roman times.

The book will be published next year.

AUTHOR'S NOTE

Transport Ep, as it was known, which left Theresienstadt on October 9th 1944 with 1,600 people on board, went to Auschwitz-Birkenau where it arrived on October 12th. As was the system, the men were separated from the women on arrival. Mothers with children, as well as the sick and aged, were taken immediately to the gas chamber and murdered. Several hundred people were admitted to the camp, including 181 women.

A little over two weeks later, on October 28th, a group of 500 women, 80 of them from Theresienstadt, were taken in cattle trucks to Austria where they were put to work, building roads and air raid shelters.

Of the original 1,600 people from transport Ep, 22 survived the war.

The last transport ever to run from Theresienstadt, transport Ev, left on October 28th 1944. There were 2,038 people on it: 949 men and boys and 1,089 women and girls. The transport reached Auschwitz-Birkenau on October 30th. After the selection, 1,689 people were murdered in the gas chamber.

137 people from this final transport survived the war.

During the existence of the Paradise Ghetto, 139,654 people were deported there. 17,472 were eventually liberated from it.

207 children were born there. Most, if not all, would have been among the 86,934 deported to the Nazi death camps.

3,097 people returned from these transports. It is highly unlikely that any of those babies would have been among them.

The Paradise Ghetto had three commandants during its life.

Siegfried Seidl ran it from November 1941 until July 1943. After the war he was arrested and tried in Austria. He was sentenced to death and executed on February 4th 1947.

The second commandant, Anton Burger, ran the camp from July 1943 until February 1944. Arrested after the war, he escaped, was rearrested and escaped again. He died of natural causes on Christmas Day 1991. He never received any punishment.

The third and final commandant was Karl Rahm. He left Theresienstadt on May 5th 1945 along with the last of the SS personnel. He was captured shortly afterwards by American forces in Austria and extradited in 1947 to Czechoslovakia. Put on trial, Rahm was found guilty of crimes against humanity and sentenced to death. He was executed on April 30th 1947, four hours after his guilty verdict had been handed down by the Czech court.

Most of the children that can be seen in this clip:

http://bit.ly/29MB0YU

of the opera *Brundibár* were murdered in Auschwitz. They include Honza Treichlinger, the little guy with the moustache:

http://bit.ly/29KklGt

The White Ship

Nicholas Salaman

Normandy in 1118 is a hotbed of malcontent barons kept in fragile order by their duke, Henry I, King of England. Fresh from early years in a monastery, Bertold - the bastard son of one of these barons - meets Juliana, a countess and daughter of the King.

He falls in love, or lust (he isn't sure), but sees that his chance could come with work in her small court. Soon, though, he finds himself caught up in a ruthless feud between Juliana and her father. Juliana's daughters are offered as hostages for a strategic castle, and even love is not enough to allay a tragedy that will change the course of history.

The Tsar's Dragons

Catrin Collier

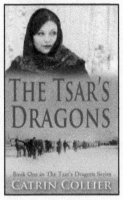

In 1869, Tsar Alexander II decided to drag Russia into the industrial age. He began by inviting Welsh businessman John Hughes to build an ironworks.

A charismatic visionary, Hughes persuaded influential people to invest in his venture, while concealing his greatest secret – he couldn't even write his own name. Hughes recruited adventurers prepared to sacrifice everything to ensure the success of Hughesovka (Donetsk, Ukraine). Young Welsh men and women fleeing violence in their home country, Jews who have accepted Russian anti-Semitism as their fate, and Russian aristocrats: all see a future in the Welshman's plans.

The Witch of Eye

Mari Griffith

A love that leads to treason …

1435, England. Eleanor Cobham has married into the highest ranks of the aristocracy – she is now the Duchess of Gloucester. She and her husband, the Duke Humphrey, set up a court of their own to rival the royal court in London, surrounding themselves with fascinating and influential people.

But Eleanor craves the one thing she lacks: a son and heir, and with him a possible route to the throne of England. Desperate, Eleanor turns to the one person she believes can help her: Margery Jourdemayne, the infamous Witch of Eye. Such help comes at a high price …

For more information about **Fergus O'Connell**

and other **Accent Press** titles

please visit

www.accentpress.co.uk